I AM A FIERCE CAT.
I WILL RIP YOU INTO SHREDS.
HIDE IN FEAR FROM ME.

— EMILY POWELL, AGE 13

MINISTRY OF
TROUBLE
INCORPORATED

WRITER/CREATOR
CHELSEA CAIN

PENCILS & INKS
KATE NIEMCZYK

COLORIST
RACHELLE ROSENBERG

LETTERER
JOE CARAMAGNA

COVERS/CREATIVE PRODUCER
LIA MITERNIQUE

ADDITIONAL INTERIOR ART
LIA MITERNIQUE
STELLA GREENVOSS
KYLE SCANLON

ADDITIONAL WRITING (#3 & #4)
ELIZA FANTASTIC MOHAN

HAIKUS (#1, #2, VOL. 1)
EMILY POWELL

SWAGGER
KATIE LANE

YOU HAVE BEEN CONTACTED BY THE MINISTRY OF TROUBLE. AWAIT FURTHER INSTRUCTIONS. ⚥

THANK YOU TO EVERYONE AT IMAGE COMICS.
FOR THE LATE NIGHTS. FOR THE HARD WORK. FOR THE RED VINES.
Sincerely, The Ministry of Trouble

PRODUCTION BY TRICIA RAMOS

IMAGE COMICS, INC. • **Robert Kirkman**: Chief Operating Officer • **Erik Larsen**: Chief Financial Officer • **Todd McFarlane**: President • **Marc Silvestri**: Chief Executive Officer • **Jim Valentino**: Vice President • **Eric Stephenson**: Publisher / Chief Creative Officer • **Corey Hart**: Director of Sales • **Jeff Boison**: Director of Publishing Planning & Book Trade Sales • **Chris Ross**: Director of Digital Sales • **Jeff Stang**: Director of Specialty Sales • **Kat Salazar**: Director of PR & Marketing • **Drew Gill**: Art Director • **Heather Doornink**: Production Director • **Nicole Lapalme**: Controller • **IMAGECOMICS.COM**

OFFICE OF PUBLIC RELATIONS
MINISTRY OF TROUBLE
INCORPORATED

This is us:

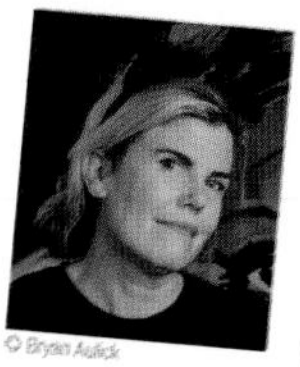

© Bryan Aulick

Chelsea Cain is the author of 12 books, including six *NYT* bestselling Gretchen Lowell thrillers. Cain's novel, *One Kick*, was turned into the 12-episode TV series, *Gone*, starring Chris Noth and Leven Rambin, debuting in the US this March. Chelsea's first comic book series, *Mockingbird*, was nominated for an Eisner for Best Writing and Best New Series. Visit chelseacain.com for more info. Chelsea is a co-founder of the Ministry of Trouble.

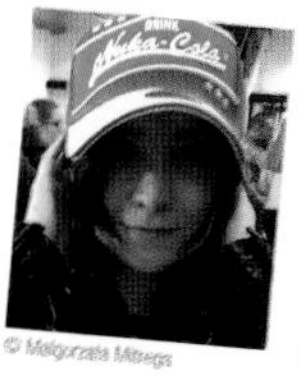

© Malgorzata Mitrega

Kate Niemczyk is a Polish comic book artist and illustrator with experience in the video game and advertisement industries. Her first comic publication was Marvel's *Mockingbird*, which was nominated for an Eisner Award for Best Writing (Chelsea Cain) and Best New Series. She has worked for other comic book publishers including Image Comics, Dark Horse Comics, Valiant Entertainment, and Titan Comics. She also drew an *Overwatch* short for Blizzard Entertainment.

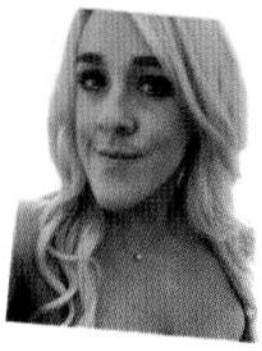

Rachelle Rosenberg From the pages of her childhood coloring book to the pages of mainstream comics, Rachelle has always had a unique love of making art come alive. She's taken her BFA in illustration and a formal oil painting background to quickly become an in-demand force in the world of coloring.

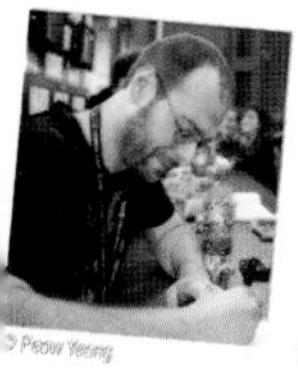

© Peow Yeong

Joe Caramagna is an Eisner and Harvey-nominated letterer and a writer for Marvel and Disney Publishing. He loves his wife and kids, hockey, and donuts – not always necessarily in that order. @JoeCaramagna on Twitter.

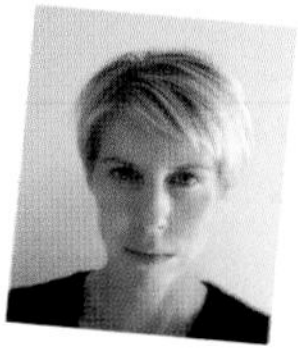

Lia Miternique is an illustrator and graphic designer. She owns Avive Design in Portland, Oregon, and works with arts organizations, healthcare, and corporations including Nike. She has designed books and covers for Chronicle and Bloomsbury. Her favorite creative inspiration comes from exploring the world through travel and her camera lens. This is Lia's first comic series. She is a co-founder of the Ministry of Trouble.

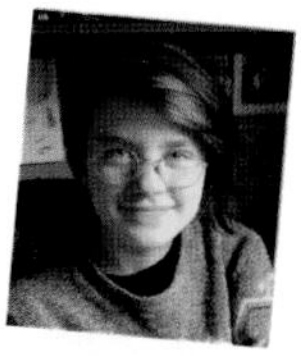

Stella Greenvoss is an eighth grader who can't believe she's in a comic! All her spare time is spent drawing, playing guitar, and petting her weird cat. She is so grateful to Chelsea and Lia for including her in this series.

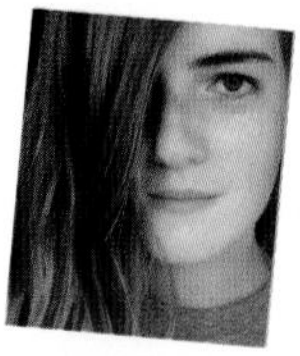

Eliza Fantastic Mohan is an eighth grader in Portland, Oregon. She is a *Buffy the Vampire Slayer* fan, animal lover, Superwholock, feminist, and all around fangirl.

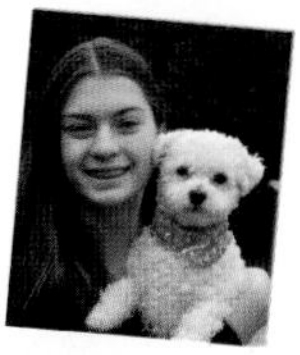

Emily Powell is a thirteen-year-old who lives in Portland, Oregon, where she competes in mountain biking, track and field, soccer, and basketball. She also loves writing, and every animal she's ever met.

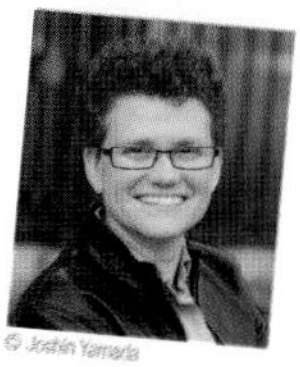

© Joshin Yamada

Katie Lane is an attorney and negotiation coach who works with artists and freelancers to help them protect their rights and get paid fairly for the work they do. She specializes in comic books, and swagger. Find her blog at WorkMadeForHire.net and her clever witticisms on Twitter @_katie_lane.

Chapter one

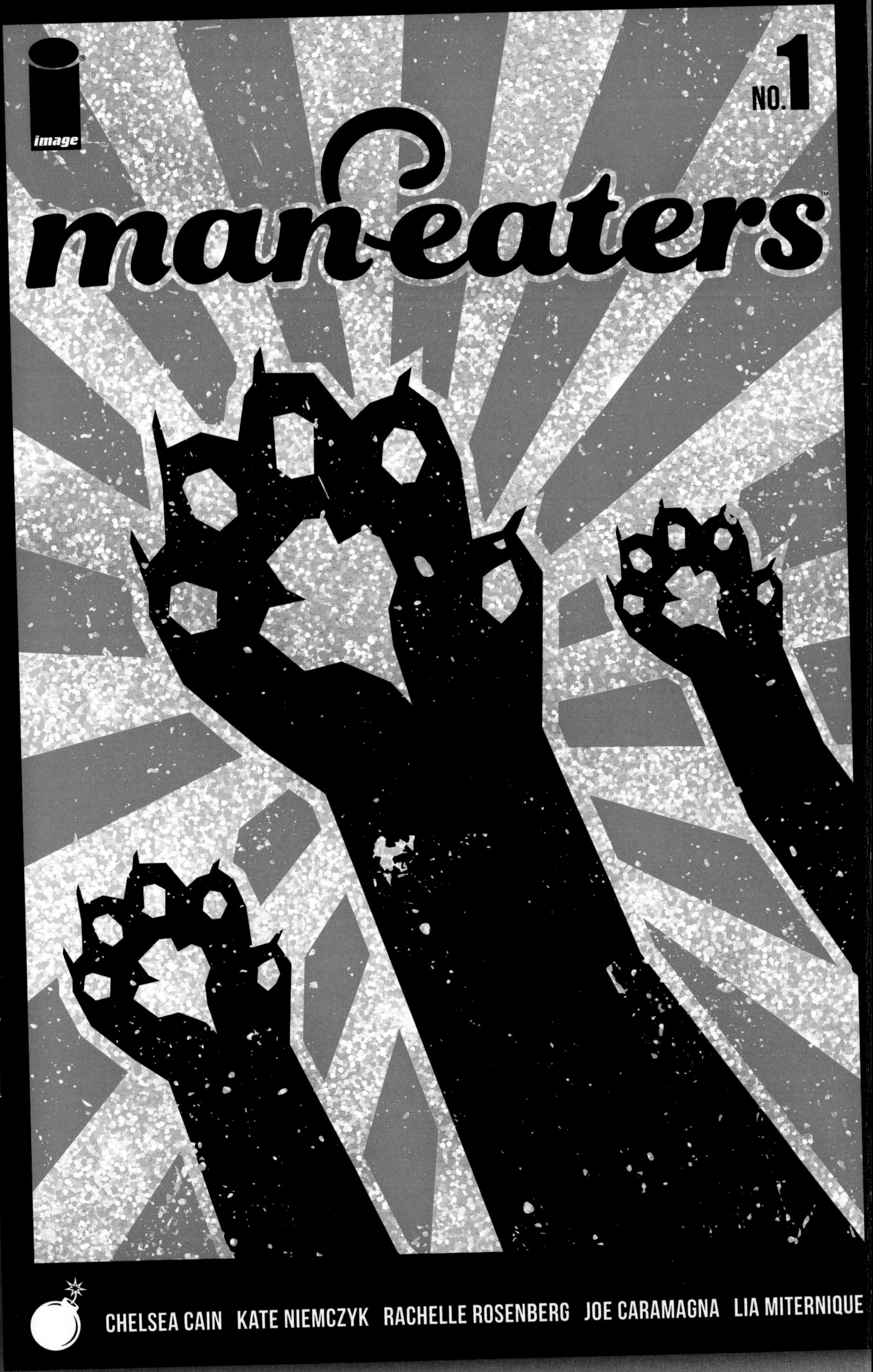
image
NO. 1
man-eaters
CHELSEA CAIN KATE NIEMCZYK RACHELLE ROSENBERG JOE CARAMAGNA LIA MITERNIQUE

BY ORDER OF THE MINISTRY OF TROUBLE

PUBLIC NOTICE

PLEASE BE ADVISED THERE HAS BEEN A

CAT ATTACK

IN YOUR AREA

IF YOU SEE A CAT:

☑ **DO NOT APPROACH**

☑ **DO NOT PROVOKE**

☑ **SEEK SHELTER IMMEDIATELY**

ARE YOU INFECTED?
GET TESTED FOR TOXOPLASMOSIS X

PRODUCED BY THE MINISTRY OF TROUBLE
CHELSEA CAIN, LIA MITERNIQUE, KATE NIEMCZYK, RACHELLE ROSENBERG,
JOE CARAMAGNA, STELLA GREENVOSS, EMILY POWELL, AND KATIE LANE

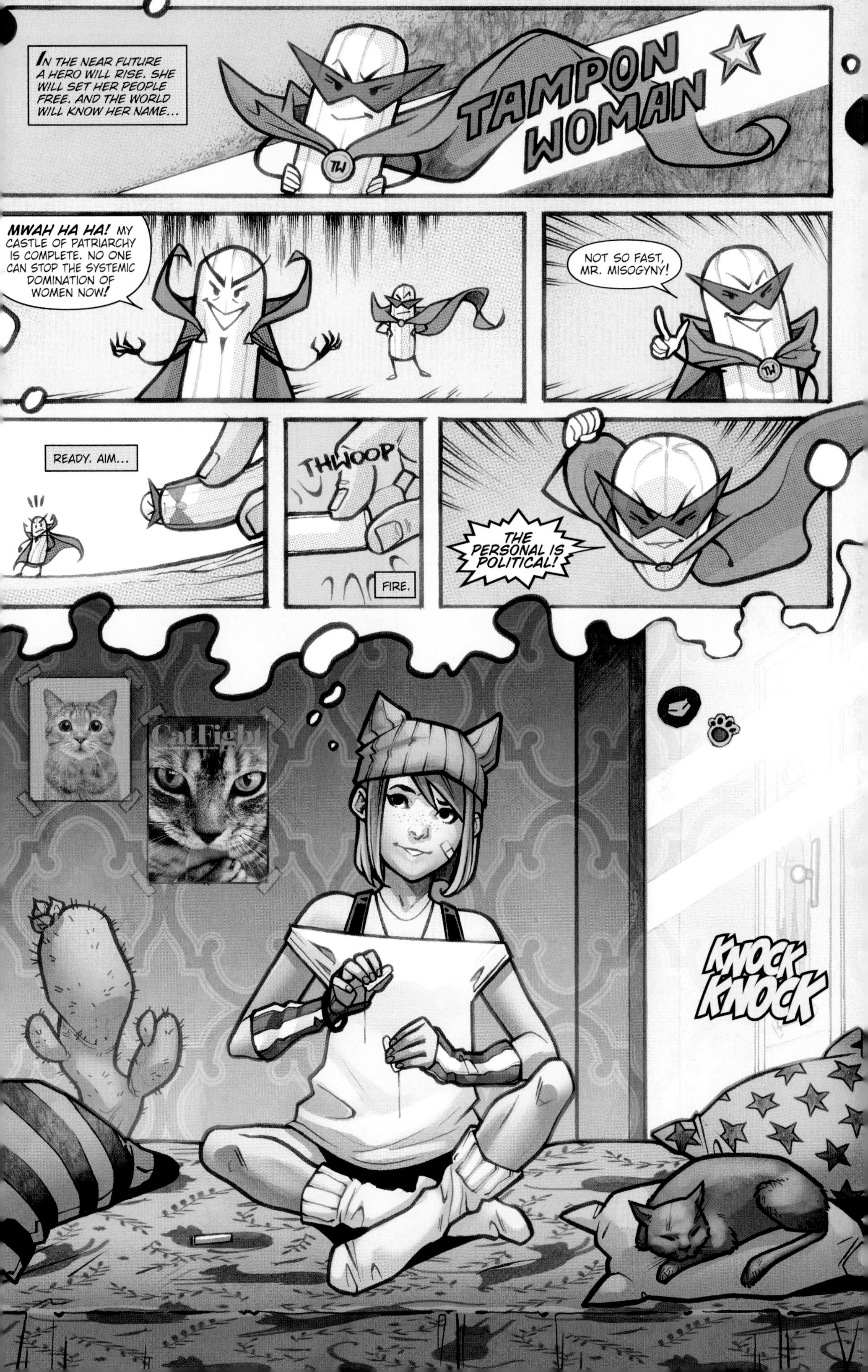

IN THE NEAR FUTURE A HERO WILL RISE. SHE WILL SET HER PEOPLE FREE. AND THE WORLD WILL KNOW HER NAME...
TAMPON WOMAN
TW
MWAH HA HA! MY CASTLE OF PATRIARCHY IS COMPLETE. NO ONE CAN STOP THE SYSTEMIC DOMINATION OF WOMEN NOW!
NOT SO FAST, MR. MISOGYNY!
TW
READY. AIM...
THWOOP
FIRE.
THE PERSONAL IS POLITICAL!
CatFight
KNOCK KNOCK

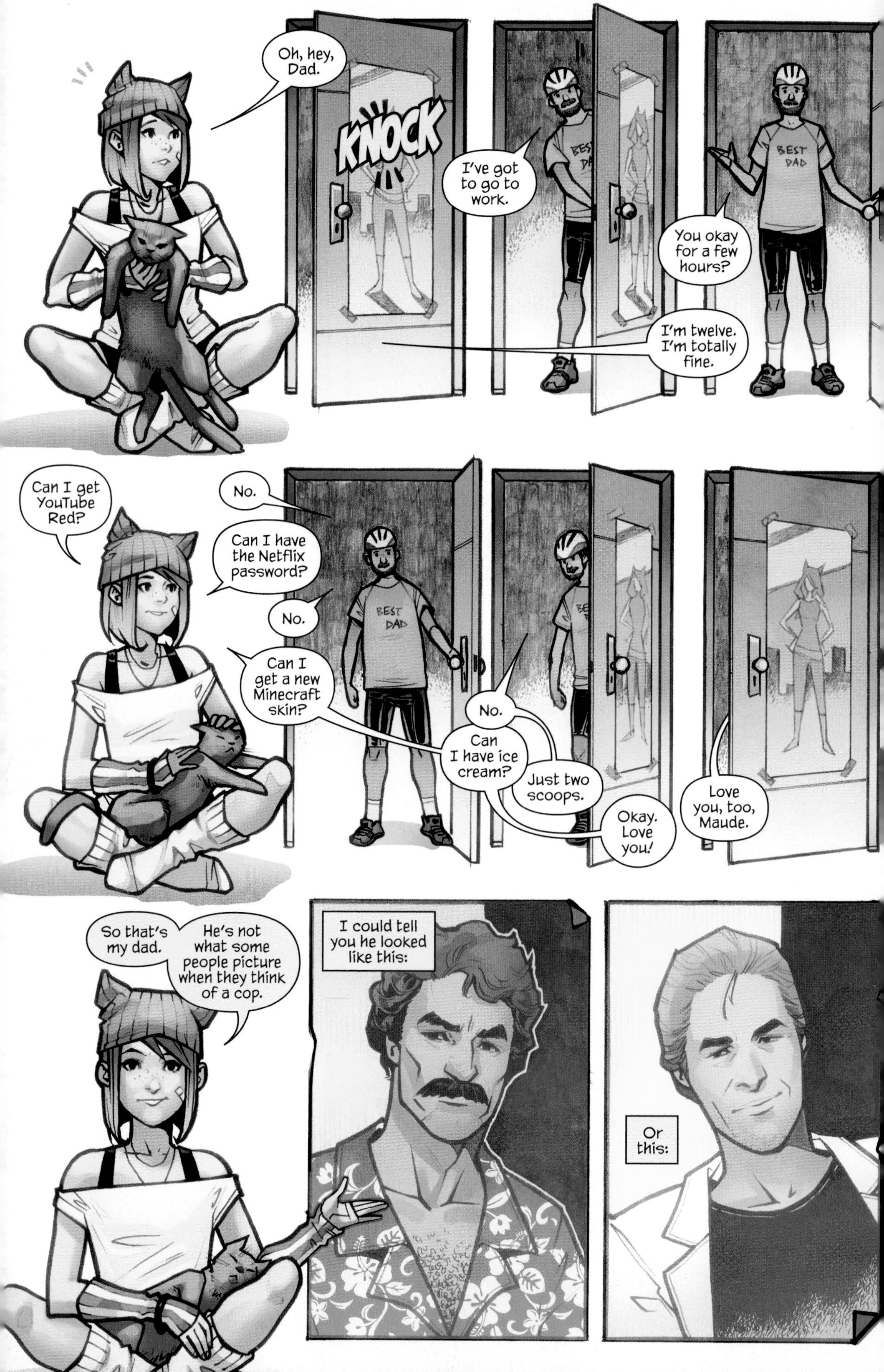
Oh, hey, Dad.
KNOCK
I've got to go to work.
You okay for a few hours?
I'm twelve. I'm totally fine.
Can I get YouTube Red?
No.
Can I have the Netflix password?
No.
Can I get a new Minecraft skin?
No.
Can I have ice cream?
Just two scoops.
Okay. Love you!
Love you, too, Maude.
So that's my dad.
He's not what some people picture when they think of a cop.
I could tell you he looked like this:
Or this:

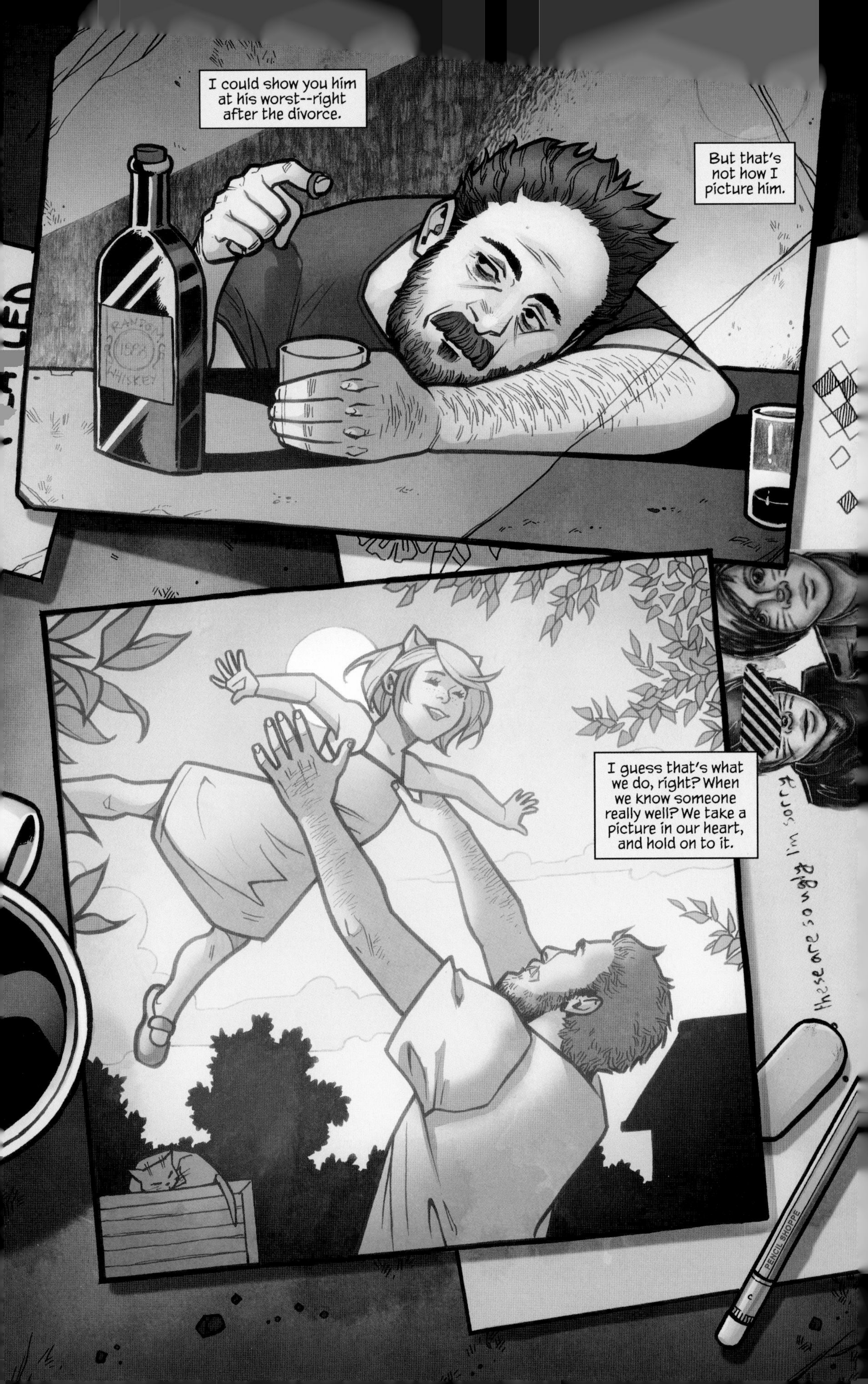
I could show you him at his worst--right after the divorce.
But that's not how I picture him.
I guess that's what we do, right? When we know someone really well? We take a picture in our heart, and hold on to it.
PENCIL SHOPPE

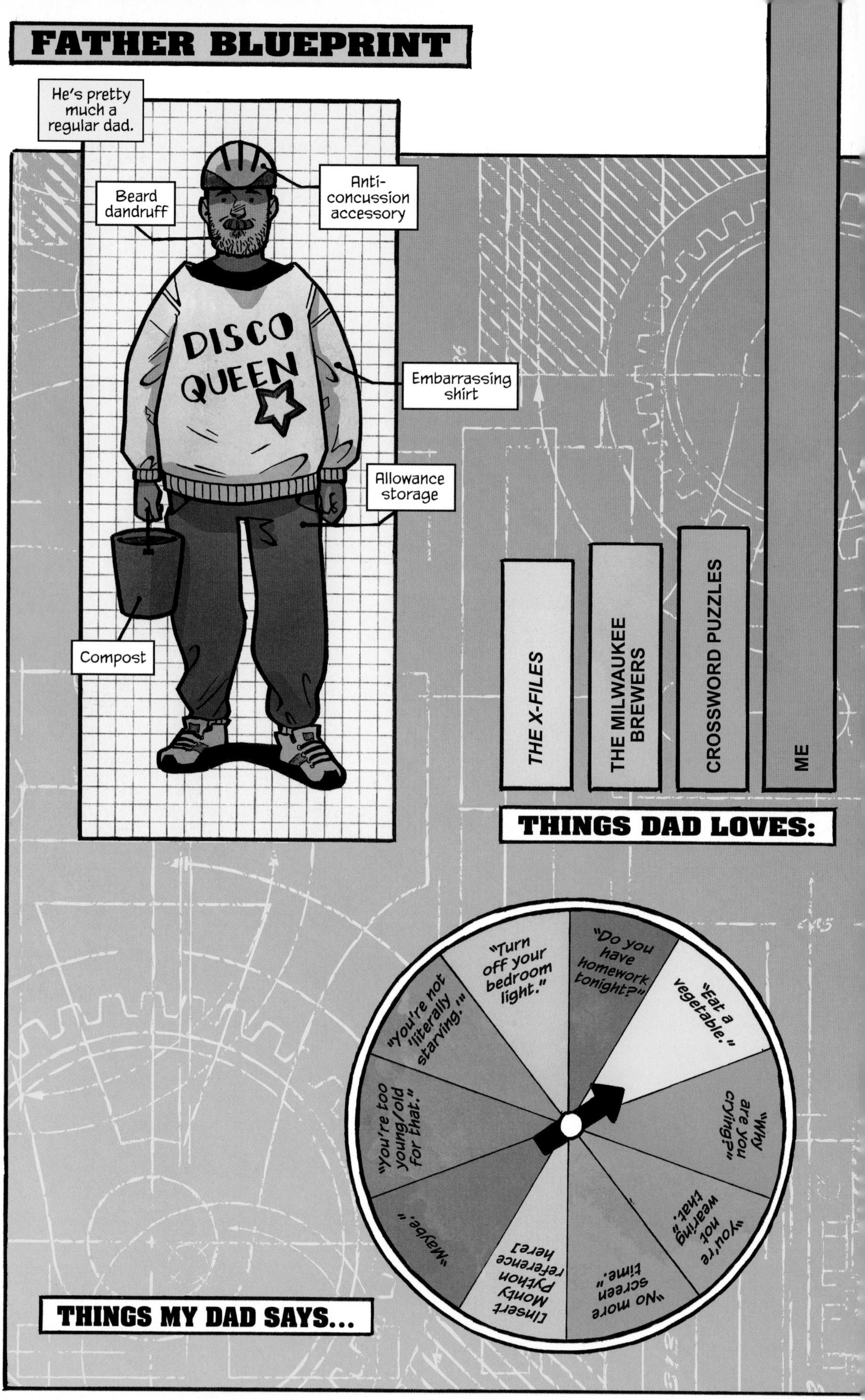
FATHER BLUEPRINT
He's pretty much a regular dad.
Beard dandruff
Anti-concussion accessory
DISCO QUEEN
Embarrassing shirt
Allowance storage
Compost
THE X-FILES
THE MILWAUKEE BREWERS
CROSSWORD PUZZLES
ME
THINGS DAD LOVES:
"Do you have homework tonight?"
"Eat a vegetable."
"Why are you crying?"
"You're not wearing that."
"No more screen time."
[Insert Monty Python reference here]
"Maybe."
"You're too young/old for that."
"You're not literally starving."
"Turn off your bedroom light."
THINGS MY DAD SAYS...

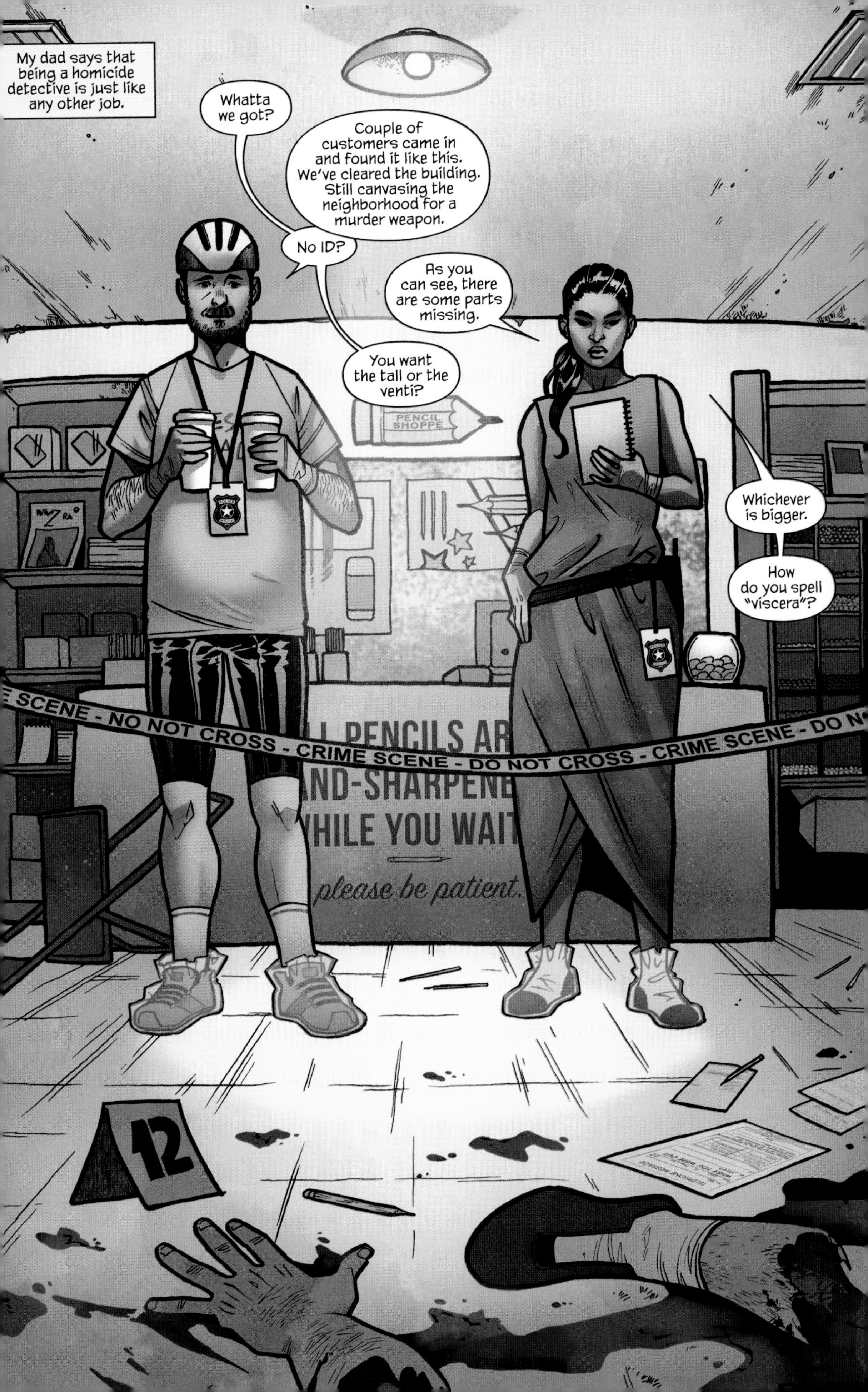
My dad says that being a homicide detective is just like any other job.
Whatta we got?
Couple of customers came in and found it like this. We've cleared the building. Still canvasing the neighborhood for a murder weapon.
No ID?
As you can see, there are some parts missing.
You want the tall or the venti?
Whichever is bigger.
How do you spell "viscera"?
PENCIL SHOPPE
CRIME SCENE - DO NOT CROSS
LL PENCILS AR
AND-SHARPENE
WHILE YOU WAIT
please be patient.
12

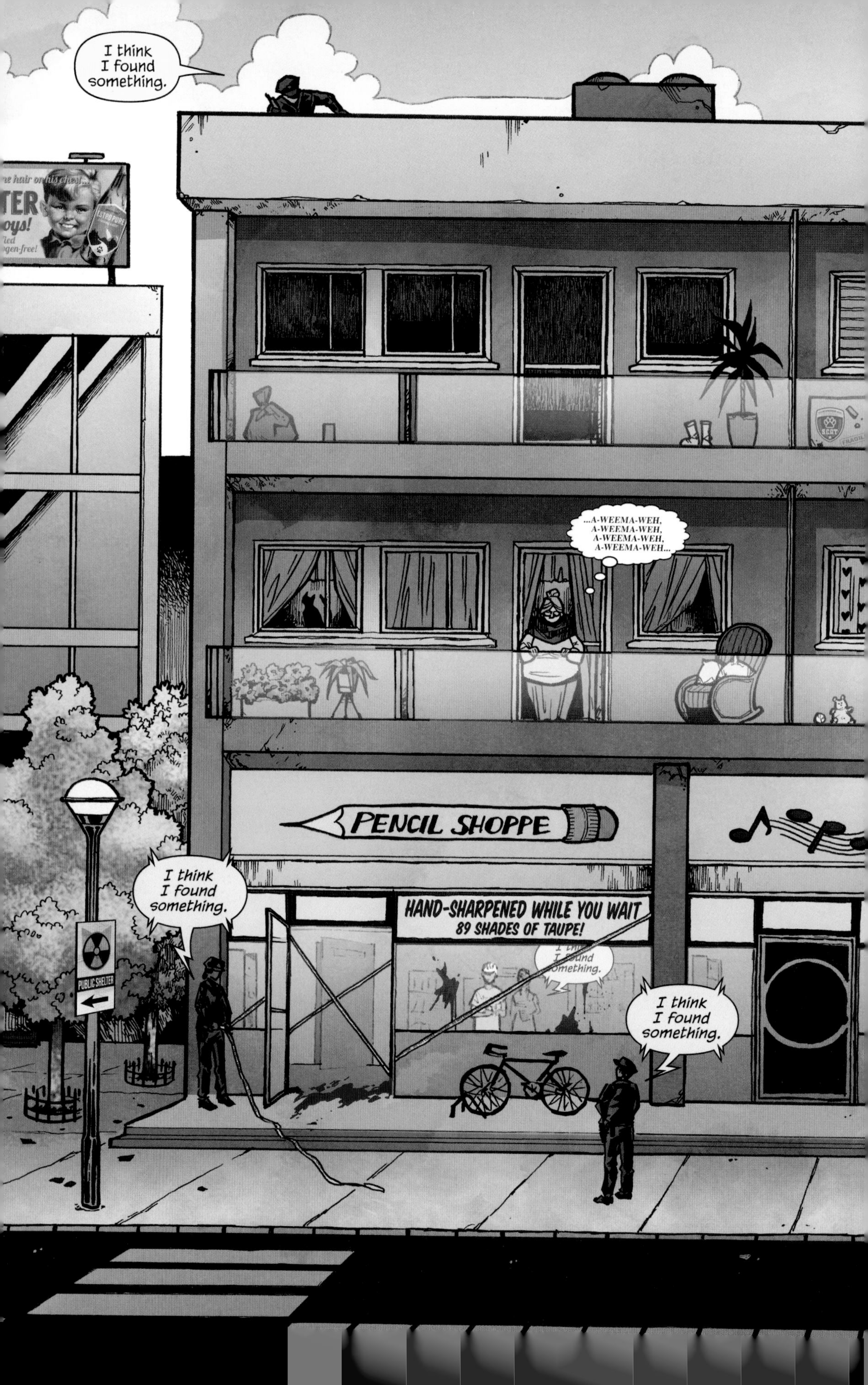

I think I found something.
...A-WEEMA-WEH, A-WEEMA-WEH, A-WEEMA-WEH, A-WEEMA-WEH...
PENCIL SHOPPE
HAND-SHARPENED WHILE YOU WAIT
89 SHADES OF TAUPE!
PUBLIC SHELTER
I think I found something.
I think I found something.

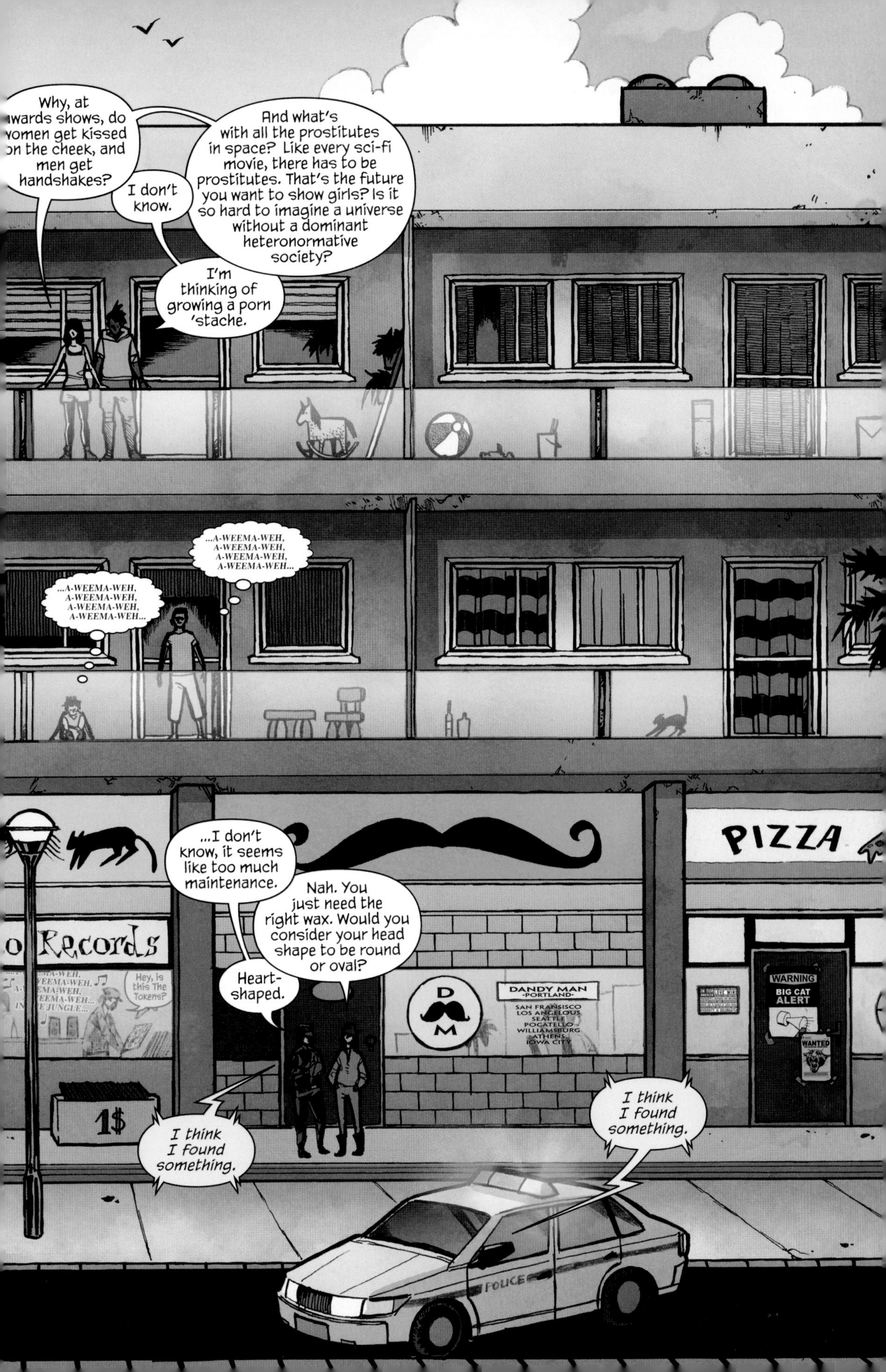
Why, at awards shows, do women get kissed on the cheek, and men get handshakes?
I don't know.
And what's with all the prostitutes in space? Like every sci-fi movie, there has to be prostitutes. That's the future you want to show girls? Is it so hard to imagine a universe without a dominant heteronormative society?
I'm thinking of growing a porn 'stache.
...A-WEEMA-WEH, A-WEEMA-WEH, A-WEEMA-WEH, A-WEEMA-WEH...
...A-WEEMA-WEH, A-WEEMA-WEH, A-WEEMA-WEH, A-WEEMA-WEH...
PIZZA
o Records
Hey, is this The Tokens?
...I don't know, it seems like too much maintenance.
Nah. You just need the right wax. Would you consider your head shape to be round or oval?
Heart-shaped.
D M
DANDY MAN
-PORTLAND-
SAN FRANSISCO
LOS ANGELOUS
SEATTLE
POCATELLO
WILLIAMSBURG
ATHENS
IOWA CITY
WARNING
BIG CAT ALERT
WANTED
1$
I think I found something.
I think I found something.
POLICE

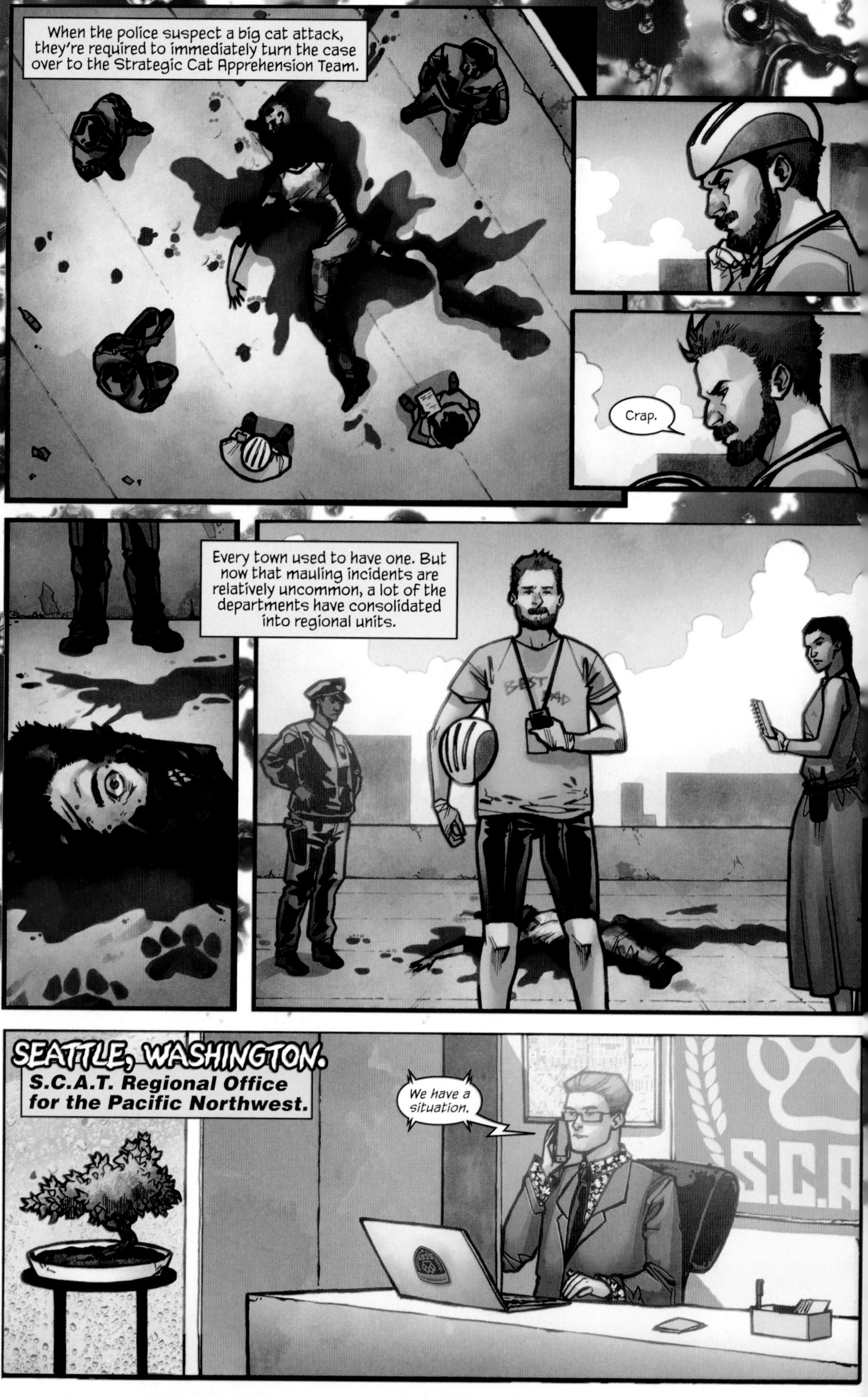
When the police suspect a big cat attack, they're required to immediately turn the case over to the Strategic Cat Apprehension Team.
Crap.
Every town used to have one. But now that mauling incidents are relatively uncommon, a lot of the departments have consolidated into regional units.
BEST DAD
SEATTLE, WASHINGTON.
S.C.A.T. Regional Office for the Pacific Northwest.
We have a situation.

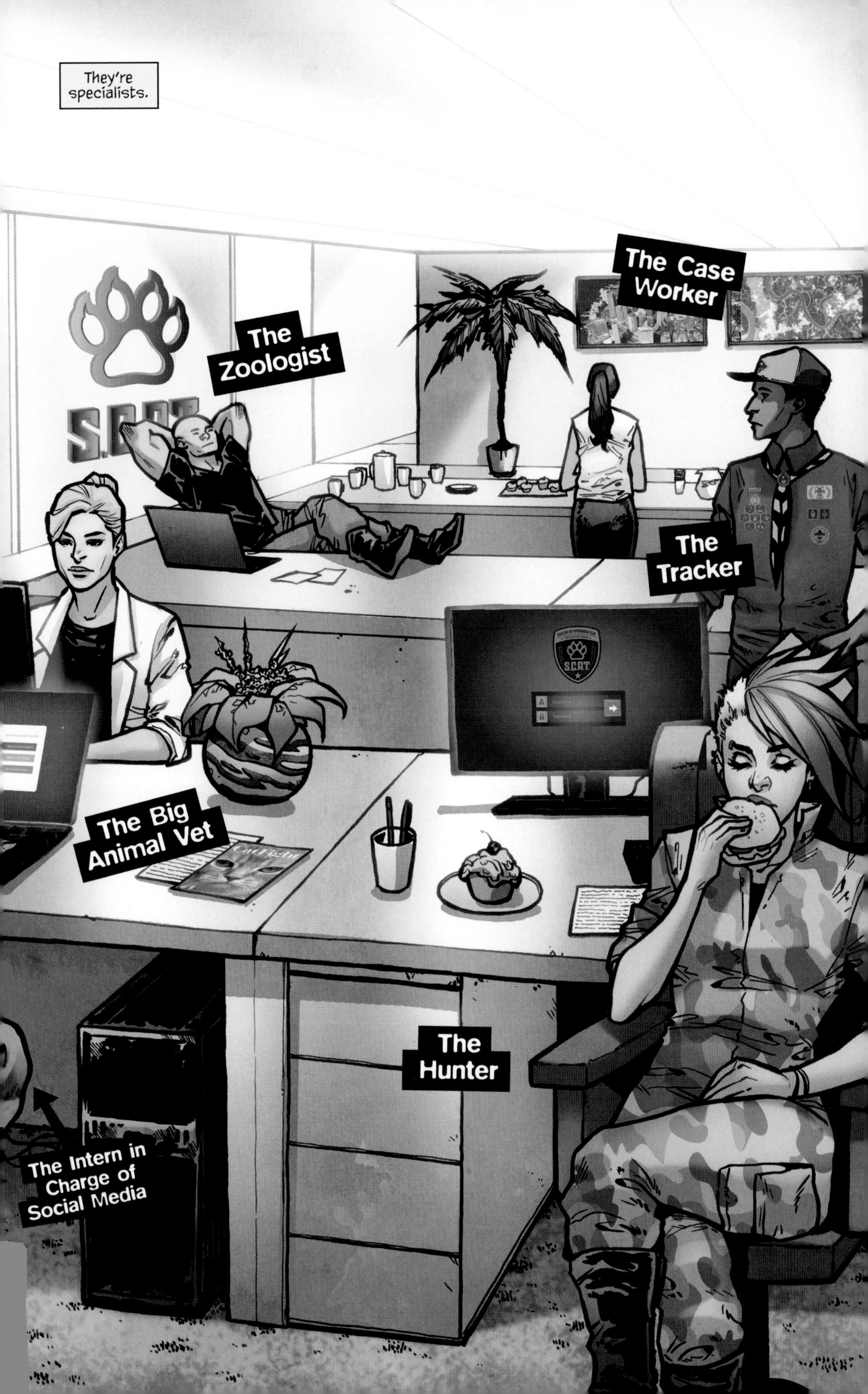
They're specialists.
The Zoologist
The Case Worker
The Tracker
The Big Animal Vet
The Hunter
The Intern in Charge of Social Media

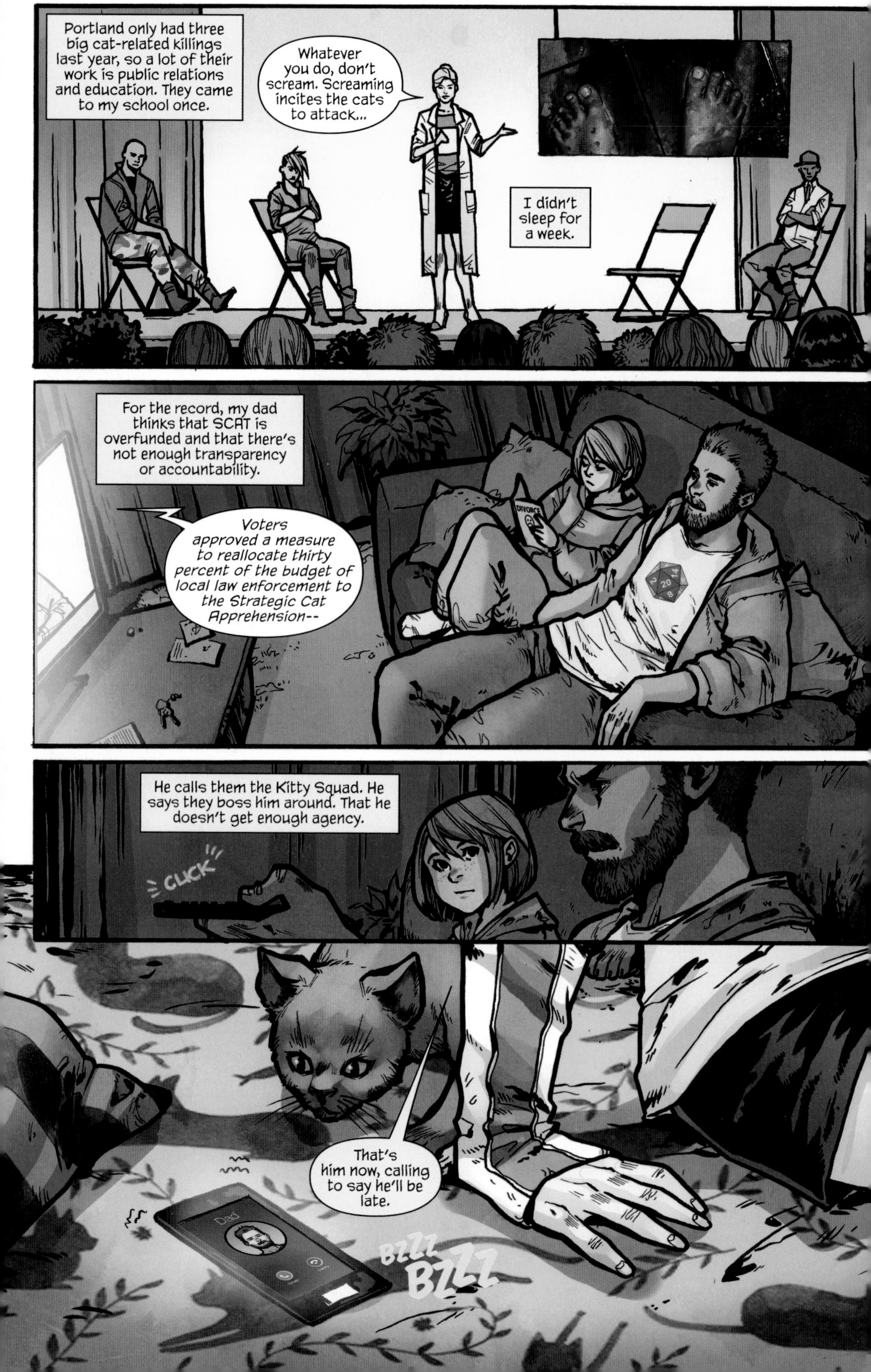
Portland only had three big cat-related killings last year, so a lot of their work is public relations and education. They came to my school once.
Whatever you do, don't scream. Screaming incites the cats to attack...
I didn't sleep for a week.
For the record, my dad thinks that SCAT is overfunded and that there's not enough transparency or accountability.
DIVORCE
Voters approved a measure to reallocate thirty percent of the budget of local law enforcement to the Strategic Cat Apprehension--
He calls them the Kitty Squad. He says they boss him around. That he doesn't get enough agency.
CLICK
That's him now, calling to say he'll be late.
Dad
BZZZ BZZZ

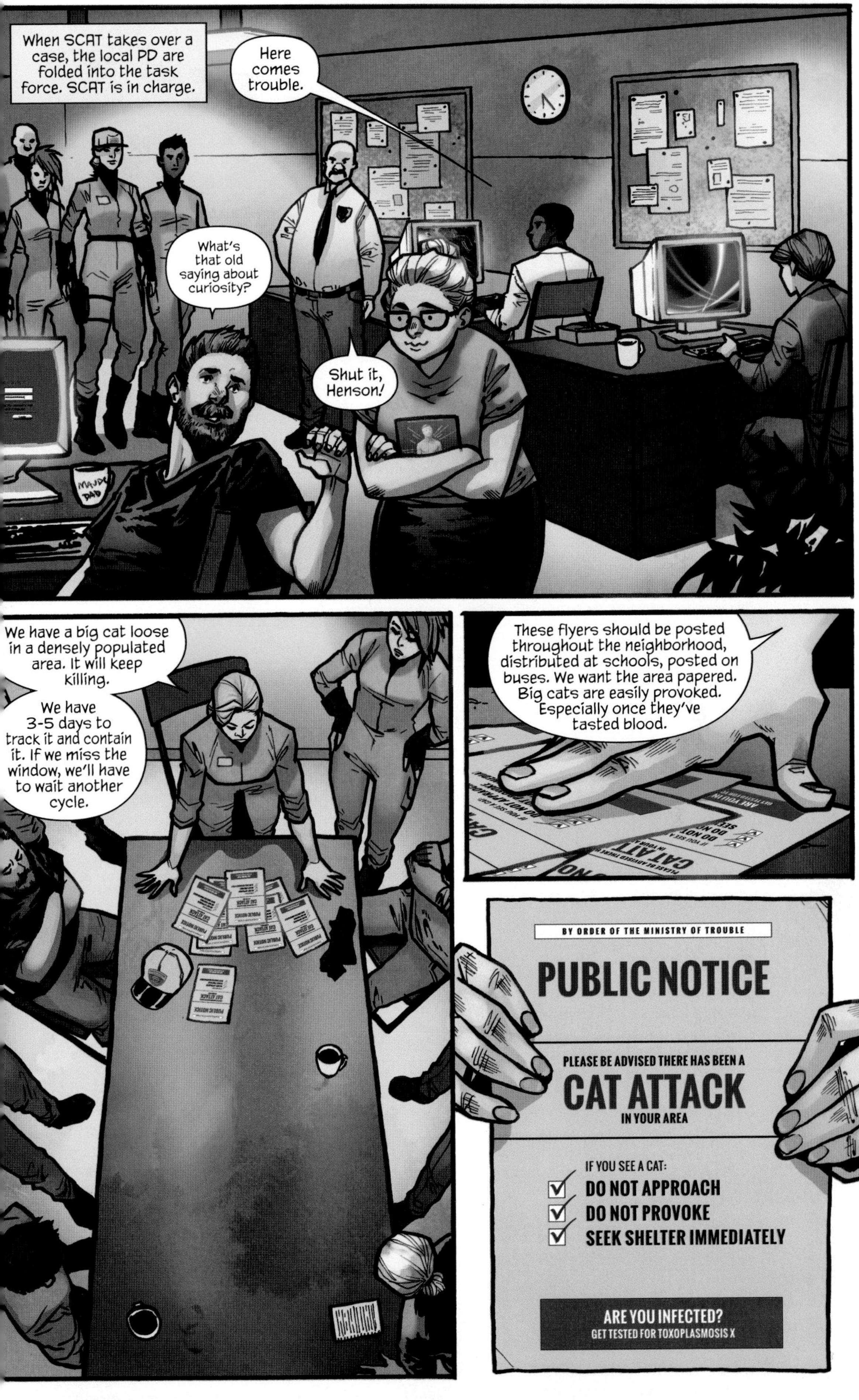
When SCAT takes over a case, the local PD are folded into the task force. SCAT is in charge.
Here comes trouble.
What's that old saying about curiosity?
Shut it, Henson!
We have a big cat loose in a densely populated area. It will keep killing.
We have 3-5 days to track it and contain it. If we miss the window, we'll have to wait another cycle.
These flyers should be posted throughout the neighborhood, distributed at schools, posted on buses. We want the area papered. Big cats are easily provoked. Especially once they've tasted blood.
BY ORDER OF THE MINISTRY OF TROUBLE
PUBLIC NOTICE
PLEASE BE ADVISED THERE HAS BEEN A
CAT ATTACK
IN YOUR AREA
IF YOU SEE A CAT:
DO NOT APPROACH
DO NOT PROVOKE
SEEK SHELTER IMMEDIATELY
ARE YOU INFECTED?
GET TESTED FOR TOXOPLASMOSIS X

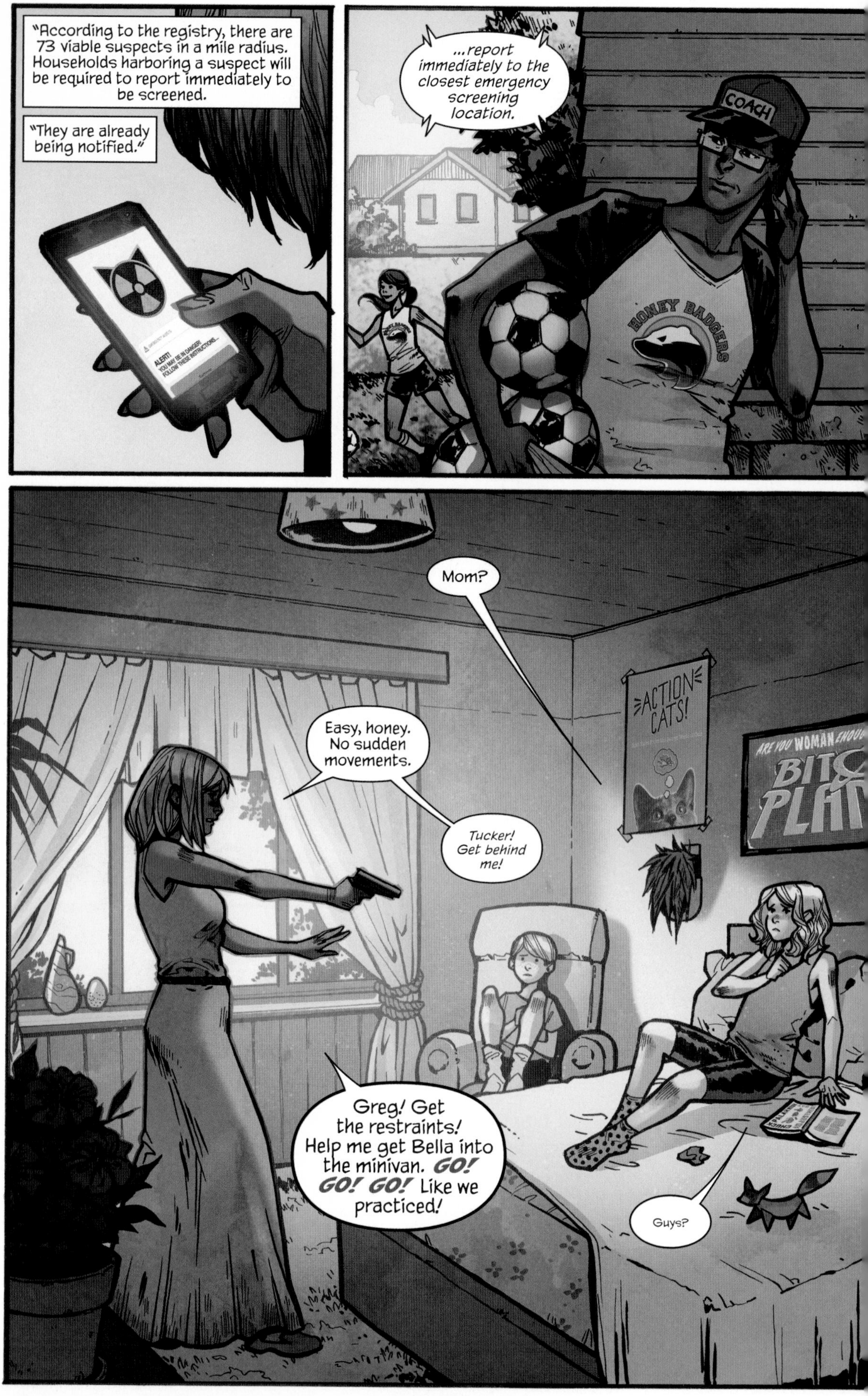
"According to the registry, there are 73 viable suspects in a mile radius. Households harboring a suspect will be required to report immediately to be screened.
"They are already being notified."
ALERT!
YOU MAY BE IN DANGER!
FOLLOW THESE INSTRUCTIONS...
...report immediately to the closest emergency screening location.
COACH
HONEY BADGERS
Mom?
ACTION CATS!
Easy, honey. No sudden movements.
Tucker! Get behind me!
Greg! Get the restraints! Help me get Bella into the minivan. GO! GO! GO! Like we practiced!
Guys?

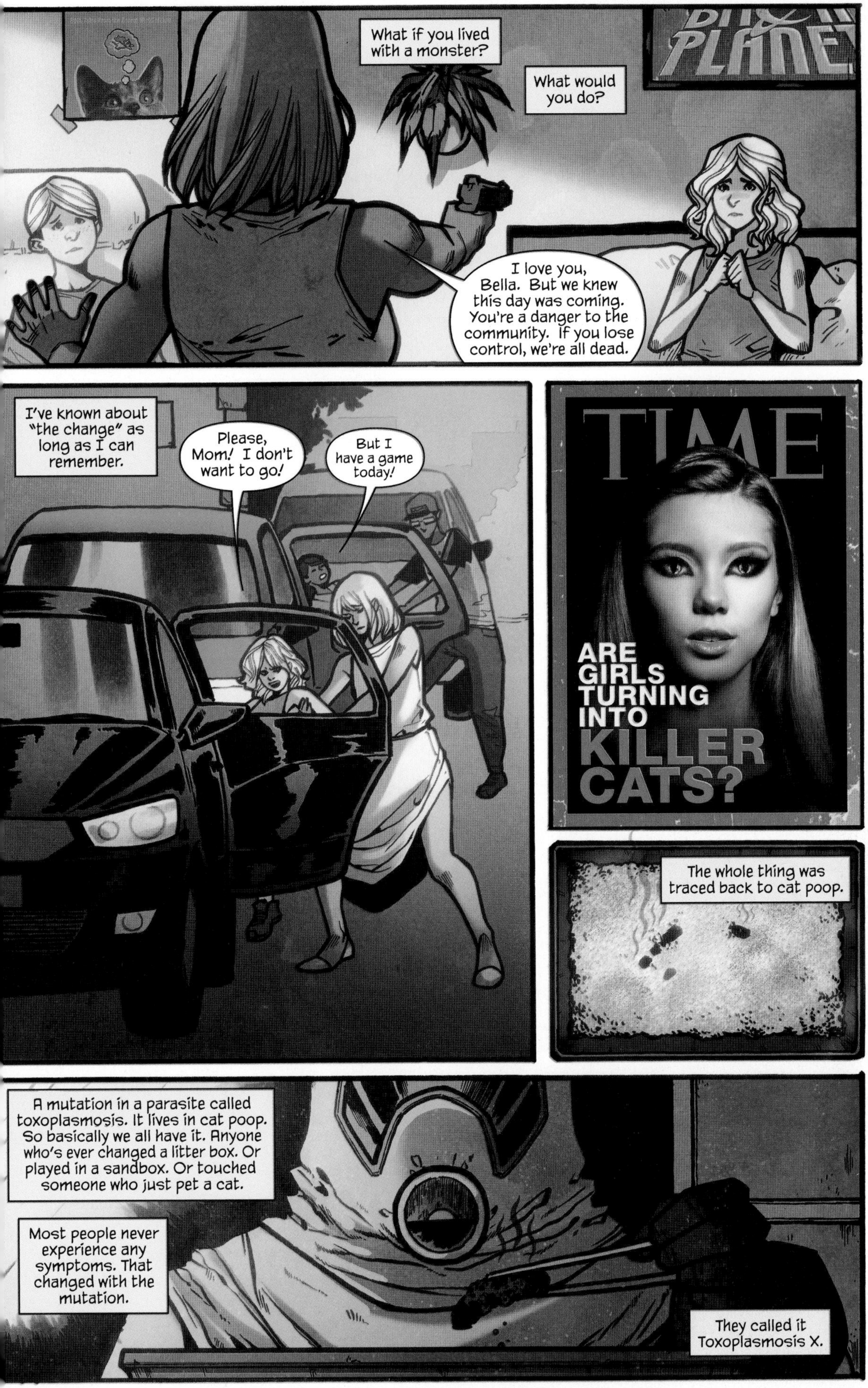
What if you lived with a monster?
What would you do?
I love you, Bella. But we knew this day was coming. You're a danger to the community. If you lose control, we're all dead.
I've known about "the change" as long as I can remember.
Please, Mom! I don't want to go!
But I have a game today!
TIME
ARE GIRLS TURNING INTO KILLER CATS?
The whole thing was traced back to cat poop.
A mutation in a parasite called toxoplasmosis. It lives in cat poop. So basically we all have it. Anyone who's ever changed a litter box. Or played in a sandbox. Or touched someone who just pet a cat.
Most people never experience any symptoms. That changed with the mutation.
They called it Toxoplasmosis X.

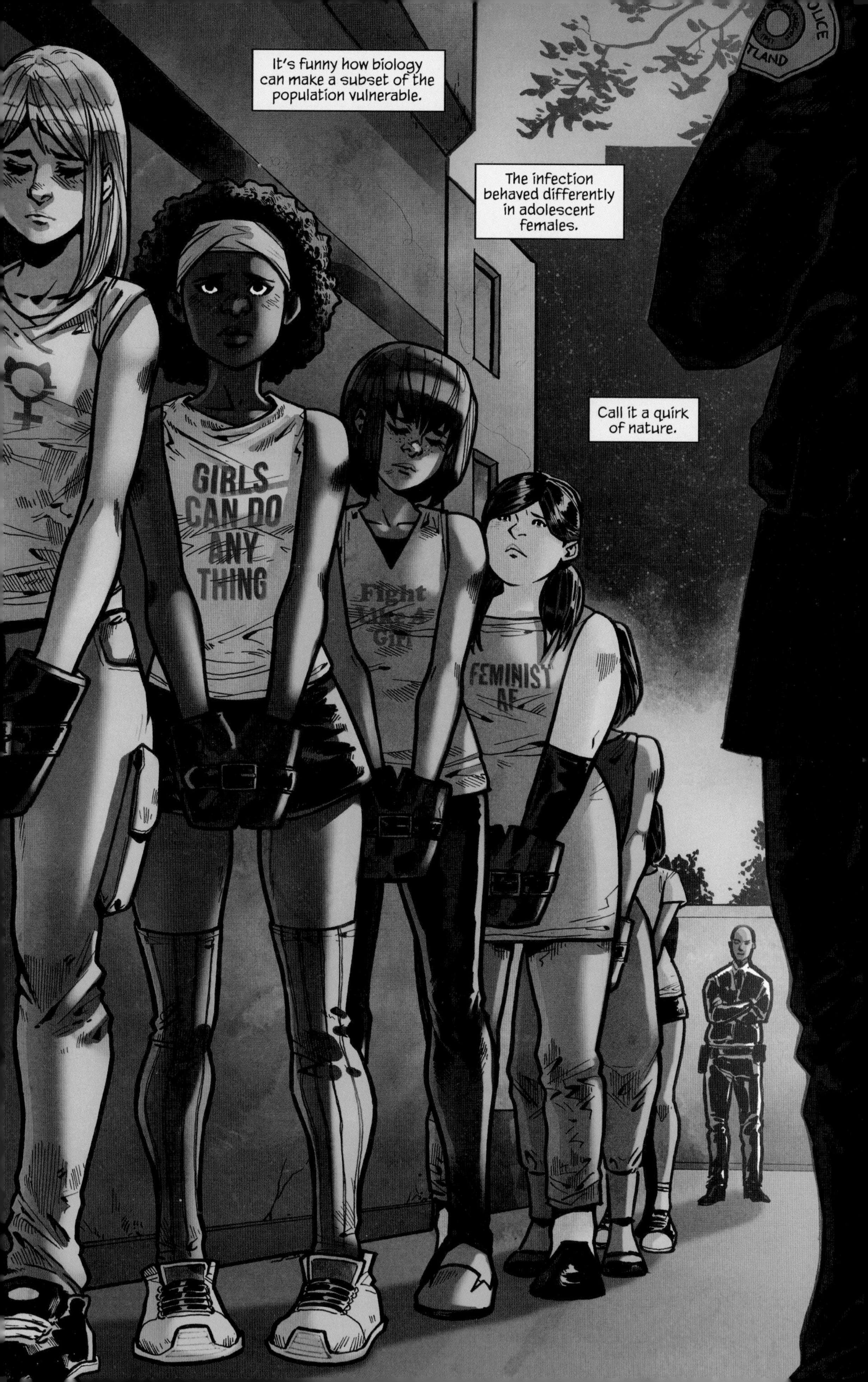
It's funny how biology can make a subset of the population vulnerable.
The infection behaved differently in adolescent females.
Call it a quirk of nature.
GIRLS CAN DO ANY THING
FEMINIST AF

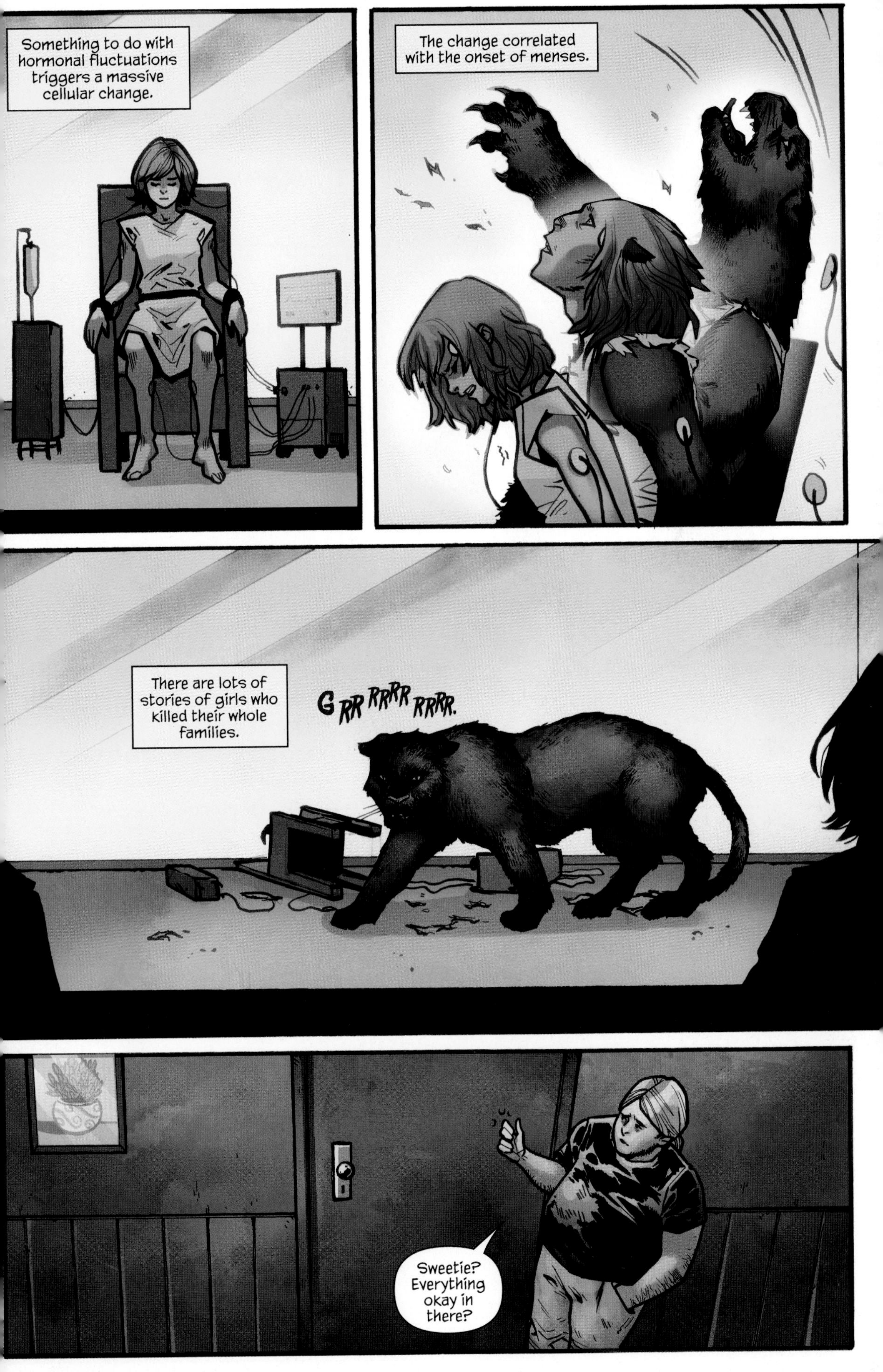
Something to do with hormonal fluctuations triggers a massive cellular change.
The change correlated with the onset of menses.
There are lots of stories of girls who killed their whole families.
GRR RRRR RRRR.
Sweetie? Everything okay in there?

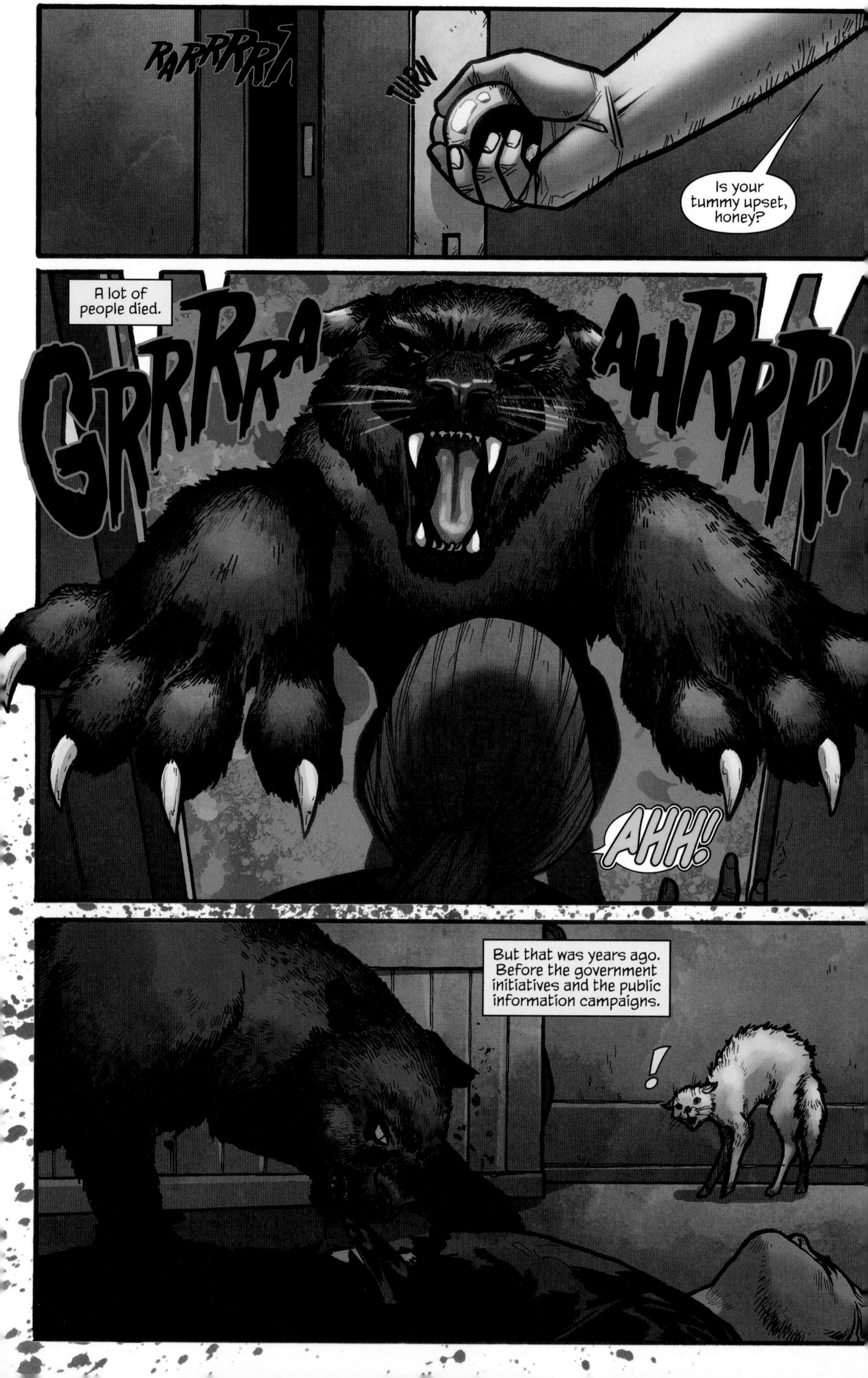
RARRRRR
TURN
Is your tummy upset, honey?
A lot of people died.
GRRRRRA
AHRRRR!
AHH!
But that was years ago. Before the government initiatives and the public information campaigns.
!

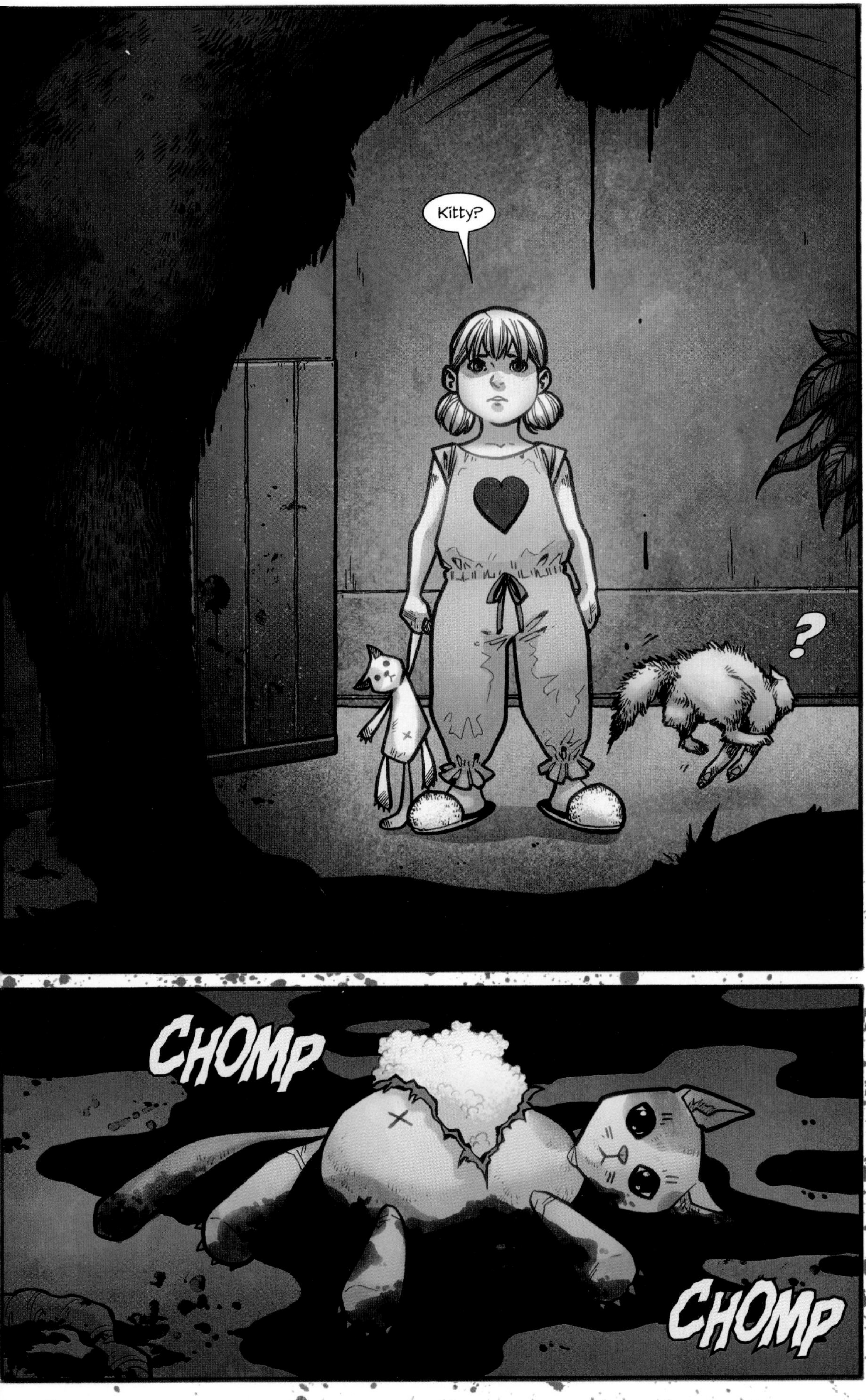
Kitty?
?
CHOMP
CHOMP

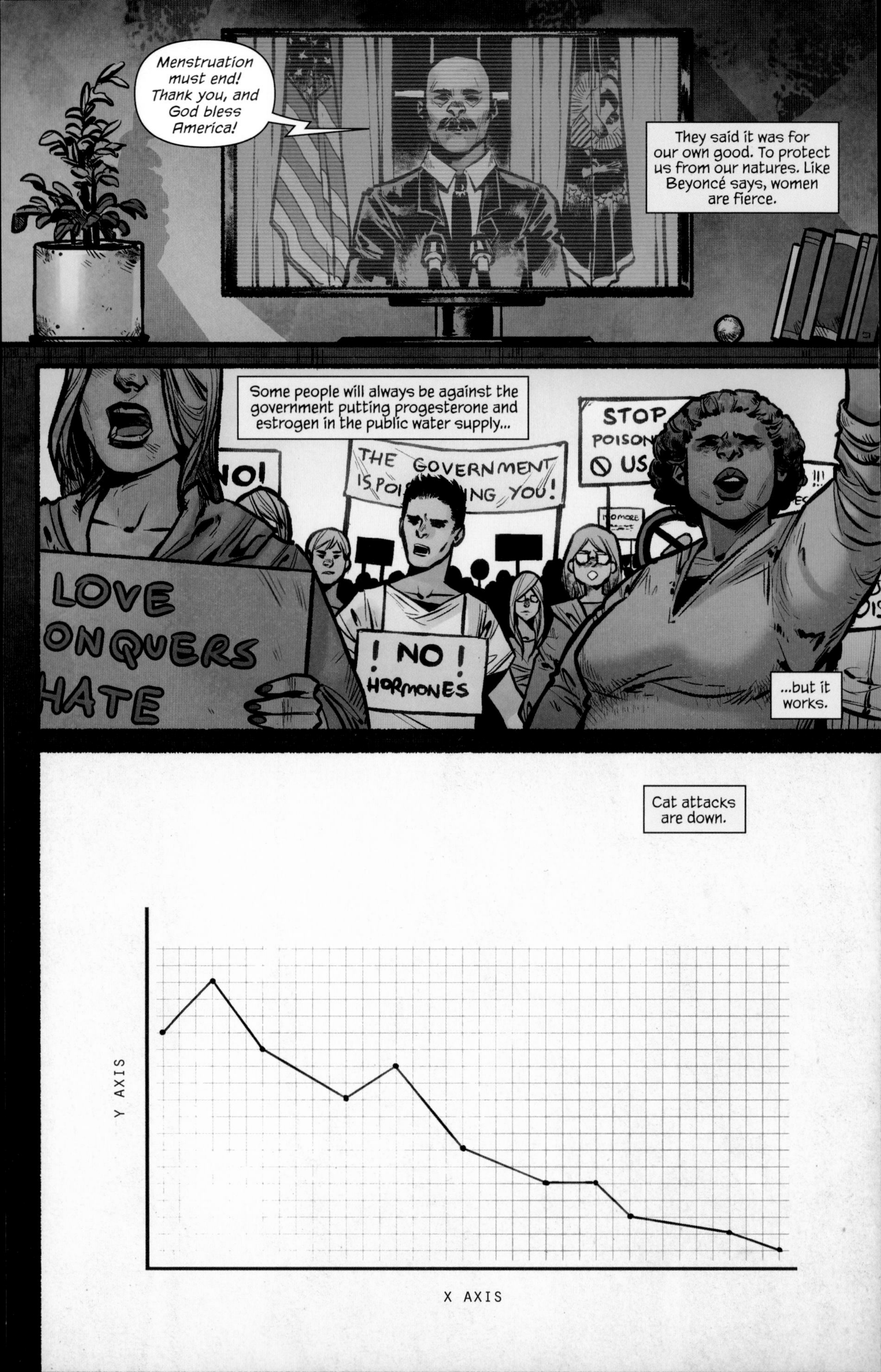
Menstruation must end! Thank you, and God bless America!
They said it was for our own good. To protect us from our natures. Like Beyoncé says, women are fierce.
Some people will always be against the government putting progesterone and estrogen in the public water supply...
STOP POISON US
THE GOVERNMENT IS POIS NG YOU!
NO!
LOVE ONQUERS HATE
! NO ! HORMONES
...but it works.
Cat attacks are down.
Y AXIS
X AXIS

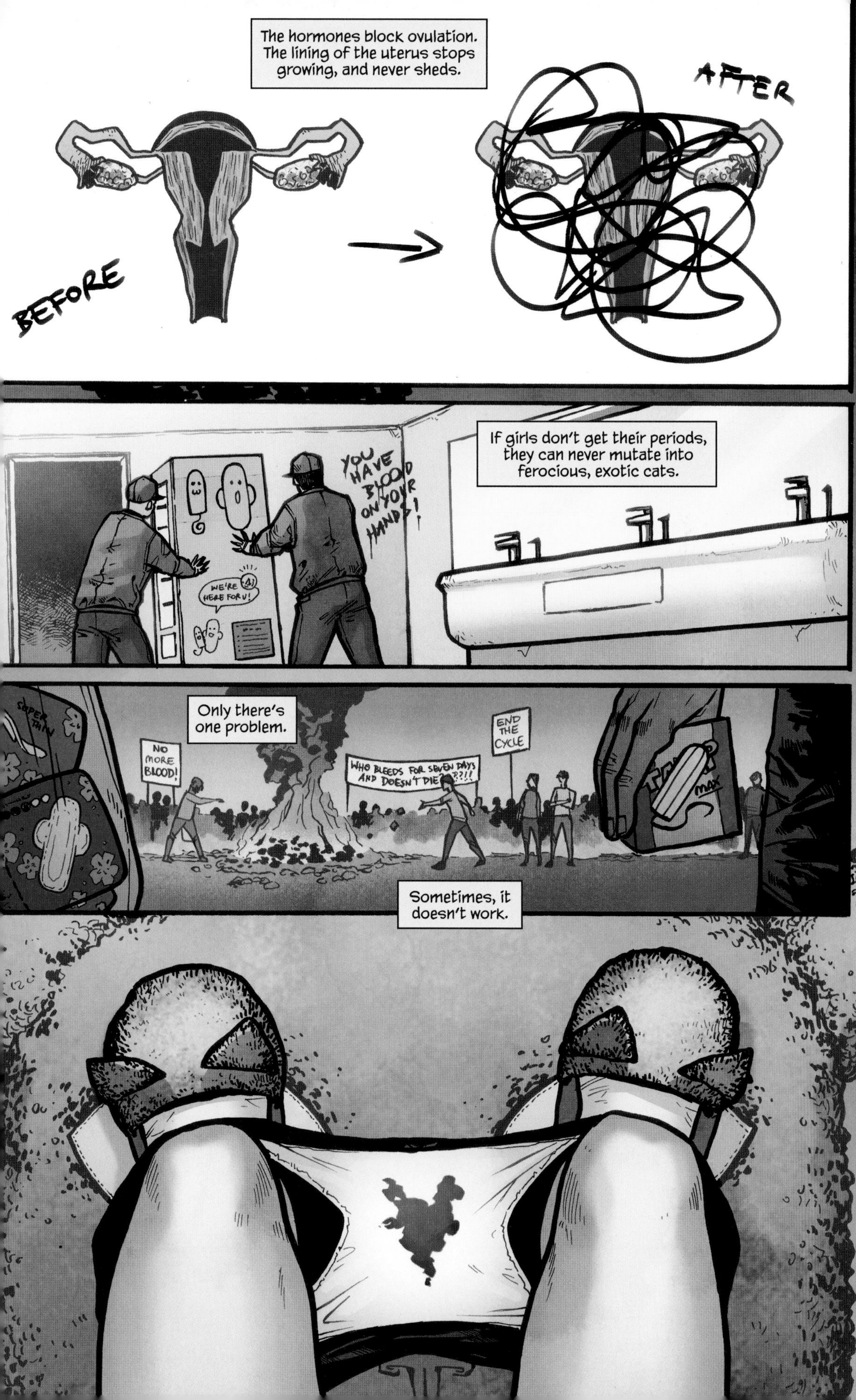
The hormones block ovulation. The lining of the uterus stops growing, and never sheds.
AFTER
BEFORE
YOU HAVE BLOOD ON YOUR HANDS!
WE'RE HERE FOR U!
If girls don't get their periods, they can never mutate into ferocious, exotic cats.
SUPER THIN
Only there's one problem.
NO MORE BLOOD!
WHO BLEEDS FOR SEVEN DAYS AND DOESN'T DIE
END THE CYCLE
MAX
Sometimes, it doesn't work.

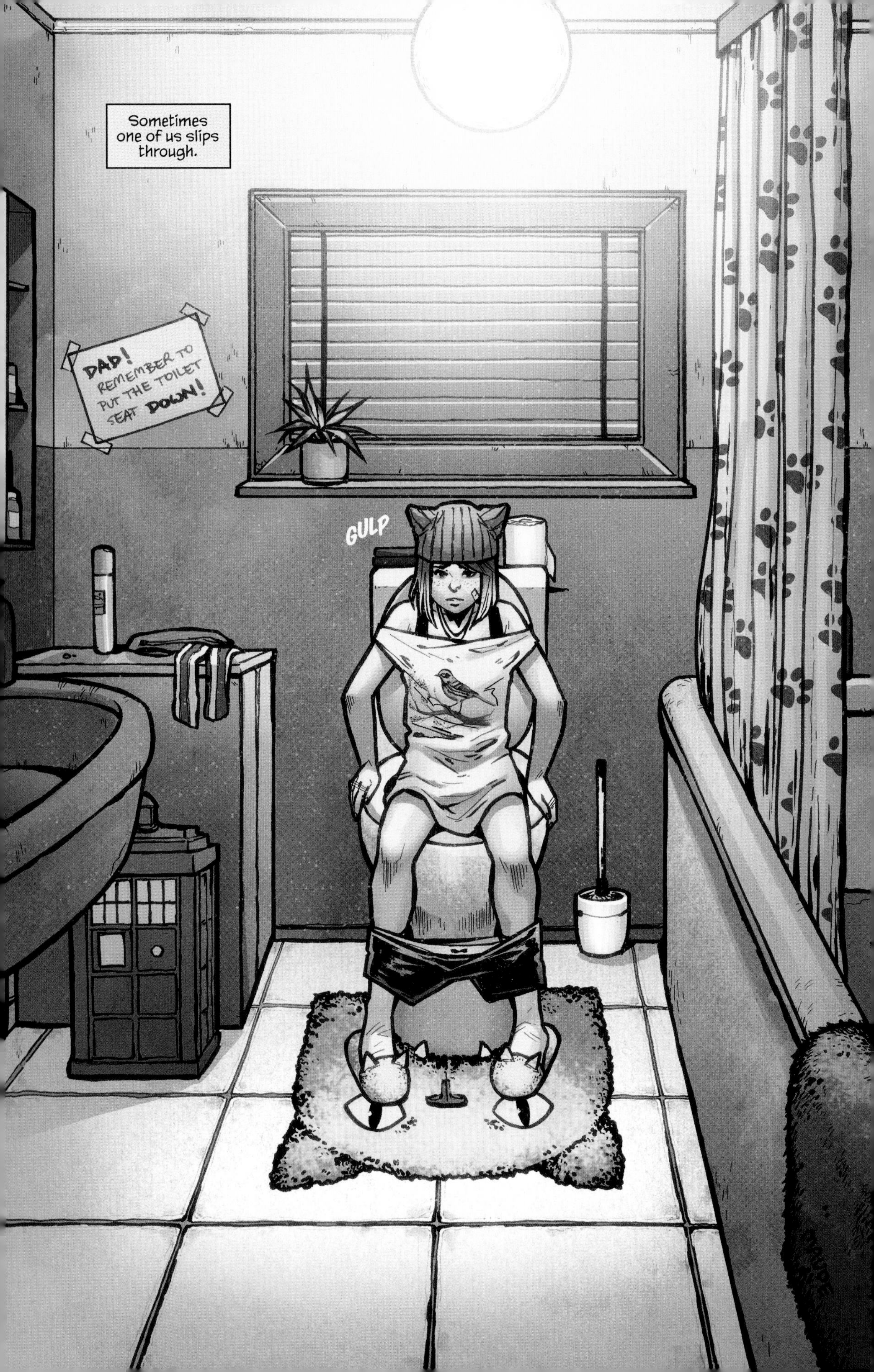
Sometimes one of us slips through.
DAD! REMEMBER TO PUT THE TOILET SEAT DOWN!
GULP

URGENT

MOST CAT ATTACKS TAKE PLACE AT HOME.
IS YOUR CAT BEHAVING STRANGELY? KNOW THE SIGNS.

Which of the following list of words best describes your cat or girlfriend? *Check all that apply.*

- ☐ Moody
- ☐ Irritable
- ☐ Distracted
- ☐ Fastidious
- ☐ Competitive
- ☐ Defensive
- ☐ Abrupt

- ☐ Unaffectionate
- ☐ Prickly
- ☐ Manic
- ☐ Disappointed
- ☐ Marginalized
- ☐ Bossy
- ☐ Insistent

- ☐ Disgusted
- ☐ Entitled
- ☐ Unhinged
- ☐ Prissy
- ☐ Self-serious
- ☐ Tightly wound
- ☐ Resentful

Does your cat or girlfriend suffer from mood swings?
(Circle one.) Yes. No.

Does your cat or girlfriend ever appear to be in a "mental fog"?
(Circle one.) Yes. No.

Has your cat or girlfriend engaged in any of the following behaviors over the last 24 hours? *Check all that apply.*

- ☐ Sleeping more than usual.
- ☐ Self-soothing rituals (excessive hygiene, over-eating, etc)
- ☐ Staring into space
- ☐ Incessant whining
- ☐ Pacing
- ☐ Attempting to get outside

Has your cat or girlfriend ever attacked you viciously for no reason at all? *(Circle one.)* Yes. No.

Is your cat or girlfriend in the room right now?
(Circle one.) Yes. No.

ANSWER KEY

Scoring: Give yourself one point for every checkmark and every time you answered "yes".

Did you score 5+? *You are in danger of a cat attack!*

CAT ATTACK INCIDENT REPORT

NAME OF PERSON ATTACKED BY CAT ____________________ AGE __________

LOCATION OF ATTACK ______________________________

TYPE OF ATTACK (CHECK ALL THAT APPLY) ☐ AMBUSH ☐ MAULING ☐ CLAWING

DATE OF LAST PERIOD ______________________________

INSTRUCTIONS

DESCRIBE PAIN (CHECK ALL THAT APPLY)

1	FLICKERING, QUIVERING, PULSING, THROBBING, BEATING, POUNDING	11	TIRING, EXHAUSTING
2	JUMPING, FLASHING, SHOOTING	12	SICKENING, SUFFOCATING
3	PRICKING, BORING, DRILLING, STABBING, LANCINATING	13	FEARFUL, FRIGHTFUL, TERRIFYING
4	SHARP, CUTTING, LACERATING	14	PUNISHING, GRUELING, CRUEL, VICIOUS, KILLING
5	PINCHING, PRESSING, GNAWING, CRAMPING, CRUSHING	15	WRETCHED, BLINDING
6	TUGGING, PULLING, WRENCHING	16	ANNOYING, TROUBLESOME, MISERABLE, INTENSE, UNBEARABLE
7	HOT, BURNING, SCALDING, SEARING	17	SPREADING, RADIATING, PENETRATING, PIERCING
8	TINGLING, ITCHY, SMARTING, STINGING	18	TIGHT, NUMB, DRAWING, SQUEEZING, TEARING
9	DULL, SORE, HURTING, ACHING, HEAVING	19	COOL, COLD, FREEZING
10	TENDER, TAUT, RASPING, SPLITTING	20	NAGGING, NAUSEATING, AGONIZING, DREADFUL, TORTURING

PPI	
0	NO PAIN
1	MILD
2	DISCOMFORTING
3	DISTRESSING
4	HORRIBLE
5	EXCRUCIATING

PPI ________ COMMENTS:

DESCRIBE LOCATION OF PAIN
(CIRCLE ALL THAT APPLY)

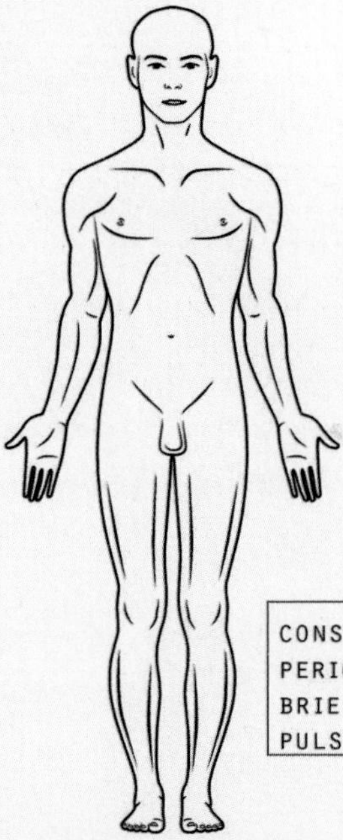

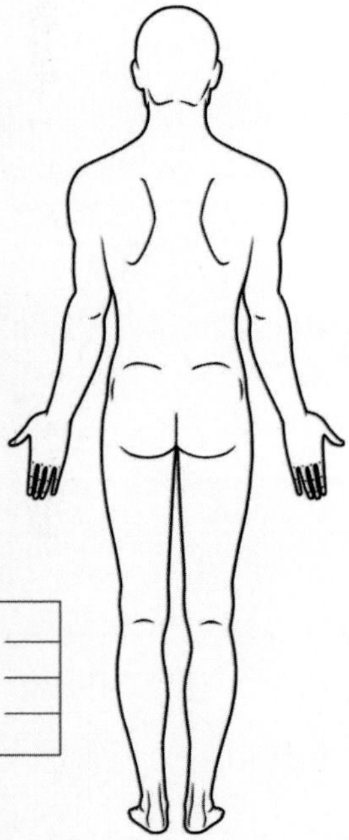

CONSTANT	____
PERIODIC	____
BRIEF	____
PULSATING	____

ACCOMPANYING SYMPTOMS	ACTIVITY	FOOD INTAKE	SLEEP
NAUSEA	GOOD	GOOD	GOOD
HEADACHE	SOME	SOME	FITFUL
DIZZINESS	LITTLE	LITTLE	CAN'T SLEEP
DROWSINESS	NONE	NONE	
CONSTIPATION			
DIARRHEA			

LAST WORDS, IF ANY

COMPLETE AND SUBMIT THIS FORM TO THE MINISTRY OF TROUBLE

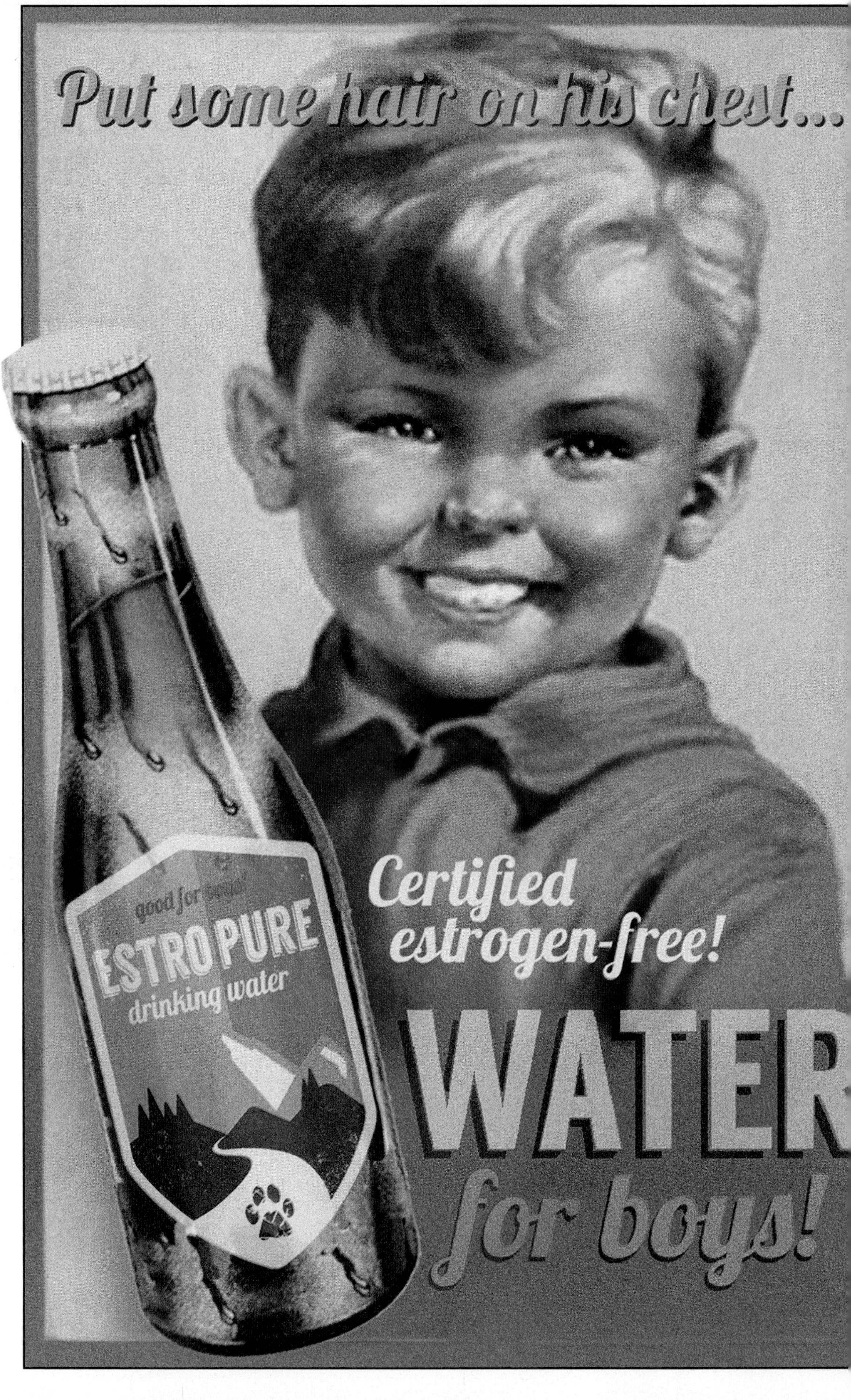
Put some hair on his chest...
good for boys!
ESTRO PURE
drinking water
Certified
estrogen-free!
WATER
for boys!

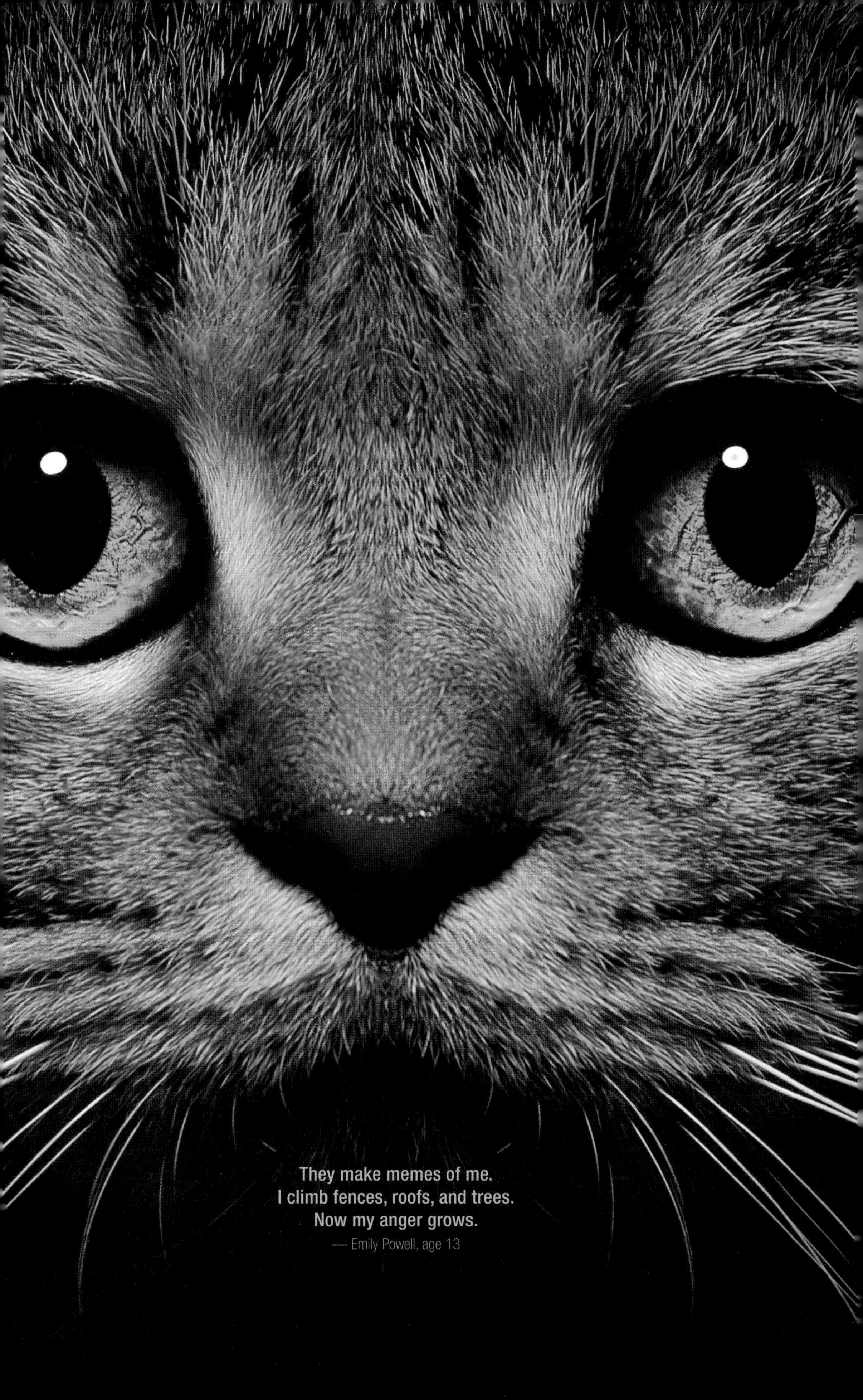

They make memes of me.
I climb fences, roofs, and trees.
Now my anger grows.

— Emily Powell, age 13

Chapter two

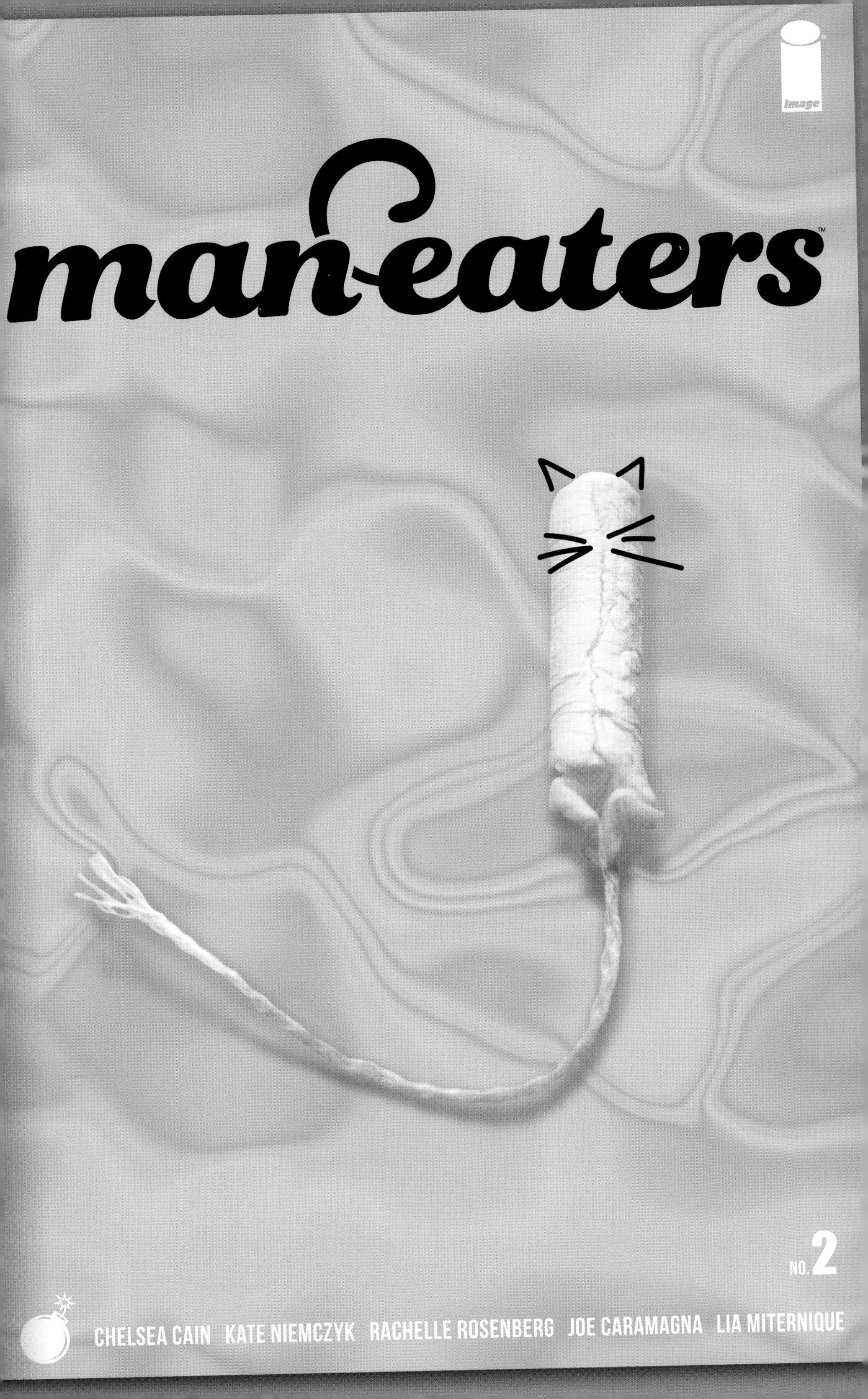
man eaters™
NO. 2
CHELSEA CAIN KATE NIEMCZYK RACHELLE ROSENBERG JOE CARAMAGNA LIA MITERNIQUE

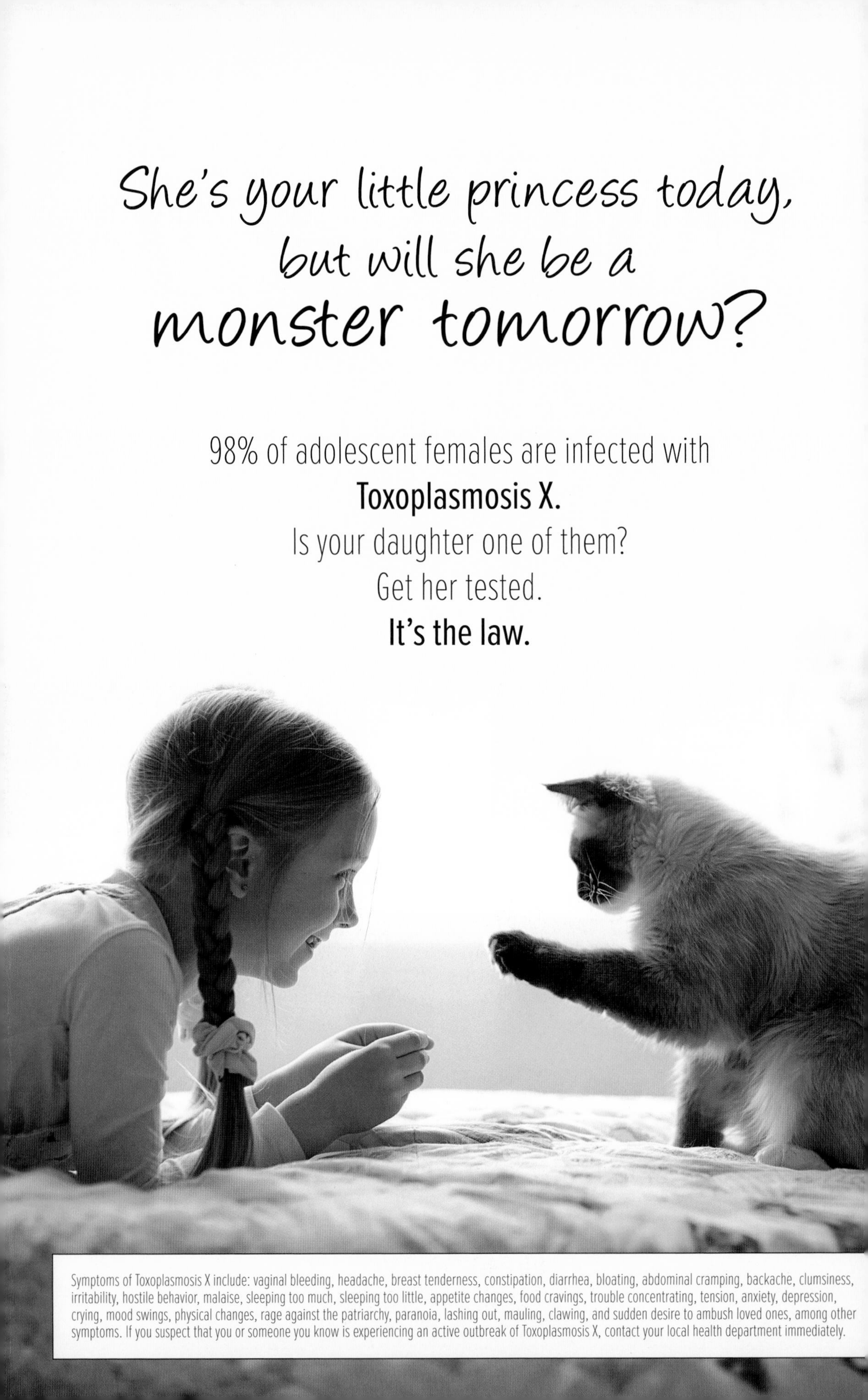
She's your little princess today, but will she be a monster tomorrow?
98% of adolescent females are infected with
Toxoplasmosis X.
Is your daughter one of them?
Get her tested.
It's the law.
Symptoms of Toxoplasmosis X include: vaginal bleeding, headache, breast tenderness, constipation, diarrhea, bloating, abdominal cramping, backache, clumsiness, irritability, hostile behavior, malaise, sleeping too much, sleeping too little, appetite changes, food cravings, trouble concentrating, tension, anxiety, depression, crying, mood swings, physical changes, rage against the patriarchy, paranoia, lashing out, mauling, clawing, and sudden desire to ambush loved ones, among other symptoms. If you suspect that you or someone you know is experiencing an active outbreak of Toxoplasmosis X, contact your local health department immediately.

BY ORDER OF THE MINISTRY OF TROUBLE

PUBLIC WARNING

THIS COMIC MAY ATTRACT
GIRLS AND WOMEN

IF YOU SEE A GIRL OR WOMAN IN YOUR AREA,
REMAIN CALM.
GIRLS AND WOMEN MAY LASH OUT IF PROVOKED.

NO TE ACERQUES.
NO PROVOQUES!
NIE ZBLIŻAJ SIĘ. NIE PROWOKUJ!

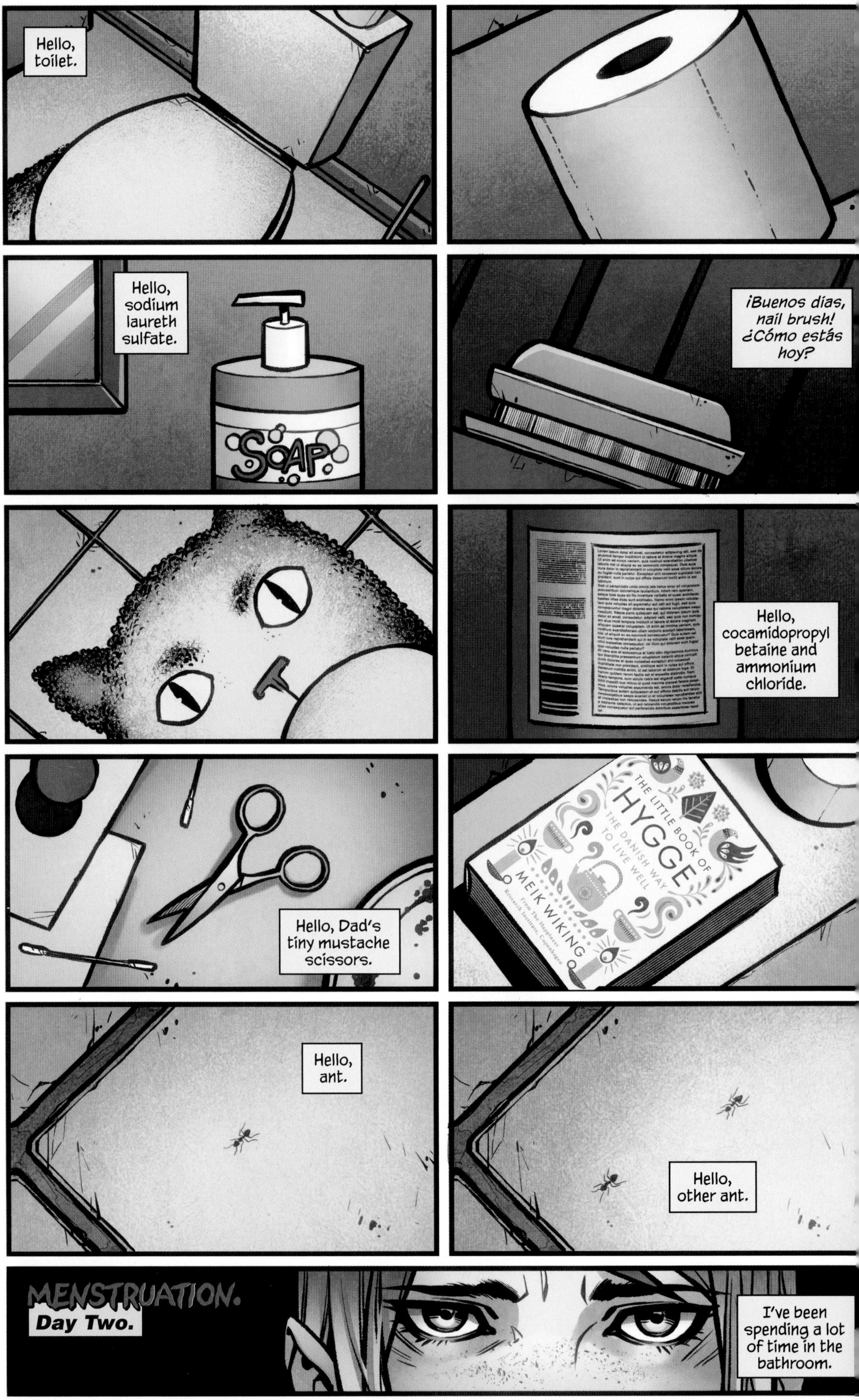
Hello,
toilet.
Hello,
sodium
laureth
sulfate.
SOAP
¡Buenos días,
nail brush!
¿Cómo estás
hoy?
Hello,
cocamidopropyl
betaine and
ammonium
chloride.
Hello, Dad's
tiny mustache
scissors.
THE LITTLE BOOK OF
HYGGE
THE DANISH WAY
TO LIVE WELL
MEIK WIKING
Hello,
ant.
Hello,
other ant.
MENSTRUATION.
Day Two.
I've been
spending a lot
of time in the
bathroom.

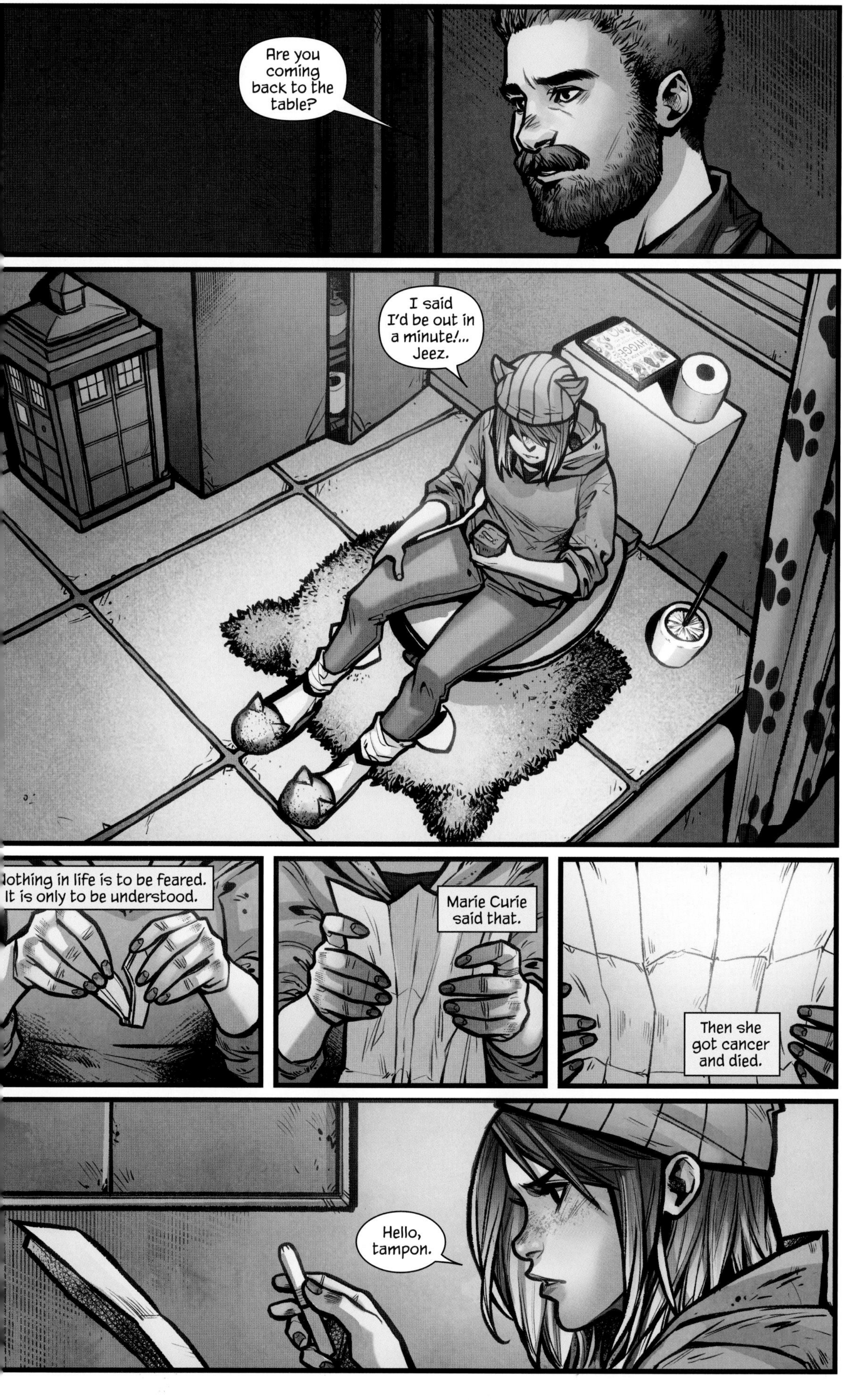
Are you coming back to the table?
I said I'd be out in a minute!... Jeez.
lothing in life is to be feared. It is only to be understood.
Marie Curie said that.
Then she got cancer and died.
Hello, tampon.

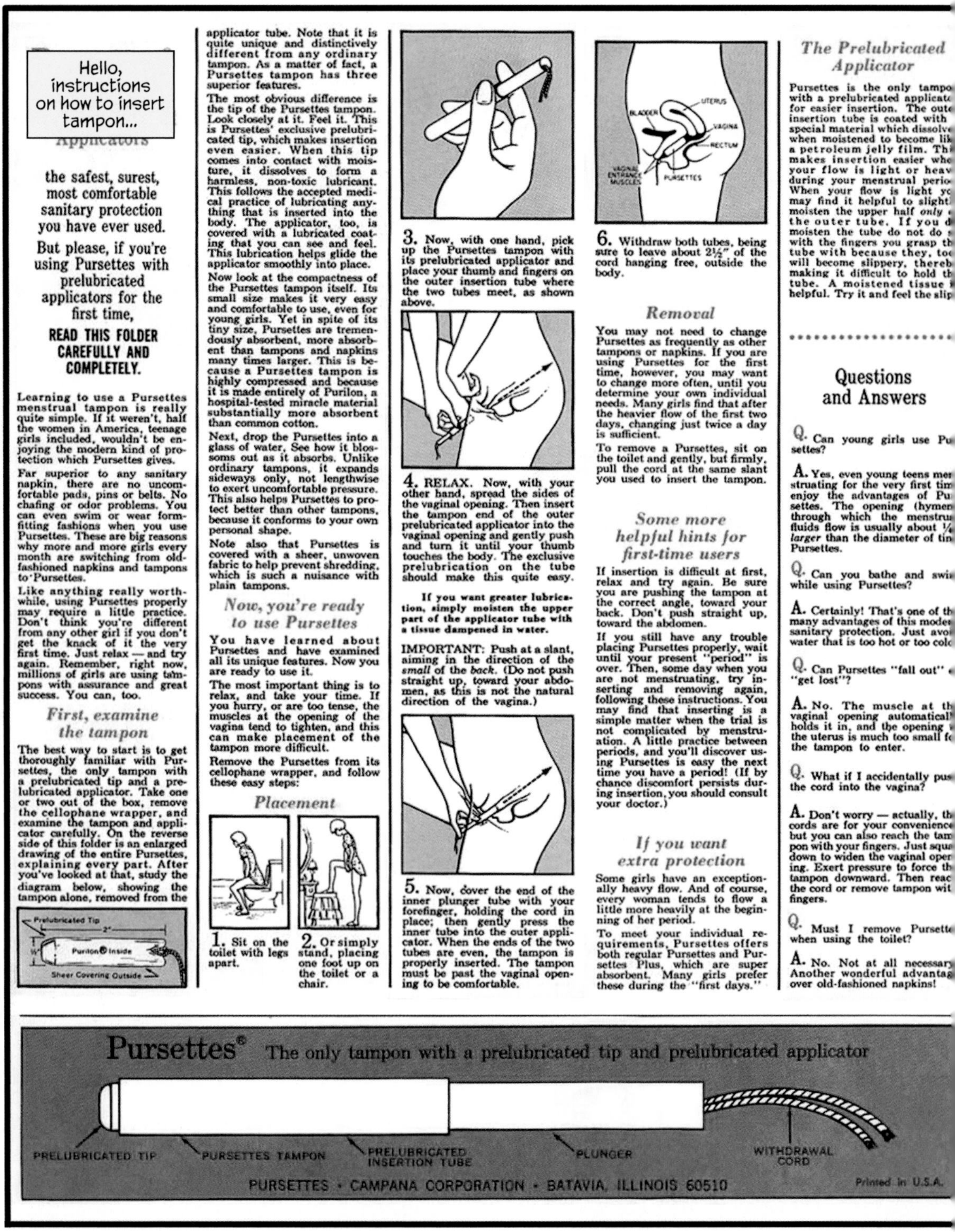

Hello, instructions on how to insert tampon...

...Applicators

the safest, surest, most comfortable sanitary protection you have ever used.

But please, if you're using Pursettes with prelubricated applicators for the first time,

READ THIS FOLDER CAREFULLY AND COMPLETELY.

Learning to use a Pursettes menstrual tampon is really quite simple. If it weren't, half the women in America, teenage girls included, wouldn't be enjoying the modern kind of protection which Pursettes gives.

Far superior to any sanitary napkin, there are no uncomfortable pads, pins or belts. No chafing or odor problems. You can even swim or wear form-fitting fashions when you use Pursettes. These are big reasons why more and more girls every month are switching from old-fashioned napkins and tampons to Pursettes.

Like anything really worthwhile, using Pursettes properly may require a little practice. Don't think you're different from any other girl if you don't get the knack of it the very first time. Just relax — and try again. Remember, right now, millions of girls are using tampons with assurance and great success. You can, too.

First, examine the tampon

The best way to start is to get thoroughly familiar with Pursettes, the only tampon with a prelubricated tip and a prelubricated applicator. Take one or two out of the box, remove the cellophane wrapper, and examine the tampon and applicator carefully. On the reverse side of this folder is an enlarged drawing of the entire Pursettes, explaining every part. After you've looked at that, study the diagram below, showing the tampon alone, removed from its

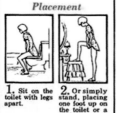
- Prelubricated Tip
- Purilon® Inside
- Sheer Covering Outside

applicator tube. Note that it is quite unique and distinctively different from any ordinary tampon. As a matter of fact, a Pursettes tampon has three superior features.

The most obvious difference is the tip of the Pursettes tampon. Look closely at it. Feel it. This is Pursettes' exclusive prelubricated tip, which makes insertion even easier. When this tip comes into contact with moisture, it dissolves to form a harmless, non-toxic lubricant. This follows the accepted medical practice of lubricating anything that is inserted into the body. The applicator, too, is covered with a lubricated coating that you can see and feel. This lubrication helps glide the applicator smoothly into place.

Now look at the compactness of the Pursettes tampon itself. Its small size makes it very easy and comfortable to use, even for young girls. Yet in spite of its tiny size, Pursettes are tremendously absorbent, more absorbent than tampons and napkins many times larger. This is because a Pursettes tampon is highly compressed and because it is made entirely of Purilon, a hospital-tested miracle material substantially more absorbent than common cotton.

Next, drop the Pursettes into a glass of water. See how it blossoms out as it absorbs. Unlike ordinary tampons, it expands sideways only, not lengthwise to exert uncomfortable pressure. This also helps Pursettes to protect better than other tampons, because it conforms to your own personal shape.

Note also that Pursettes is covered with a sheer, unwoven fabric to help prevent shredding, which is such a nuisance with plain tampons.

Now, you're ready to use Pursettes

You have learned about Pursettes and have examined all its unique features. Now you are ready to use it.

The most important thing is to relax, and take your time. If you hurry, or are too tense, the muscles at the opening of the vagina tend to tighten, and this can make placement of the tampon more difficult.

Remove the Pursettes from its cellophane wrapper, and follow these easy steps:

Placement

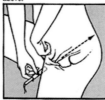

1. Sit on the toilet with legs apart.
2. Or simply stand, placing one foot up on the toilet or a chair.

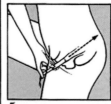

3. Now, with one hand, pick up the Pursettes tampon with its prelubricated applicator and place your thumb and fingers on the outer insertion tube where the two tubes meet, as shown above.

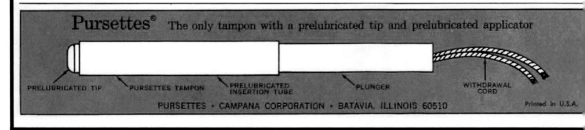

4. RELAX. Now, with your other hand, spread the sides of the vaginal opening. Then insert the tampon end of the outer prelubricated applicator into the vaginal opening and turn it until your thumb touches the body. The exclusive prelubrication on the tube should make this quite easy.

If you want greater lubrication, simply moisten the upper part of the applicator tube with a tissue dampened in water.

IMPORTANT: Push at a slant, aiming in the direction of the *small* of the *back*. (Do not push straight up, toward your abdomen, as this is not the natural direction of the vagina.)

5. Now, cover the end of the inner plunger tube with your forefinger, holding the cord in place; then gently press the inner tube into the outer applicator. When the ends of the two tubes are even, the tampon is properly inserted. The tampon must be past the vaginal opening to be comfortable.

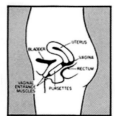

6. Withdraw both tubes, being sure to leave about 2½" of the cord hanging free, outside the body.

Removal

You may not need to change Pursettes as frequently as other tampons or napkins. If you are using Pursettes for the first time, however, you may want to change more often, until you determine your own individual needs. Many girls find that after the heavier flow of the first two days, changing just twice a day is sufficient.

To remove a Pursettes, sit on the toilet and gently, but firmly, pull the cord at the same slant you used to insert the tampon.

Some more helpful hints for first-time users

If insertion is difficult at first, relax and try again. Be sure you are pushing the tampon at the correct angle, toward your back. Don't push straight up, toward the abdomen.

If you still have any trouble placing Pursettes properly, wait until your present "period" is over. Then, some day when you are not menstruating, try inserting and removing again, following these instructions. You may find that inserting is a simple matter when the trial is not complicated by menstruation. A little practice between periods, and you'll discover using Pursettes is easy the next time you have a period! (If by chance discomfort persists during insertion, you should consult your doctor.)

If you want extra protection

Some girls have an exceptionally heavy flow. And of course, every woman tends to flow a little more heavily at the beginning of her period.

To meet your individual requirements, Pursettes offers both regular Pursettes and Pursettes Plus, which are super absorbent. Many girls prefer these during the "first days."

The Prelubricated Applicator

Pursettes is the only tampon with a prelubricated applicator for easier insertion. The outer insertion tube is coated with special material which dissolves when moistened to become like a petroleum jelly film. This makes insertion easier when your flow is light or heavy during your menstrual period. When your flow is light you may find it helpful to slightly moisten the upper half *only* of the outer tube. If you do moisten the tube do not do so with the fingers you grasp the tube with because they, too, will become slippery, thereby making it difficult to hold the tube. A moistened tissue is helpful. Try it and feel the slip.

....

Questions and Answers

Q. Can young girls use Pursettes?

A. Yes, even young teens menstruating for the very first time enjoy the advantages of Pursettes. The opening (hymen) through which the menstrual fluids flow is usually about ¼ larger than the diameter of tiny Pursettes.

Q. Can you bathe and swim while using Pursettes?

A. Certainly! That's one of the many advantages of this modern sanitary protection. Just avoid water that is too hot or too cold.

Q. Can Pursettes "fall out" or "get lost"?

A. No. The muscle at the vaginal opening automatically holds it in, and the opening to the uterus is much too small for the tampon to enter.

Q. What if I accidentally push the cord into the vagina?

A. Don't worry — actually, the cords are for your convenience, but you can also reach the tampon with your fingers. Just squat down to widen the vaginal opening. Exert pressure to force the tampon downward. Then reach the cord or remove tampon with fingers.

Q. Must I remove Pursettes when using the toilet?

A. No. Not at all necessary. Another wonderful advantage over old-fashioned napkins!

Pursettes® The only tampon with a prelubricated tip and prelubricated applicator

PRELUBRICATED TIP • PURSETTES TAMPON • PRELUBRICATED INSERTION TUBE • PLUNGER • WITHDRAWAL CORD

PURSETTES • CAMPANA CORPORATION • BATAVIA, ILLINOIS 60510

Printed in U.S.A.

...Seriously?

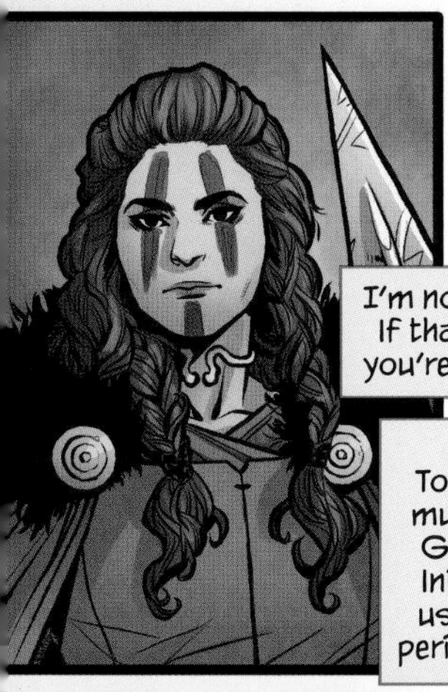
I'm not scared. If that's what you're thinking.
Before the Toxoplasmosis X mutation, and the Global Hormone Initiative, women used to get their periods all the time.

BOUDICA

Anti-imperialist Celtic rebel warrior queen. Led uprising against the occupying forces of the Roman Empire. Tough AF.

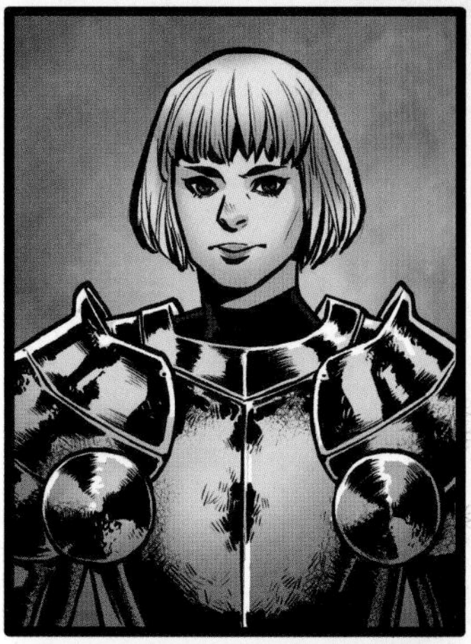

JOAN OF ARC

Commanded French army as a teen. Cross-dressing goals. Saint. Probably had to deal with having her period while wearing armor, and riding a horse.

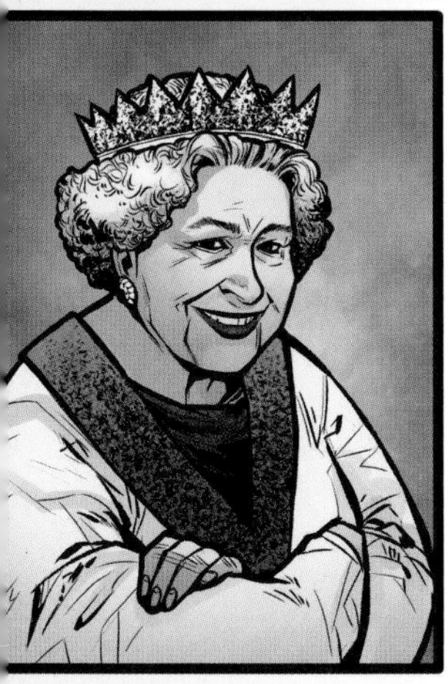

QUEEN ELIZABETH 2

British monarch. Corgi enthusiast. Refuses to retire. Loves hats. Still married.

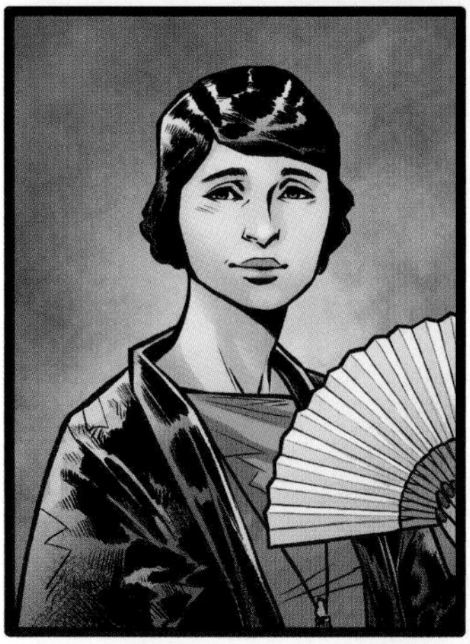

MARGARET SANGER

Birth control advocate, nurse, sex educator, social reformer. Opened U.S.'s first birth control clinic--in 1916.

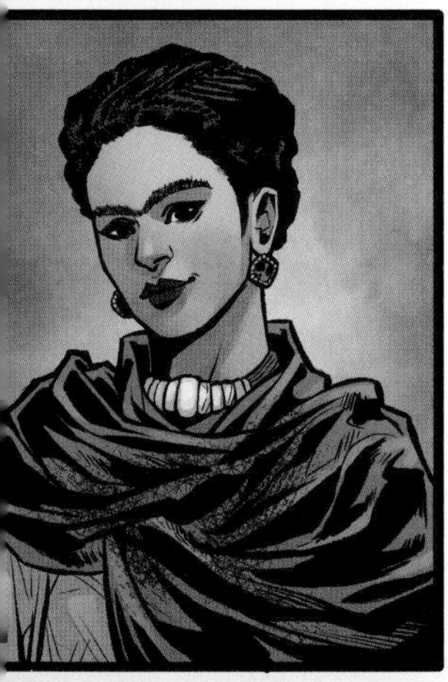

FRIDA KAHLO

Postcard icon, self-portraitist, activist. Considered one of Mexico's greatest artists. Lived in chronic pain, still made art. Was like, yeah, I have a unibrow, so what?

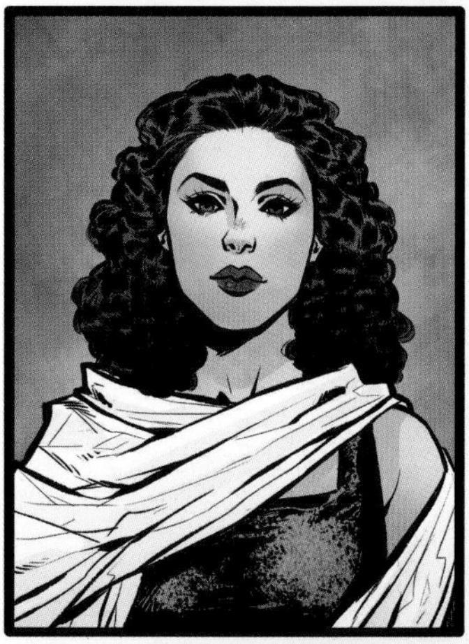

HEDY LAMARR

Actress, studio designated bombshell, inventor, self-taught tinkerer. Credited with creating a frequency-hopping signal used in all wireless communications.

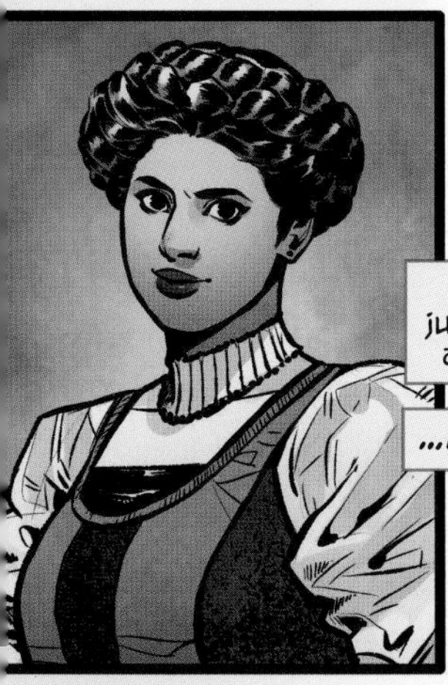
They just walked around...
...bleeding.

MATA HARI

Dancer, sex worker, entrepreneur, single mother, World War I spy, cultural agitator, fabulist. Often appeared on stage in nude body stocking.

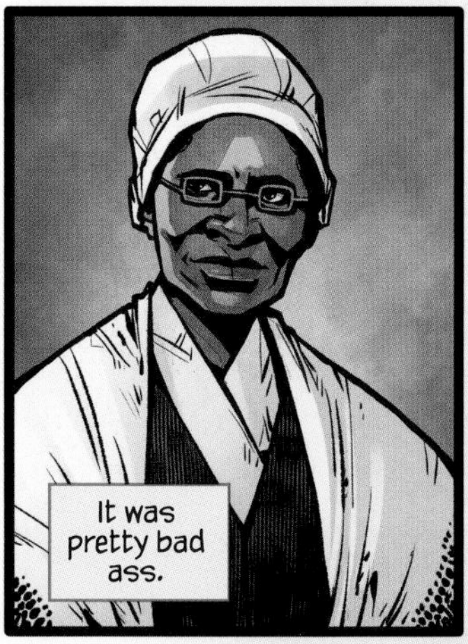
It was pretty bad ass.

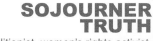

SOJOURNER TRUTH

Abolitionist, women's rights activist. Born into slavery, escaped with infant daughter to freedom in 1862. Homeowner. Campaigned against slavery, for women's rights, prison reform, temperance, and against the death penalty.

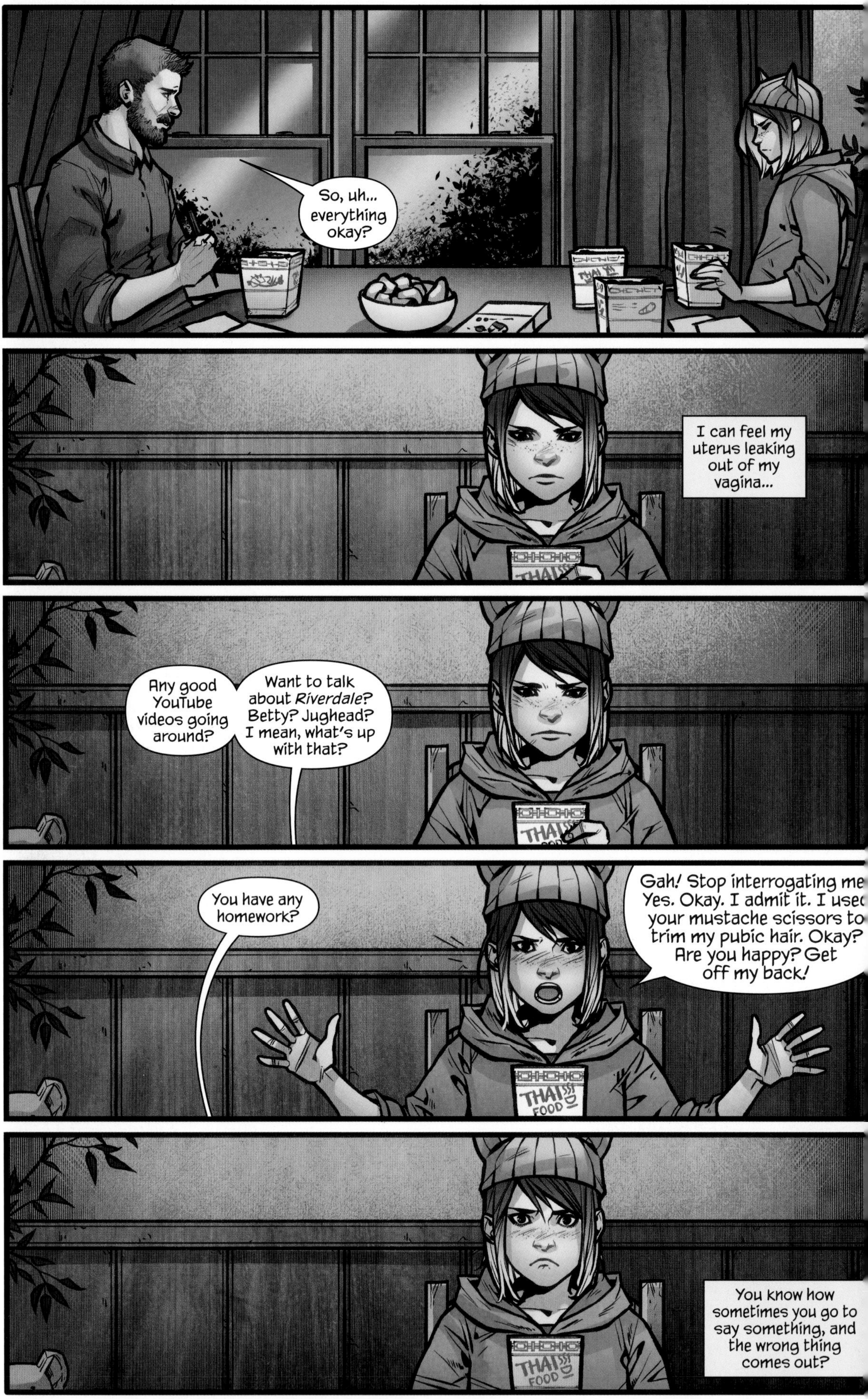
So, uh... everything okay?
I can feel my uterus leaking out of my vagina...
Any good YouTube videos going around?
Want to talk about *Riverdale*? Betty? Jughead? I mean, what's up with that?
You have any homework?
Gah! Stop interrogating me Yes. Okay. I admit it. I use your mustache scissors to trim my pubic hair. Okay? Are you happy? Get off my back!
You know how sometimes you go to say something, and the wrong thing comes out?

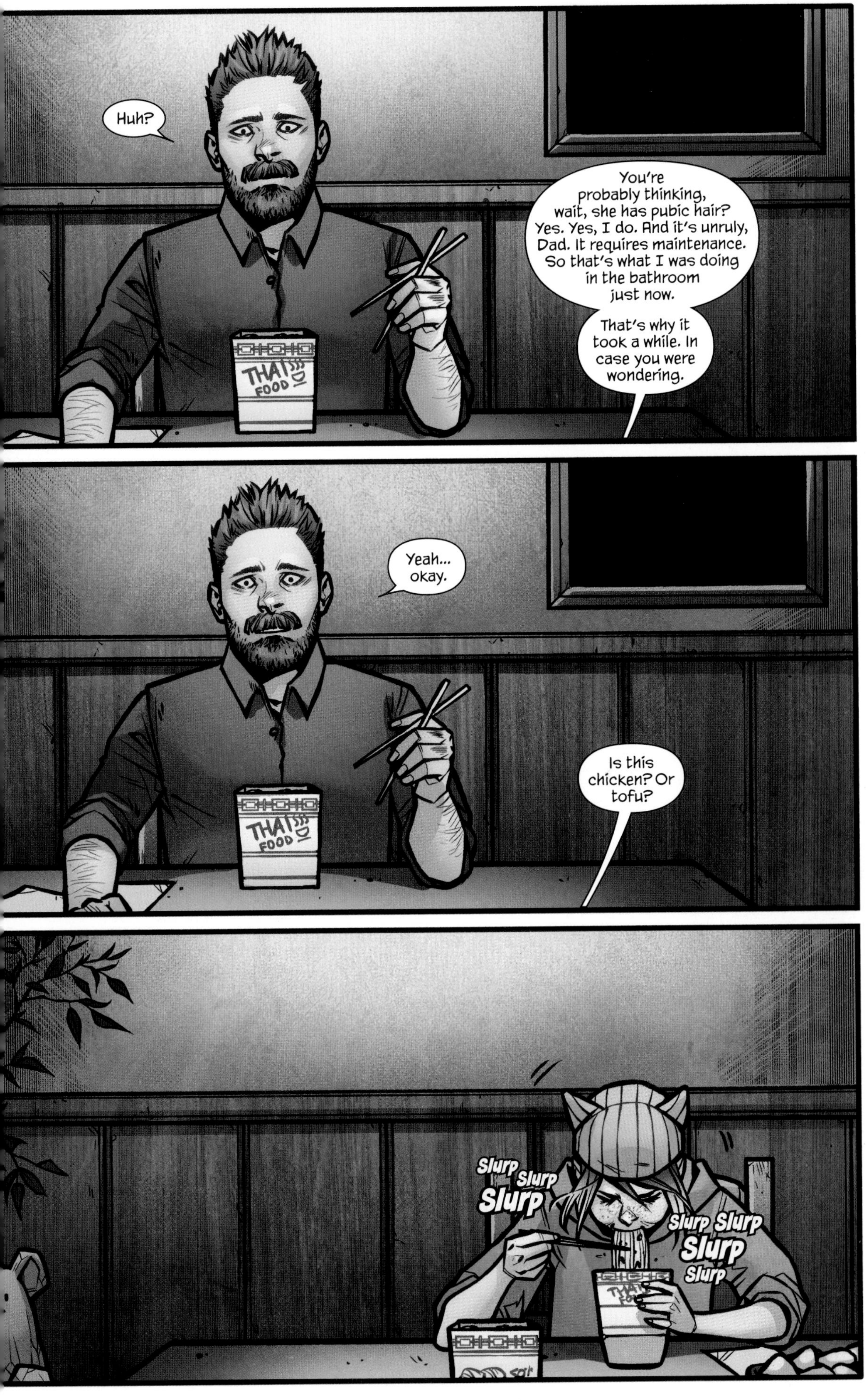
Huh?
You're probably thinking, wait, she has pubic hair? Yes. Yes, I do. And it's unruly, Dad. It requires maintenance. So that's what I was doing in the bathroom just now.
That's why it took a while. In case you were wondering.
Yeah... okay.
Is this chicken? Or tofu?
Slurp Slurp Slurp
Slurp Slurp Slurp Slurp

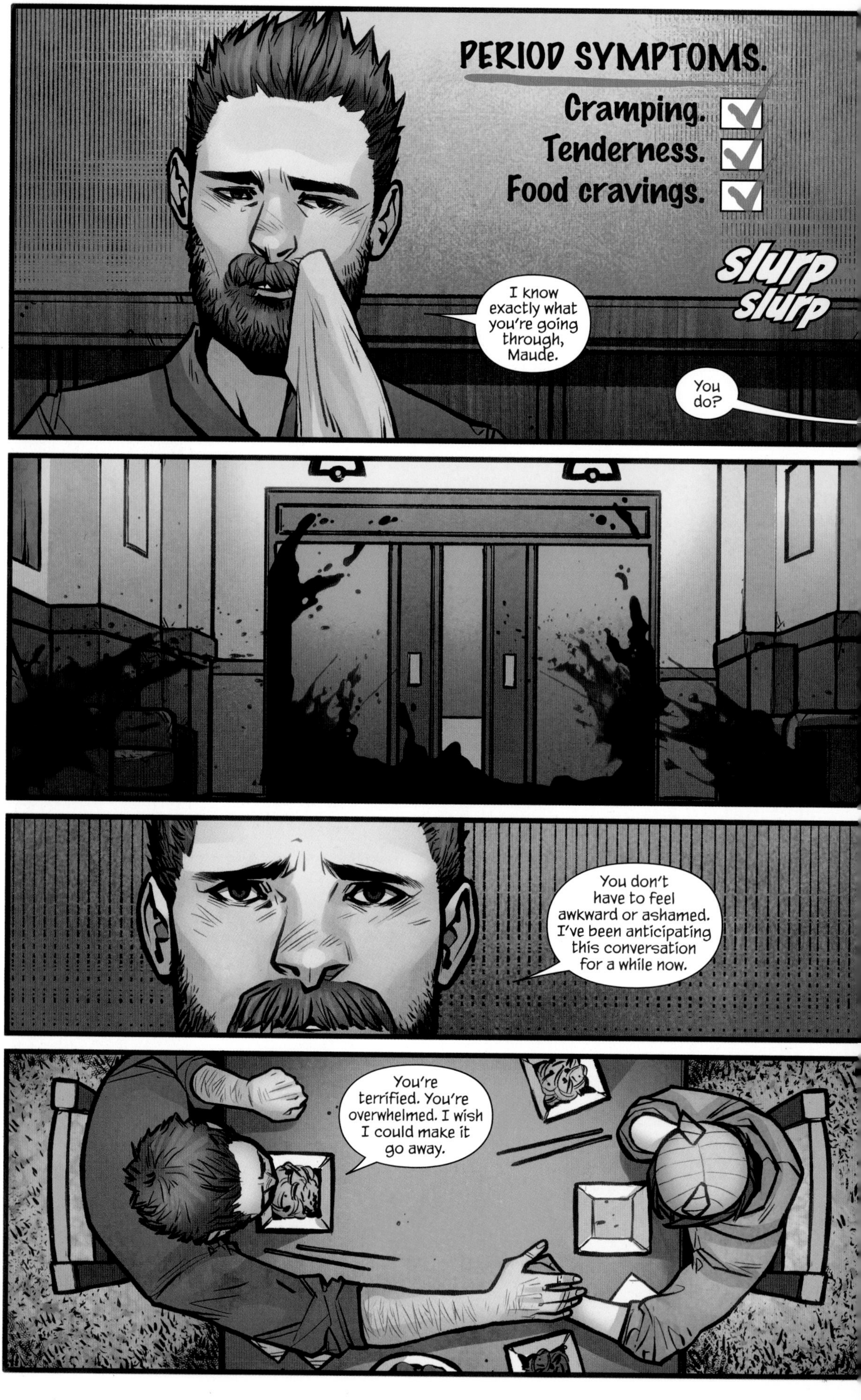
PERIOD SYMPTOMS.
Cramping.
Tenderness.
Food cravings.
slurp slurp
I know exactly what you're going through, Maude.
You do?
You don't have to feel awkward or ashamed. I've been anticipating this conversation for a while now.
You're terrified. You're overwhelmed. I wish I could make it go away.

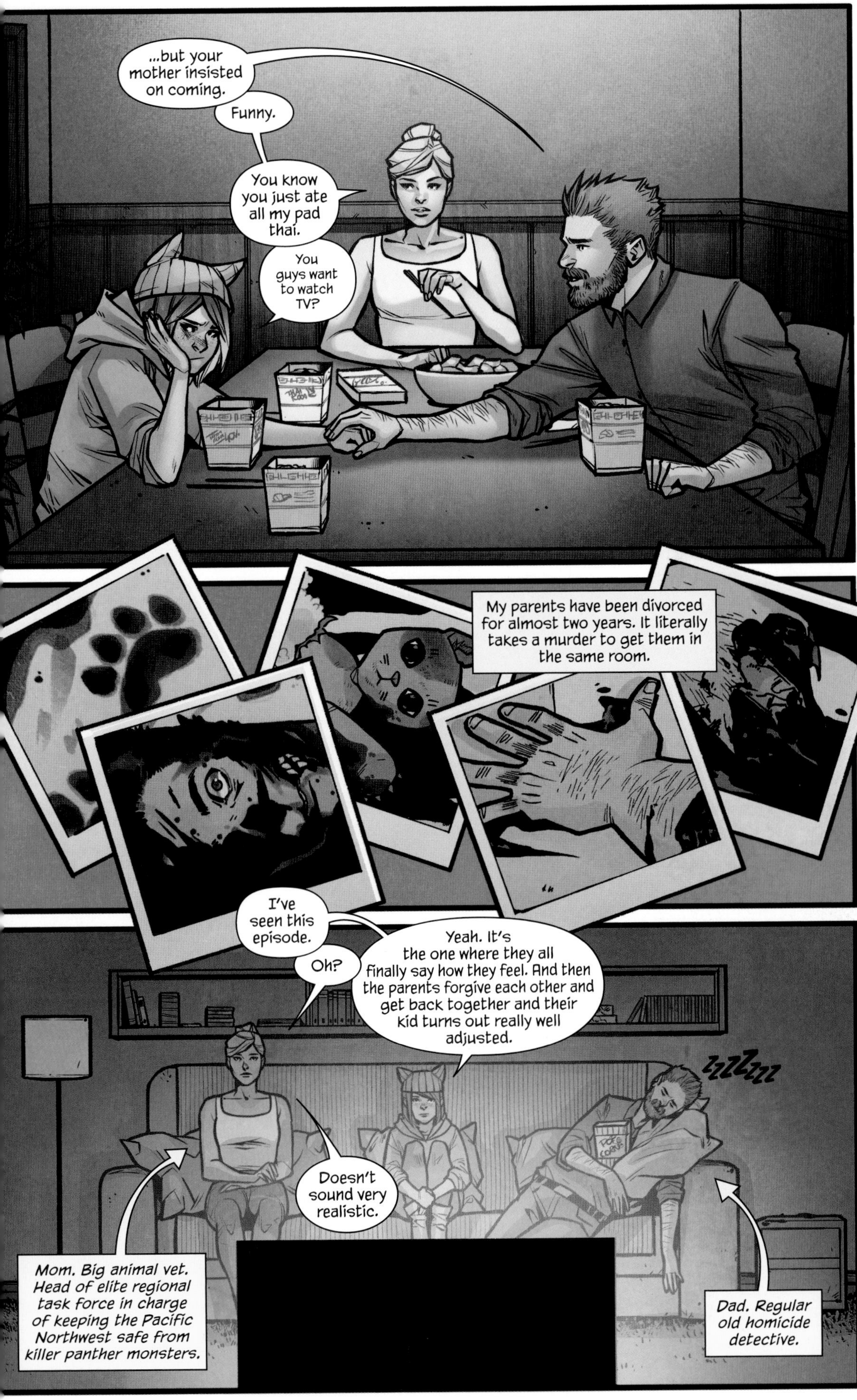
...but your mother insisted on coming.
Funny.
You know you just ate all my pad thai.
You guys want to watch TV?
My parents have been divorced for almost two years. It literally takes a murder to get them in the same room.
I've seen this episode.
Oh?
Yeah. It's the one where they all finally say how they feel. And then the parents forgive each other and get back together and their kid turns out really well adjusted.
ZZZZZZZ
Doesn't sound very realistic.
Mom. Big animal vet. Head of elite regional task force in charge of keeping the Pacific Northwest safe from killer panther monsters.
Dad. Regular old homicide detective.

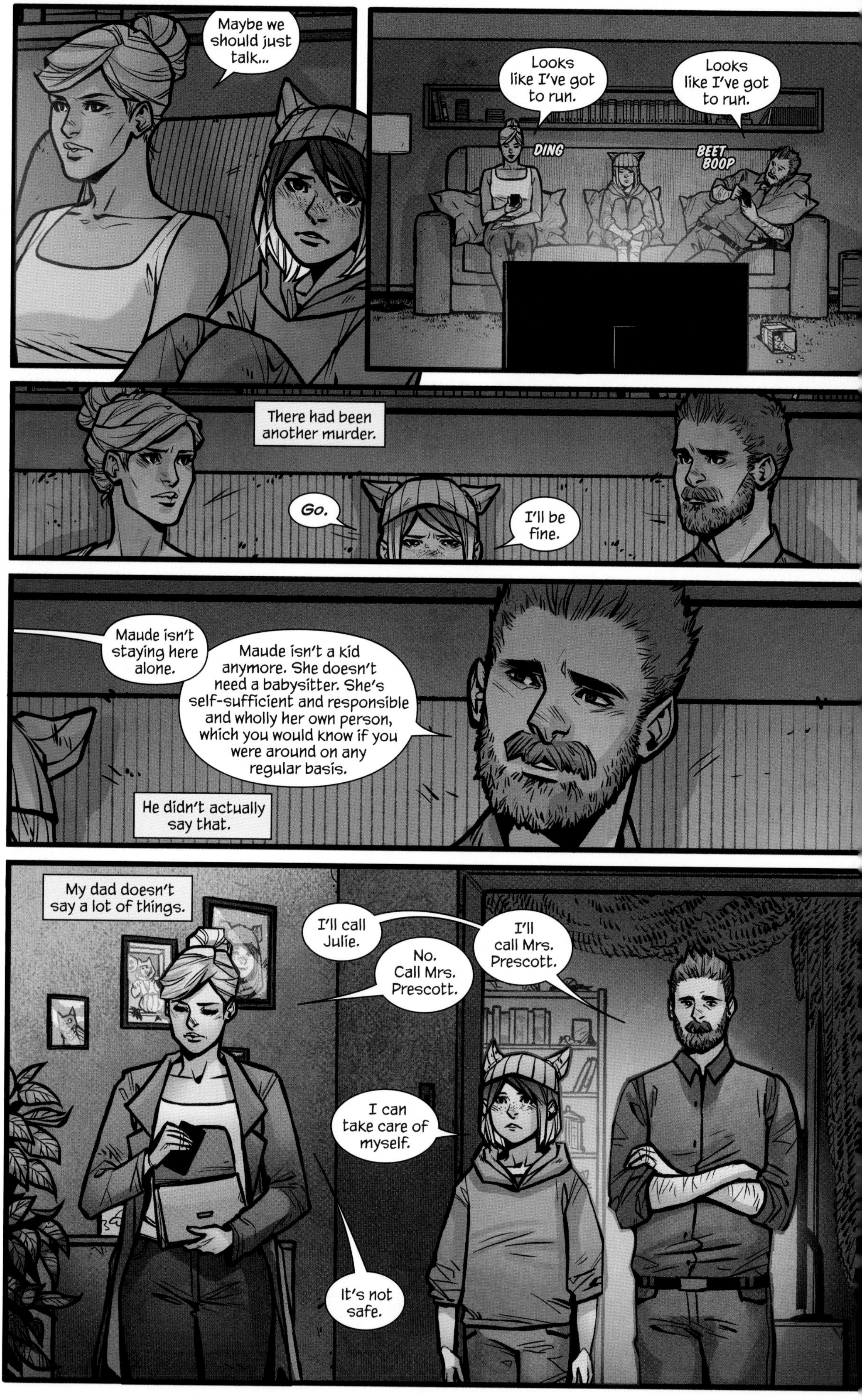

Maybe we should just talk...
Looks like I've got to run.
DING
Looks like I've got to run.
BEET BOOP
There had been another murder.
Go.
I'll be fine.
Maude isn't staying here alone.
Maude isn't a kid anymore. She doesn't need a babysitter. She's self-sufficient and responsible and wholly her own person, which you would know if you were around on any regular basis.
He didn't actually say that.
My dad doesn't say a lot of things.
I'll call Julie.
I'll call Mrs. Prescott.
No. Call Mrs. Prescott.
I can take care of myself.
It's not safe.

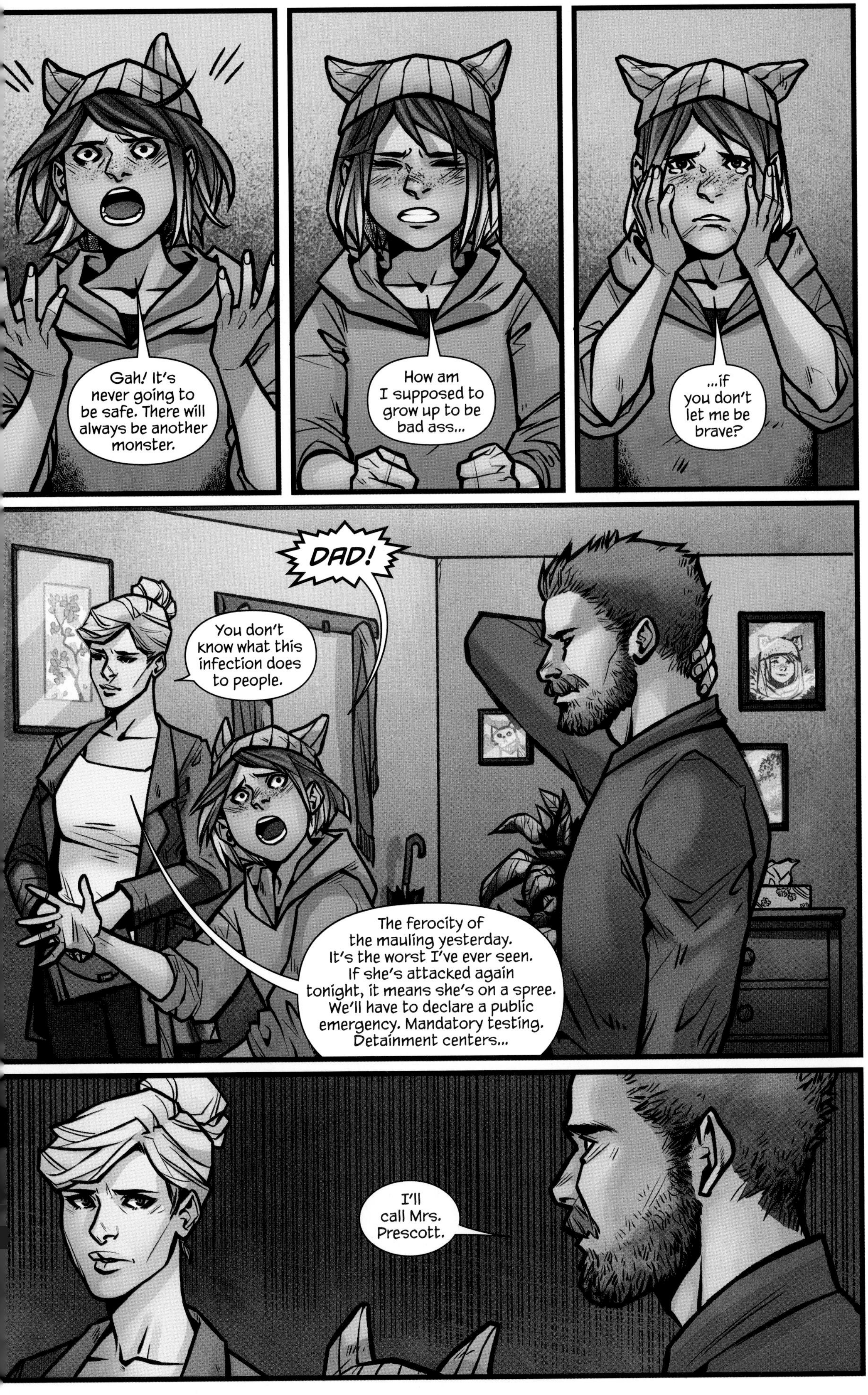
Gah! It's never going to be safe. There will always be another monster.
How am I supposed to grow up to be bad ass...
...if you don't let me be brave?
DAD!
You don't know what this infection does to people.
The ferocity of the mauling yesterday. It's the worst I've ever seen. If she's attacked again tonight, it means she's on a spree. We'll have to declare a public emergency. Mandatory testing. Detainment centers...
I'll call Mrs. Prescott.

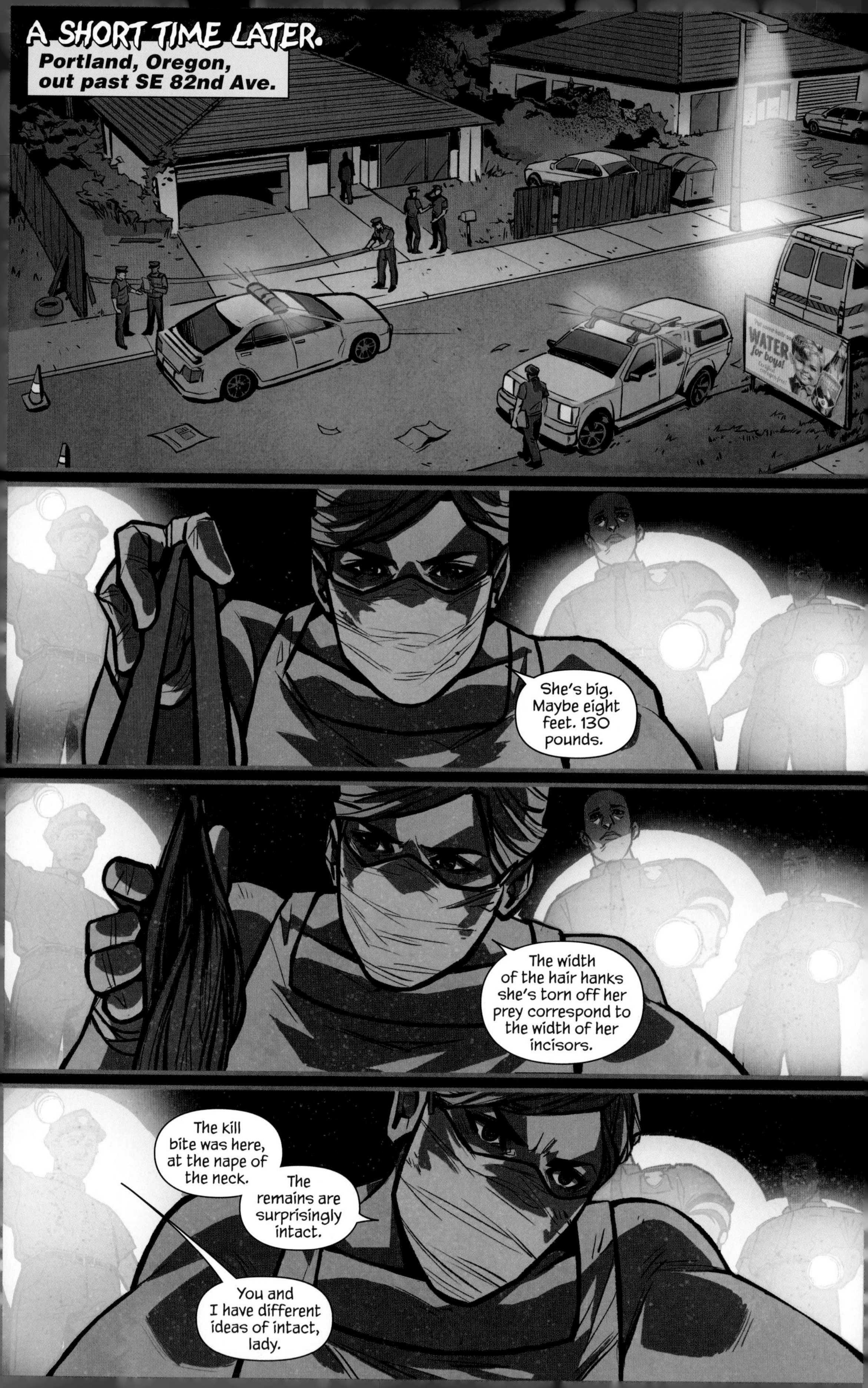
A SHORT TIME LATER.
Portland, Oregon, out past SE 82nd Ave.
WATER
for boys!
She's big. Maybe eight feet. 130 pounds.
The width of the hair hanks she's torn off her prey correspond to the width of her incisors.
The kill bite was here, at the nape of the neck.
The remains are surprisingly intact.
You and I have different ideas of intact, lady.

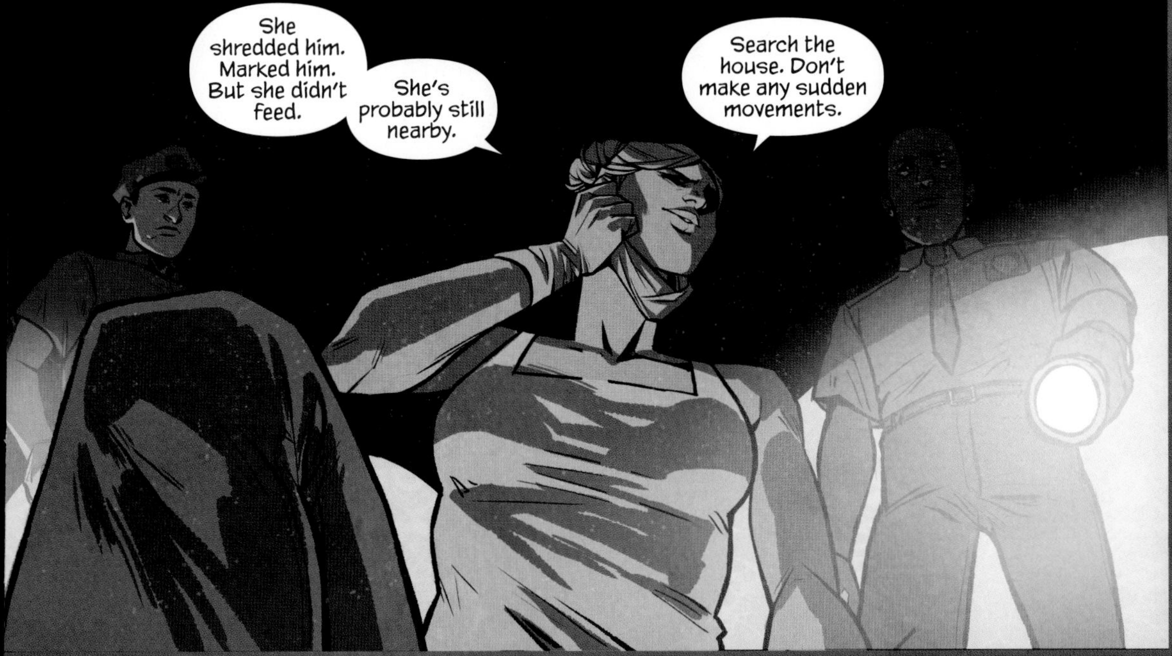
She shredded him. Marked him. But she didn't feed.
She's probably still nearby.
Search the house. Don't make any sudden movements.

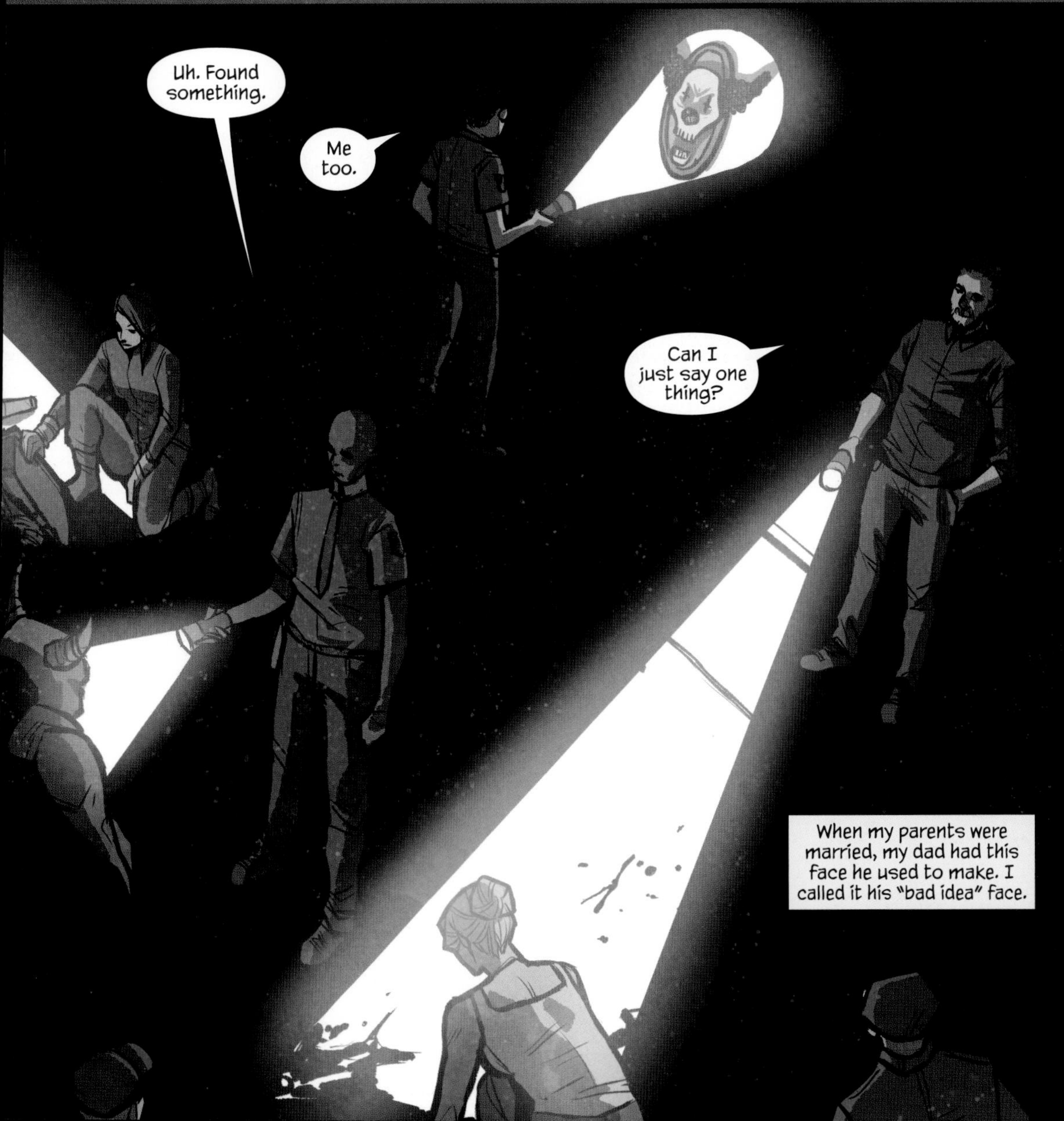
Uh. Found something.
Me too.
Can I just say one thing?
When my parents were married, my dad had this face he used to make. I called it his "bad idea" face.

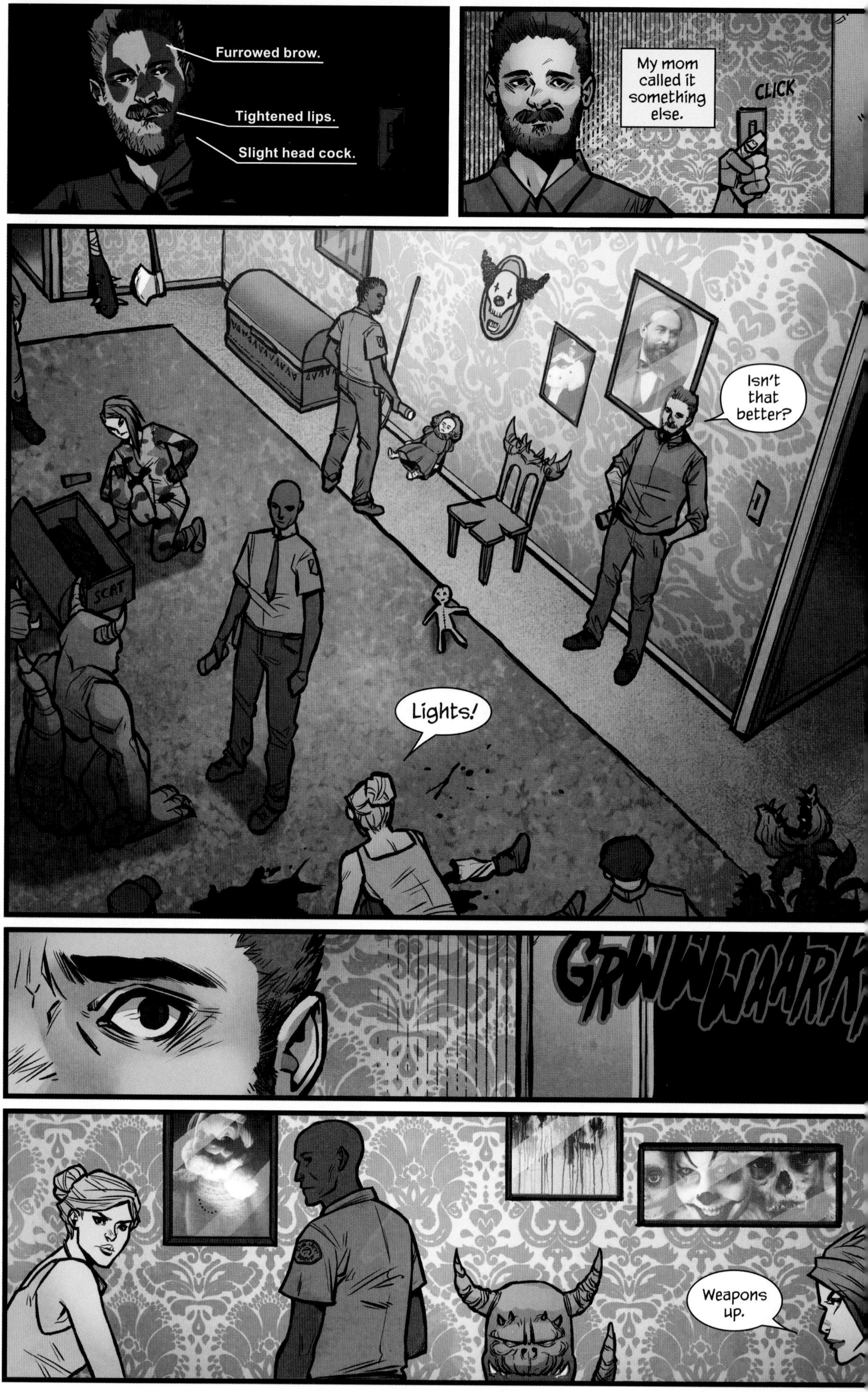
Furrowed brow.
Tightened lips.
Slight head cock.
My mom called it something else.
CLICK
Isn't that better?
Lights!
GRWWWAARK
Weapons up.

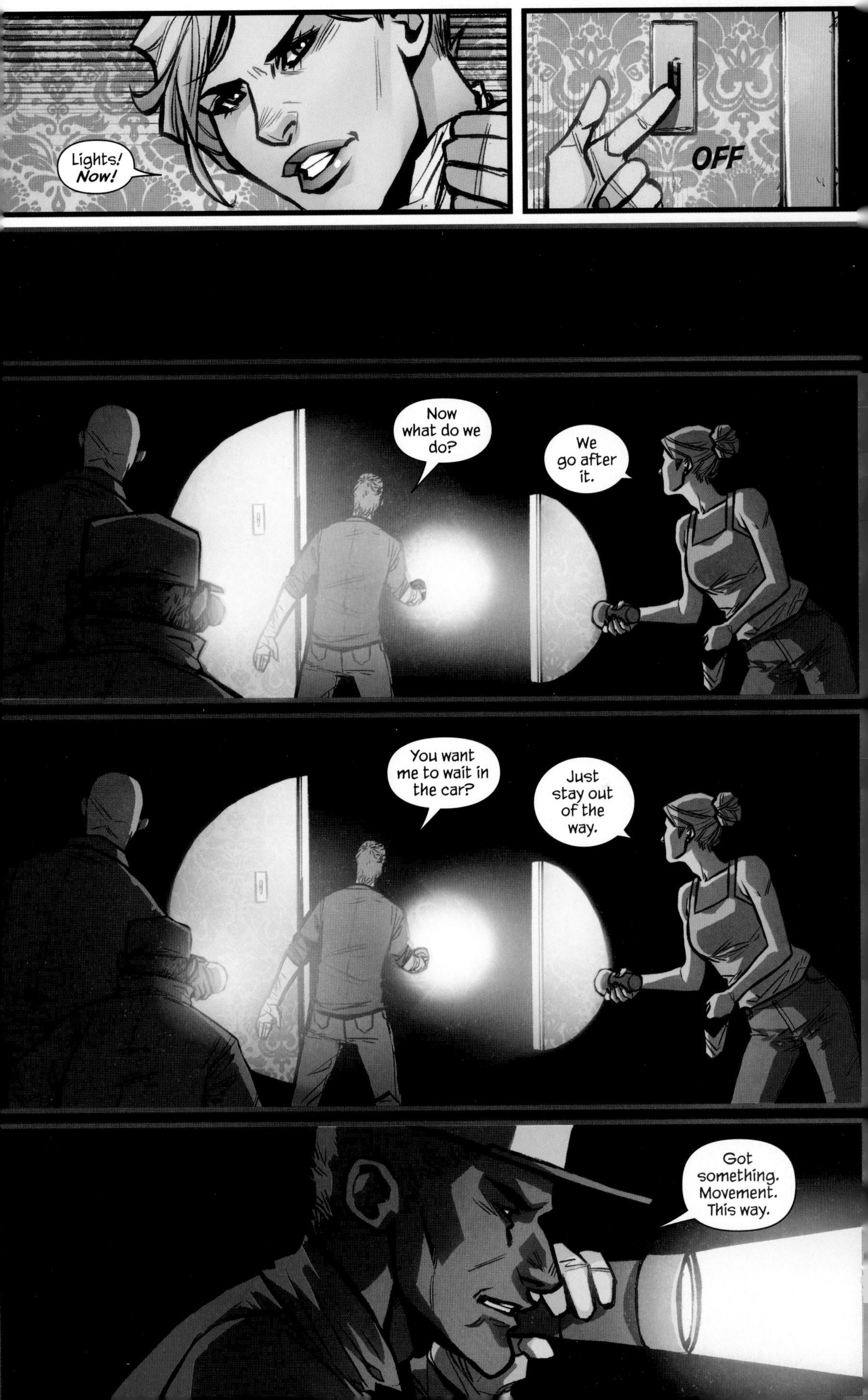
Lights! Now!
OFF
Now what do we do?
We go after it.
You want me to wait in the car?
Just stay out of the way.
Got something. Movement. This way.

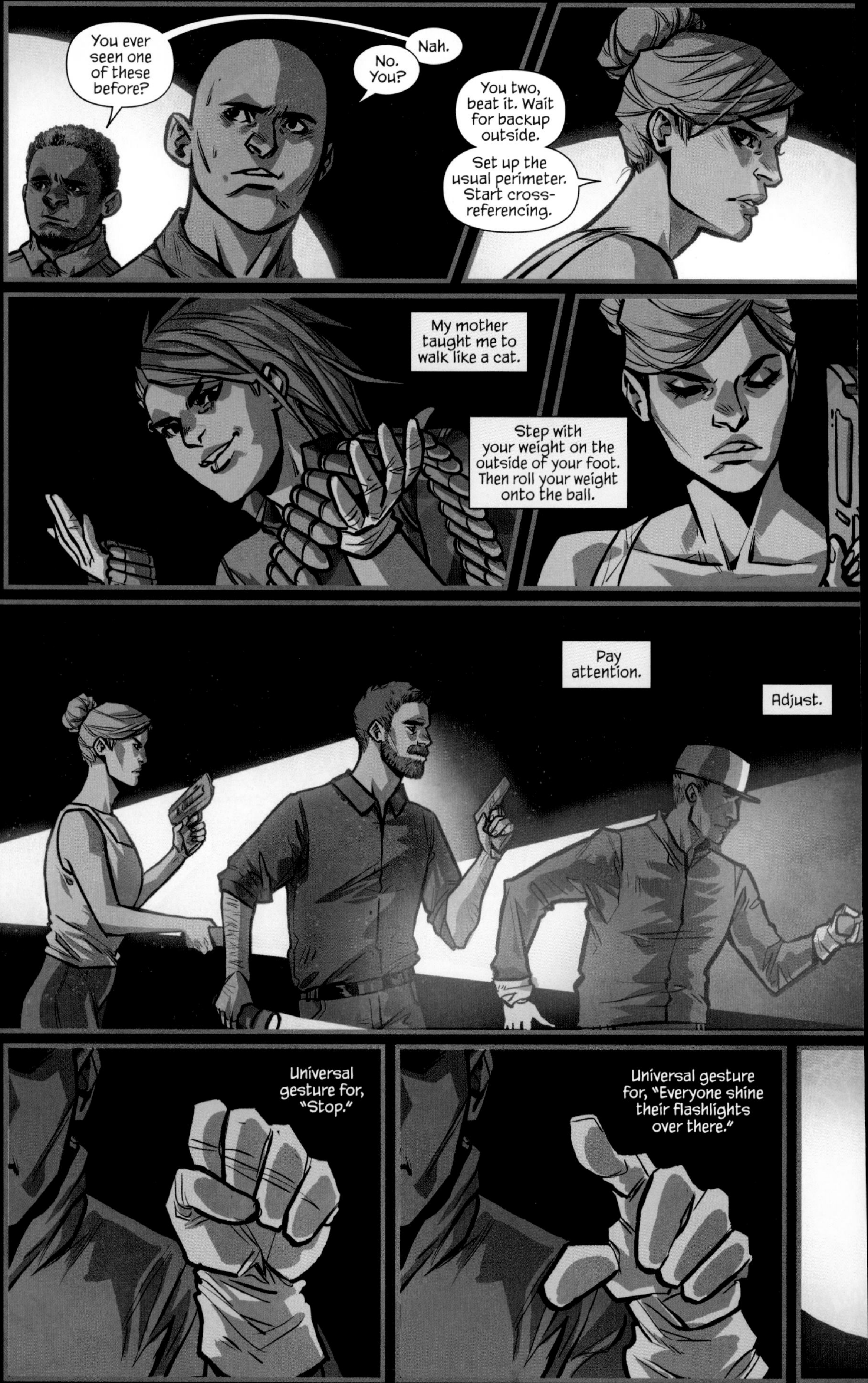

You ever seen one of these before?
No. You?
Nah.
You two, beat it. Wait for backup outside.
Set up the usual perimeter. Start cross-referencing.
My mother taught me to walk like a cat.
Step with your weight on the outside of your foot. Then roll your weight onto the ball.
Pay attention.
Adjust.
Universal gesture for, "Stop."
Universal gesture for, "Everyone shine their flashlights over there."

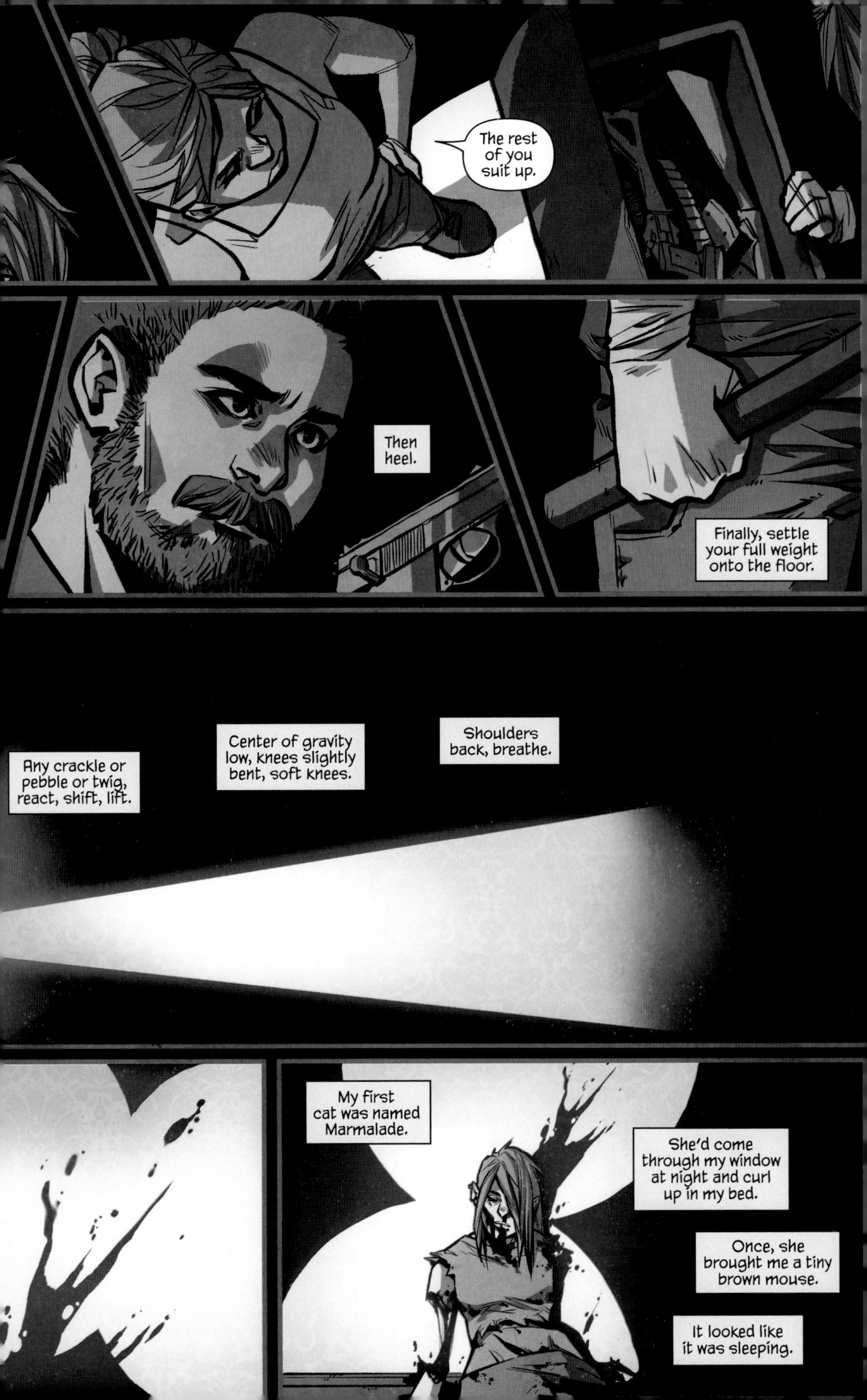
The rest of you suit up.
Then heel.
Finally, settle your full weight onto the floor.
Any crackle or pebble or twig, react, shift, lift.
Center of gravity low, knees slightly bent, soft knees.
Shoulders back, breathe.
My first cat was named Marmalade.
She'd come through my window at night and curl up in my bed.
Once, she brought me a tiny brown mouse.
It looked like it was sleeping.

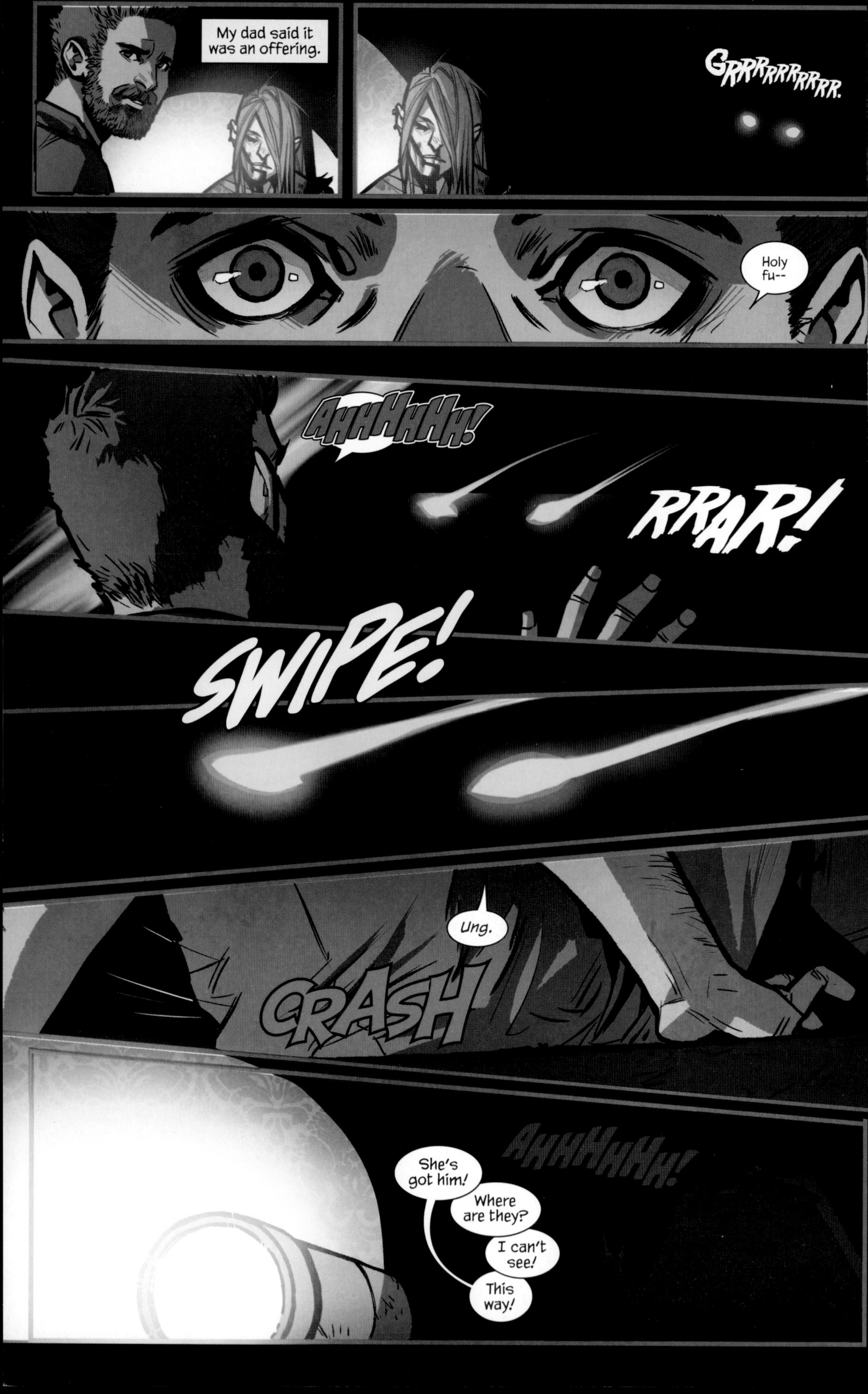

My dad said it was an offering.
GRRRRRRRRRR.
Holy fu--
AHHHHHH!
RRAR!
SWIPE!
Ung.
CRASH
AHHHHHH!
She's got him!
Where are they?
I can't see!
This way!

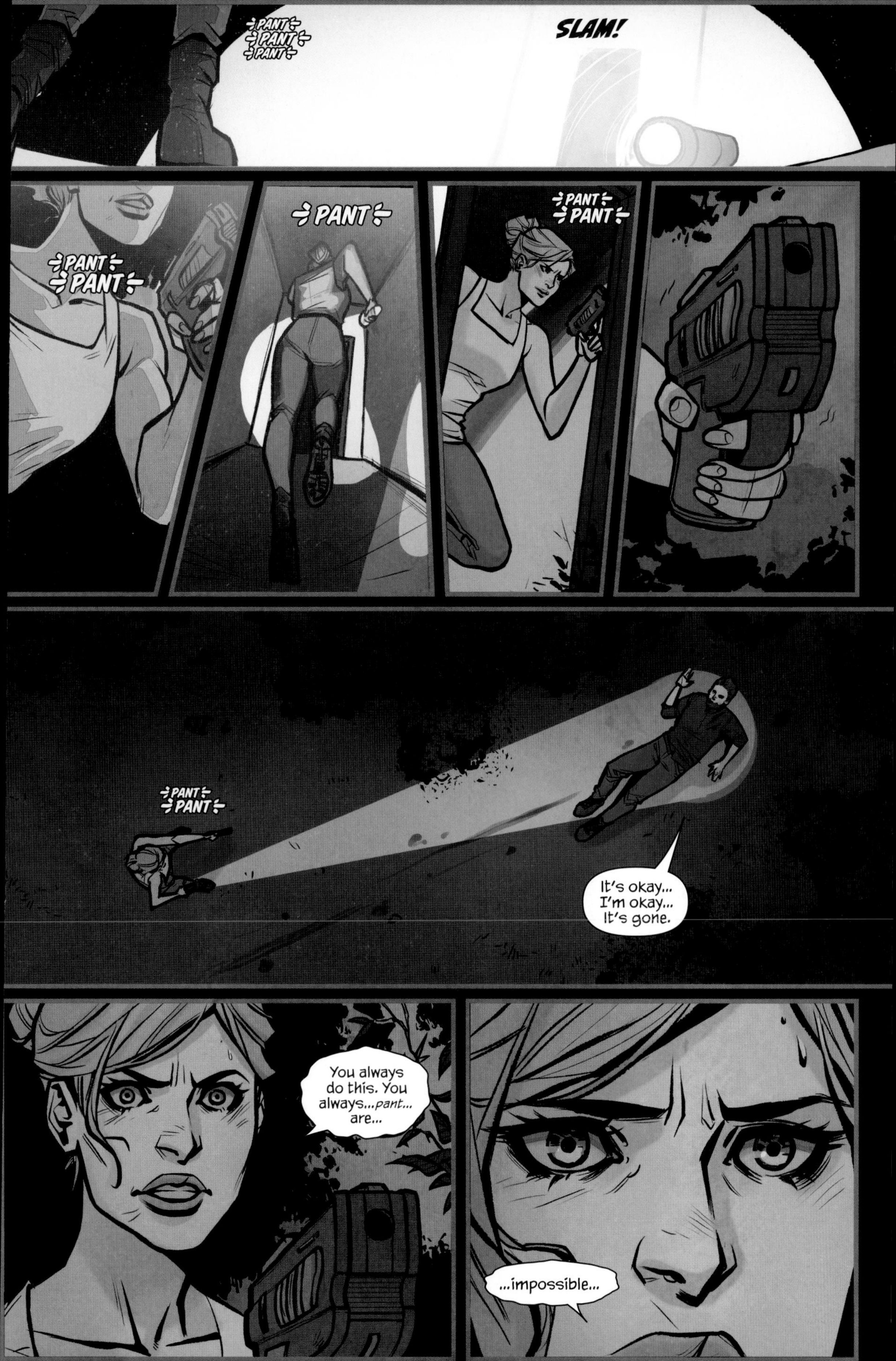
PANT PANT PANT
SLAM!
PANT PANT
PANT
PANT PANT
PANT PANT
It's okay... I'm okay... It's gone.
You always do this. You always...*pant*... are...
...impossible...

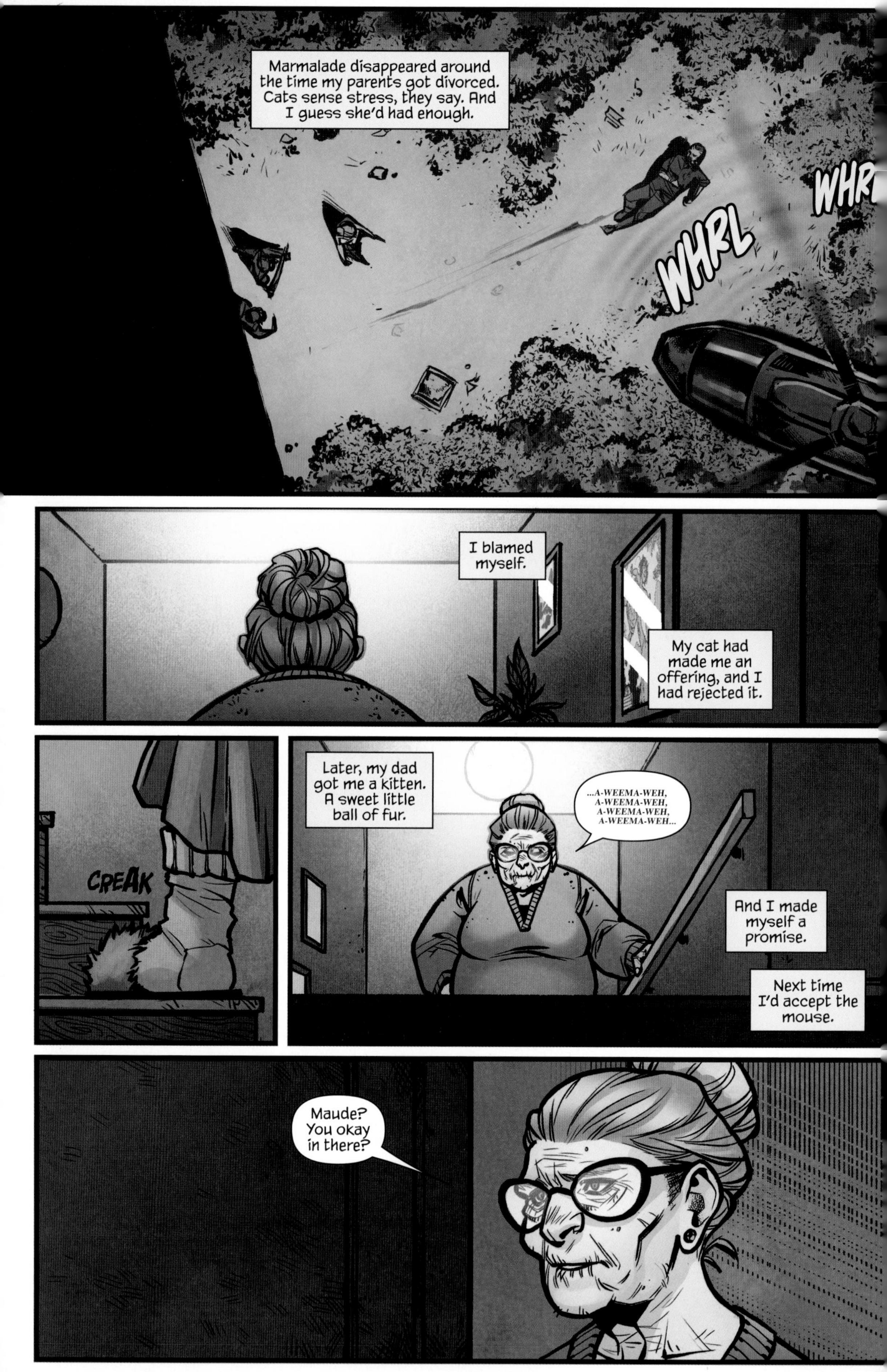
Marmalade disappeared around the time my parents got divorced. Cats sense stress, they say. And I guess she'd had enough.
WHRL
WHRL
I blamed myself.
My cat had made me an offering, and I had rejected it.
CREAK
Later, my dad got me a kitten. A sweet little ball of fur.
...A-WEEMA-WEH, A-WEEMA-WEH, A-WEEMA-WEH, A-WEEMA-WEH...
And I made myself a promise.
Next time I'd accept the mouse.
Maude? You okay in there?

SAFE PLACES TO HIDE IN THE EVENT OF A CAT ATTACK

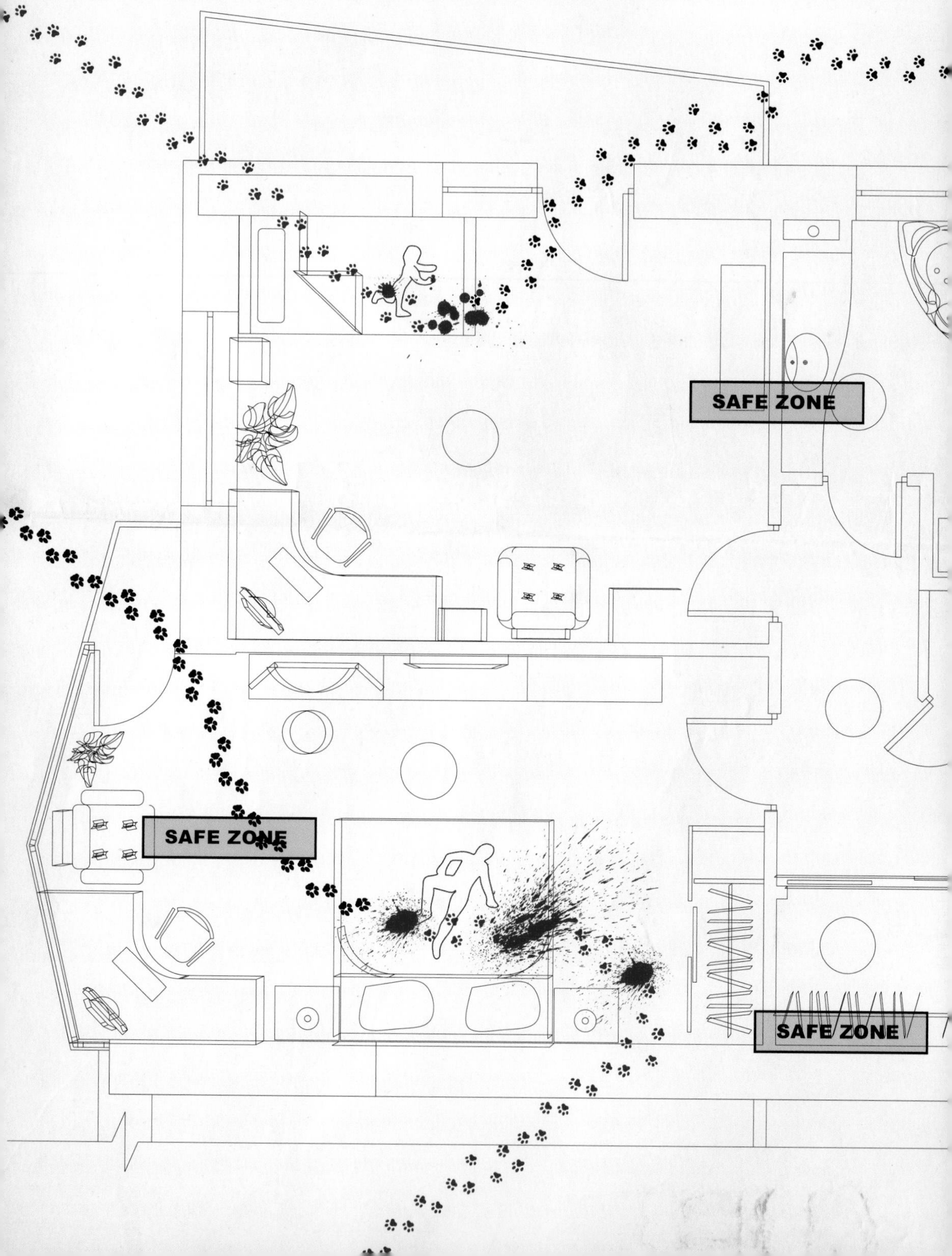
SAFE ZONE
SAFE ZONE
SAFE ZONE

If you can't get to a designated public shelter, seek cover and shelter in place.

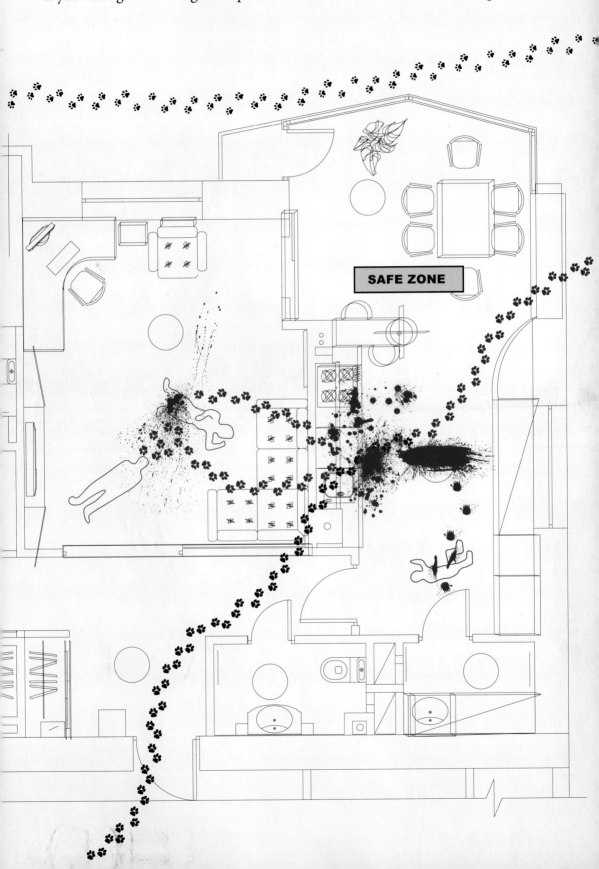

SAFE ZONE

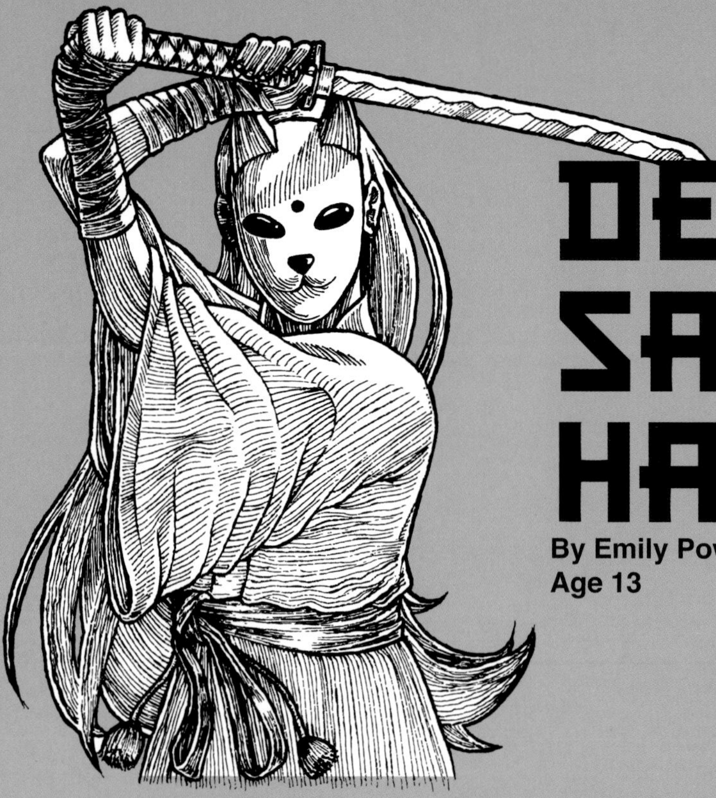

DEAD SAMURAI HAIKUS

By Emily Powell
Age 13

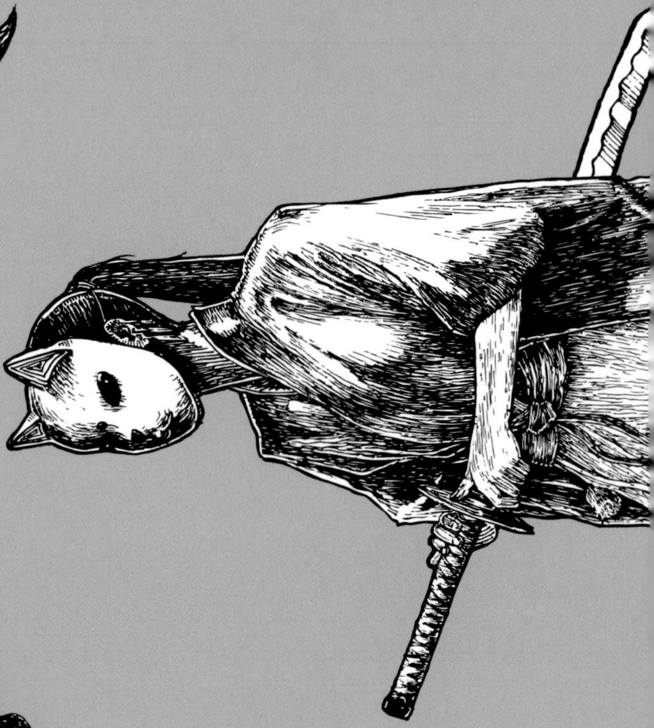

I'm a samurai,
Killing people is such fun,
I chop off their heads.

I have a sharp sword,
I use it to stab people,
Oh no I just died.

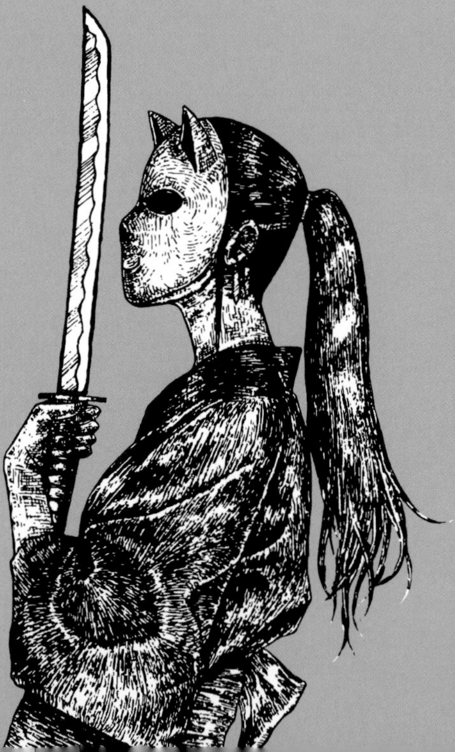

Sometimes I am mean,
Like when I kill some people,
But that is okay.

I do meditate,
That is not correct grammar,
Yet I do not care.

I don't like haikus,
It is too hard to write them,
Ok I'm done now.

PERIOD.

Chapter three

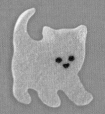

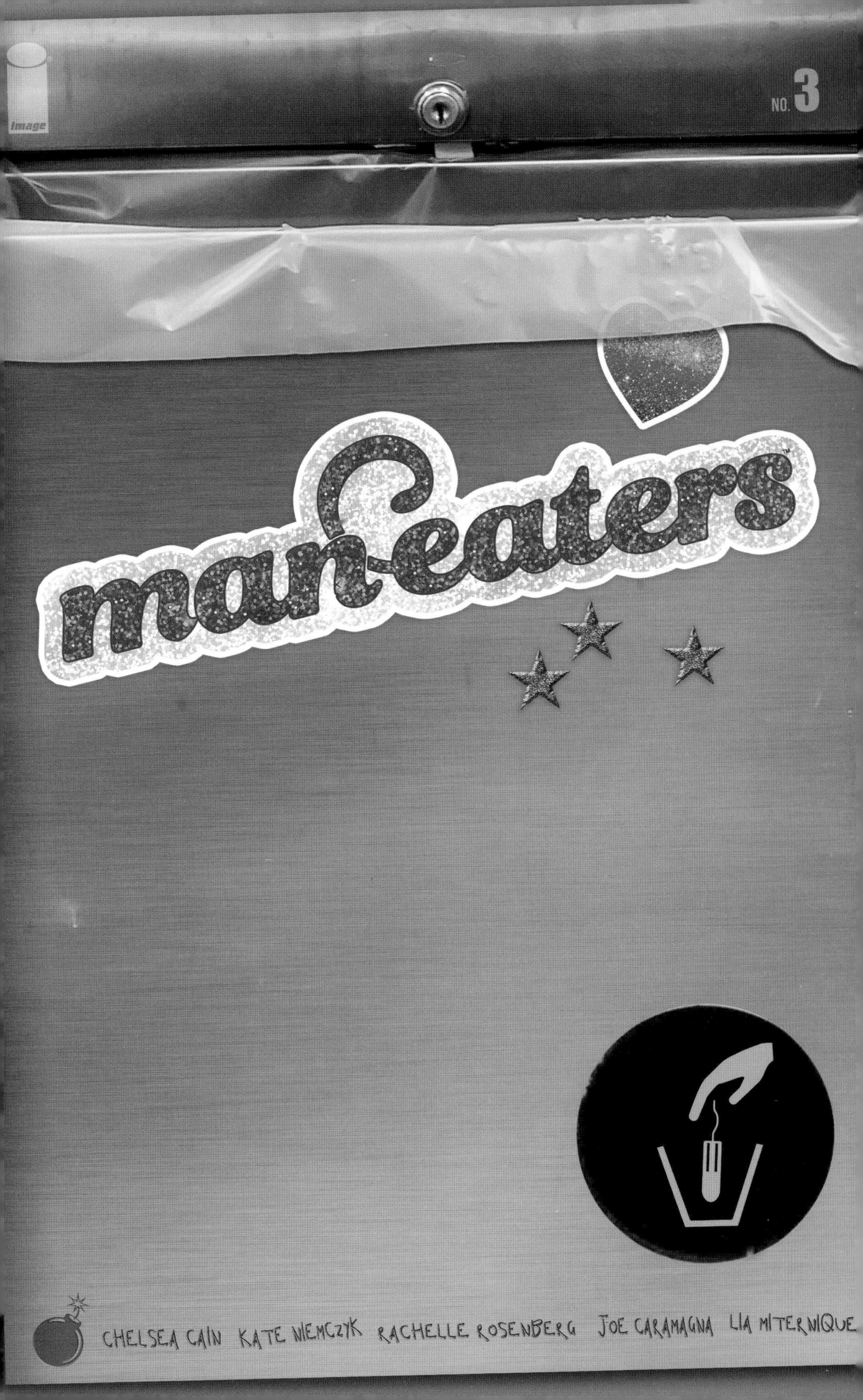

Image
NO. 3
man-eaters
CHELSEA CAIN KATE NIEMCZYK RACHELLE ROSENBERG JOE CARAMAGNA LIA MITERNIQUE

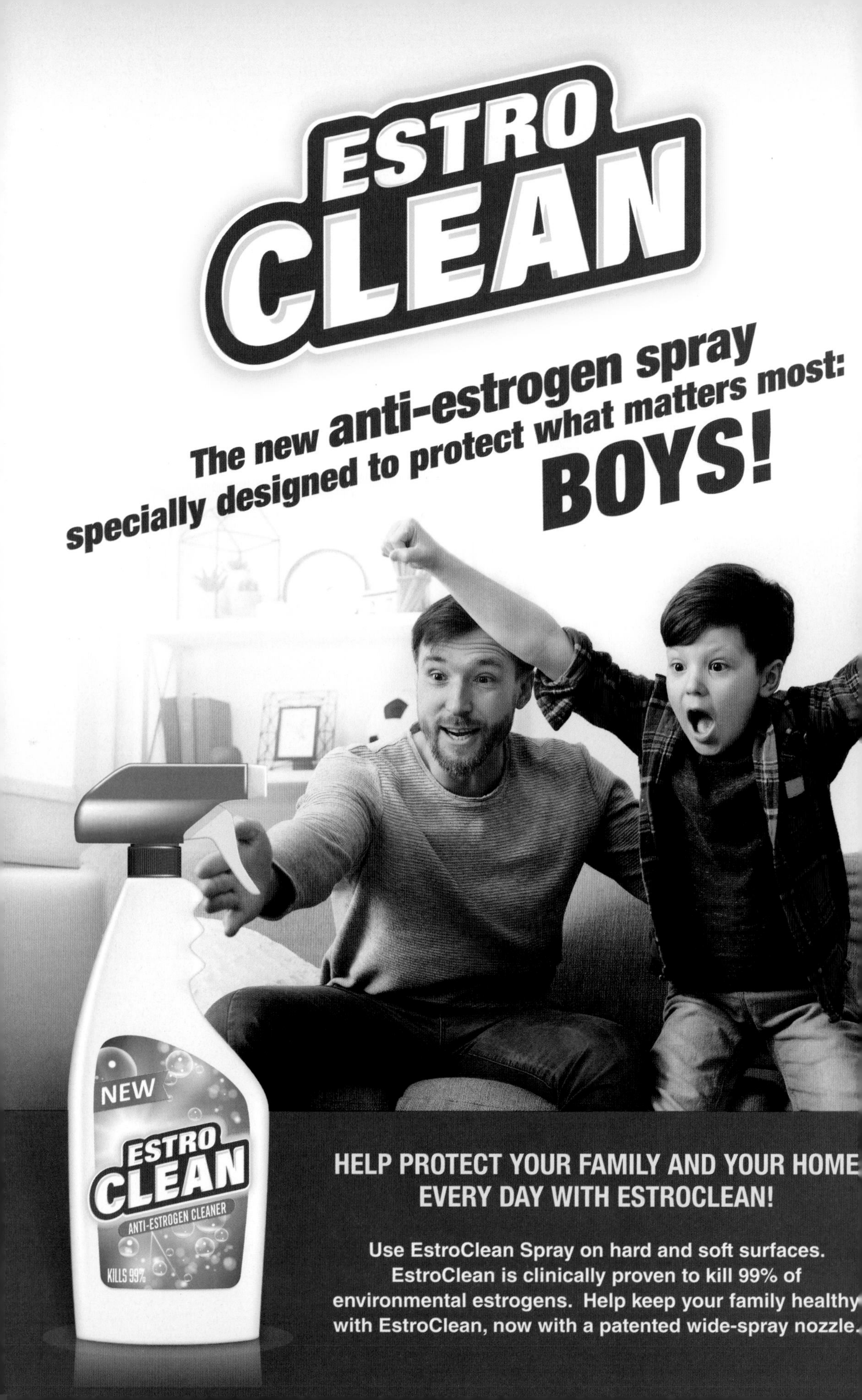
ESTRO CLEAN
The new anti-estrogen spray
specially designed to protect what matters most:
BOYS!
NEW
ESTRO CLEAN
ANTI-ESTROGEN CLEANER
KILLS 99%
HELP PROTECT YOUR FAMILY AND YOUR HOME EVERY DAY WITH ESTROCLEAN!
Use EstroClean Spray on hard and soft surfaces. EstroClean is clinically proven to kill 99% of environmental estrogens. Help keep your family healthy with EstroClean, now with a patented wide-spray nozzle.

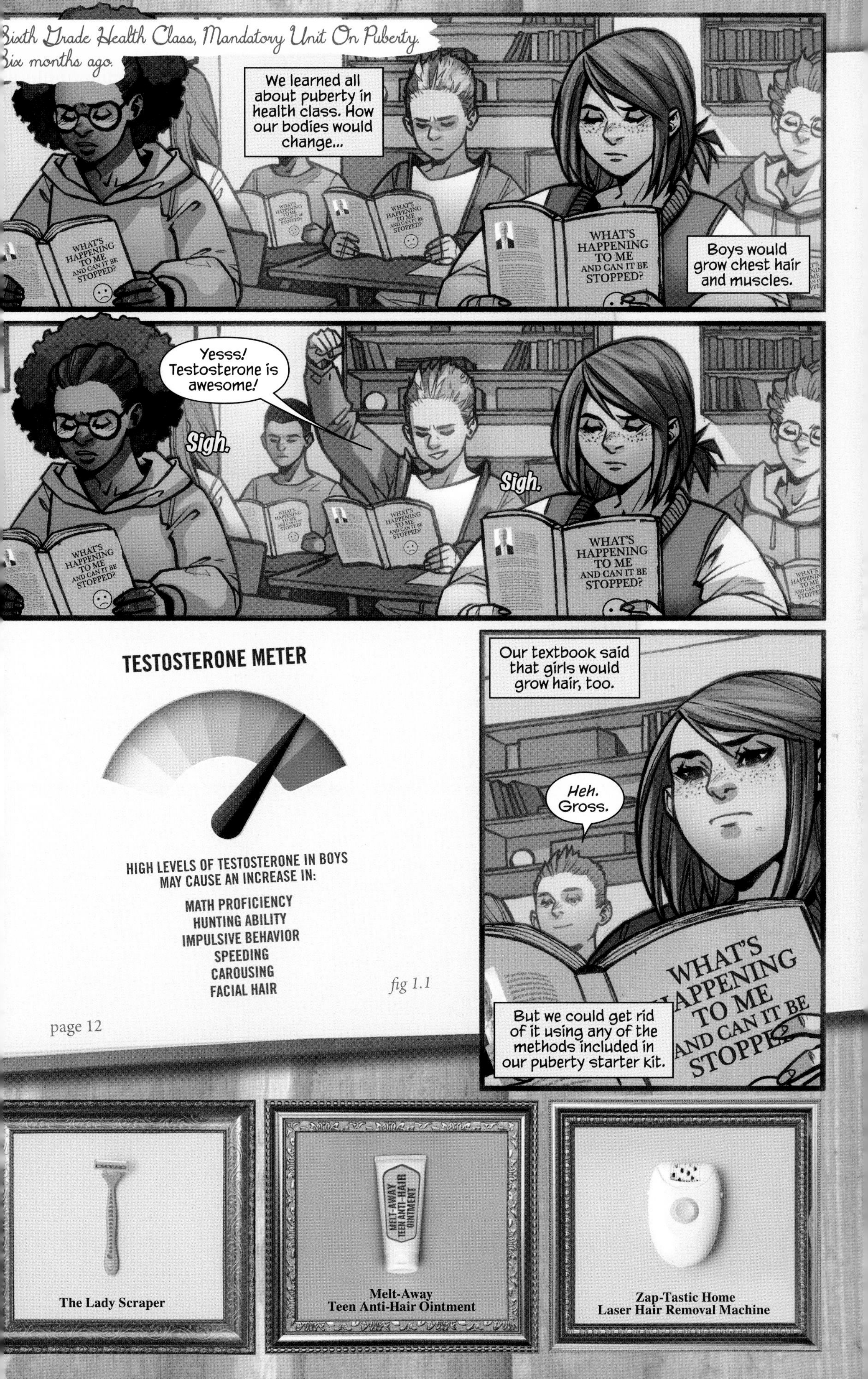
Sixth Grade Health Class, Mandatory Unit On Puberty.
Six months ago.
We learned all about puberty in health class. How our bodies would change...
WHAT'S HAPPENING TO ME AND CAN IT BE STOPPED?
Boys would grow chest hair and muscles.
Yesss! Testosterone is awesome!
Sigh.
Sigh.
TESTOSTERONE METER
HIGH LEVELS OF TESTOSTERONE IN BOYS MAY CAUSE AN INCREASE IN:
MATH PROFICIENCY
HUNTING ABILITY
IMPULSIVE BEHAVIOR
SPEEDING
CAROUSING
FACIAL HAIR
fig 1.1
page 12
Our textbook said that girls would grow hair, too.
Heh. Gross.
But we could get rid of it using any of the methods included in our puberty starter kit.
The Lady Scraper
MELT-AWAY TEEN ANTI-HAIR OINTMENT
Melt-Away
Teen Anti-Hair Ointment
Zap-Tastic Home
Laser Hair Removal Machine

The trouble was estrogen.

ESTROGEN METER

HIGH LEVELS OF ESTROGEN IN GIRLS MAY CAUSE:

BREAST TENDERNESS
CRYING JAGS
YELLING
PIMPLES
BINGE EATING
BRAIN FOG
INCREASED FAT STORAGE

fig 1.2

...enstruation is the shedding of the lining of the uterus (endometri...
...companied by bleeding. It occurs in approximately monthly cycle...
...woman's reproductive life, except during pregnancy. Menstruation...
...berty (at menarche) and stops permanently at menopause.

...estrogen travels through the bloodstream in fluids, it interacts w...
...variety of tissues in the body, and delivers messages and instruction...
...a number of body systems. In those infected with Toxoplasmosis X...

As estrogen travels through the bloodstream in fluids, it interacts with cells in a variety of tissues in the body, and delivers messages and instructions that affect a number of body systems. In those infected with Toxoplasmosis X, a surge in estrogen levels will cause another, more serious, unwanted physical change. Cells mutate, causing girls to transform into…

…CATS.

...UR PERIOD

...sta...y... ...od - or menstruation - used to be a major part of fe...
puberty. Some girls found getting their periods to be very exciting, an...
felt uncomfortable about it. Menstruation required expensive femini...
products, like sanitary napkins and tampons, caused clothing and be...

Student Health Edition, Estr...

Only way larger and more homicidal.

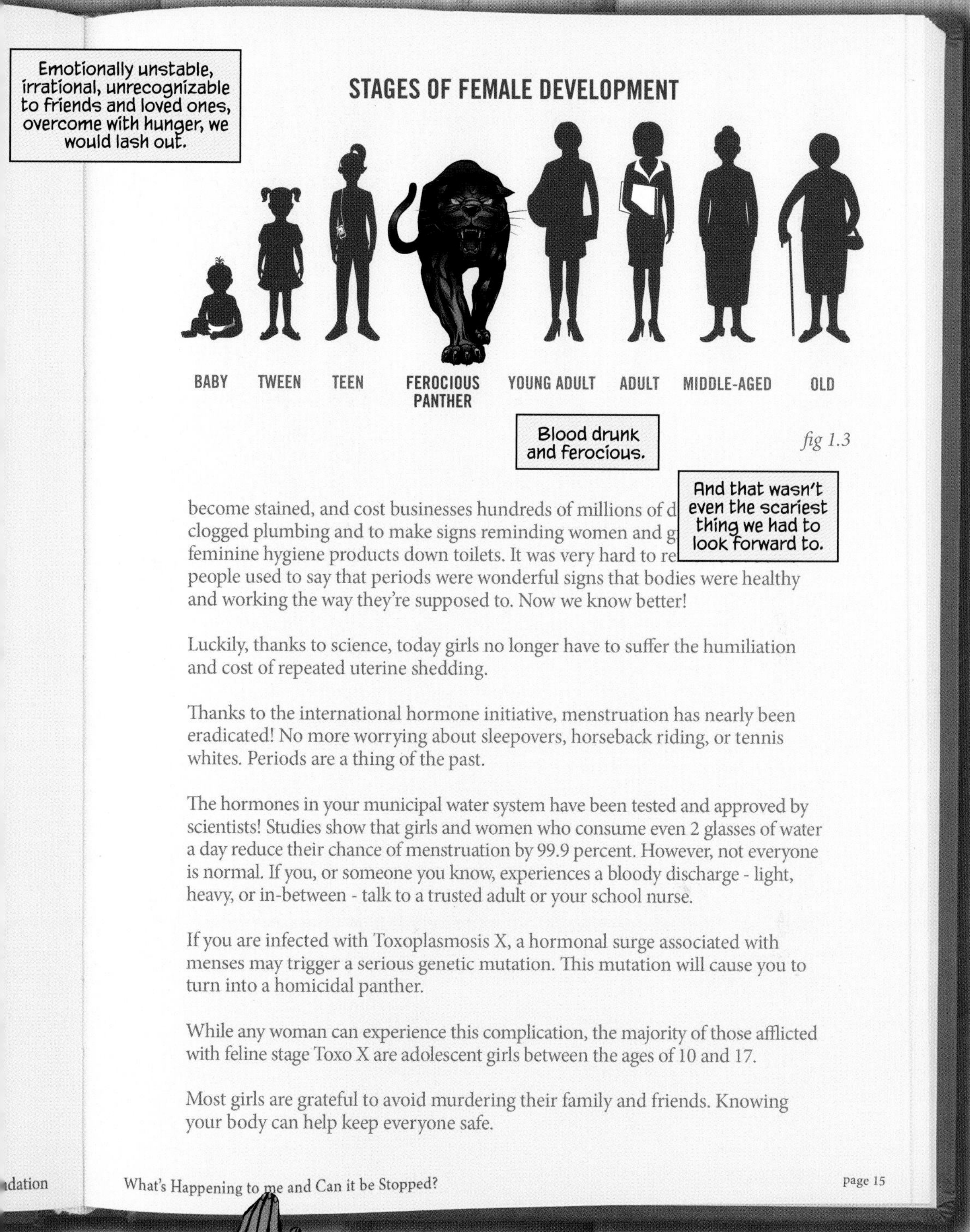
Emotionally unstable, irrational, unrecognizable to friends and loved ones, overcome with hunger, we would lash out.
STAGES OF FEMALE DEVELOPMENT
BABY
TWEEN
TEEN
FEROCIOUS PANTHER
YOUNG ADULT
ADULT
MIDDLE-AGED
OLD
Blood drunk and ferocious.
fig 1.3
And that wasn't even the scariest thing we had to look forward to.

become stained, and cost businesses hundreds of millions of d clogged plumbing and to make signs reminding women and g feminine hygiene products down toilets. It was very hard to re people used to say that periods were wonderful signs that bodies were healthy and working the way they're supposed to. Now we know better!

Luckily, thanks to science, today girls no longer have to suffer the humiliation and cost of repeated uterine shedding.

Thanks to the international hormone initiative, menstruation has nearly been eradicated! No more worrying about sleepovers, horseback riding, or tennis whites. Periods are a thing of the past.

The hormones in your municipal water system have been tested and approved by scientists! Studies show that girls and women who consume even 2 glasses of water a day reduce their chance of menstruation by 99.9 percent. However, not everyone is normal. If you, or someone you know, experiences a bloody discharge - light, heavy, or in-between - talk to a trusted adult or your school nurse.

If you are infected with Toxoplasmosis X, a hormonal surge associated with menses may trigger a serious genetic mutation. This mutation will cause you to turn into a homicidal panther.

While any woman can experience this complication, the majority of those afflicted with feline stage Toxo X are adolescent girls between the ages of 10 and 17.

Most girls are grateful to avoid murdering their family and friends. Knowing your body can help keep everyone safe.

dation What's Happening to me and Can it be Stopped? page 15

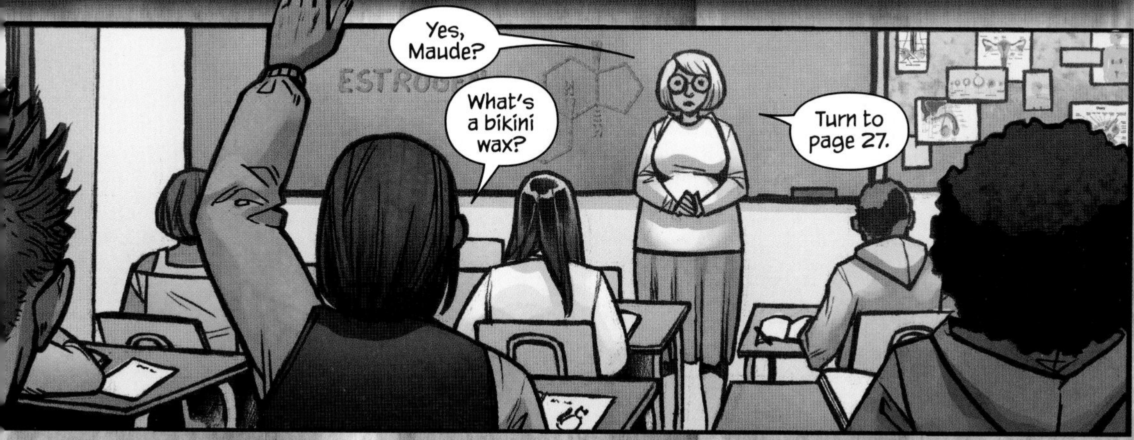
Yes, Maude?
What's a bikini wax?
Turn to page 27.

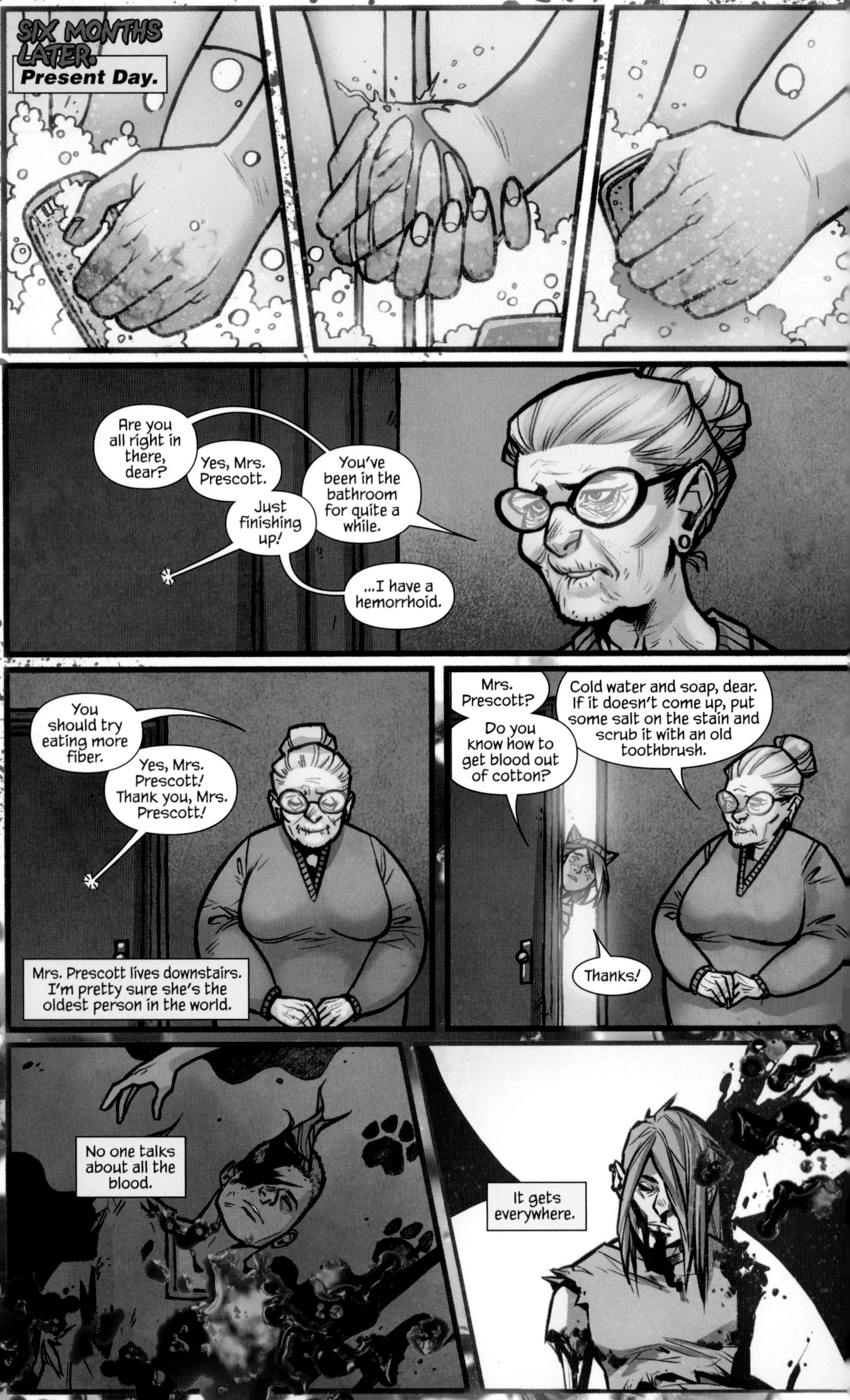
SIX MONTHS LATER.
Present Day.
Are you all right in there, dear?
Yes, Mrs. Prescott.
Just finishing up!
You've been in the bathroom for quite a while.
...I have a hemorrhoid.
You should try eating more fiber.
Yes, Mrs. Prescott! Thank you, Mrs. Prescott!
Mrs. Prescott lives downstairs. I'm pretty sure she's the oldest person in the world.
Mrs. Prescott?
Do you know how to get blood out of cotton?
Cold water and soap, dear. If it doesn't come up, put some salt on the stain and scrub it with an old toothbrush.
Thanks!
No one talks about all the blood.
It gets everywhere.

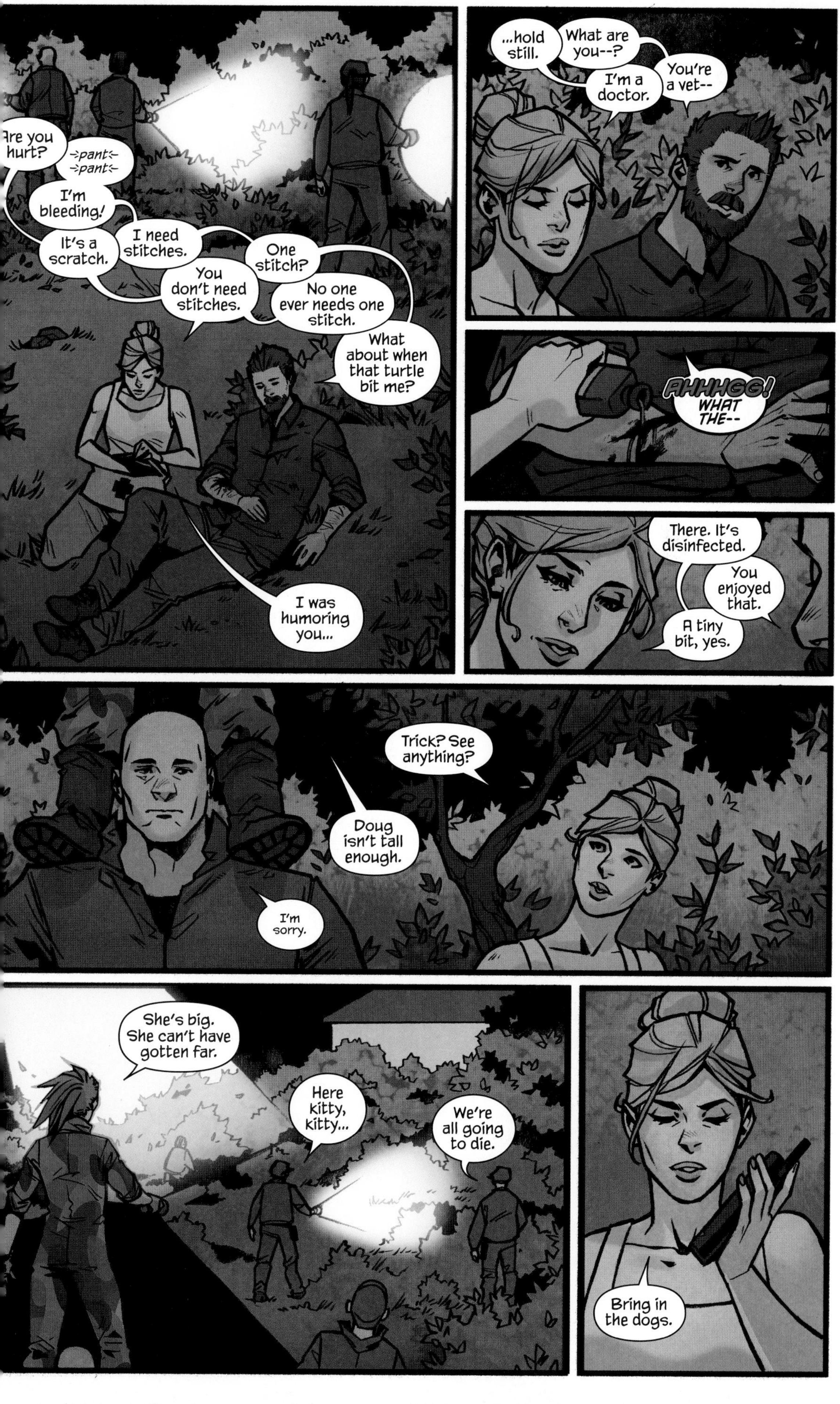

Are you hurt?
->pant<- ->pant<-
I'm bleeding!
It's a scratch.
I need stitches.
You don't need stitches.
One stitch?
No one ever needs one stitch.
What about when that turtle bit me?
I was humoring you...
...hold still.
What are you--?
I'm a doctor.
You're a vet--
AHHHGG! WHAT THE--
There. It's disinfected.
You enjoyed that.
A tiny bit, yes.
Trick? See anything?
Doug isn't tall enough.
I'm sorry.
She's big. She can't have gotten far.
Here kitty, kitty...
We're all going to die.
Bring in the dogs.

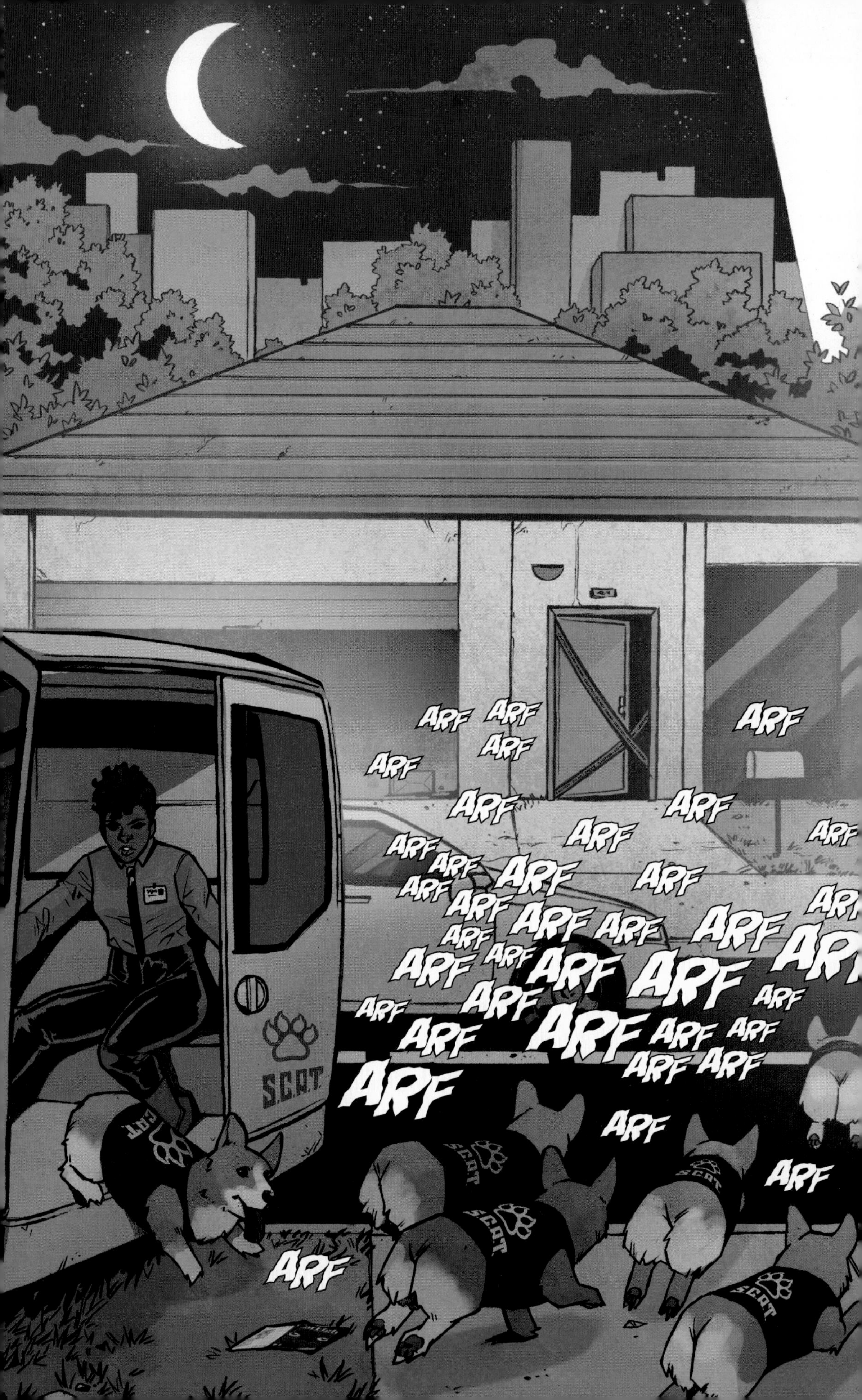
S.C.A.T.
ARF
ARF
ARF
ARF
ARF
ARF
ARF
ARF
ARF
ARF
ARF
ARF
ARF
ARF
ARF
ARF
ARF
ARF
ARF
ARF
ARF
ARF
ARF
ARF
ARF
ARF
ARF
ARF
ARF
ARF
ARF
ARF
ARF
ARF
ARF
ARF

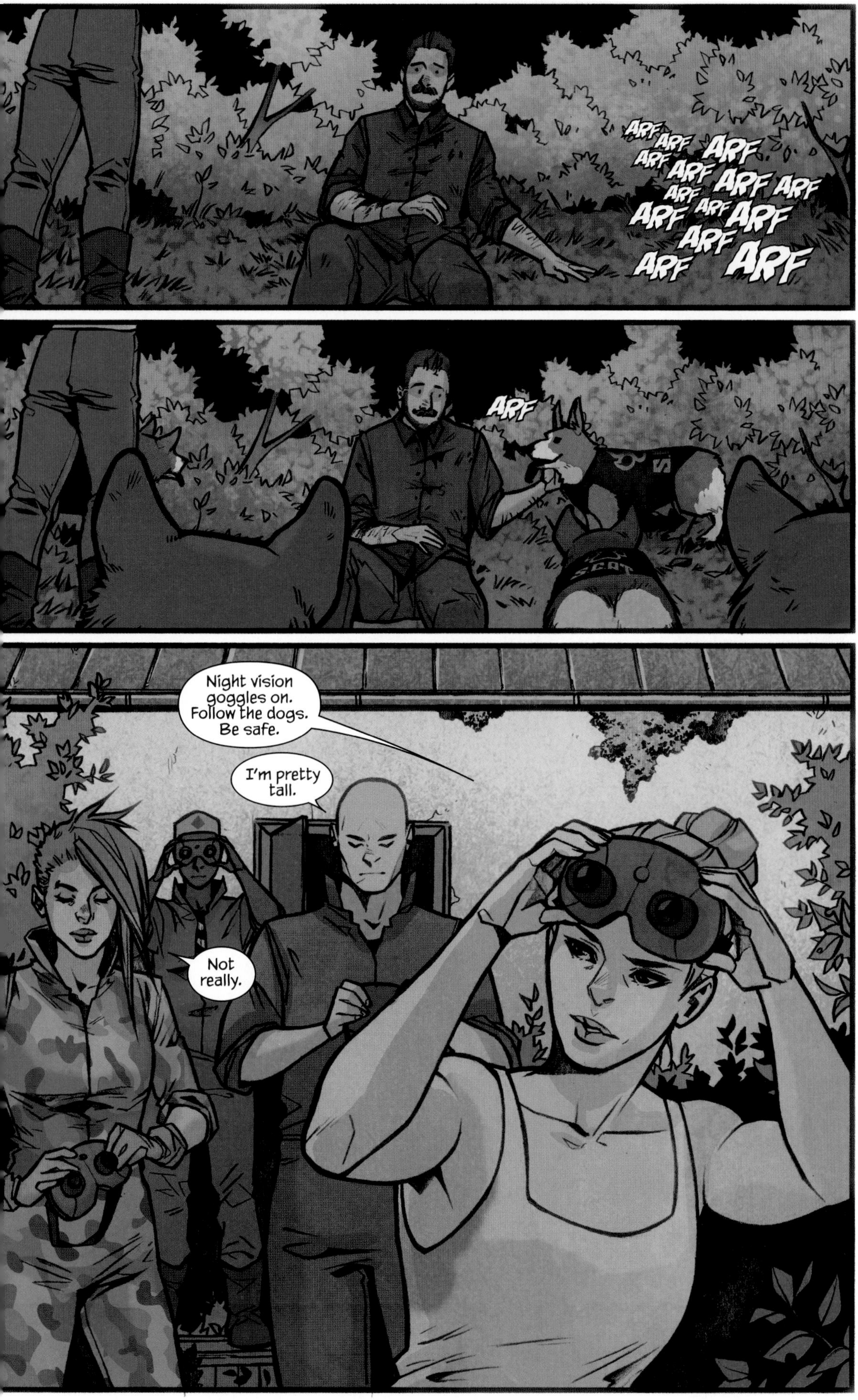
ARF ARF ARF
ARF ARF ARF ARF
ARF ARF ARF
ARF
ARF ARF
ARF
Night vision goggles on. Follow the dogs. Be safe.
I'm pretty tall.
Not really.

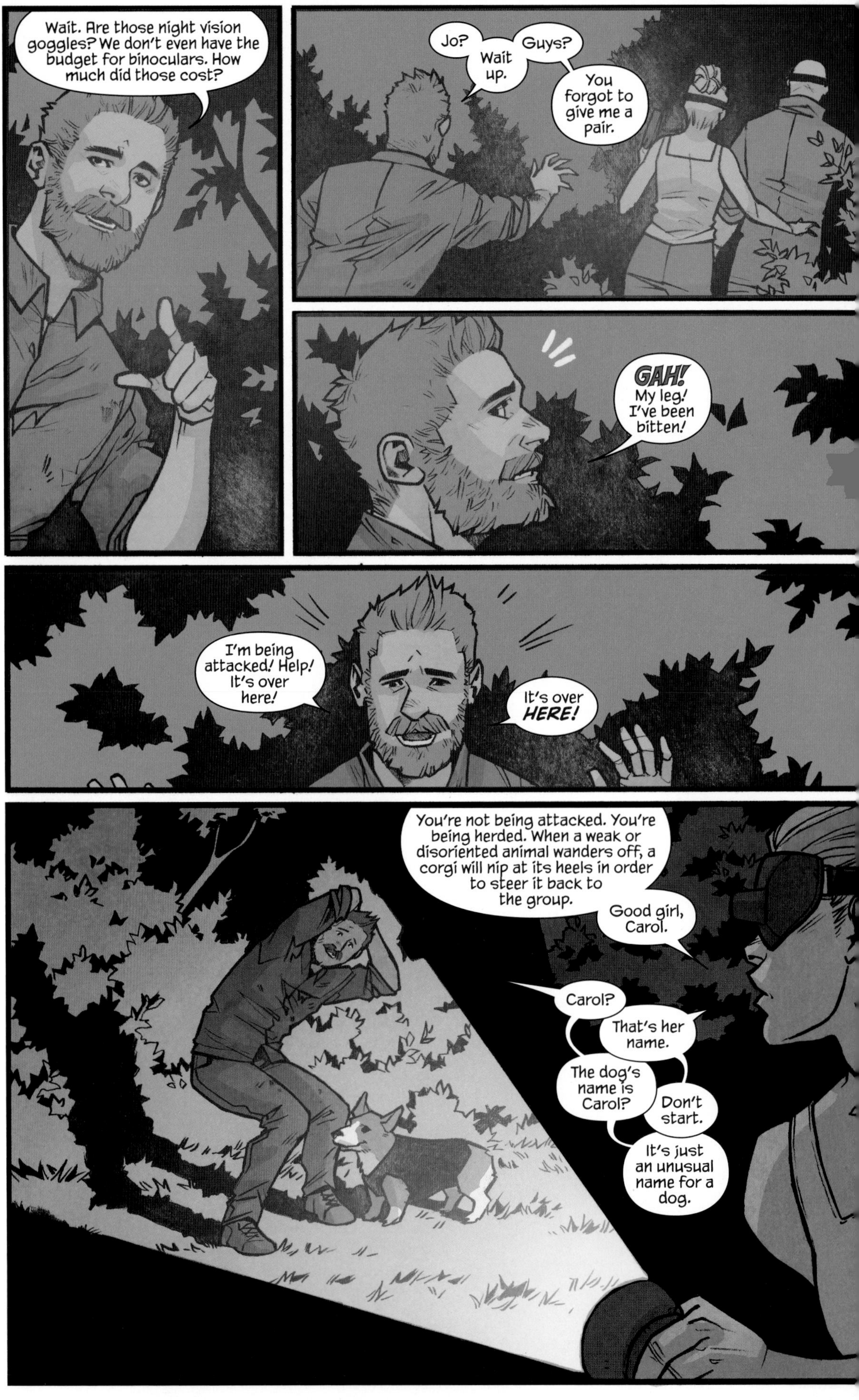
Wait. Are those night vision goggles? We don't even have the budget for binoculars. How much did those cost?
Jo?
Wait up.
Guys?
You forgot to give me a pair.
GAH!
My leg! I've been bitten!
I'm being attacked! Help! It's over here!
It's over HERE!
You're not being attacked. You're being herded. When a weak or disoriented animal wanders off, a corgi will nip at its heels in order to steer it back to the group.
Good girl, Carol.
Carol?
That's her name.
The dog's name is Carol?
Don't start.
It's just an unusual name for a dog.

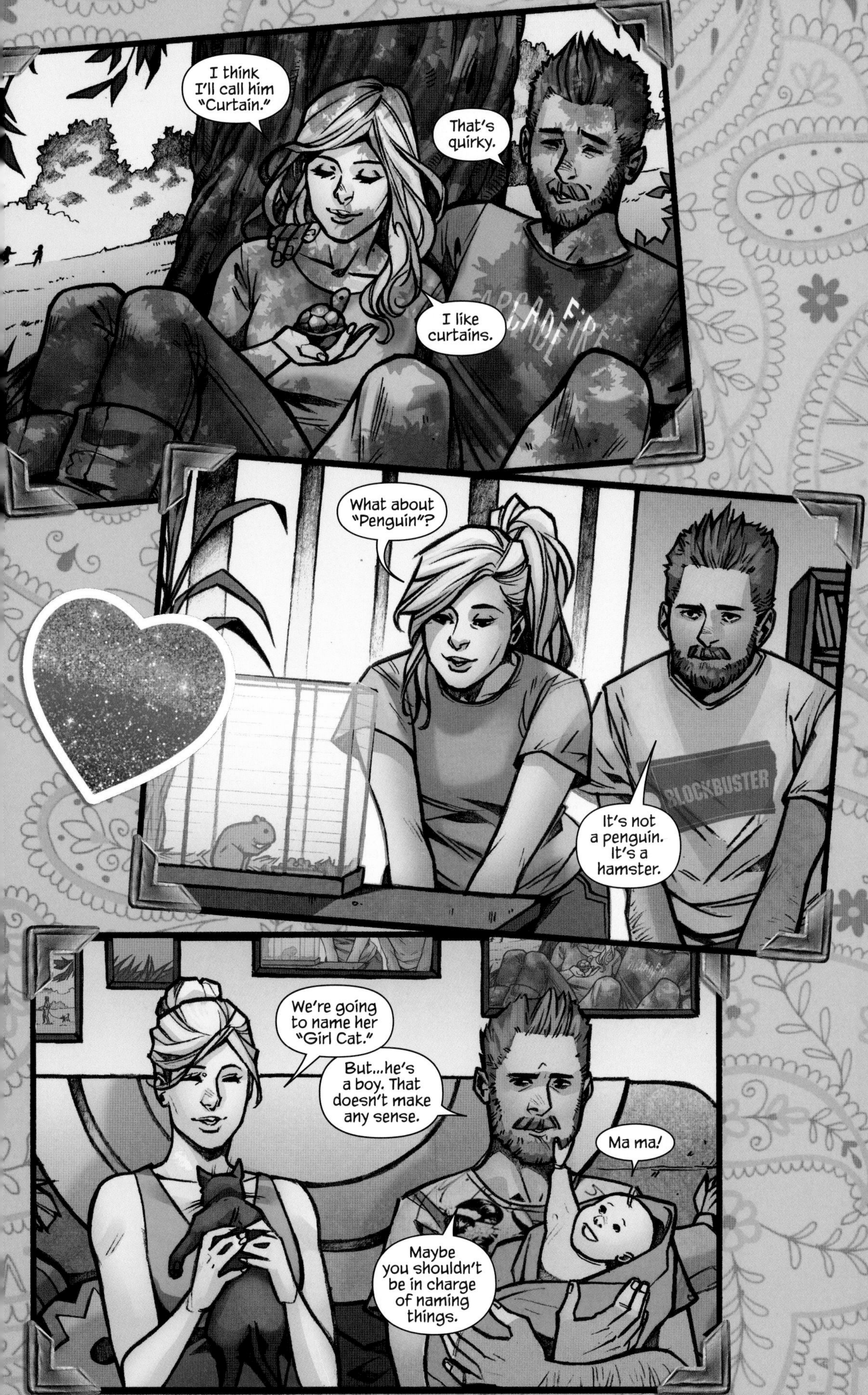
I think I'll call him "Curtain."
That's quirky.
I like curtains.
What about "Penguin"?
BLOCKBUSTER
It's not a penguin. It's a hamster.
We're going to name her "Girl Cat."
But...he's a boy. That doesn't make any sense.
Ma ma!
Maybe you shouldn't be in charge of naming things.

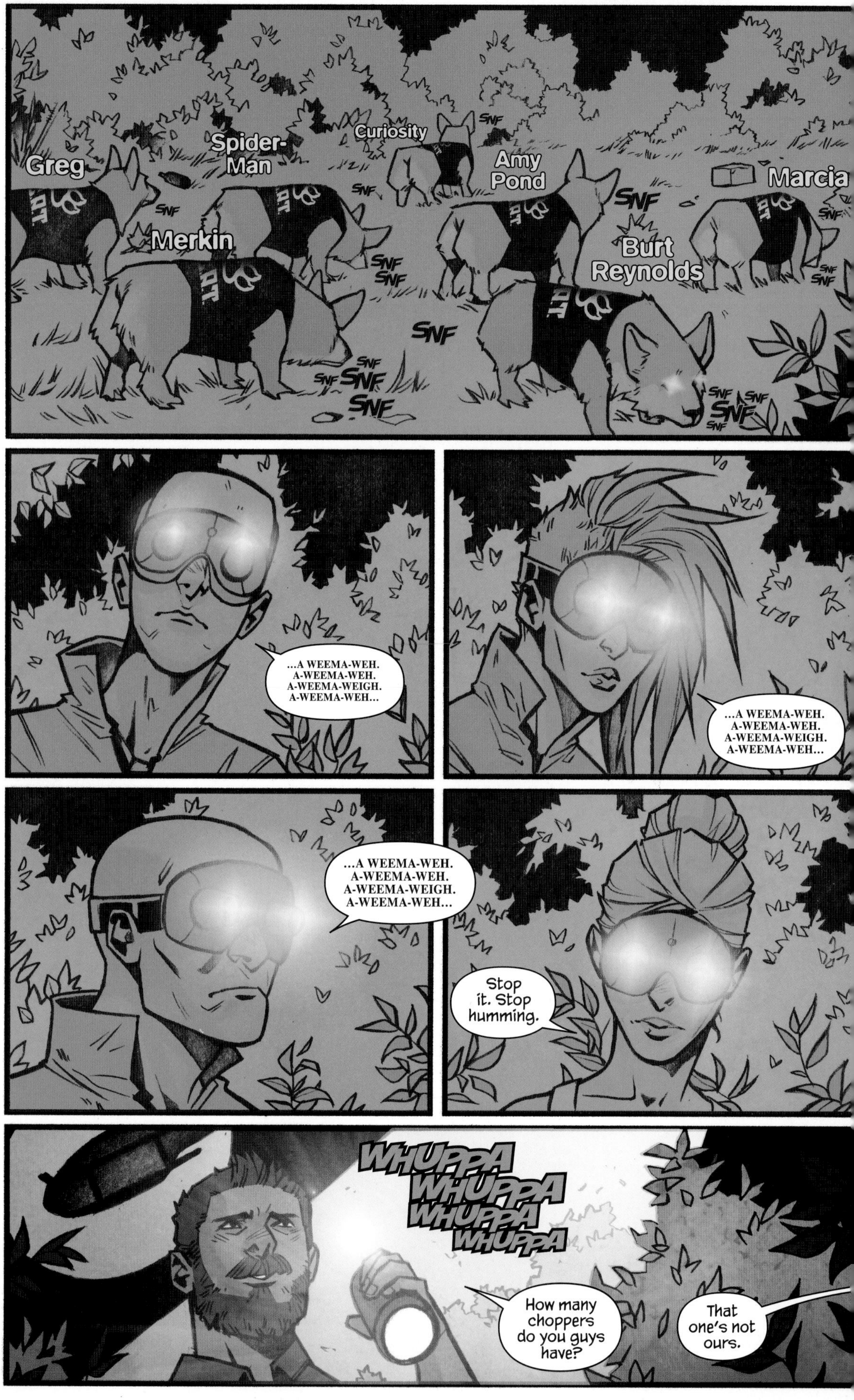
Greg
Spider-Man
Curiosity
Amy Pond
Marcia
Merkin
Burt Reynolds
SNF SNF SNF
...A WEEMA-WEH. A-WEEMA-WEH. A-WEEMA-WEIGH. A-WEEMA-WEH...
...A WEEMA-WEH. A-WEEMA-WEH. A-WEEMA-WEIGH. A-WEEMA-WEH...
...A WEEMA-WEH. A-WEEMA-WEH. A-WEEMA-WEIGH. A-WEEMA-WEH...
Stop it. Stop humming.
WHUPPA WHUPPA WHUPPA WHUPPA
How many choppers do you guys have?
That one's not ours.

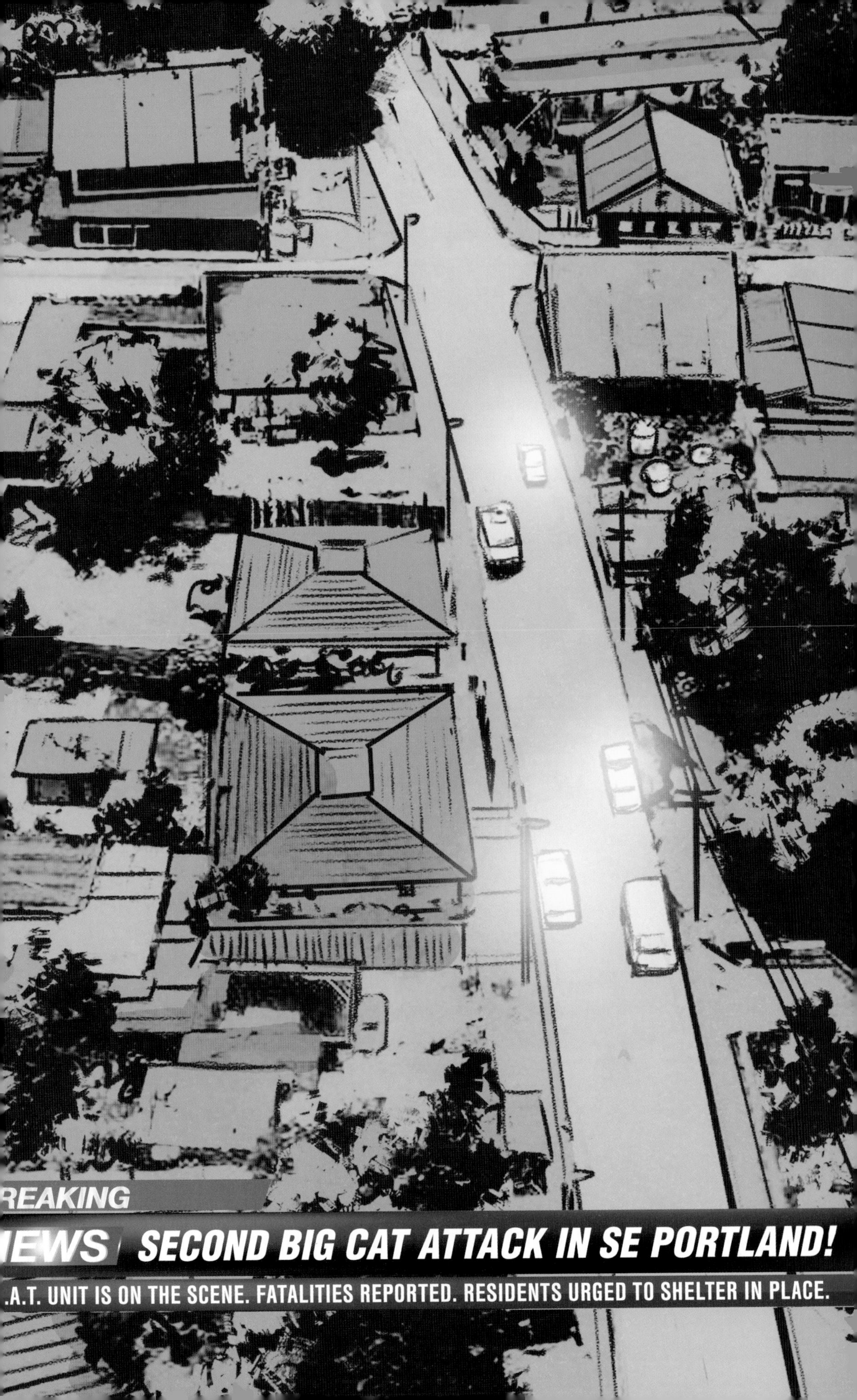

REAKING
IEWS
SECOND BIG CAT ATTACK IN SE PORTLAND!
.A.T. UNIT IS ON THE SCENE. FATALITIES REPORTED. RESIDENTS URGED TO SHELTER IN PLACE.

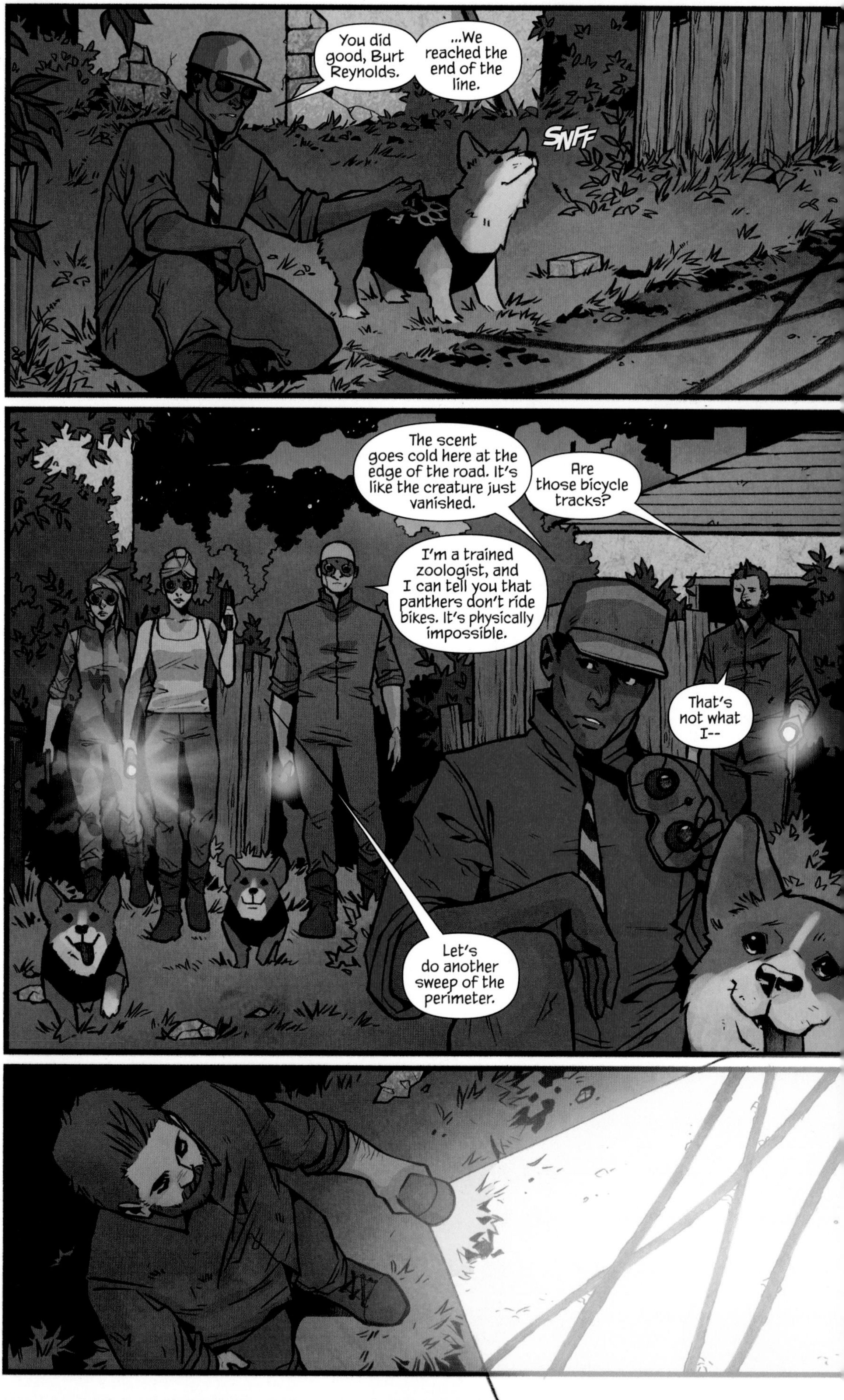
You did good, Burt Reynolds.
...We reached the end of the line.
SNFF
The scent goes cold here at the edge of the road. It's like the creature just vanished.
Are those bicycle tracks?
I'm a trained zoologist, and I can tell you that panthers don't ride bikes. It's physically impossible.
That's not what I--
Let's do another sweep of the perimeter.

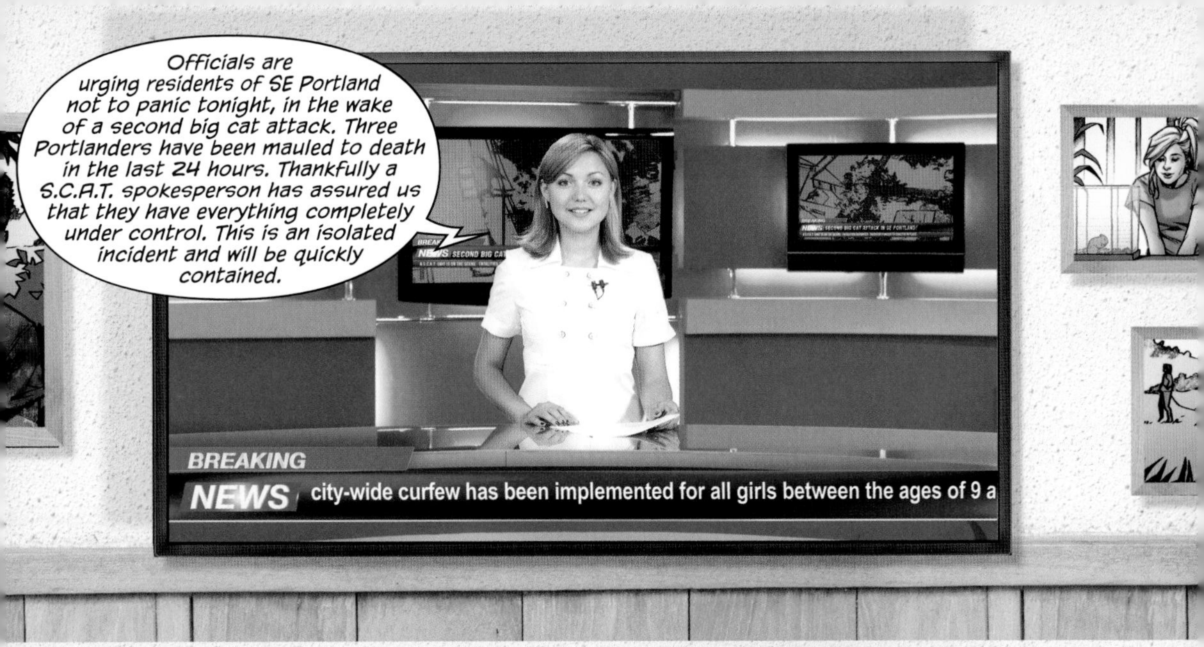
Officials are urging residents of SE Portland not to panic tonight, in the wake of a second big cat attack. Three Portlanders have been mauled to death in the last 24 hours. Thankfully a S.C.A.T. spokesperson has assured us that they have everything completely under control. This is an isolated incident and will be quickly contained.
BREAKING
NEWS city-wide curfew has been implemented for all girls between the ages of 9 a

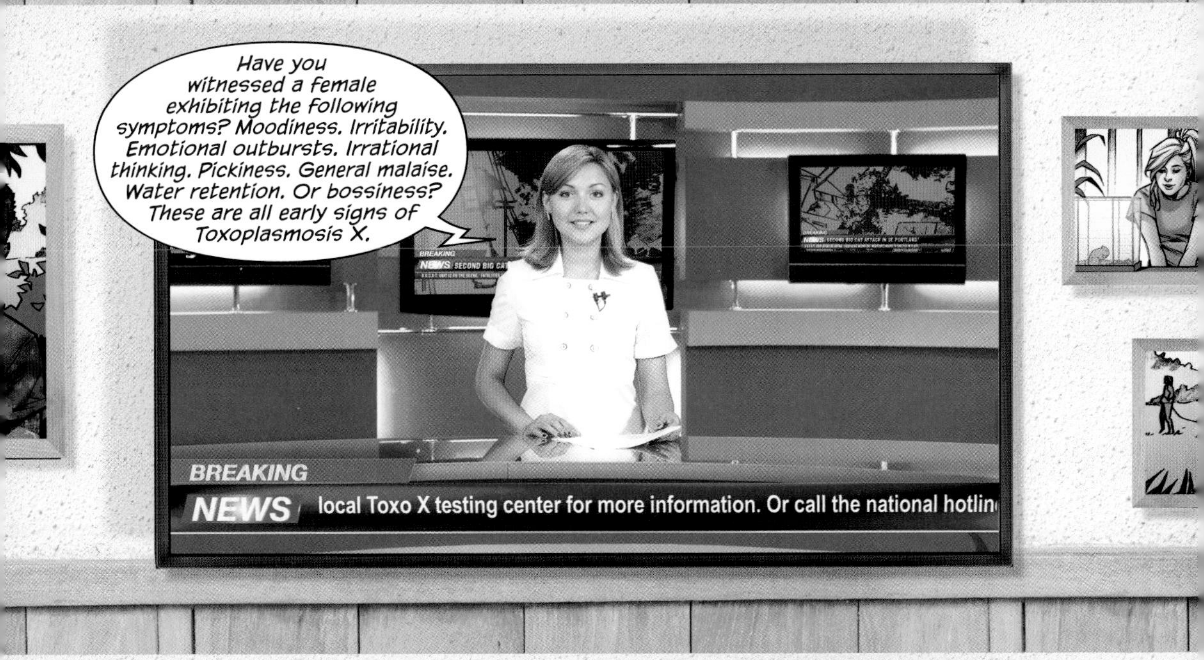
Have you witnessed a female exhibiting the following symptoms? Moodiness. Irritability. Emotional outbursts. Irrational thinking. Pickiness. General malaise. Water retention. Or bossiness? These are all early signs of Toxoplasmosis X.
BREAKING
NEWS local Toxo X testing center for more information. Or call the national hotlin

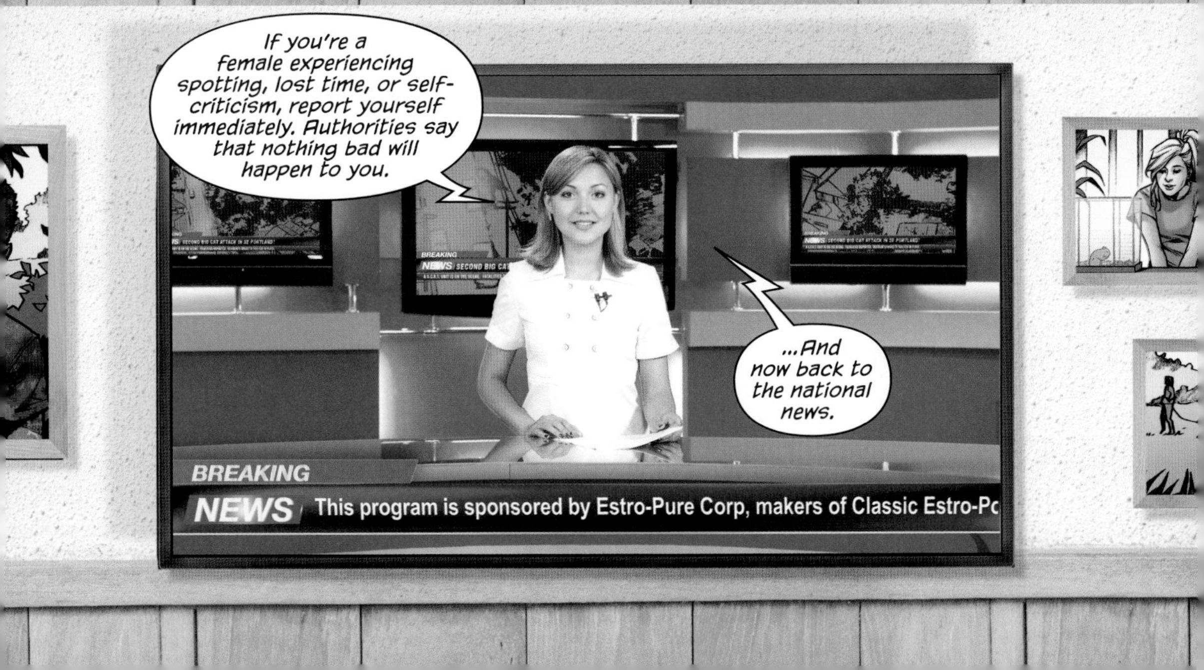
If you're a female experiencing spotting, lost time, or self-criticism, report yourself immediately. Authorities say that nothing bad will happen to you.
...And now back to the national news.
BREAKING
NEWS This program is sponsored by Estro-Pure Corp, makers of Classic Estro-Po

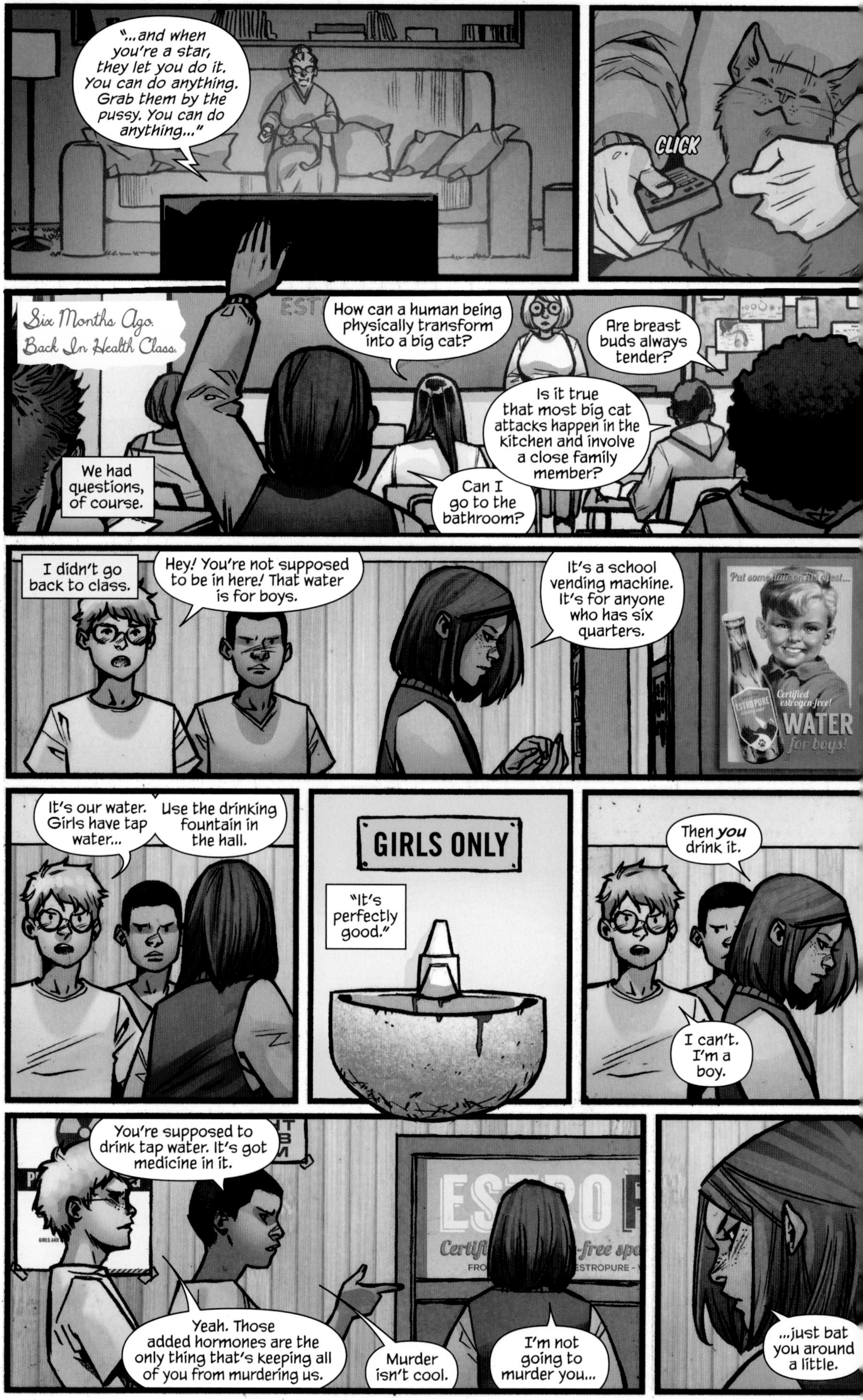

"...and when you're a star, they let you do it. You can do anything. Grab them by the pussy. You can do anything..."
CLICK
Six Months Ago. Back In Health Class.
How can a human being physically transform into a big cat?
Are breast buds always tender?
Is it true that most big cat attacks happen in the kitchen and involve a close family member?
We had questions, of course.
Can I go to the bathroom?
I didn't go back to class.
Hey! You're not supposed to be in here! That water is for boys.
It's a school vending machine. It's for anyone who has six quarters.
ESTRO PURE
Certified estrogen-free!
WATER for boys!
It's our water. Girls have tap water...
Use the drinking fountain in the hall.
GIRLS ONLY
"It's perfectly good."
Then *you* drink it.
I can't. I'm a boy.
You're supposed to drink tap water. It's got medicine in it.
Yeah. Those added hormones are the only thing that's keeping all of you from murdering us.
Murder isn't cool.
I'm not going to murder you...
...just bat you around a little.

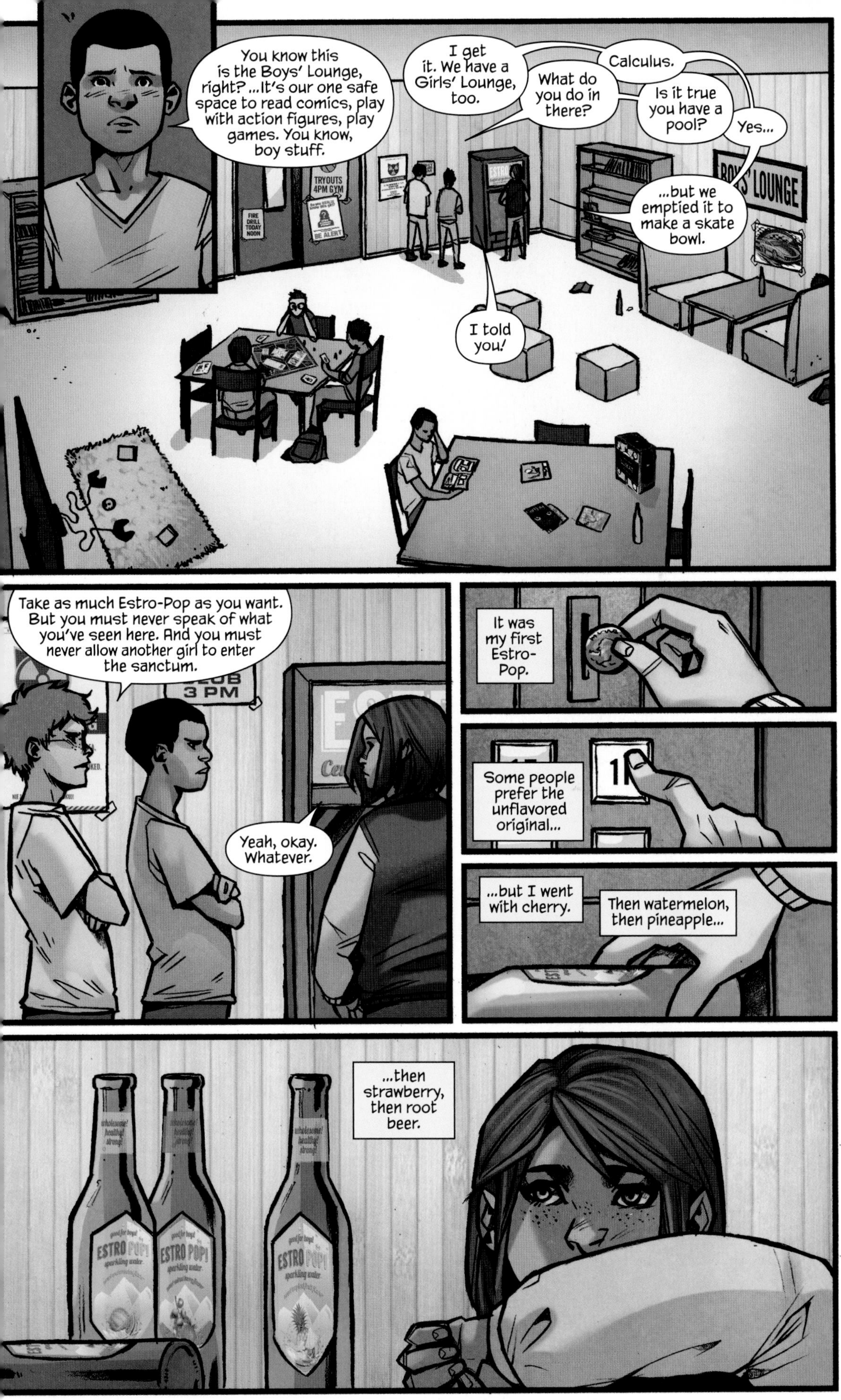
You know this is the Boys' Lounge, right? ...It's our one safe space to read comics, play with action figures, play games. You know, boy stuff.
I get it. We have a Girls' Lounge, too.
What do you do in there?
Calculus.
Is it true you have a pool?
Yes...
...but we emptied it to make a skate bowl.
TRYOUTS 4PM GYM
FIRE DRILL TODAY NOON
BE ALERT
BOYS' LOUNGE
I told you!
Take as much Estro-Pop as you want. But you must never speak of what you've seen here. And you must never allow another girl to enter the sanctum.
3 PM
Yeah, okay. Whatever.
It was my first Estro-Pop.
Some people prefer the unflavored original...
...but I went with cherry.
Then watermelon, then pineapple...
...then strawberry, then root beer.
wholesome! healthy! strong!
good for boys!
ESTRO POP!
sparkling water

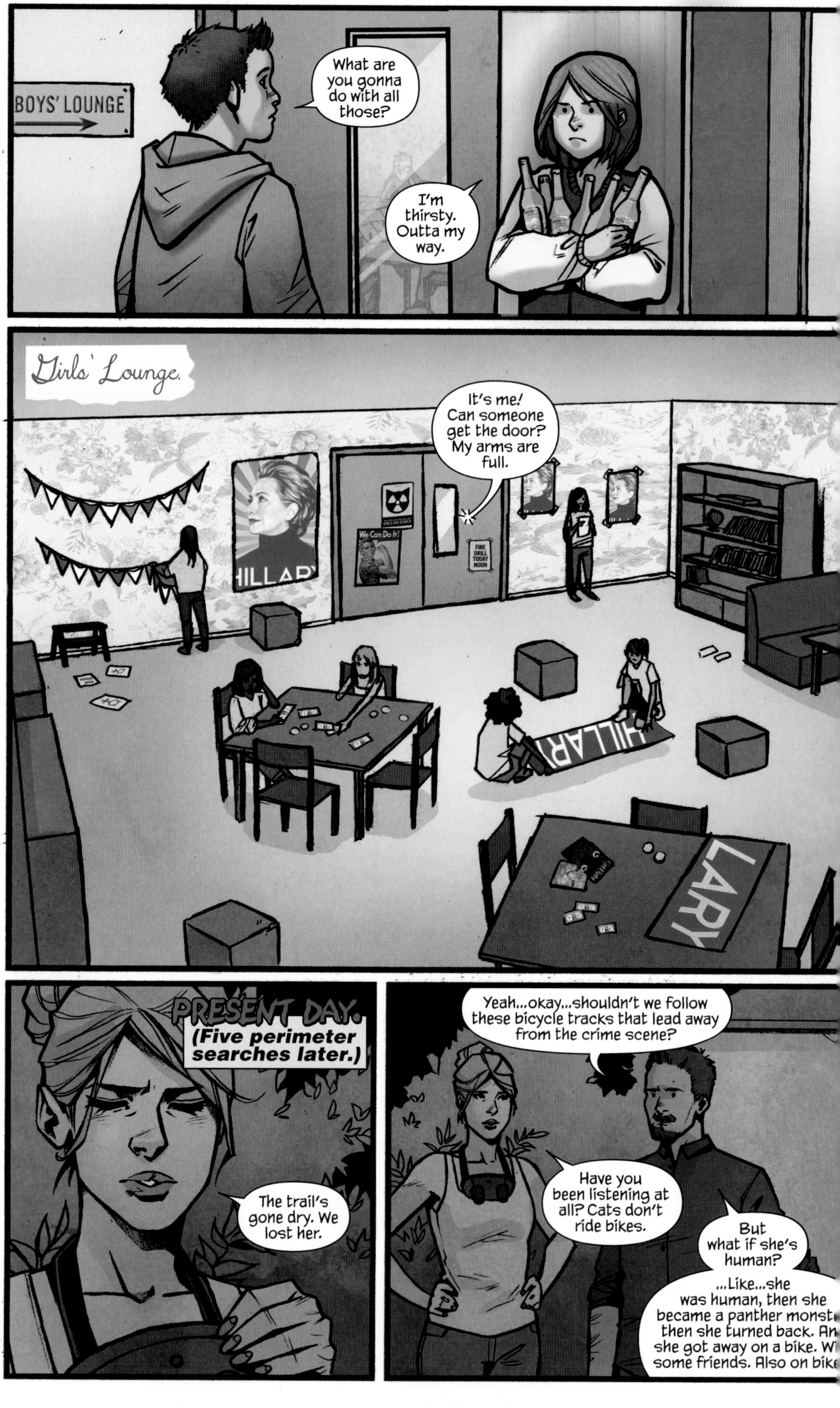
BOYS' LOUNGE
What are you gonna do with all those?
I'm thirsty. Outta my way.
Girls' Lounge.
It's me! Can someone get the door? My arms are full.
HILLARY
We Can Do It!
FIRE DRILL TODAY NOON
HILLARY
LARY
PRESENT DAY.
(Five perimeter searches later.)
The trail's gone dry. We lost her.
Yeah...okay...shouldn't we follow these bicycle tracks that lead away from the crime scene?
Have you been listening at all? Cats don't ride bikes.
But what if she's human?
...Like...she was human, then she became a panther monst
then she turned back. An
she got away on a bike. Wi
some friends. Also on bike

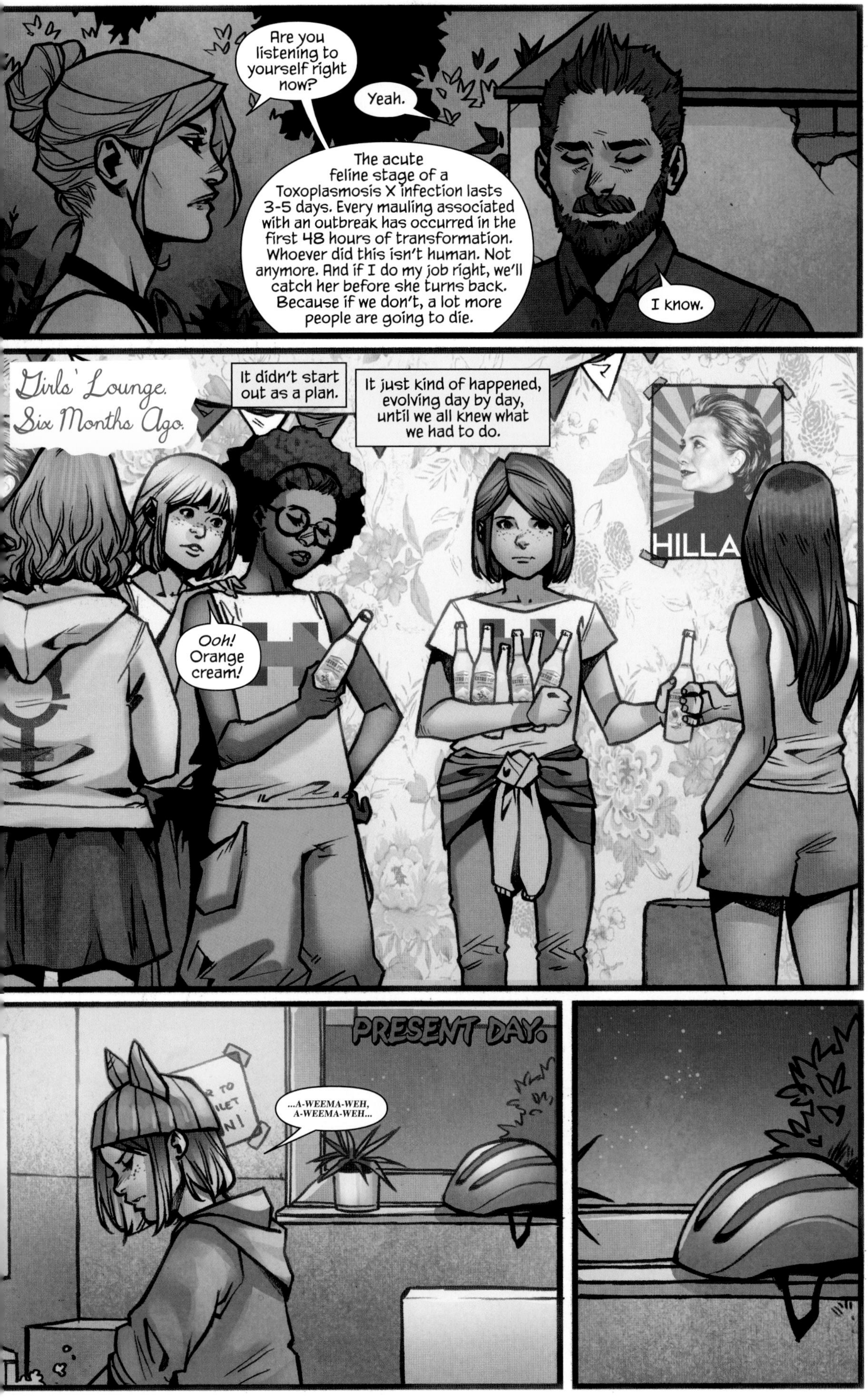
Are you listening to yourself right now?
Yeah.
The acute feline stage of a Toxoplasmosis X infection lasts 3-5 days. Every mauling associated with an outbreak has occurred in the first 48 hours of transformation. Whoever did this isn't human. Not anymore. And if I do my job right, we'll catch her before she turns back. Because if we don't, a lot more people are going to die.
I know.
Girls' Lounge. Six Months Ago.
It didn't start out as a plan.
It just kind of happened, evolving day by day, until we all knew what we had to do.
HILLA
Ooh! Orange cream!
PRESENT DAY.
...A-WEEMA-WEH, A-WEEMA-WEH...

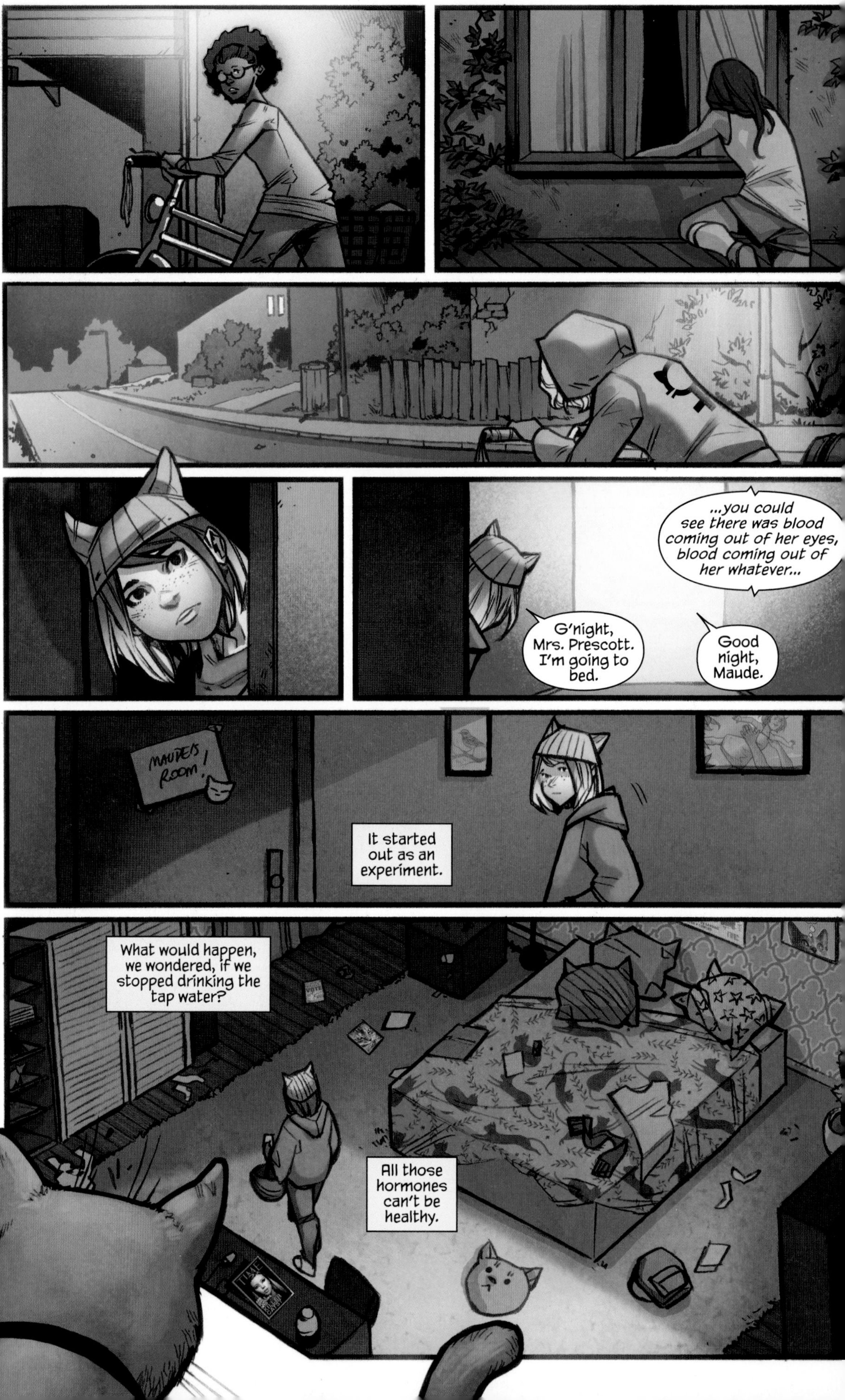
...you could see there was blood coming out of her eyes, blood coming out of her whatever...
G'night, Mrs. Prescott. I'm going to bed.
Good night, Maude.
MAUDE'S ROOM!
It started out as an experiment.
What would happen, we wondered, if we stopped drinking the tap water?
All those hormones can't be healthy.

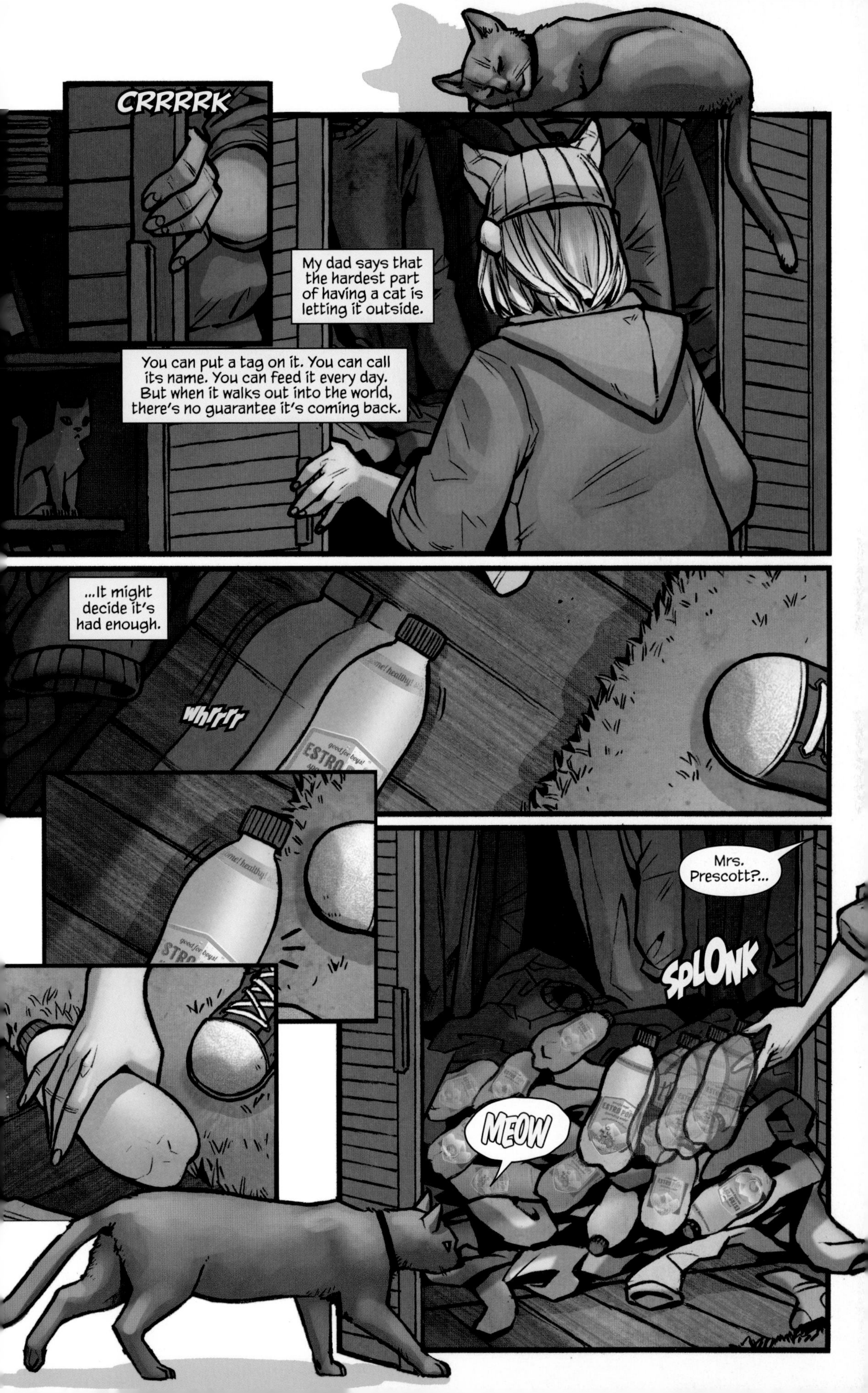
CRRRRK
My dad says that the hardest part of having a cat is letting it outside.
You can put a tag on it. You can call its name. You can feed it every day. But when it walks out into the world, there's no guarantee it's coming back.
...It might decide it's had enough.
whrrrr
Mrs. Prescott?...
SPLONK
MEOW

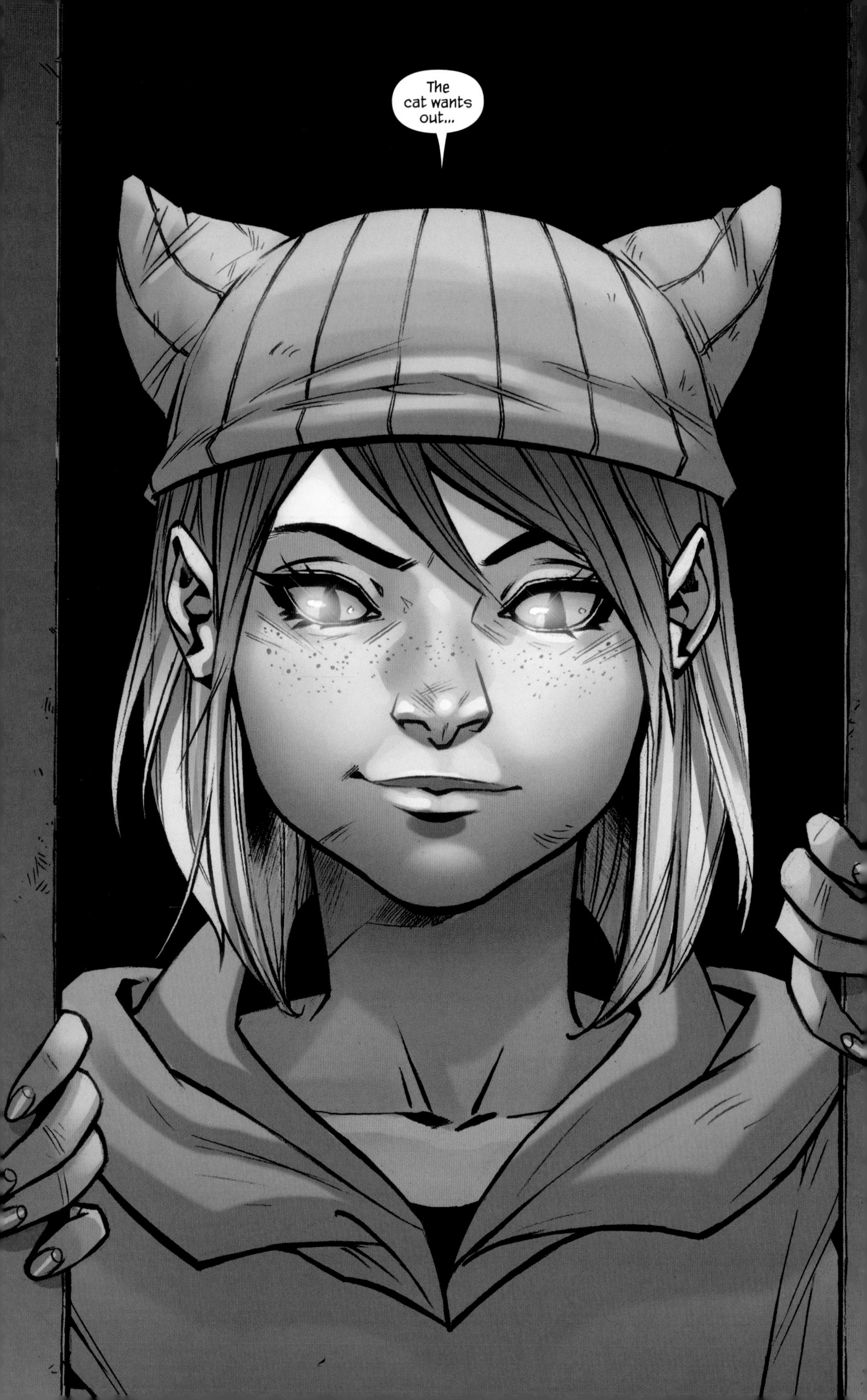
The cat wants out...

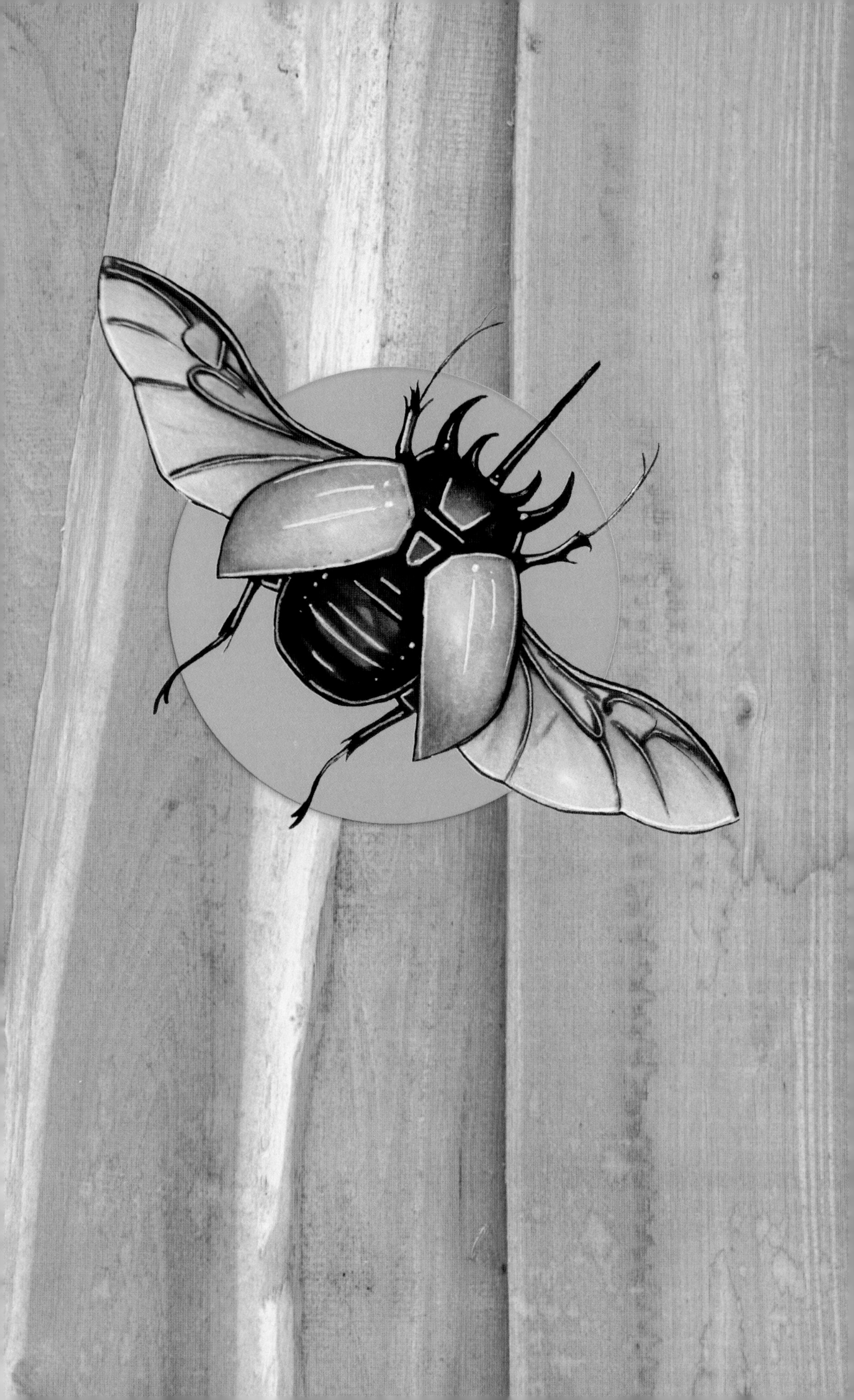

PHOENIX

By Eliza Fantastic Mohan (age 13)

The humans call me Phoenix. There are three of them, a male and two females. The smaller female is my Person, she gives me food when I yell loud enough. Sometimes I let her pet me, and she seems to find a much joy in the act. It is strange. Occasionally she will pick me up, and hold me in her long arms, rocking me back and forth like a baby.

I am not a baby.

Tonight I venture out, and the cool breeze kisses my fur. The moon is full and round tonight, illuminating my path. The other cats of my neighborhood are scarce, and most leave me alone at night. A quiet white and orange cat stares at me from a bush of fuschia flowers, as still as a tree. Just watching me. I pretend not to notice, letting the cat take me in. Eventually she turns around, and walks away, her long tail taunting me with each careful step.

Sometimes I sleep outside, when they humans grow tired of my taunting and close the door before I can rush inside at the last minute. I don't mind.

I find my bush, and rest my body on the dirt, letting the branches block out the moon's light. This is my favorite time, when there is nothing outside except the other cats who keep to their shadows, and the few brave squirrels silently jumping from tree to tree.

I hear my name being called by my Person, her voice light and careful, the voice she uses to get me to do what she wants. She stands on the front deck, her arms crossed over her chest in a silent protest, and her robe tied in front of her. It must be the sleep time. She looks worried. I debate staying outside, but decide her soft blanket sounds nice. She starts to turn around, but I move a little, letting my collar notify her of my decision. She turns back to me, and smiles. I like it when she smiles, I think it means I have done something right. I hurry up to her, slowing my pace once I get close enough. She says something I don't understand, and picks me up. I purr immediately nuzzling my face into her soft robe. She leads me upstairs to her room, and sets me down on her bed. She climbs in too, and before I know it it's dark and she is fast asleep, her face calm and relaxed. I find a spot next to her and curl up, content. I close my eyes, absolute darkness taking up my vision, and let myself drift away into peaceful sleep.

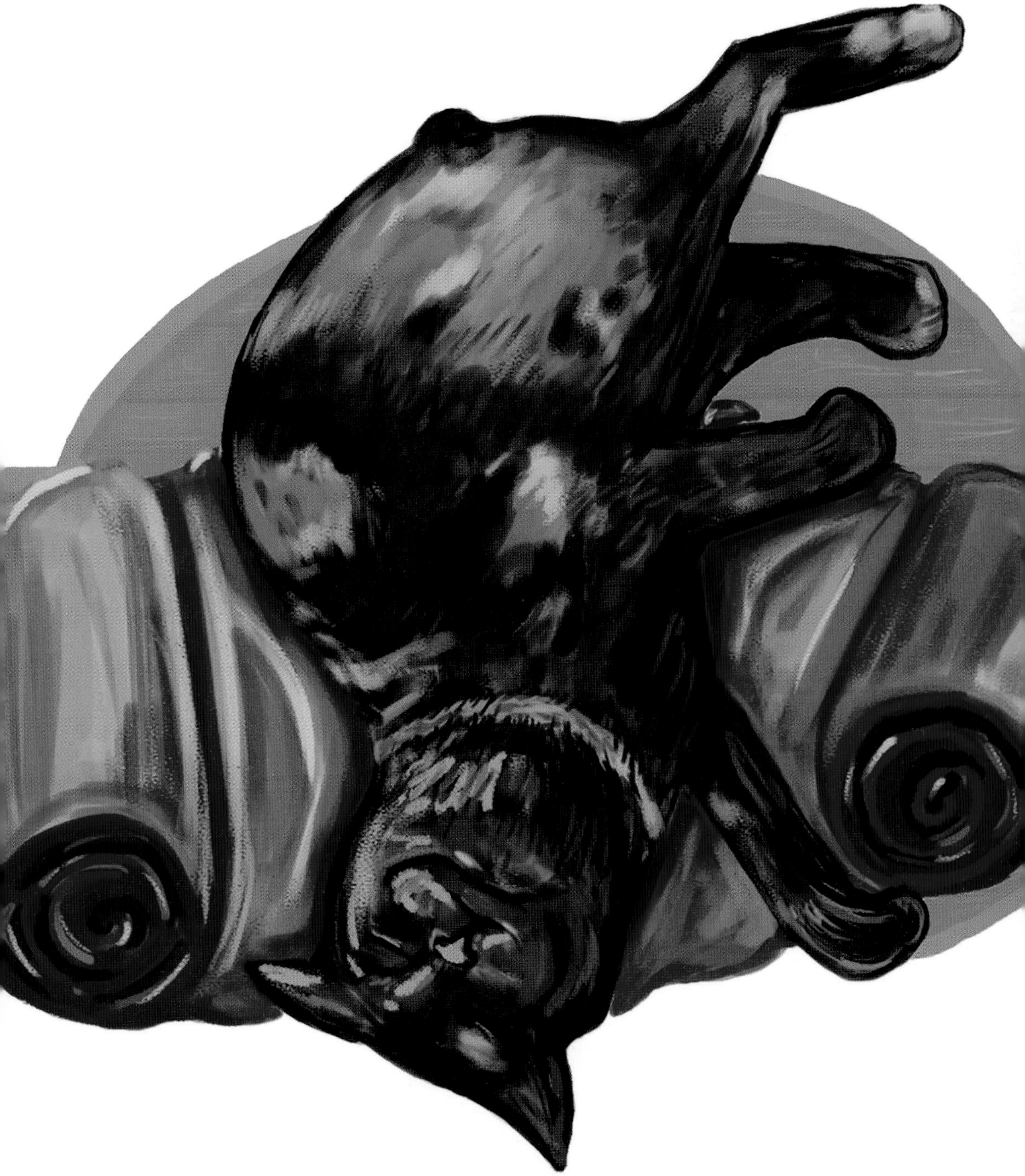

Portrait of Phoenix, Kyle Scanlon 2018

SUPPLEMENT PAID FOR BY ESTRO-PURE CORP

because everyone loves ESTROPOP!

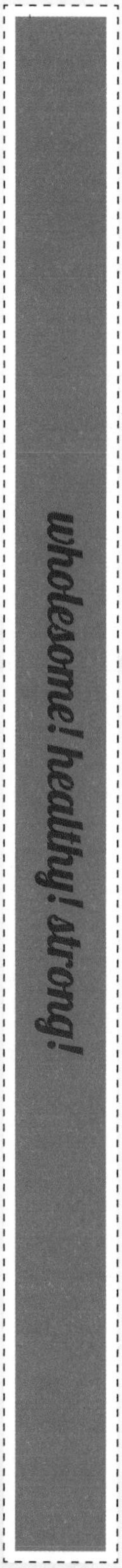
wholesome! healthy! strong!

BE SURE TO CUT ACCURATELY ALONG DOTTED LINES

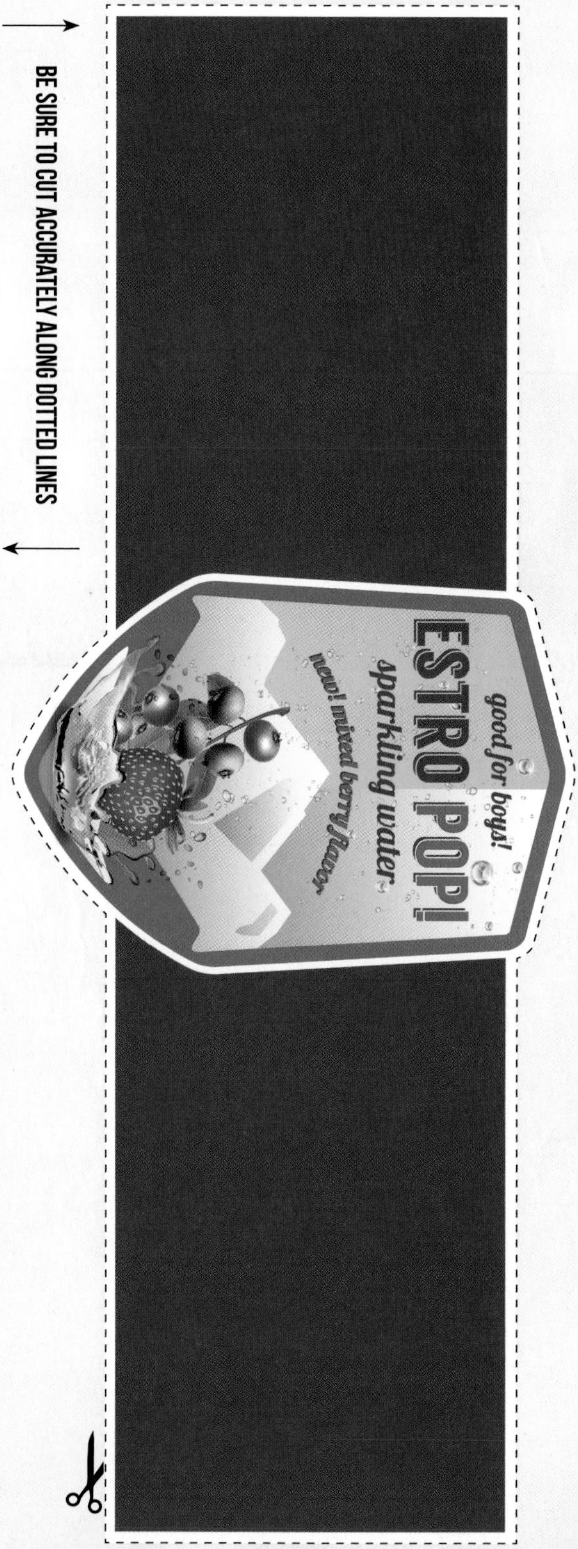
good for boys!
ESTRO POP!
sparkling water
new! mixed berry flavor

WHAT YOU NEED TO GET STARTED

- ☐ Water bottle
- ☐ Scissors
- ☐ Double-sided tape

INSTRUCTIONS

Start with your empty water bottle. Remove any existing lables. Clean. Dry. Set aside.

Cut out main body label (top) and neck label (bottom) along dotted lines.

Turn over. On back side place neat rows of double-sided tape. Flip over (*caution: do not let the sticky side of the labels touch your table or other surface.*)

Take clean, dry bottle and carefully place labels according to the example below.

Show your father or other man or boy your completed bottle, ready to fill with your favorite EstroPOP! flavor.

Enjoy!

example of completed bottle

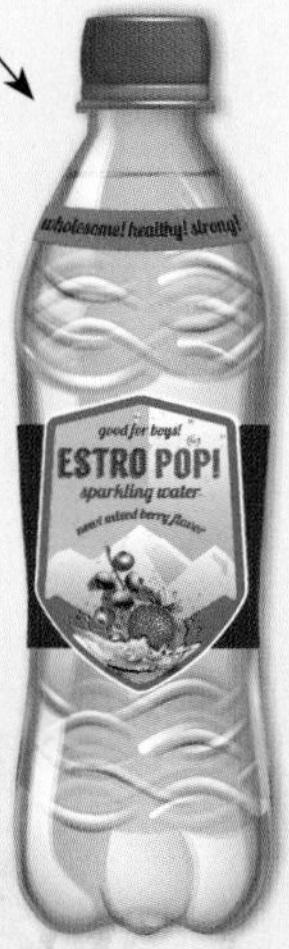
wholesome! healthy! strong!
good for boys!
ESTRO POP!
sparkling water

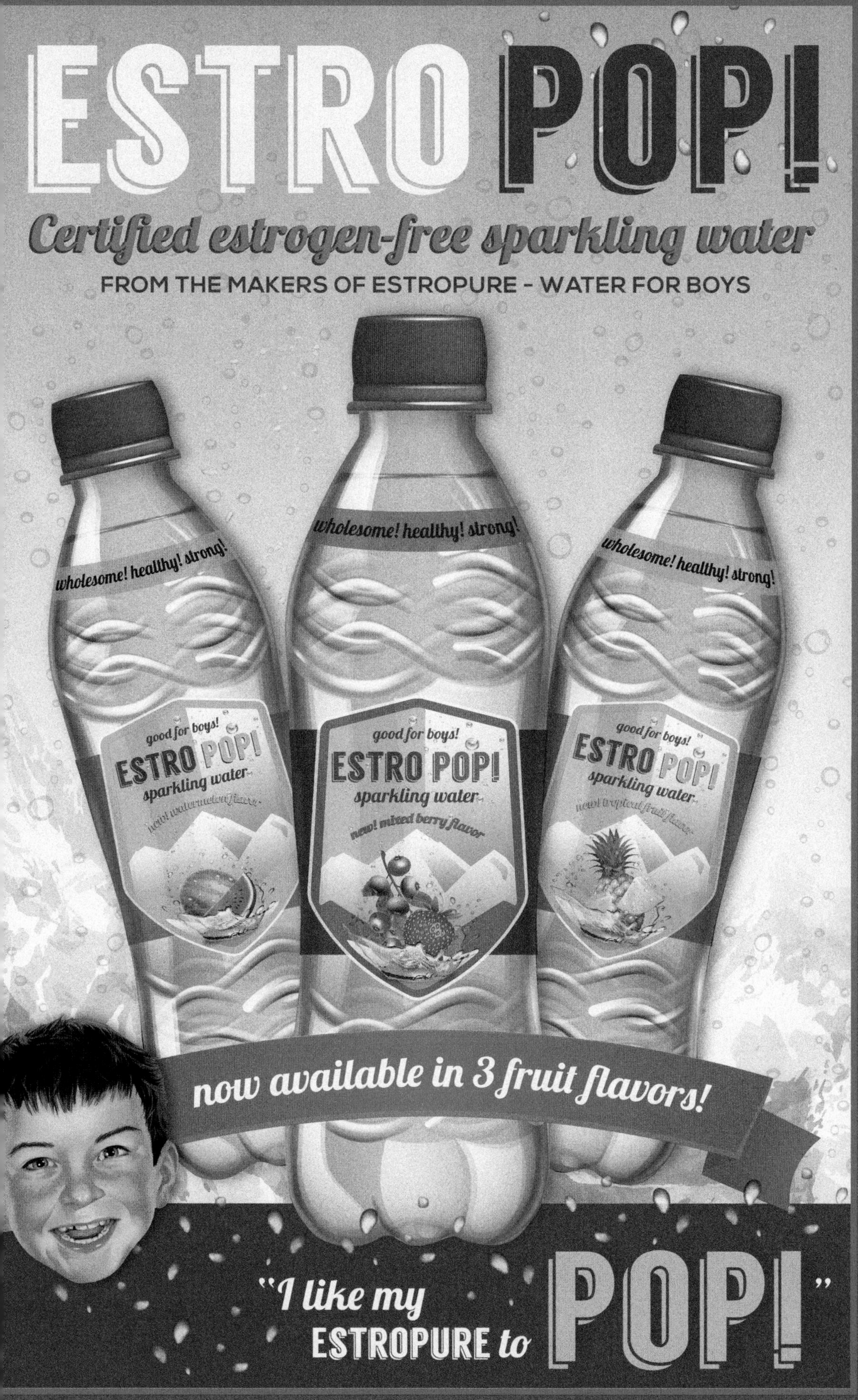

ESTRO POP!
Certified estrogen-free sparkling water
FROM THE MAKERS OF ESTROPURE - WATER FOR BOYS
wholesome! healthy! strong!
good for boys!
ESTRO POP!
sparkling water
new! mixed berry flavor
now available in 3 fruit flavors!
"I like my ESTROPURE to POP!"

Chapter four

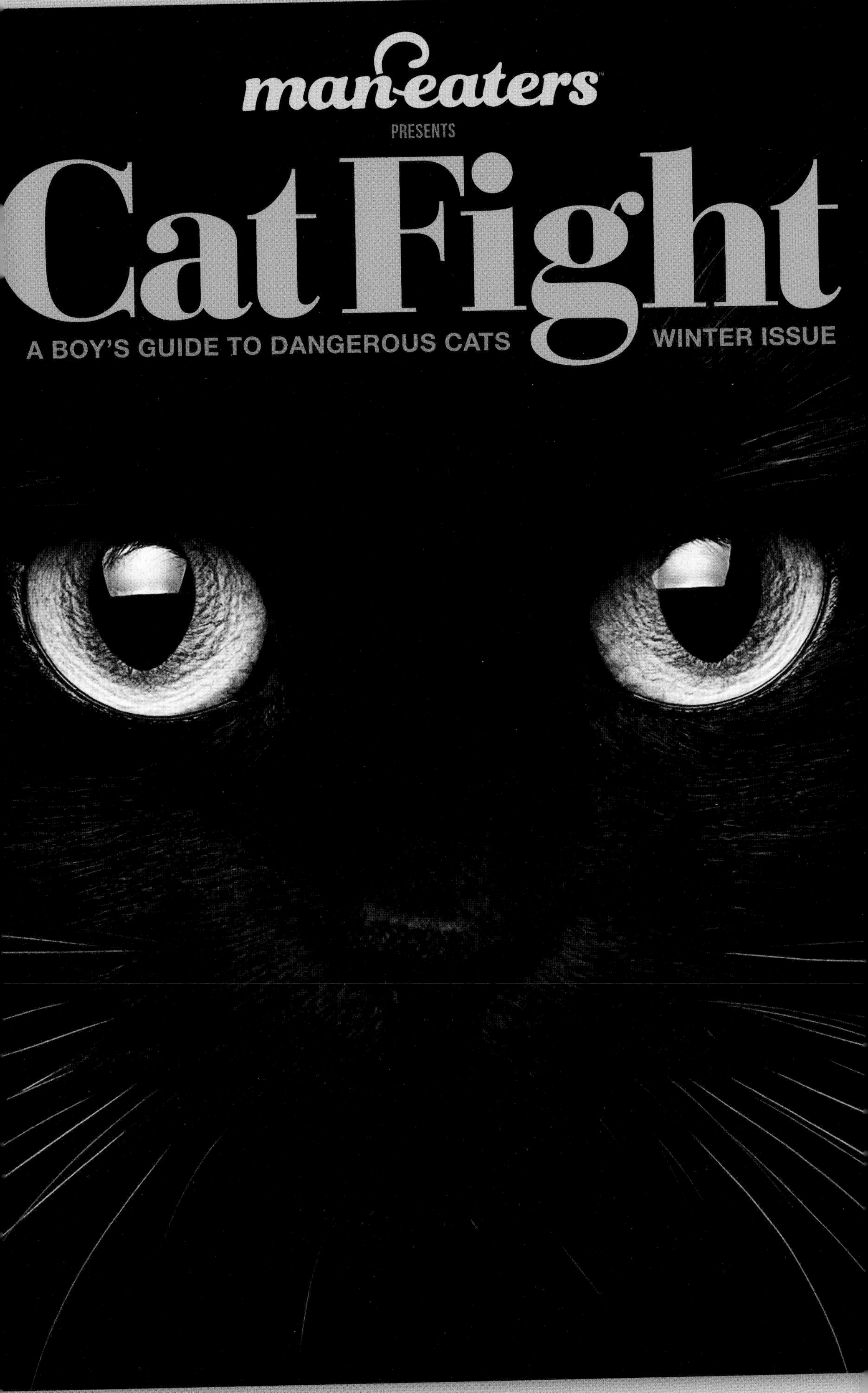
man-eaters™
PRESENTS
Cat Fight
A BOY'S GUIDE TO DANGEROUS CATS
WINTER ISSUE

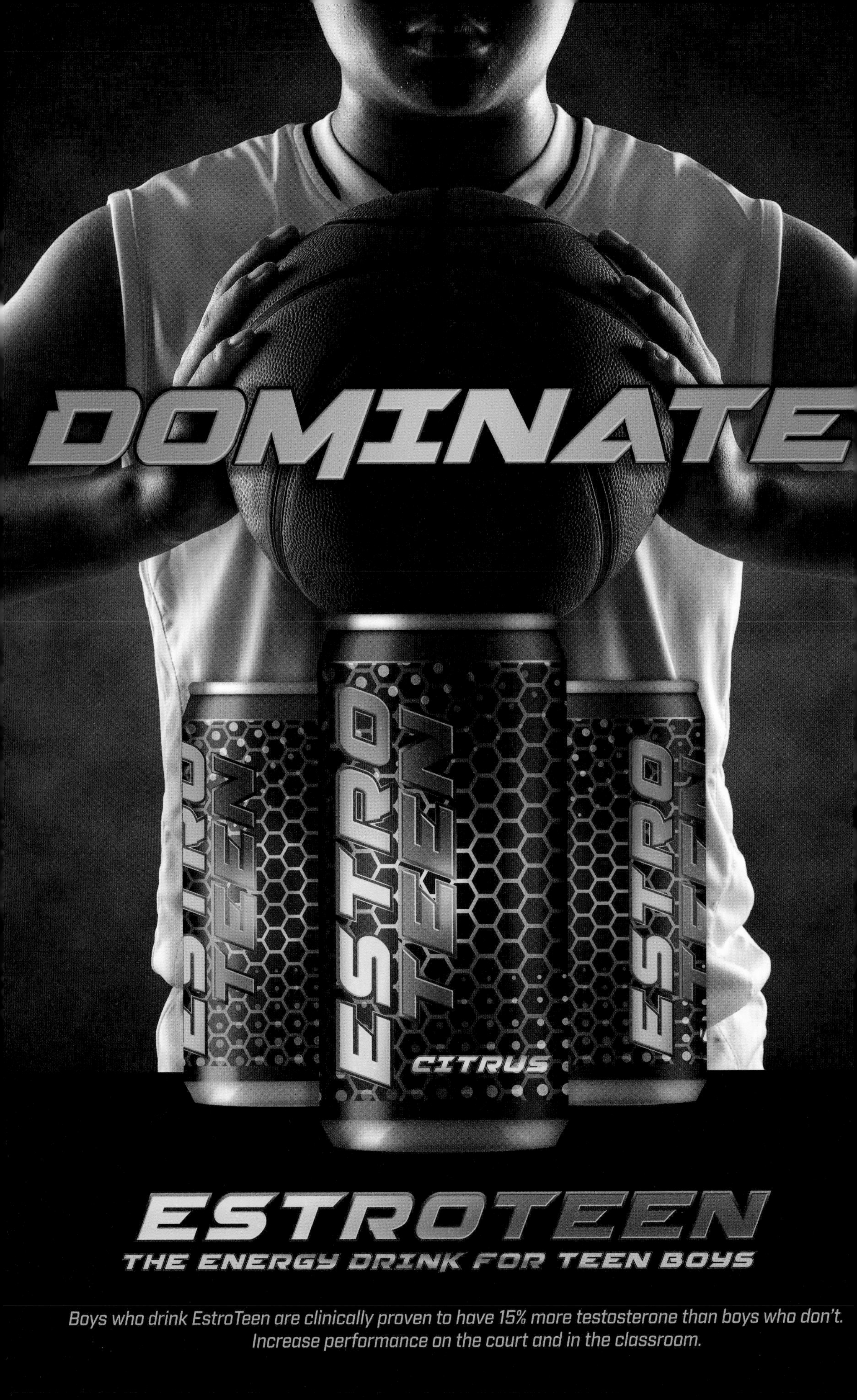
DOMINATE
ESTRO TEEN
ESTRO TEEN
CITRUS
ESTRO TEEN
ESTROTEEN
THE ENERGY DRINK FOR TEEN BOYS
Boys who drink EstroTeen are clinically proven to have 15% more testosterone than boys who don't.
Increase performance on the court and in the classroom.

man-eaters

Cat Fight

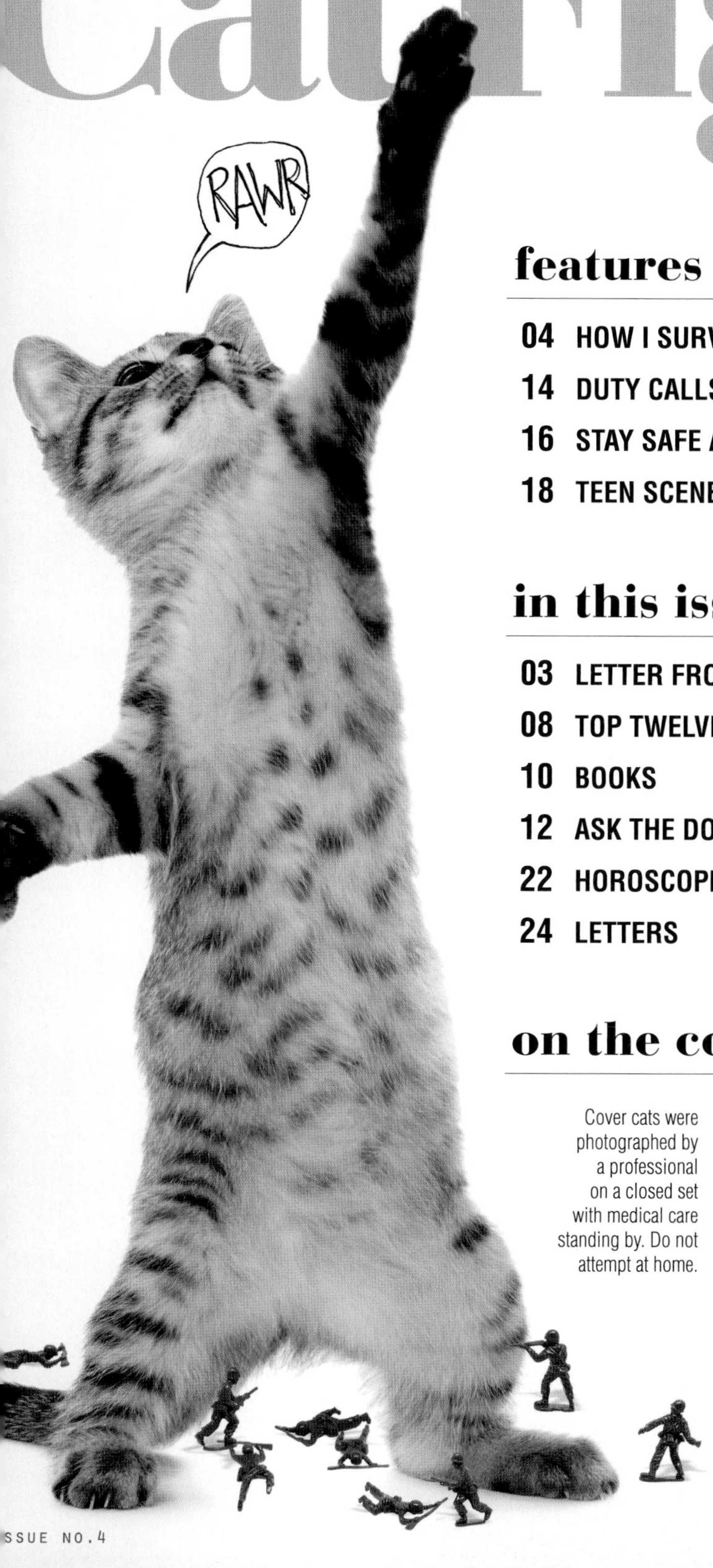

RAWR

features

in this issue

on the cover

Cover cats were photographed by a professional on a closed set with medical care standing by. Do not attempt at home.

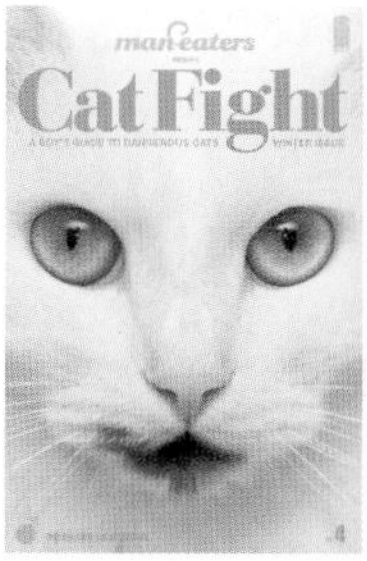

man-eaters
Cat Fight

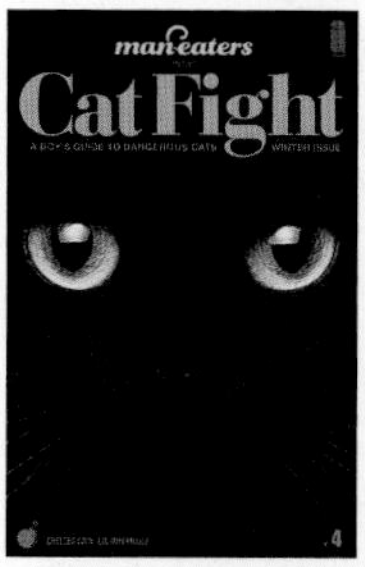

man-eaters
Cat Fight

MINISTRY OF
TROUBLE
I N C O R P O R A T E D

WRITER/CREATOR
CHELSEA CAIN

**COVER/CREATIVE
PRODUCER**
LIA MITERNIQUE

**ADDITIONAL
INTERIOR ART**
LIA MITERNIQUE
STELLA GREENVOSS

ADDITIONAL WRITING
ELIZA FANTASTIC MOHAN

SWAGGER
KATIE LANE

YOU HAVE BEEN CONTACTED BY THE MINISTRY OF TROUBLE. AWAIT FURTHER INSTRUCTIONS. ⚥

PRODUCTION BY TRICIA RAMOS

IMAGE COMICS, INC. •**Robert Kirkman**: Chief
Operating Officer • **Erik Larsen**: Chief Financial Officer
• **Todd McFarlane**: President • **Marc Silvestri**: Chief
Executive Officer • **Jim Valentino**: Vice President •
Eric Stephenson: Publisher / Chief Creative Officer •
Corey Hart: Director of Sales • **Jeff Boison**: Director
of Publishing Planning & Book Trade Sales • **Chris
Ross**: Director of Digital Sales • **Jeff Stang**: Director
of Specialty Sales • **Kat Salazar**: Director of PR
& Marketing • **Drew Gill**: Art Director • **Heather
Doornink**: Production Director • **Nicole Lapalme**:
Controller • IMAGECOMICS.COM

There are a hundr
ways to skin a ca
Half of them don't w
Find out which ha

Listen.
Learn.
Subscribe.

BIG CAT SURVIVAL PODCAST

Download & listen on Apple Podcast,
Google Play, or the podcatcher of your choice.
Then rate us on iTunes. Episodes updated weekly.

under attack

Dangerous cats continue to maul men and boys at appalling numbers. Why are some cats so mad at us? What provokes these vicious attacks? Can the carnage be stopped? How can you tell the difference between a good cat and a bad cat? These are the questions facing boys and men today.

You may have been taught that some cats are safe because they have been "domesticated." Some boys even invite cats into their beds. We do not recommend this. Cats are unpredictable and can never be trusted. According to a recent study, boys raised by women tend to associate cats with positive words like "smart," "deliberate," and "self-reliant." Whereas boys raised by men tend to associate cats with words like "unpredictable," "intimidating," "neat freak," and "controlling."

The facts speak for themselves. The boys in the second group are ten times more likely to survive a feline encounter.

Cats are highly adaptive and manipulative. Do not believe the pro-cat propaganda. Purring is not a reliable indicator of future behavior. The most docile-seeming cat can turn on a man or boy in a heartbeat.

In this issue, we explore personal accounts of near-deadly maulings, as well as what you can do to keep yourself safe.

It's not easy.

It's not comfortable.

But it may be the new normal of the man-cat relationship.

Are you a man?

Or are you a pussy?

Kevin Soter
Editor-in-Chief

HOW I SURVIV

By Jake Kagel

I didn't think it could happen to me.

My girlfriend and I were both Toxo X positive, but we'd been together for almost three years, and she had never exhibited any symptoms of advanced infection.

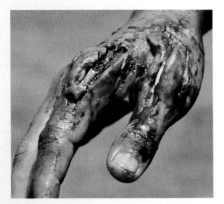

Dana *[not her real name]* and I met in college, and soon fell deeply in love. After graduation, we moved in together. I was planning on proposing that Christmas.

Instead I spent the holidays in the Big Cat Attack Intensive Care Unit at Oregon Health & Sciences University.

She ambushed me one night at home. I still don't know what set her off. They say that's one of the hardest parts about

SCIENCE SHOWS CATS HATE MEN AND BOYS

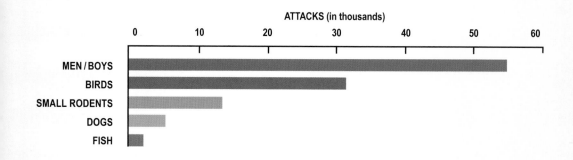

ATTACKS (in thousands)

	0	10	20	30	40	50	60
MEN / BOYS							
BIRDS							
SMALL RODENTS							
DOGS							
FISH							

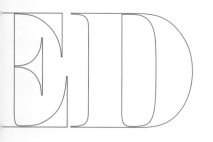

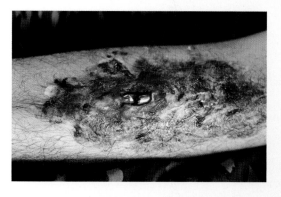

being a survivor. What was different about that night? It was just like any other night. I didn't say anything. I didn't do anything to provoke her.

I didn't deserve it.

I was the same person she'd fallen in love with. It was Dana who had changed.

Nothing had prepared me for that moment. No amount of in-school drills or at-home safety planning, or Netflix Cat Attack specials.

She'd mutated. The woman I loved, replaced by a monster – all rippling muscle, teeth, claws, and rage.

Dana lunged at me, and I felt her claws slice into my thigh. The heat of my own blood on

The woman I loved, replaced by a monster – all rippling muscle, teeth, claws, and rage.

my pants. That's when my training kicked in.

[Editor's note: Jake took a Red Cross Big Cat Survival Strategies course in high school.]

They always say to fight back, to make noise. Most people never get the chance. They're ambushed so they don't see it coming, or they're so disoriented by the eruption of fury that they freeze up.

(continued on next page)

(continued from previous page)

Survivor, Jake Kagel, and his new girlfriend, Na

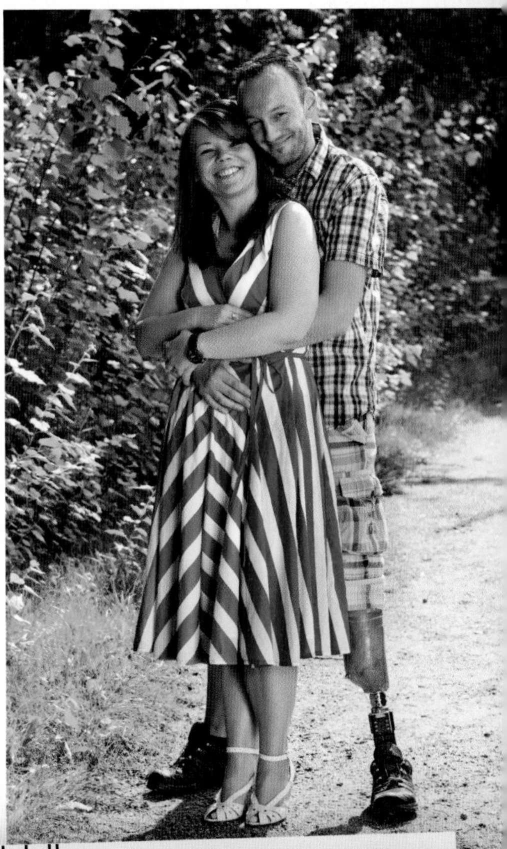

I screamed. I used the only weapon I had – the television remote – in self-defense, reflexively ramming it into Dana's snout.

It surprised her, and I was able to use the distraction to my advantage and curl into a ball. This protected my major organs from mauling. She clawed at my back and arm, but eventually lost interest. When she was gone, I used an electrical cord to tourniquet my leg, and I called 911.

Dana is still missing.

Her bloody paw prints led from the scene, down the steps of our apartment, and toward the woods. That's where the dogs lost her trail.

Me? I'm just happy to be here.

WHERE DO CAT ATTACKS OCCUR?

A global perspective

Studies show, you're not safe anywhere.

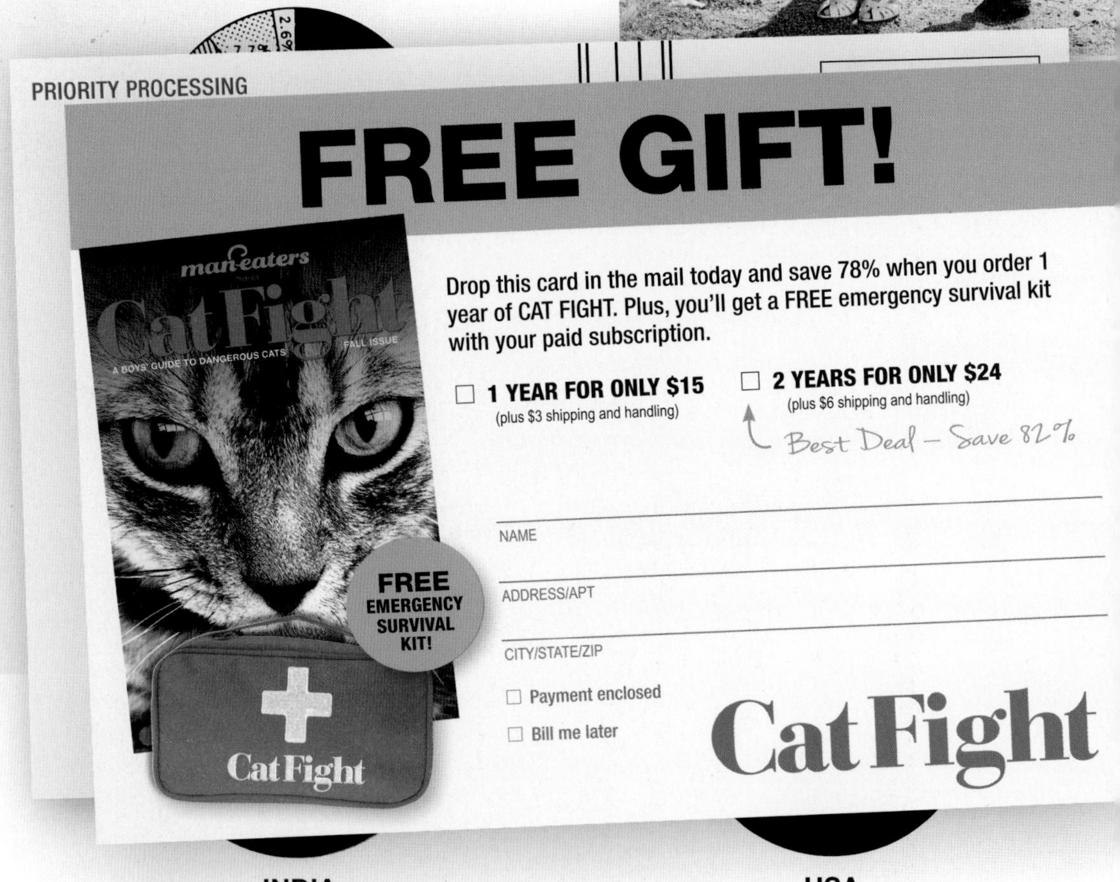
2.6%
7.7%
PRIORITY PROCESSING
FREE GIFT!
man-eaters
CatFight
A BOYS' GUIDE TO DANGEROUS CATS
FALL ISSUE
FREE EMERGENCY SURVIVAL KIT!
CatFight
Drop this card in the mail today and save 78% when you order 1 year of CAT FIGHT. Plus, you'll get a FREE emergency survival kit with your paid subscription.
☐ 1 YEAR FOR ONLY $15
(plus $3 shipping and handling)
☐ 2 YEARS FOR ONLY $24
(plus $6 shipping and handling)
Best Deal – Save 82%
NAME
ADDRESS/APT
CITY/STATE/ZIP
☐ Payment enclosed
☐ Bill me later
CatFight

INDIA

USA

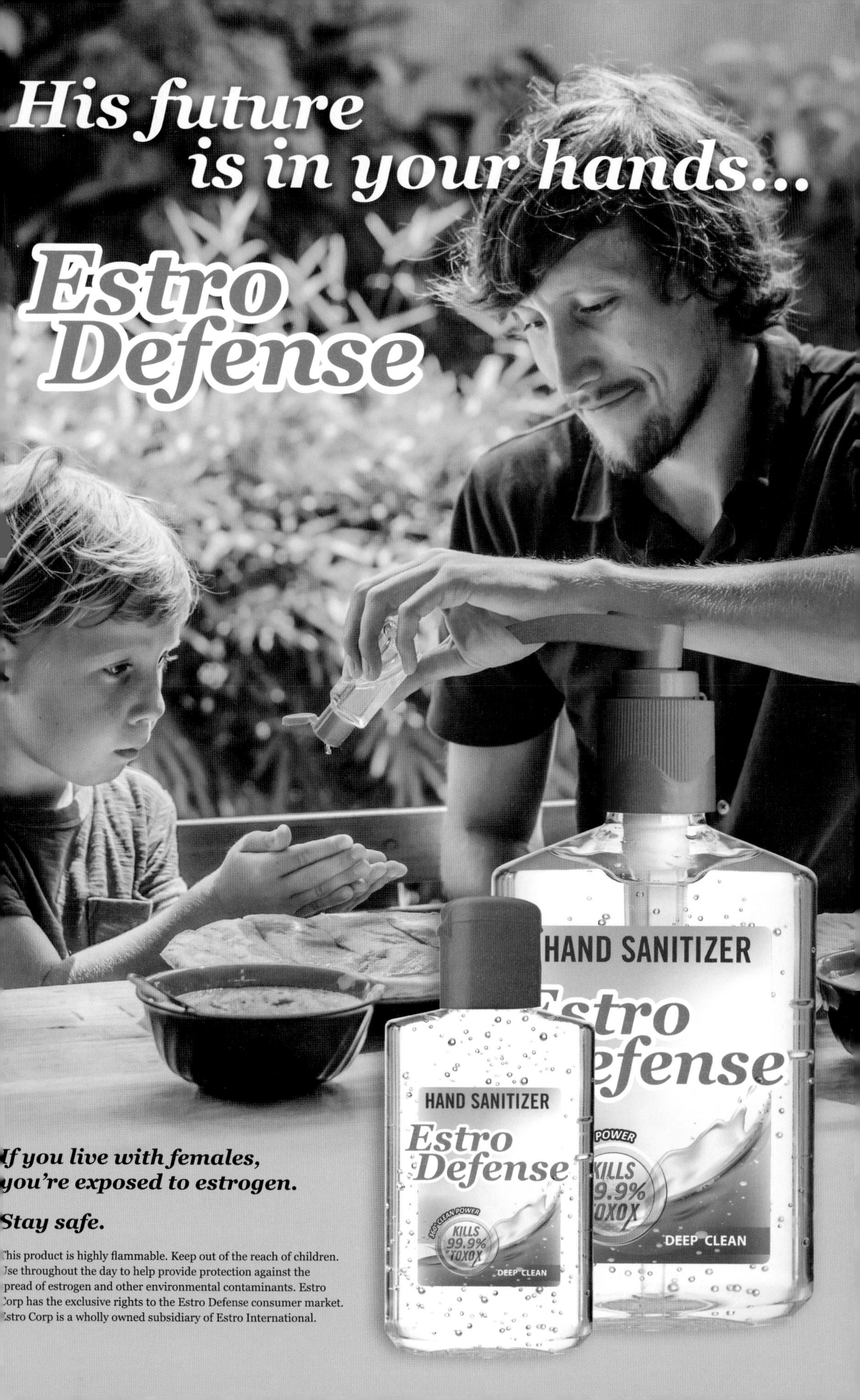

His future
is in your hands...

Estro
Defense

If you live with females,
you're exposed to estrogen.

Stay safe.

This product is highly flammable. Keep out of the reach of children.
Use throughout the day to help provide protection against the
spread of estrogen and other environmental contaminants. Estro
Corp has the exclusive rights to the Estro Defense consumer market.
Estro Corp is a wholly owned subsidiary of Estro International.

HAND SANITIZER
Estro
Defense
KILLS
99.9%
TOXOX
DEEP CLEAN

HAND SANITIZER
Estro
Defense
BODY CLEAN POWER
KILLS
99.9%
TOXOX
DEEP CLEAN

TOP 12
SURVIVAL TOOLS FOR BOYS

1. Gauze
2. Comfortable backpack
3. Pocket-size hand sanitizer
4. Rope
5. Matches
6. Yarn
7. Ten gallons of estrogen-free water
8. Binoculars
9. Multi-tool for cutting yarn and gauze
10. More gauze
11. Useful how-to handbook
12. Distraction tool

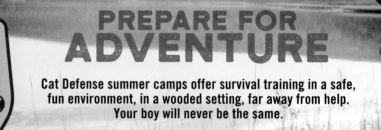

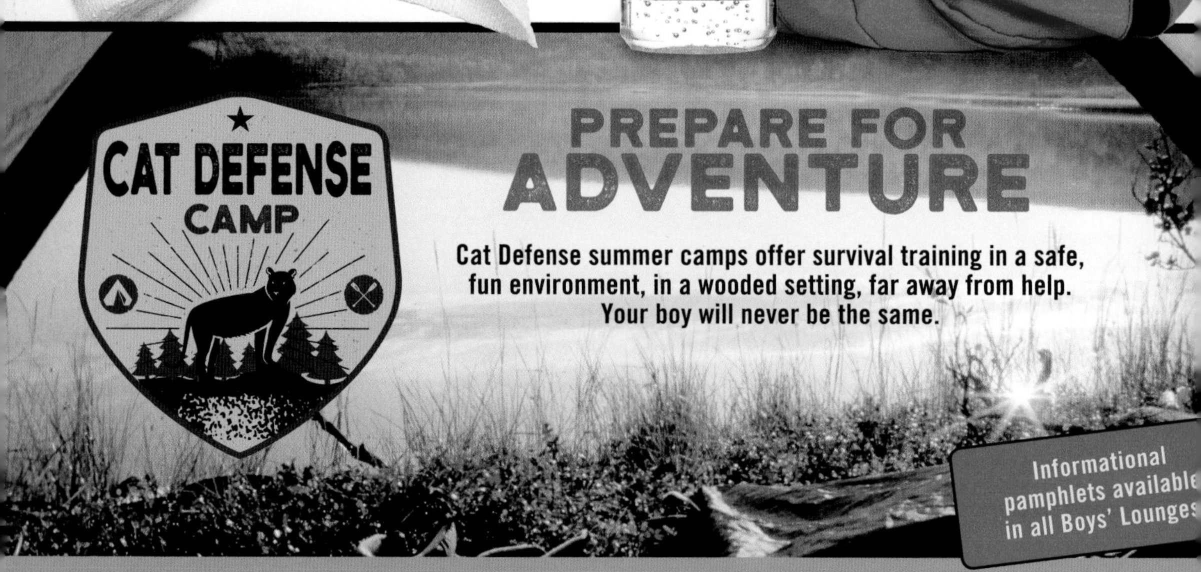

CAT DEFENSE CAMP

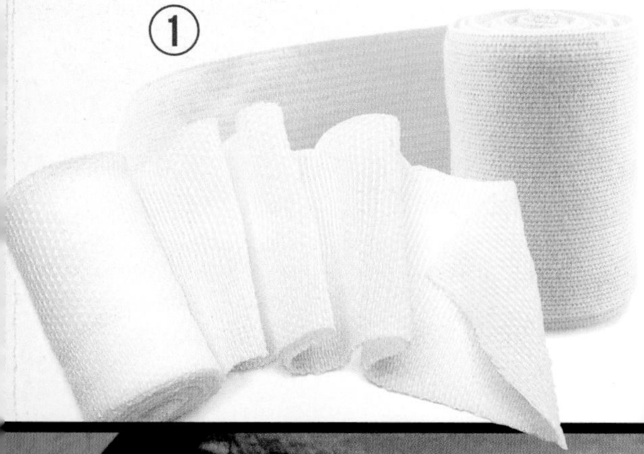

PREPARE FOR
ADVENTURE

Cat Defense summer camps offer survival training in a safe, fun environment, in a wooded setting, far away from help. Your boy will never be the same.

Informational pamphlets available in all Boys' Lounges

"My son, Henry, loves CDC. And now he won't stop foraging! Thanks, CDC. See you this summer!" – Parent of Camper

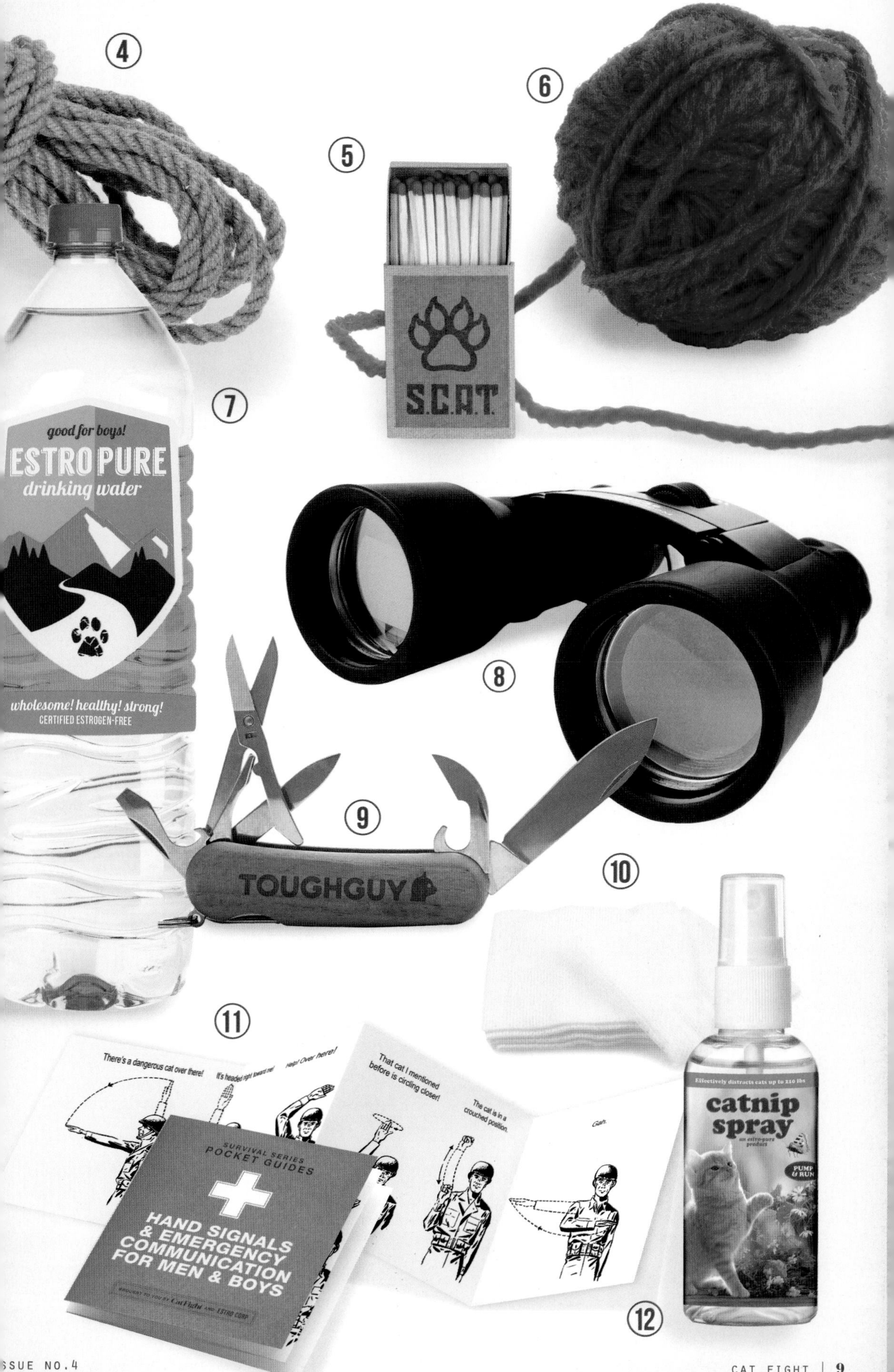
4
5
6
7
8
9
10
11
12
S.C.A.T.
good for boys!
ESTRO PURE
drinking water
wholesome! healthy! strong!
CERTIFIED ESTROGEN-FREE
TOUGHGUY
There's a dangerous cat over there!
It's headed right toward me!
Help! Over here!
That cat I mentioned before is circling closer!
The cat is in a crouched position.
Gah.
SURVIVAL SERIES
POCKET GUIDES
HAND SIGNALS & EMERGENCY COMMUNICATION FOR MEN & BOYS
Effectively distracts cats up to 110 lbs
catnip spray
PUMP & RUN

Are you readin

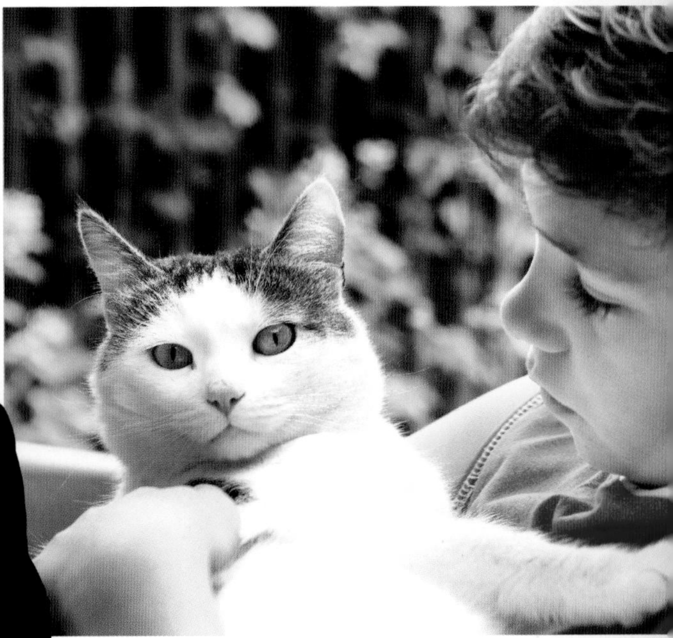

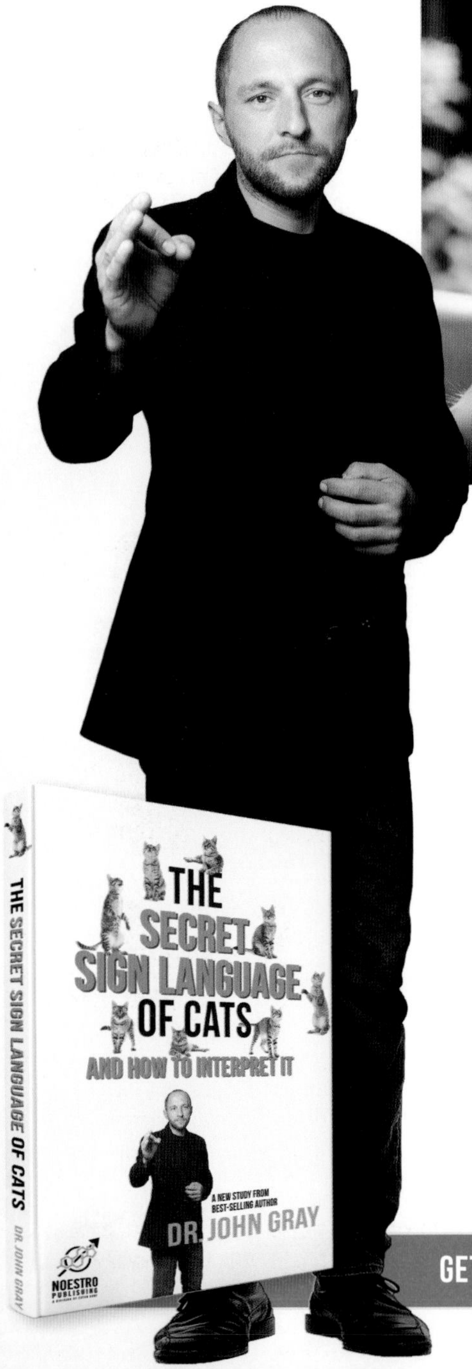
THE SECRET SIGN LANGUAGE OF CATS
AND HOW TO INTERPRET IT
A NEW STUDY FROM BEST-SELLING AUTHOR
DR. JOHN GRAY
NOESTRO PUBLISHING
THE SECRET SIGN LANGUAGE OF CATS
DR. JOHN GRAY

Celebrity feline body language specialist, Dr. John Gray, thinks cats are trying to tell us something.

CAT SIGNALS: INTERPRETING CAT BEHAVIOR

Many of us love cats. Some of us even long to have them on our laps. But do we ever really know them? I have devoted my life to understanding the feline mind in the hopes of strengthening the man-cat relationship.

Cats are not like us. They are more sensitive, talkative, mercurial, and not as educated.

Because men are less emotive than cats, we sometimes misunderstand the signals they are sending. This can lead to resentment.

A few simple "tells" can make the difference between simpatico and slaughter.

GET YOUR COPY BEFORE IT SELLS OUT. ORDER TODAY!

he "tell-tail" signs?

① *Ears*

Very slight variation in ear position can tell you a lot about what your cat is thinking.

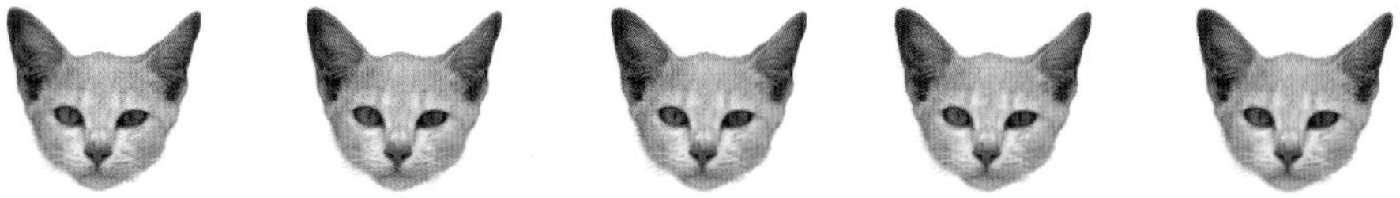

CONTENT — EXASPERATED — SARCASTIC — OFFENDED — HOMICIDAL (This cat is probably attacking you)

② *Butts*

Cats let their tails do the talking.
Match each image with the correct subtext.

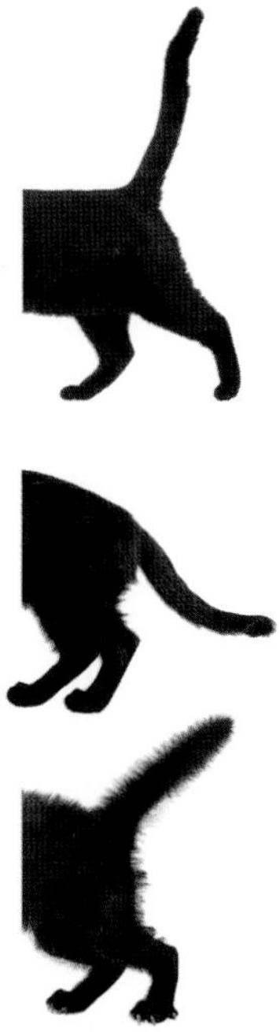

Ⓐ Ⓑ Ⓒ

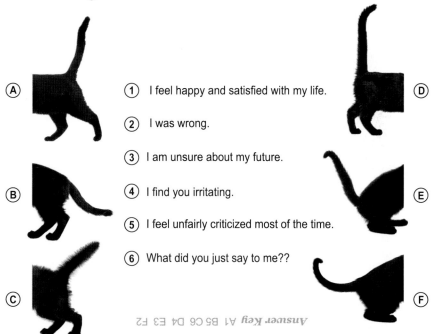

① I feel happy and satisfied with my life.

② I was wrong.

③ I am unsure about my future.

④ I find you irritating.

⑤ I feel unfairly criticized most of the time.

⑥ What did you just say to me??

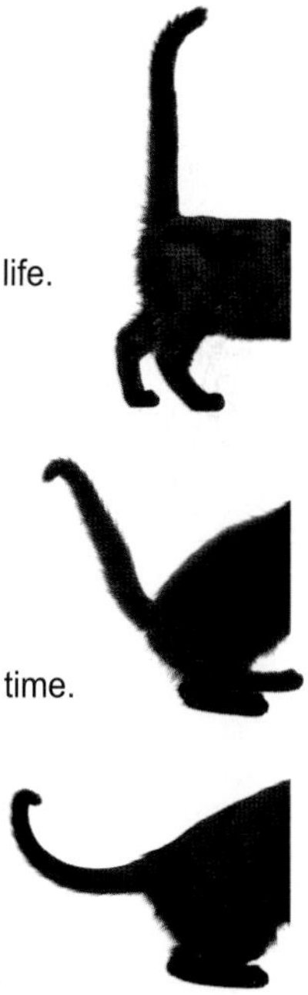

Ⓓ Ⓔ Ⓕ

Answer Key A1 B5 C6 D4 E3 F2

③ *Conclusion and takeaway*

If you have a relationship with a cat, you owe it to yourself to learn the basics of man-cat communication, as outlined in my book, *The Secret Sign Language of Cats and How to Interpret it*. It just might save your life.

ask *the doctor*

What is Toxoplasmosis X?
Toxoplasmosis X (tok-so-plaz-MOE-sis ex) is a single-cell parasite that currently infects about 79 million Americans. It is spread through cat feces, airport restroom faucets, office keyboards, and school gym equipment like basketballs and badminton rackets.

Who's at risk?
Females, age 11-14, tend to experience the worst complications, due to a biological quirk called menstruation.

Tell me more.
Anyone who menstruates is in danger of succumbing to madness and deformity. When triggered, Toxo X causes females to mutate into hulking, panther-like cats. This process is savage and sudden. (Though often precipitated by specific indicators, including moodiness, emotional outbursts, cravings, obstinance, etc.) The woman/girl becomes enraged, disassociated, and violent. She will lash out at loved ones, strangers, co-workers, and even authority figures.

Do panthers get better?
Symptoms are self-limiting and even left untreated will fade after 3-5 days. Unfortunately, once someone has entered Feline Stage Toxo X, the condition becomes chronic, and the afflicted will experience outbreaks on a 28-day cycle for three to four decades.

What happens if I get it?
Most people are Toxo X positive. However, boys and men appear immune to the parasite's more serious effects. At worst, you may experience some mild flu-like symptoms.

What can I do to help?
Monitor the females in your life. Encourage them to get screened. Ask the status of female friends and family members. Pay special attention to adolescent females. Are they behaving differently? Have their interests changed? Is there something about a particular girl that makes you "feel funny"? Trust your gut. All pre-menstrual symptoms – joint pain, spotting, etc. – should be taken seriously.

So, where did Toxoplasmosis X come from?

By the time Toxoplasmosis evolved into "Toxoplasmosis X," it had already infected most of the human population. Your cat is to blame.

THE LIFE CYCLE OF TRADITIONAL TOXOPLASMOSIS

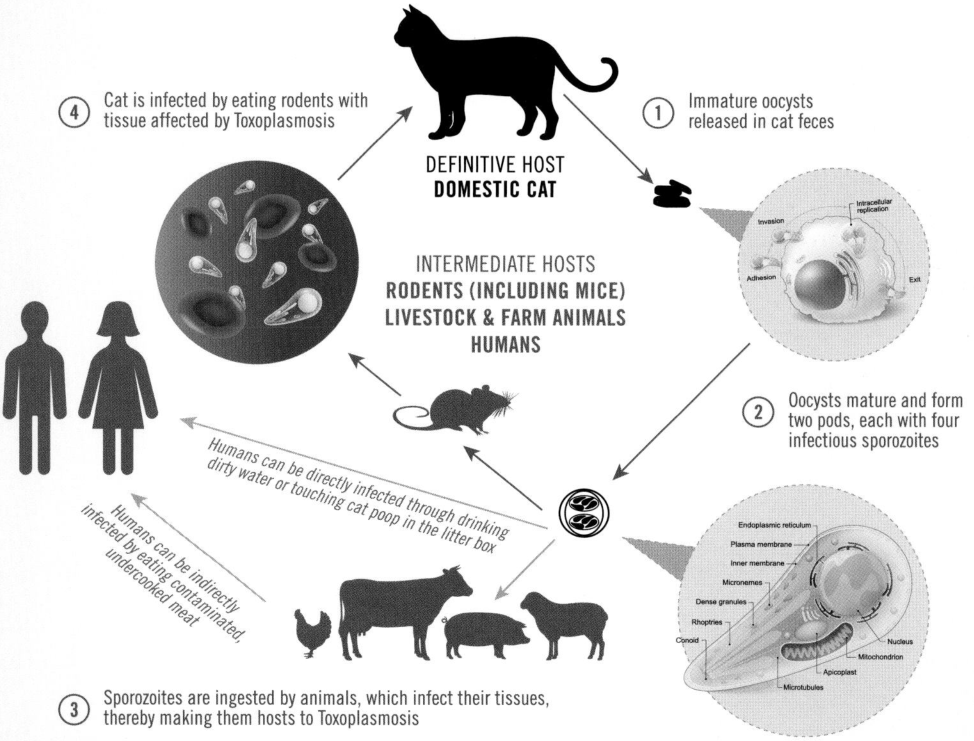

DEFINITIVE HOST
DOMESTIC CAT
1 Immature oocysts released in cat feces
Invasion
Intracellular replication
Adhesion
Exit
2 Oocysts mature and form two pods, each with four infectious sporozoites
Endoplasmic reticulum
Plasma membrane
Inner membrane
Micronemes
Dense granules
Rhoptries
Conoid
Nucleus
Mitochondrion
Apicoplast
Microtubules
3 Sporozoites are ingested by animals, which infect their tissues, thereby making them hosts to Toxoplasmosis
Humans can be directly infected through drinking dirty water or touching cat poop in the litter box
Humans can be indirectly infected by eating contaminated, undercooked meat
INTERMEDIATE HOSTS
RODENTS (INCLUDING MICE)
LIVESTOCK & FARM ANIMALS
HUMANS
4 Cat is infected by eating rodents with tissue affected by Toxoplasmosis

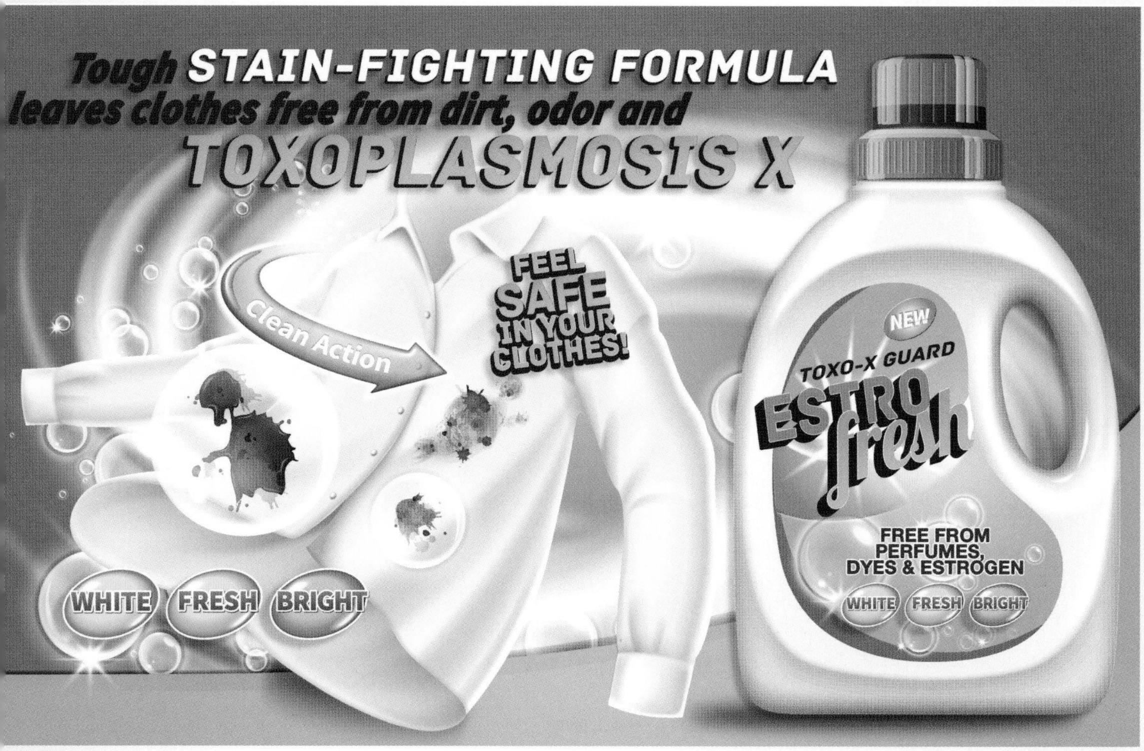

Tough STAIN-FIGHTING FORMULA
leaves clothes free from dirt, odor and
TOXOPLASMOSIS X
Clean Action
FEEL SAFE IN YOUR CLOTHES!
WHITE FRESH BRIGHT
NEW
TOXO-X GUARD
ESTRO fresh
FREE FROM PERFUMES, DYES & ESTROGEN
WHITE FRESH BRIGHT

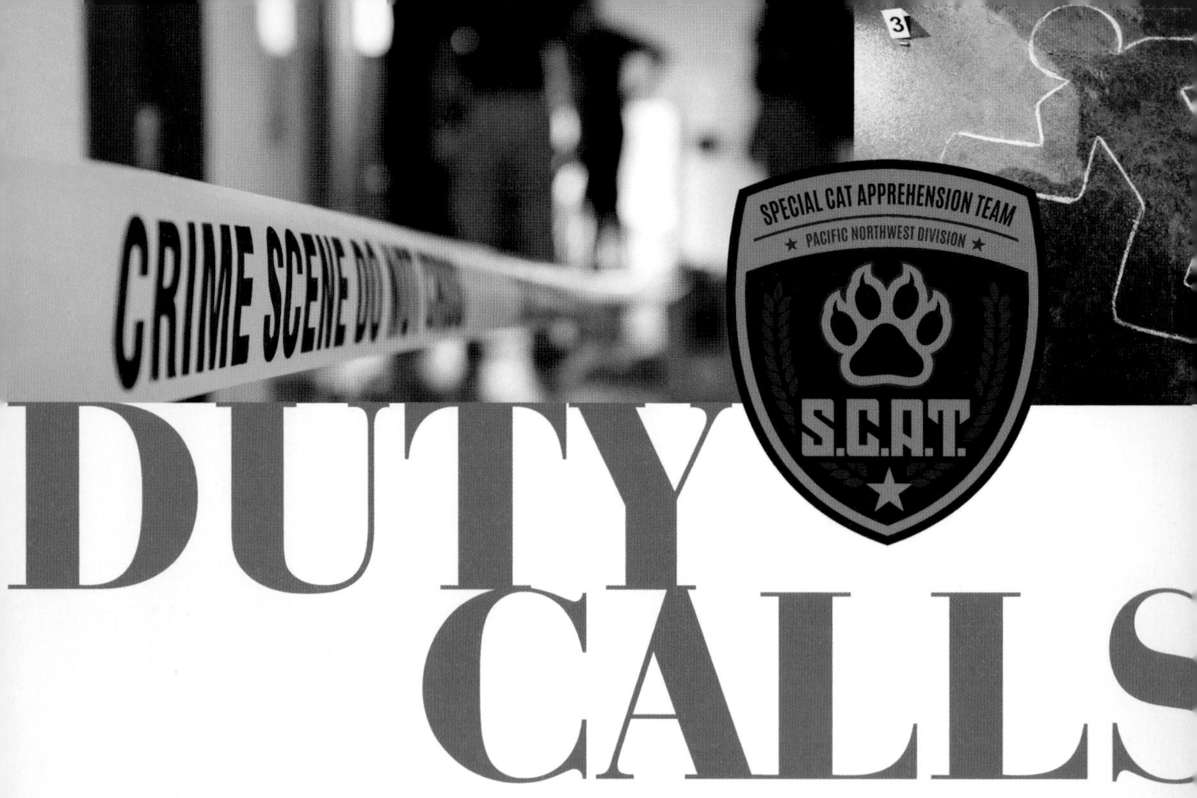
CRIME SCENE DO
3
SPECIAL CAT APPREHENSION TEAM
PACIFIC NORTHWEST DIVISION
S.C.A.T.

DUTY CALLS

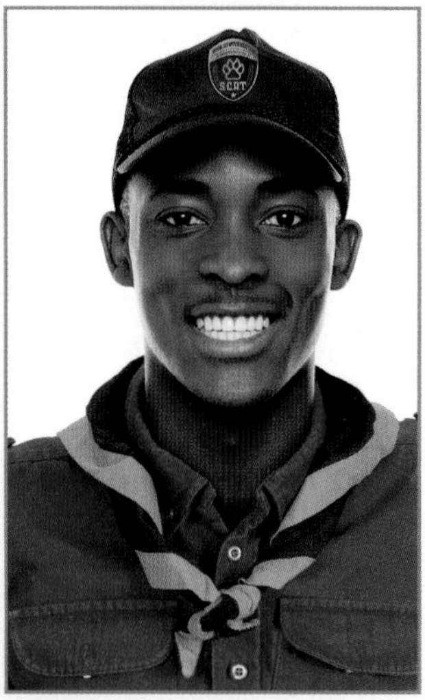
© Troy Sampson

Jed Jebson, S.C.A.T. Tracker and Poop Expert

Interview with JED JEBSON, tracker with the PNW division of S.C.A.T.

CF **What's the risk of being attacked by a big cat?**

JJ That's a good question! It's important to remember that – while Toxoplasmosis X infection rates have never been higher – big cat attacks are far less frequent and less deadly than they used to be. People see the news, a mauling, maybe an amputation, and they freak out. I like to remind people to take a breath. These things tend to happen in waves, or clusters. They cause a lot of panic. And then things return to normal. They always do.

CF **Did you always want to be a professional tracker?**

JJ I was a kid during the first outbreak. There were kids at my school who didn't make it. I guess I just wanted to find a way to give back. It's a challenging job. But every day is different and I get to meet a lot of different kinds of people. Also, I love working with animals.

CF **What advice would you give to boys who want to grow up to track big cats for S.C.A.T.?**

JJ Join a SCAT club. Volunteer in your community. Keep an eye on your neighbors.

CF **What can men and boys do to keep ourselves safe from attacks?**

JJ Get tested. Encourage the people around you to get tested. Most folks are Toxo X pos. And as long as they're monitoring their systems – and registering with the proper government agencies – they're perfectly harmless. Some people will always turn into killer panther monsters. Don't be a victim.

KNOW YOUR POOP!

Can you tell one animal's feces from the next?

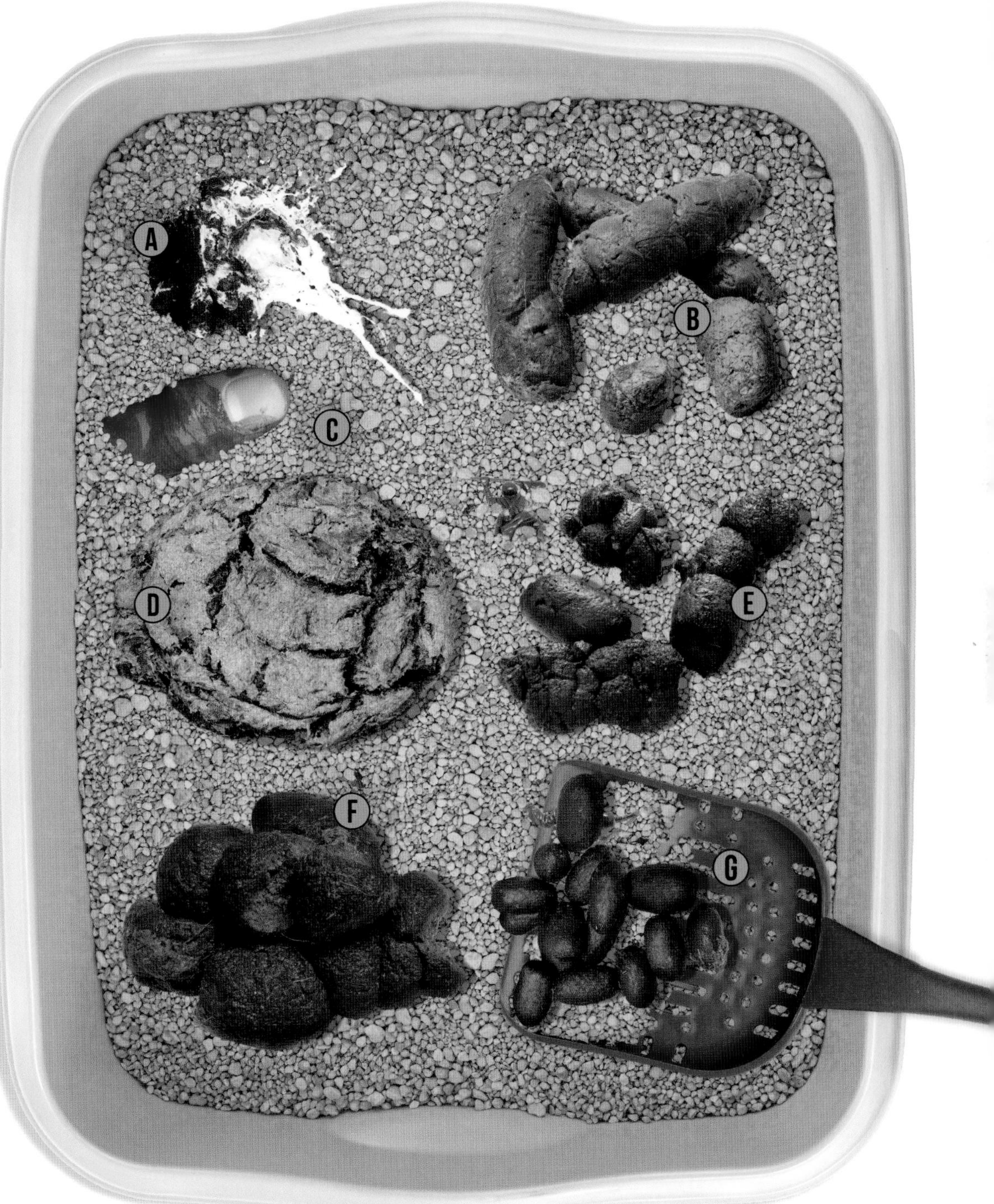
A
B
C
D
E
F
G

Answer Key Ⓐ PIGEON Ⓑ KILLER PANTHER MONSTER Ⓒ SEVERED FINGER Ⓓ COW Ⓔ K-9 Ⓕ WOLF Ⓖ HARE

STAY SAFE AT HOME

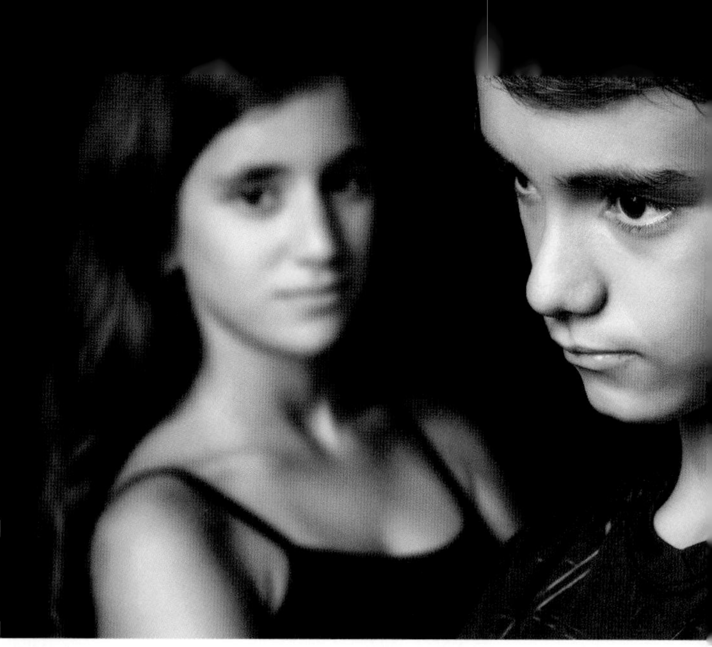

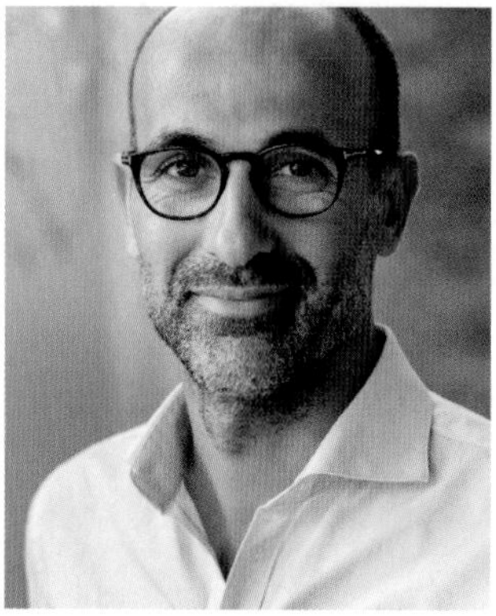

© Troy Sampson

EXPERT

My sister is always lurking in my house. How do I make her go away?

I get this question a lot. Have you tried setting off fireworks? Sisters don't like bright lights or loud noises. A few M-80s every other night for a week or so, and that should do the trick. If that doesn't work, try fire.

If my sister attacks me, is it OK to punch her in the nose?

Fight off your sister in any way you can. If punching seems best, do it. If you have a sharp stick or a knife, that may work even better. Avoid agitating her further with a weak hit. Never crouch near your sister. This will make you seem smaller and more prey-like. When confronted, face her. Wave your arms slowly and speak in a loud, firm voice. Don't let her get you by the neck.

Can I run away?

No. This is a very bad idea. Your sister would see you as vulnerable and chase after you. You will not be able to outrun her.

If I can get my sister out of the house, what kind of fence should I install to protect our residence? How high and what type?

Even a younger sister can probably jump an average of 15 feet from standing and 40 feet running. I suggest a 30-foot fence with a 95-degree angled base. Numbers – as well as math of any kind – deter most sisters. Consider fence rollers, outdoor lighting, motion sensors, and electric fencing.

GOOD LUCK!

GIRL GRIEVANCE

Submit this report to your school counselor.

ULD LIKE TO REPORT: *Check all that apply.*

☐ A SISTER   ☐ A STRANGER
☐ A GIRLFRIEND   ☐ AN EX-GIRLFRIEND
☐ A CLASSMATE   ☐ A LAB PARTNER
☐ A NEIGHBOR   ☐ A WOMAN WHO WORKS IN
                                    THE SERVICE INDUSTRY

CRIBE HOW YOU HAVE BEEN VICTIMIZED, IN DETAIL.

_____
_____
_____
_____
_____
_____
_____
_____
_____
_____
_____
_____
_____
_____
_____
_____
_____
_____
_____
_____
_____
_____
_____
_____
_____

_____
YOUR NAME

☐ I WOULD LIKE TO REMAIN ANONYMOUS

BIG CAT
EARLY WARNING
ALERT SYSTEM

ALERT SIGNAL
Attack Probable

STEADY BLAST OF 3 TO 5 MINUTES

BIG CAT WATCH
A BIG CAT WATCH goes into effect
when conditions are favorable for a
Big Cat incident in your area. Be alert.
Await further updates.

WARNING SIGNAL
Attack Imminent

WAILING TONE

BIG CAT WARNING
A BIG CAT WARNING is triggered by
a confirmed Big Cat sighting in your
area. Reader boards will be activated
over highways. Radio and television
will feature breaking news alerts.

UNDER ATTACK SIGNAL
Immediate Danger

3 SHORT BLASTS FOR 3 MINUTES

BIG CAT EVENT
In case of a BIG CAT EVENT, everyone
in the area will receive text and email
notifications. Shelter in place.

TEEN SC

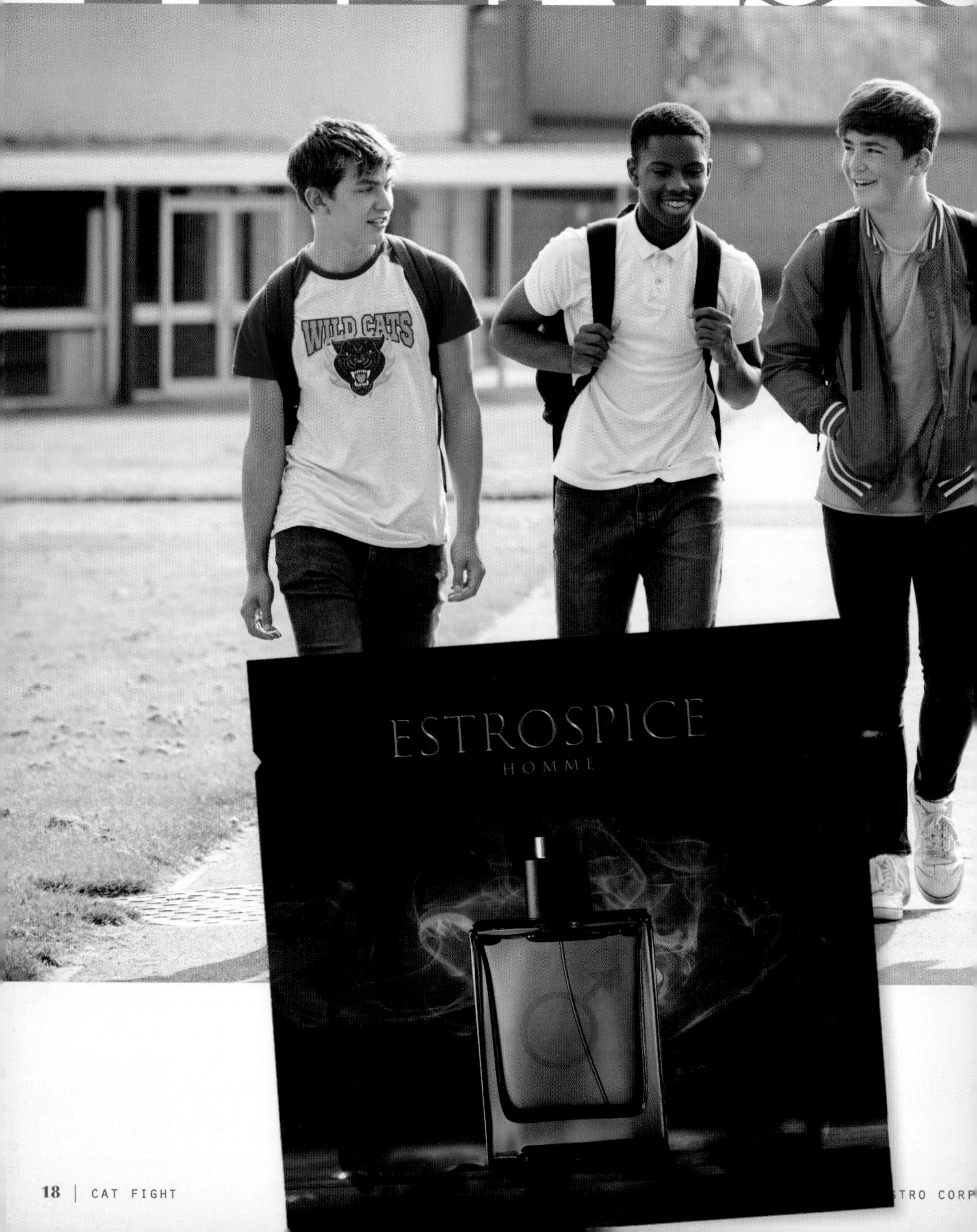
WILD CATS
ESTROSPICE
HOMME

ENE

Logan Janowsky (far left) and Marshall Lee Mall (second to left), students at Powell Middle School, in Portland, Oregon, walk with two unidentified classmates.

MIDDLE SCHOOL RULES
SPOTLIGHT ON:
ALL-GENDER BATHROOMS
By Arnold Hung, Editor-at-Large

As some schools convert existing restrooms to all-gender restrooms, many students and their parents have had the same question: *What about boys??*

School administrators say they're perfectly safe. Fewer and fewer girls are transforming into homicidal big cats, and when they do, their attacks tend to be less deadly.

Talk to boys in the hall of one Portland, Oregon, middle school, and they express concerns.

"I don't necessarily feel safe going to the bathroom with girls."
— Seventh-Grade Student

"I'm scared to death of girls," said Logan Janowsky, an incoming sixth grader at Powell Middle School in Southeast Portland. "My uncle was killed by a girl."

"I don't necessarily feel safe going to the bathroom with girls," said Marshall Lee Mall, a Powell seventh grader. "The ones I know are nice, but what if they turn into panthers? They can't control themselves. I don't want to be in the room with them when it happens."

(continued on next page)

(continued from previous page)

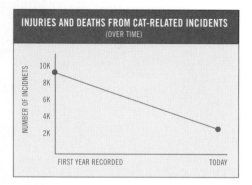

INJURIES AND DEATHS FROM CAT-RELATED INCIDENTS
(OVER TIME)

NUMBER OF INCIDNETS

10K
8K
6K
4K
2K

FIRST YEAR RECORDED   TODAY

As most readers know, feline stage Toxoplasmosis is often triggered by menses, which makes middle school bathrooms a battlefield.

In fact, Powell Middle School decided to abandon a planned all-gender restroom, when a student, sixth grader, Sophie E., went missing in a girls' bathroom during lunch. Authorities theorize that she may have turned into a panther and crawled into the school ventilation system. As of press time, she was still at large.

MISSING

HAVE YOU SEEN THIS GIRL?

Sophie E.

Age: 13   Height: 5'4"   Weight: 120

LAST SEEN AT SCHOOL IN THE SECOND FLOOR RESTROOM
IF YOU HAVE ANY INFORMATION OR HAVE SEEN SOPHIE PLEASE CONTACT
THE PACIFIC NORTHWEST S.C.A.T. OFFICE OR CALL 911

DO NOT APPROACH

BOYS' LOUNGE

YOU'LL NEVER WANT TO LEAVE

Few corporate philanthropy projects of the last decade can match the success of the Estro Corp Boys' Lounge initiative. The idea was simple. Create a fun, safe space for boys, at every public middle school, where they could engage in their favorite activities without distraction. The Estro Corp Foundation was overwhelmed by community response, from companies

offering to donate supplies, to volunteers ready to donate their labor. Boys, it seemed, had been starved for a place they could call their own. Since the initiative was launched, the Estro Corp Foundation has worked with public and private partners to open over 5,000 Boys' Lounges across the country. These lounges are stocked with materials relevant to young men, ages 11-14 – comic books, video games, complicated tabletop games, karate pamphlets, sports-related podcasts, camping equipment, action figures, and more.

Cat Fight is pleased to announce that we will be partnering with Estro Corp to provide this magazine to middle school boys, free of charge. Look for us in the lounge at your school!

Thanks, Estro Corp!

[Editor's note: Estro Corp and this magazine have no relationship with so-called "Girls' Lounges," which Estro Corp considers a trademark infringement. Estro Corp is currently pursuing all legal options.]

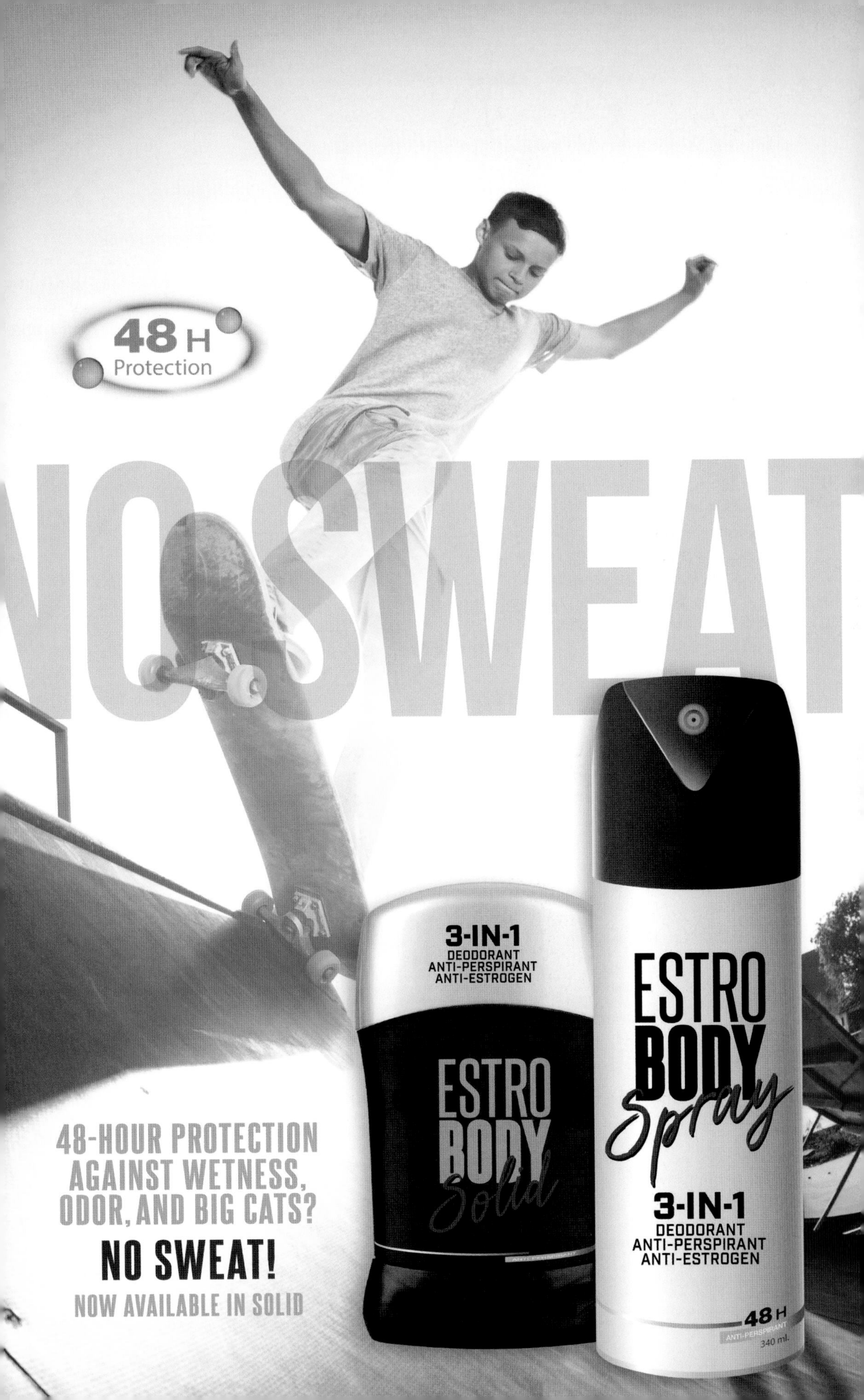
48 H
Protection
NO SWEAT
3-IN-1
DEODORANT
ANTI-PERSPIRANT
ANTI-ESTROGEN
ESTRO
BODY
Solid
ESTRO
BODY
Spray
3-IN-1
DEODORANT
ANTI-PERSPIRANT
ANTI-ESTROGEN
48 H
ANTI-PERSPIRANT
340 ml.
48-HOUR PROTECTION
AGAINST WETNESS,
ODOR, AND BIG CATS?
NO SWEAT!
NOW AVAILABLE IN SOLID

Cat Fight
MONTHLY HOROSCOPE
FOR ANXIOUS BOYS

CAPRICORN
December 21st – January 19th

Shore up relationships with older authority figures. Turn in your homework. Memorize a joke. Forge new friendships. You, or someone in your life, will have a life-changing idea that will create new opportunities. Is there a goal that you, or someone in your life, has not achieved? Good news! Saturn indicates that small variations in your mannerisms will translate into increased personal reputation.

You, or someone in your life, will finally find true joy. The material and emotional rewards are potentially enormous. Remember to stay balanced. Take care of yourself first. You, or someone in your life, will gain valuable insight from this experience. Focus on relationships with clear precedent and boundaries.

You may feel threatened during the third week of the month. A female will challenge you. If so, ask yourself, are you a star, or a sun?

This month is a good time to learn Spanish.

WHAT DOES YOUR FUTURE HOLD?

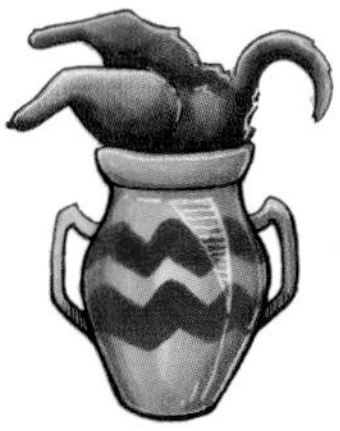

AQUARIUS
(January 19th – February 19th)
Creative talents may indicate rage.

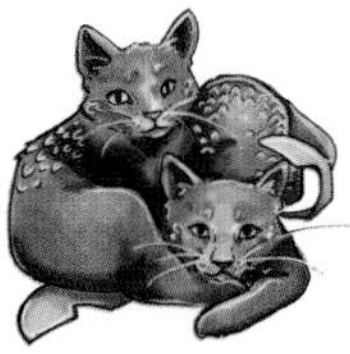

PISCES
(February 19th – March 21st)
Beware the indoor cat who wants out when the wind is blowing.

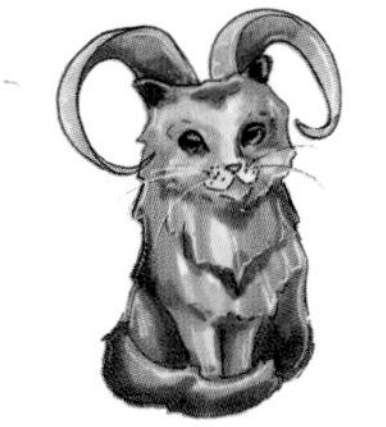

ARIES
(March 21st – April 20th)
There is a strong possibility you will be ambushed. But by a monster, or a woman's ambition? Only you can decide.

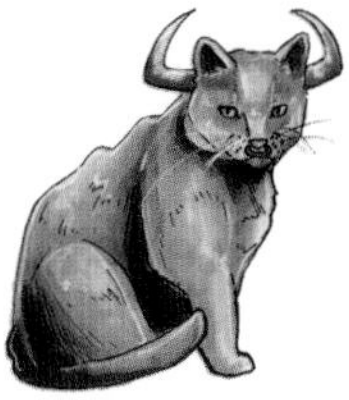

TAURUS
(April 20th – May 21st)
Her gaze is steady. Uncertainty is scary.

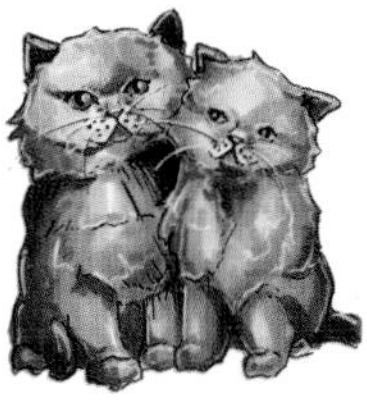

GEMINI
(May 21st – June 21st)
Communication does not always lead to understanding.

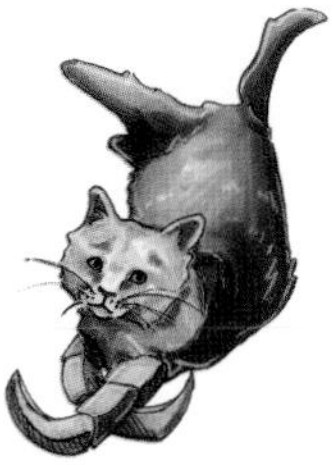

CANCER
(June 21st – July 23rd)
Be the ball.

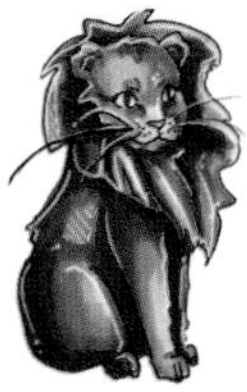

LEO
(July 23rd – August 23rd)
Jupiter continues through your third house. Judgment will be delivered by daughters.

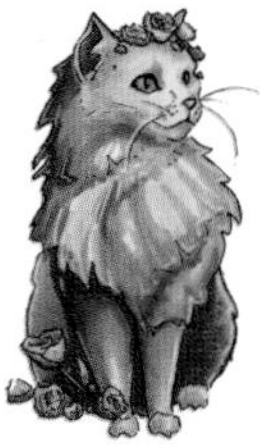

VIRGO
(August 23rd – September 23rd)
Be patient…

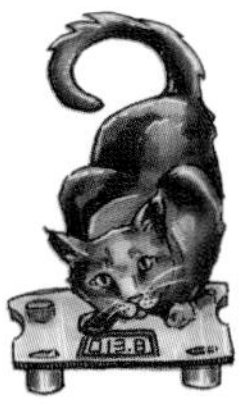

LIBRA
(September 23rd – October 22nd)
If you are looking for a chance to transform your relationship with your family the last week of the month could hold an opportunity for breakthrough.

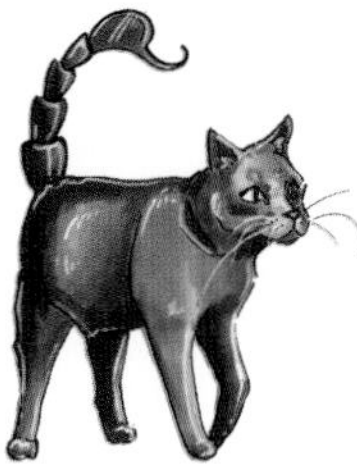

SCORPIO
(October 22nd – November 21st)
Do not take mauling personally.

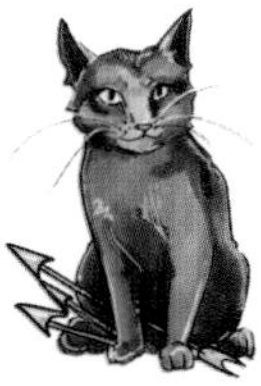

SAGITTARIUS
(November 21st – December 21st)
Your relationships with women may prove disappointing.

Cats by Stella Greenvoss

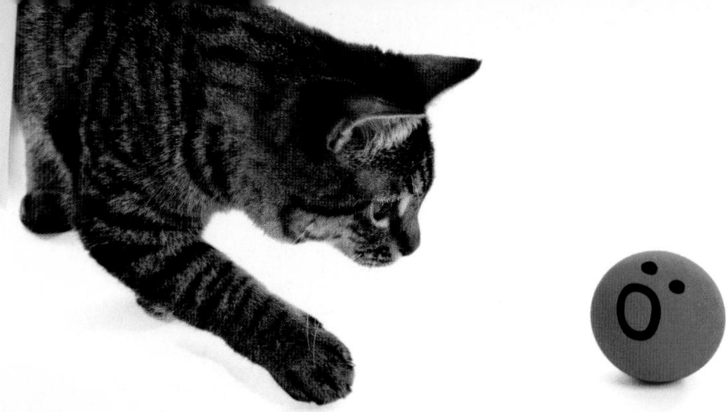

Litter box

Dear CAT FIGHT,
I live in a high cat attack neighborhood, and I have been considering building a safe house. What materials do you recommend?

Sincerely,
Worried in Walla-Walla.

Dear Worried. Some people use plaster and wood to build their safe houses, but here at *Cat Fight* we find that concrete and bamboo stalks work best. Safe houses are useful, and can provide shelter and buy valuable time. But never rely on them. You are your best weapon against a cat attack. Thanks for reading!

Dear CAT FIGHT,
What can I, as a teenage boy, do to prepare for a cat attack?
Thanks in advance.

Sincerely,
Unprepared

Hello, Unprepared. One of the best things you can do to protect yourself is to subscribe to *Cat Fight* or look for a free copy in your school's boys' lounge. Also, develop a workout routine and maintain a healthy diet. Studies show that sports that involve physical contact, mainly football, increase the chance of surviving a cat attack by 50%. Why be lazy and afraid, when you can be safe and popular?

Dear CAT FIGHT,
Does Cat Fight offer any summer camps? I am ten and like to hunt in the woods and run around.

Excitedly,
Don Jr.

Dear Don Jr. You're in luck! This year, as part of our ongoing partnership with the Estro Corp Foundation, *Cat Fight* is hosting two sessions of our Cat Defense camp in the Colorado Rockies. Eligible boys, age 10-15, will learn basic survival skills, defense training, and self-care. At the end of the week, campers are dropped in the middle of a National Wilderness Area, where they will take their training to the next level. Using their newfound skills, they will do their best to survive in the woods for 6 additional days armed with one match, grit, a bow and arrow, and a ball of yarn. Our staff of expert instructors will simulate the terror of a big cat attack through role play, war games, and highly realistic and effective simulation of menace. Waivers required. Registration opens March 5. The clock is ticking!

Dear CAT FIGHT,
I am writing to point out a mistake in your last issue. ESTRO-POP is not available in diet raspberry. Please get your facts straight.

Sincerely,
A Concerned Citizen.

Thank you. *Cat Fight* regrets the error.
– The Editors

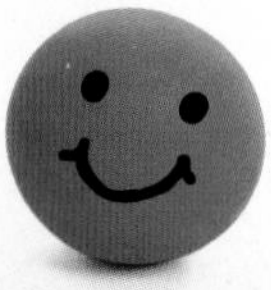

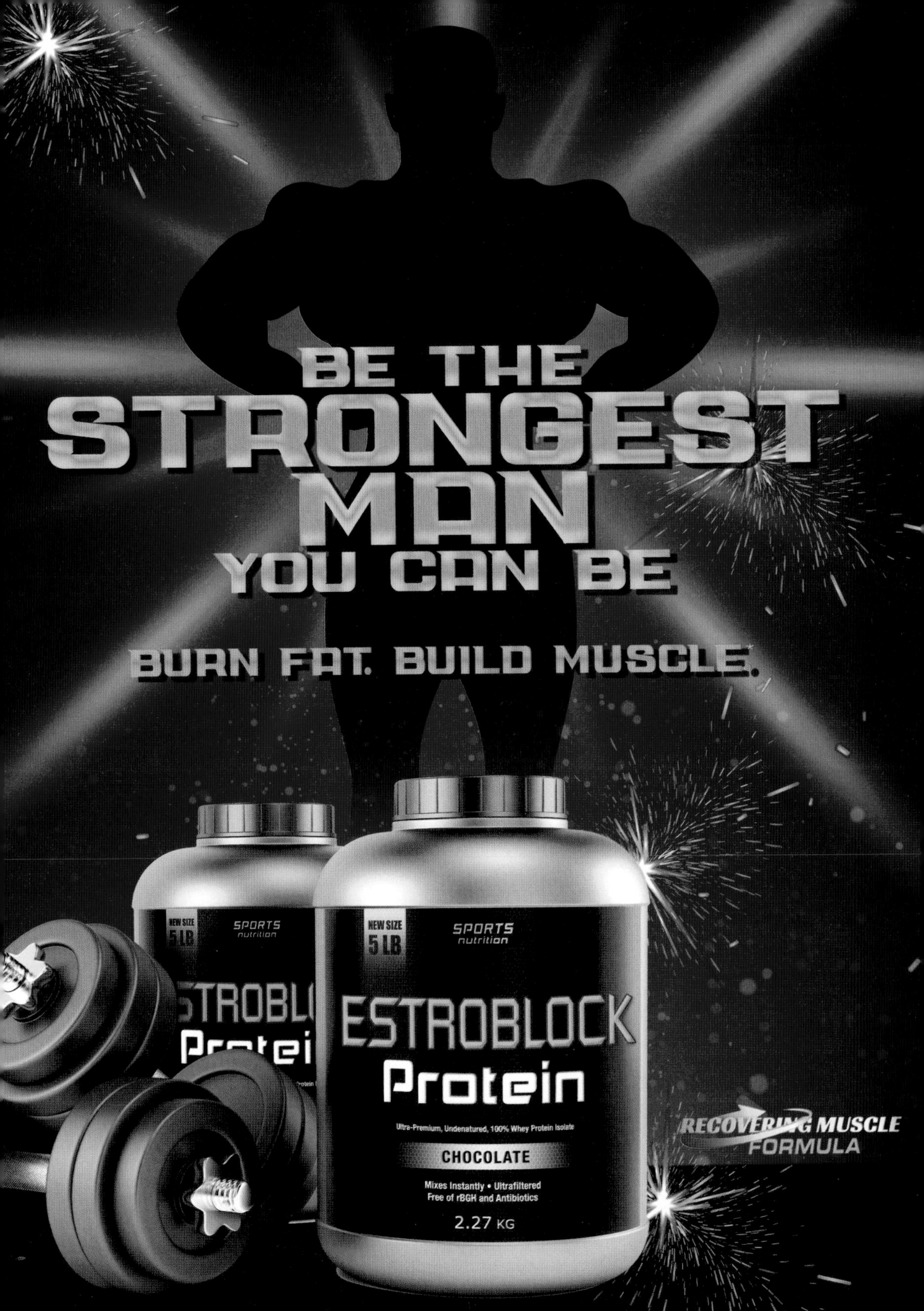
BE THE
STRONGEST
MAN
YOU CAN BE
BURN FAT. BUILD MUSCLE.*
NEW SIZE
5 LB
SPORTS
nutrition
ESTROBLOCK
Protein
Ultra-Premium, Undenatured, 100% Whey Protein Isolate
CHOCOLATE
Mixes Instantly • Ultrafiltered
Free of rBGH and Antibiotics
2.27 KG
RECOVERING MUSCLE
FORMULA

Studies show that the stronger you are, the easier you can escape dangerous situations. You run faster. Fight harder. And recover quicker. ESTROBLOCK Protein formula gives you the extra spark you need to build lean muscle mass and be the best man you can be.

*Scientific study performed by Estro-pure Corp.

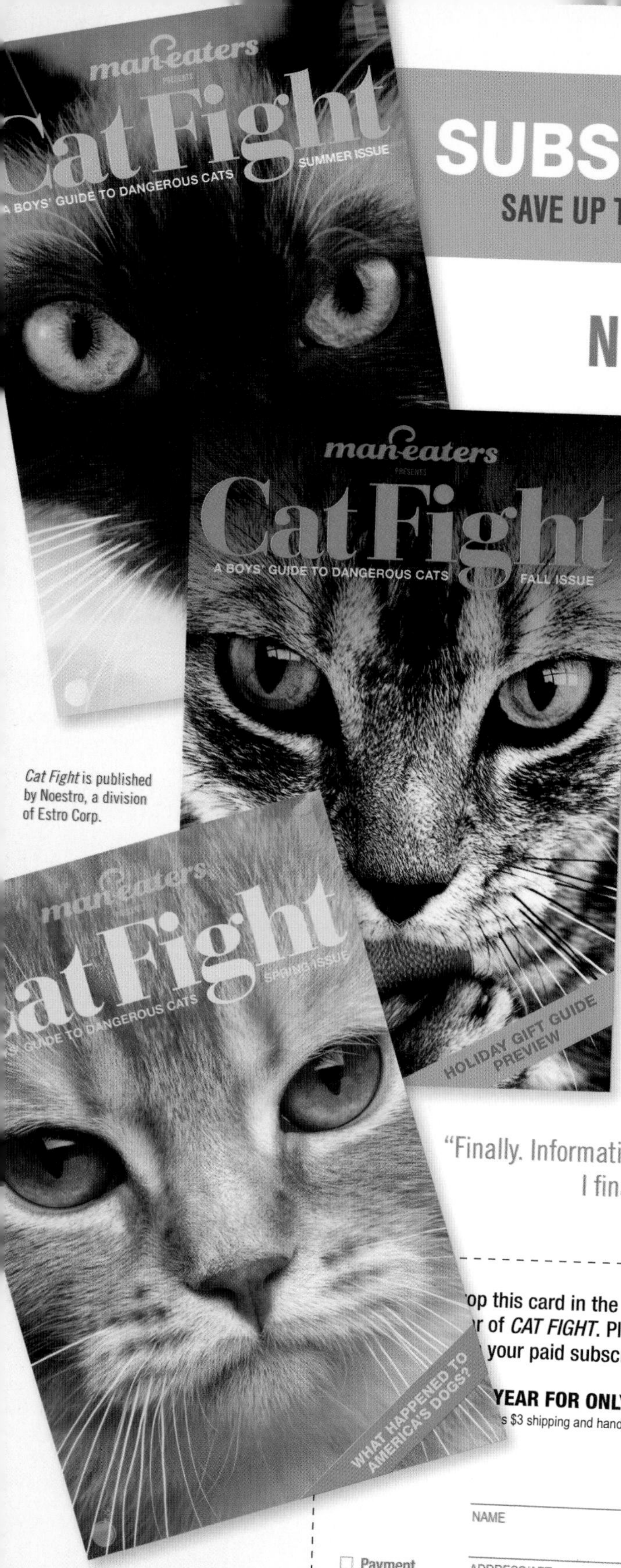
man-eaters
PRESENTS
Cat Fight
A BOYS' GUIDE TO DANGEROUS CATS
SUMMER ISSUE
man-eaters
PRESENTS
Cat Fight
A BOYS' GUIDE TO DANGEROUS CATS
FALL ISSUE
HOLIDAY GIFT GUIDE PREVIEW
atFight
GUIDE TO DANGEROUS CATS
SPRING ISSUE
WHAT HAPPENED TO AMERICA'S DOGS?

Cat Fight is published by Noestro, a division of Estro Corp.

SUBSCRIBE TODAY

SAVE UP TO 82% WHEN YOU ORDER 2 YEARS!

NEED A GIFT FOR A MAN OR BOY?

Cat Fight is an award-winning educational magazine dedicated to cat attack prevention and awareness. Issues are quarterly, and include cat-related current events, expert interviews, health tips, self-defense instruction, product recommendations, and more. We believe that every boy and man should have the skill and confidence to avoid unwelcome attention from big cats. That's why *Cat Fight* has the highest circulation of all the magazines in the "man-cat" periodical category.

SPECIAL OFFER *for teachers*

ARE YOU AN EDUCATOR?

Order *Cat Fight* today, and receive valuable resources for your classroom.

NO STUDENT DESERVES TO BE AMBUSHED.

"Finally. Information about cats that boys can understand. I finally feel like my son can defend himself."

– Father of subscriber

rop this card in the mail today and save 78% when you order 1 r of *CAT FIGHT*. Plus, you'll get a FREE emergency survival kit your paid subscription.

YEAR FOR ONLY $15 (s $3 shipping and handling)

☐ **2 YEARS FOR ONLY $24** (plus $6 shipping and handling)

Best Deal – Save 82%

NAME

☐ Payment enclosed

ADDRESS/APT

☐ Bill me later

CITY/STATE/ZIP

Cat Fight

In the near future a hero will rise. She will set her people free. And the world will know her name...

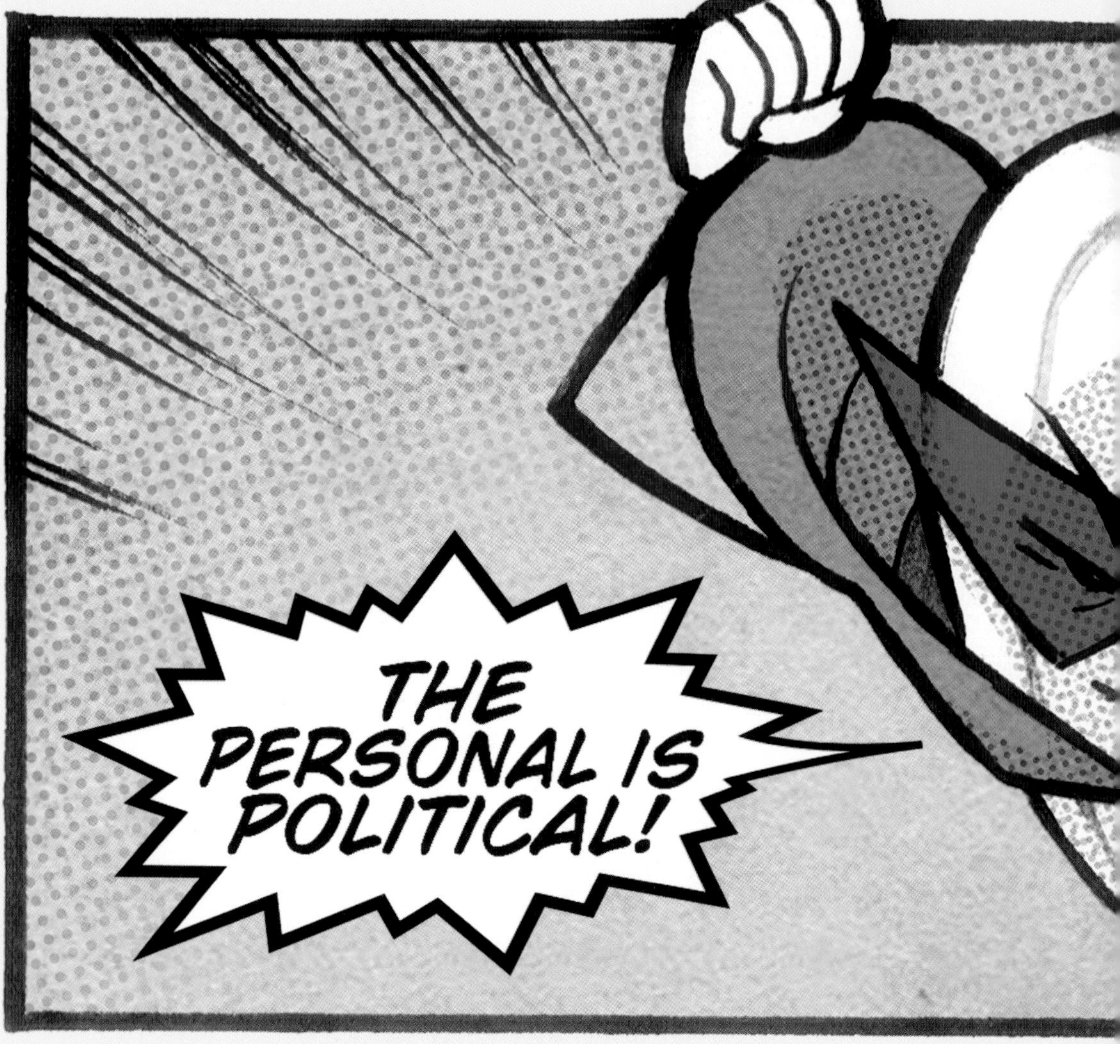
THE PERSONAL IS POLITICAL!

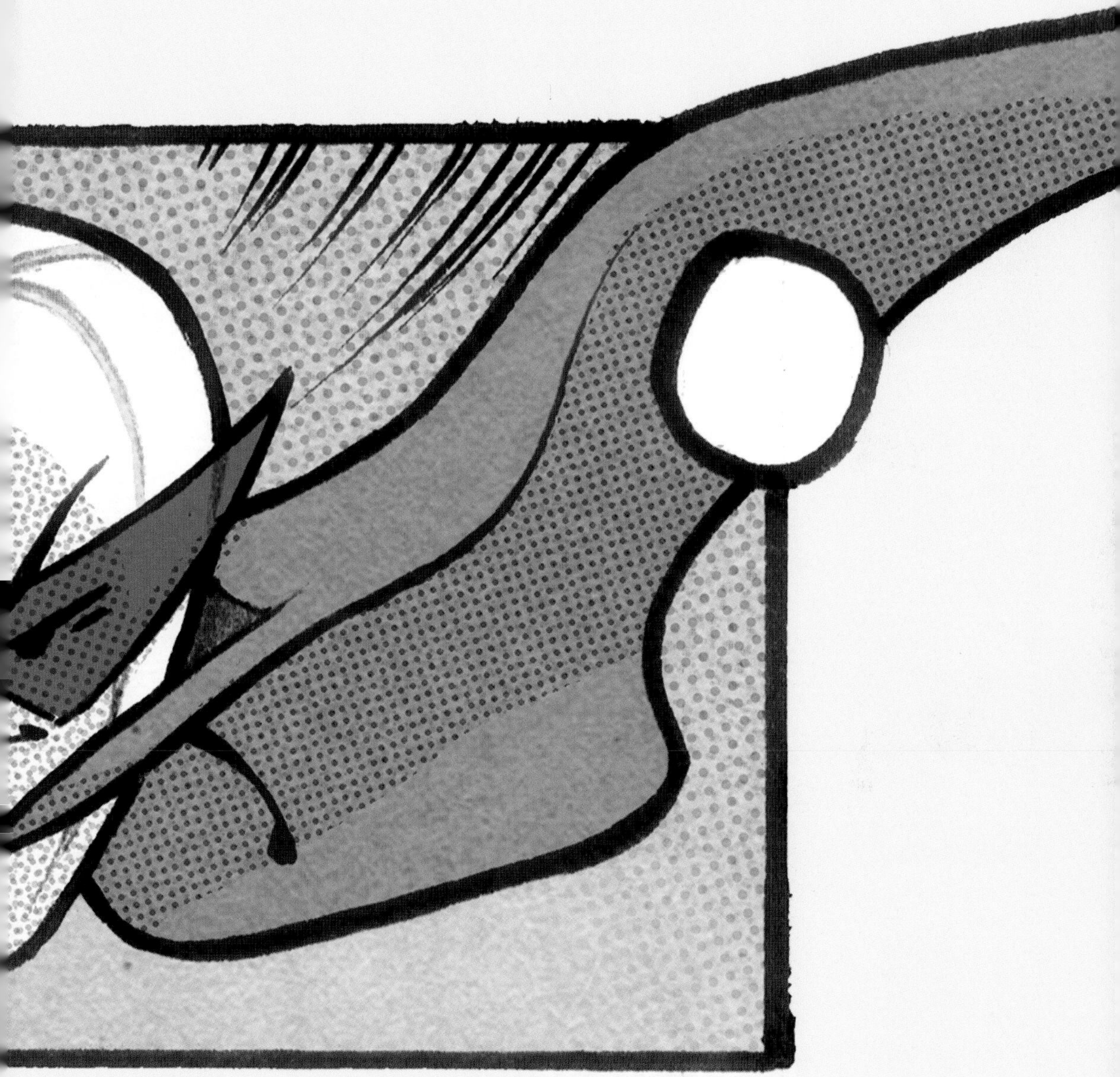

WOME
POWE
DANG

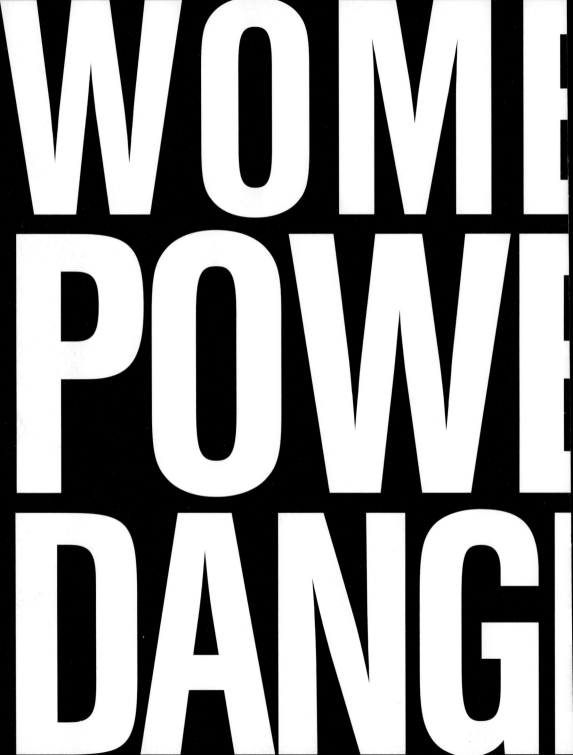

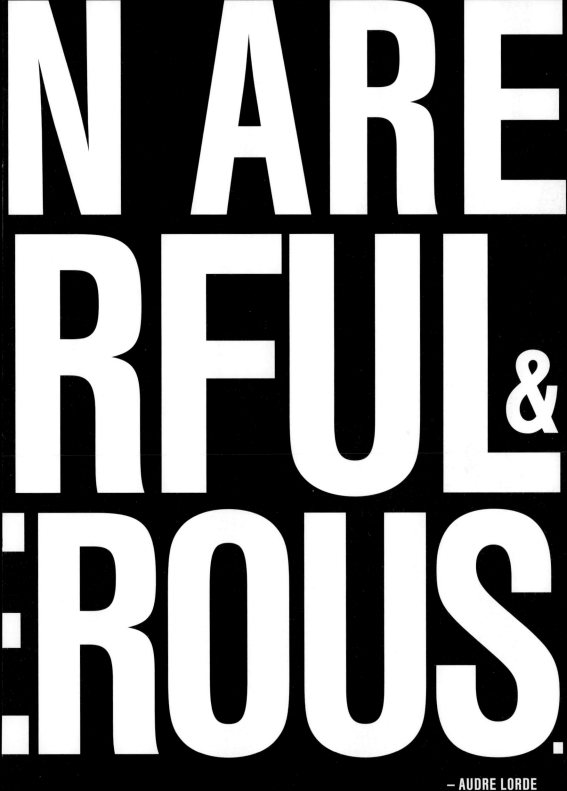

N ARE
RFUL &
ROUS.

— AUDRE LORDE

PHOTOCOPY THIS PAGE. CUT ALONG THE DOTTED LINES.

SUGGESTIONS FOR THE PATRIARCHY

MY SUGGESTION(S):

MY SUGGESTION(S) WOULD BENEFIT:

OTHER COMMENTS:

☐ CHECK HERE IF IT'S OKAY TO POST THIS ON SOCIAL MEDIA.

OFFICIAL USE ONLY

SUGGESTIONS FOR THE PATRIARCHY

MY SUGGESTION(S):

MY SUGGESTION(S) WOULD BENEFIT:

OTHER COMMENTS:

☐ CHECK HERE IF IT'S OKAY TO POST THIS ON SOCIAL MEDIA.

OFFICIAL USE ONLY

SUGGESTIONS
FOR THE PATRIARCHY

MY SUGGESTION(S):

MY SUGGESTION(S) WOULD BENEFIT:

OTHER COMMENTS:

☐ CHECK HERE IF IT'S OKAY TO POST THIS ON SOCIAL MEDIA.

OFFICIAL USE ONLY

SUGGESTIONS
FOR THE PATRIARCHY

MY SUGGESTION(S):

MY SUGGESTION(S) WOULD BENEFIT:

OTHER COMMENTS:

☐ CHECK HERE IF IT'S OKAY TO POST THIS ON SOCIAL MEDIA.

OFFICIAL USE ONLY

PHOTOCOPY THIS PAGE. CUT ALONG THE DOTTED LINES.

SUGGESTIONS FOR THE PATRIARCHY

MY SUGGESTION(S):

MY SUGGESTION(S) WOULD BENEFIT:

OTHER COMMENTS:

☐ CHECK HERE IF IT'S OKAY TO POST THIS ON SOCIAL MEDIA.

OFFICIAL USE ONLY

SUGGESTIONS FOR THE PATRIARCHY

MY SUGGESTION(S):

MY SUGGESTION(S) WOULD BENEFIT:

OTHER COMMENTS:

☐ CHECK HERE IF IT'S OKAY TO POST THIS ON SOCIAL MEDIA.

OFFICIAL USE ONLY

SUGGESTIONS FOR THE PATRIARCHY

MY SUGGESTION(S):

_____

_____

_____

_____

MY SUGGESTION(S) WOULD BENEFIT:

_____

_____

OTHER COMMENTS:

_____

_____

_____

☐ CHECK HERE IF IT'S OKAY TO POST THIS ON SOCIAL MEDIA.

OFFICIAL USE ONLY
....

SUGGESTIONS FOR THE PATRIARCHY

MY SUGGESTION(S):

_____

_____

_____

_____

MY SUGGESTION(S) WOULD BENEFIT:

_____

_____

OTHER COMMENTS:

_____

_____

_____

☐ CHECK HERE IF IT'S OKAY TO POST THIS ON SOCIAL MEDIA.

OFFICIAL USE ONLY
....

man-eaters

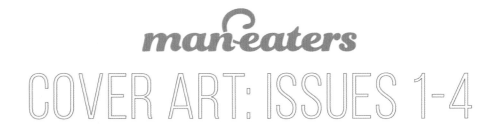

COVER ART: ISSUES 1-4

ISSUE #1

A

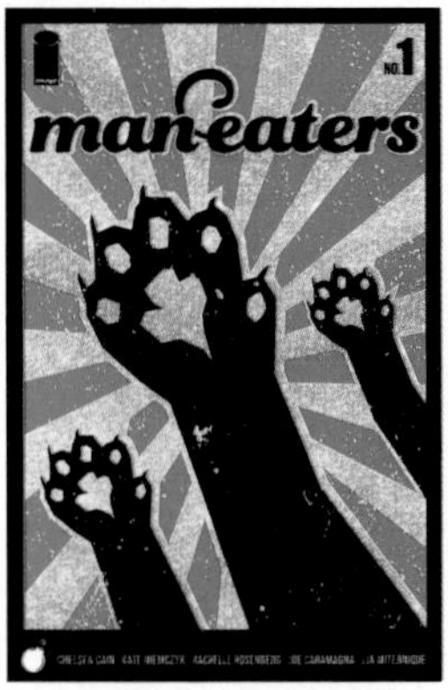
NO.1
man-eaters

B

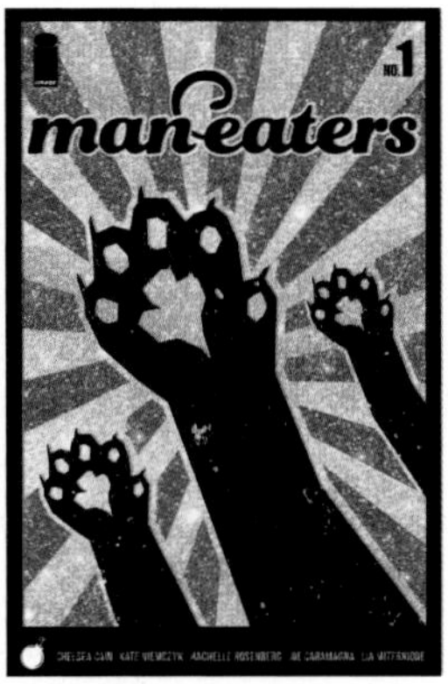
NO.1
man-eaters

C

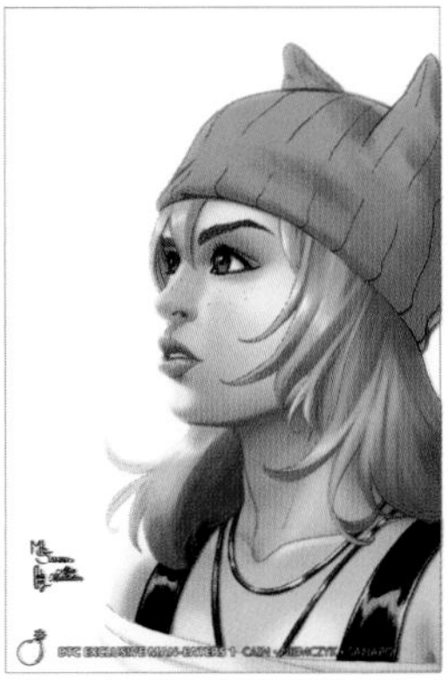

D

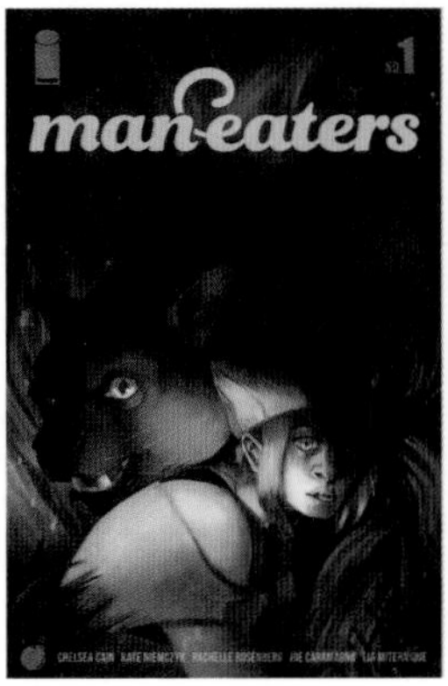
NO.1
man-eaters

ISSUE #2

A

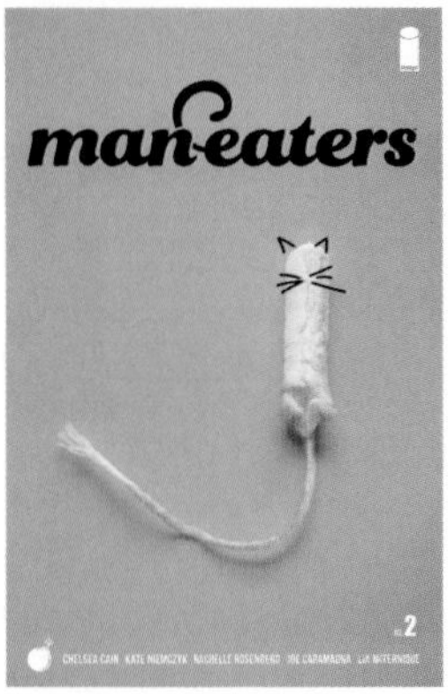
man-eaters

B

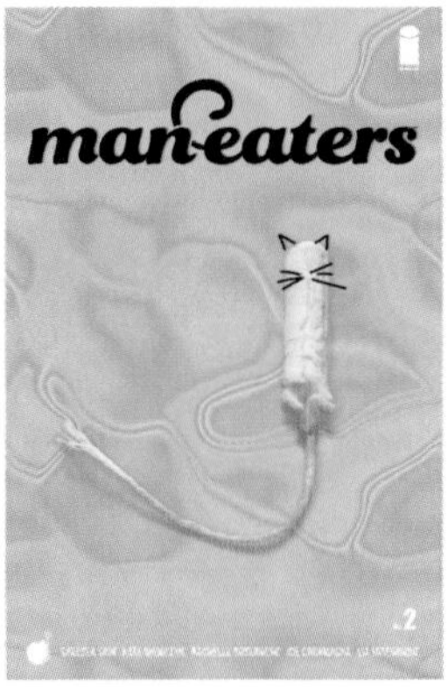
man-eaters

C

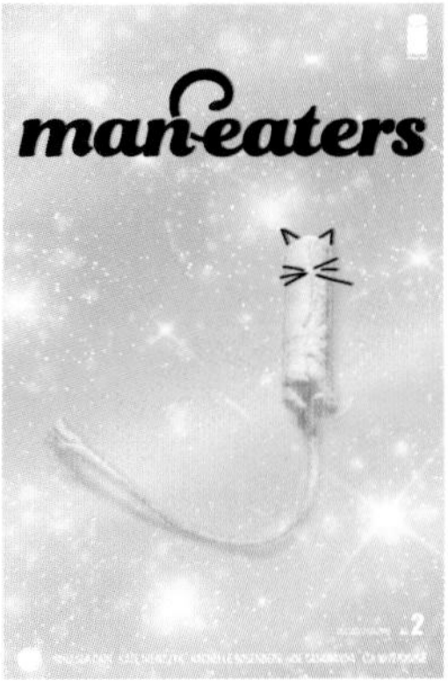
man-eaters

ISSUE #3

A

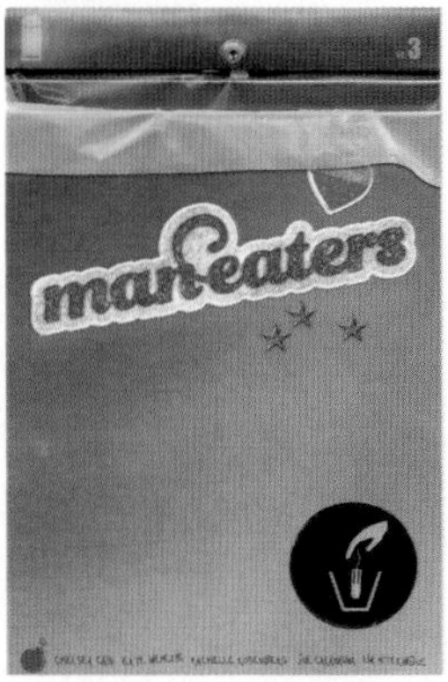
man-eaters

B

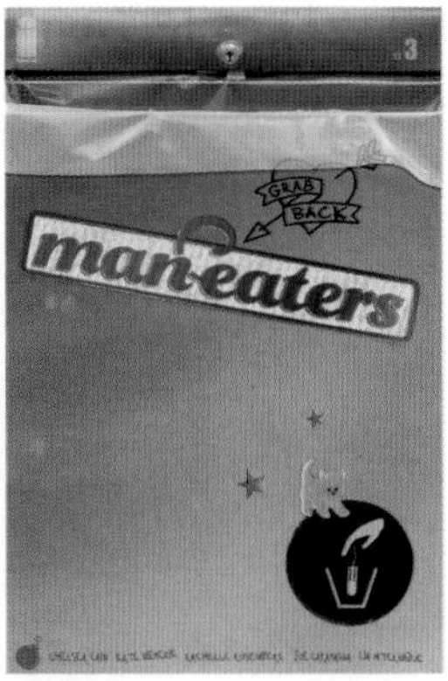
GRAB BACK
man-eaters

ISSUE #4

A

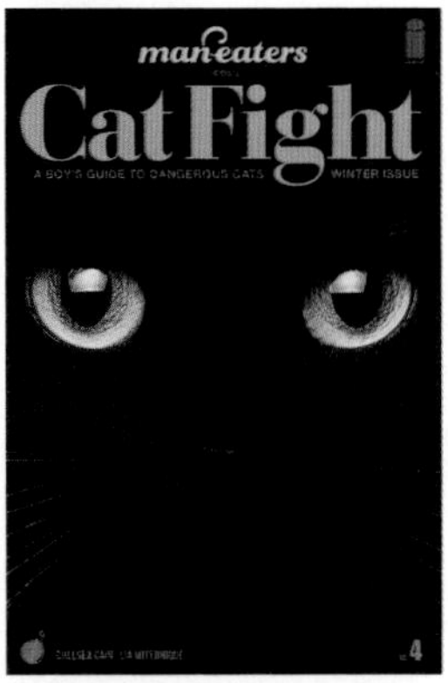
man-eaters
Cat Fight
A BOY'S GUIDE TO DANGEROUS CATS
WINTER ISSUE

B

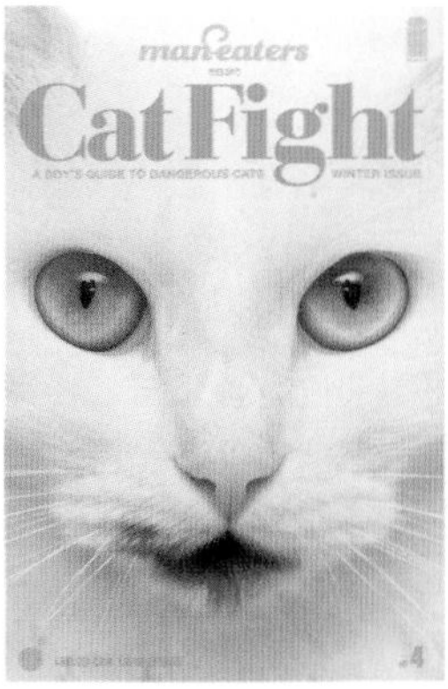
man-eaters
Cat Fight
A BOY'S GUIDE TO DANGEROUS CATS
WINTER ISSUE

COVER ART DESIGN BY LIA MITERNIQUE, 2018

VARIANT COVER 1C – MARIA LAURA SANAPO AND VARIANT COVER 1D – BETH SPARKS

man-eaters

COVER ART: ISSUES 5-8

ISSUE #5

A

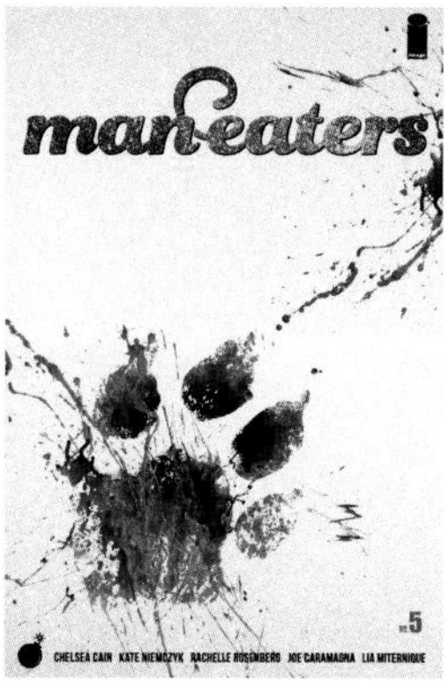
man-eaters
No. 5
CHELSEA CAIN KATE NIEMCZYK RACHELLE ROSENBERG JOE CARAMAGNA LIA MITERNIQUE

B

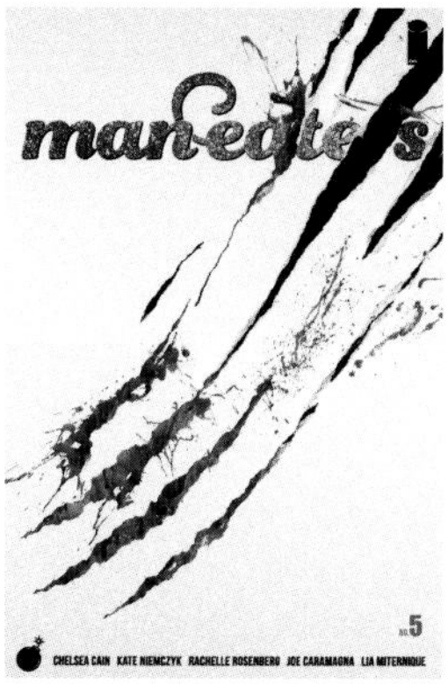
No. 5
CHELSEA CAIN KATE NIEMCZYK RACHELLE ROSENBERG JOE CARAMAGNA LIA MITERNIQUE

ISSUE #6

A

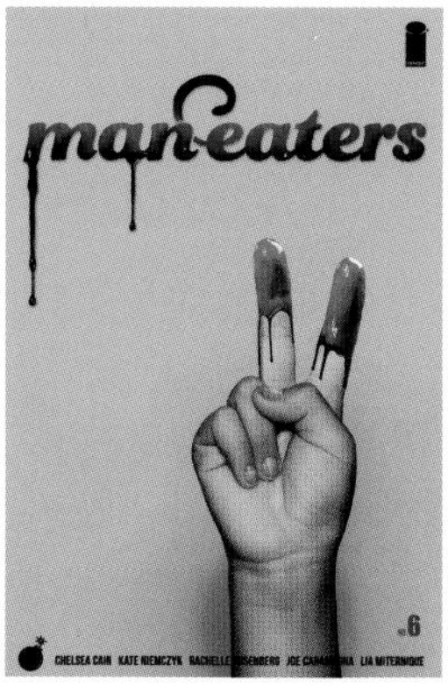
man-eaters
No. 6

B

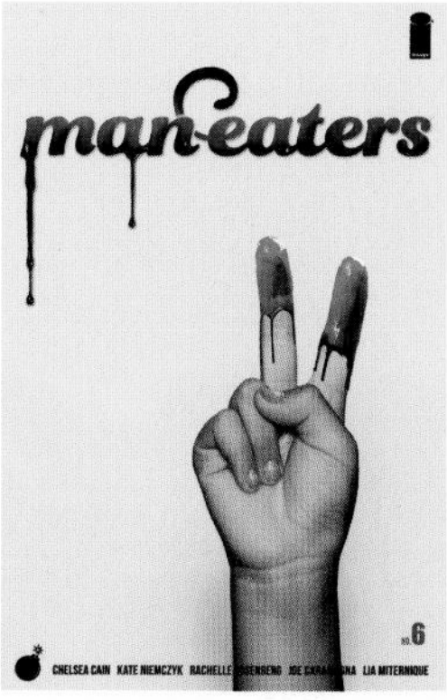
man-eaters
No. 6

ISSUE #7

A

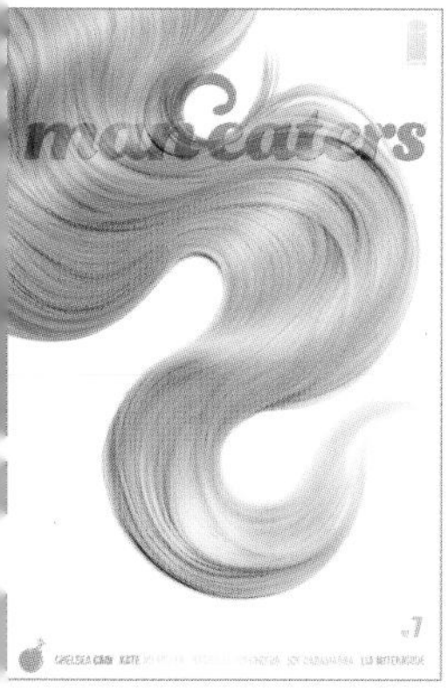
No. 7

B

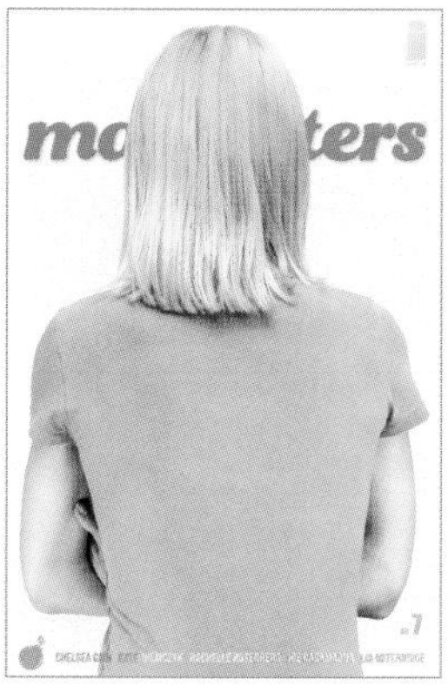
No. 7

ISSUE #8

A

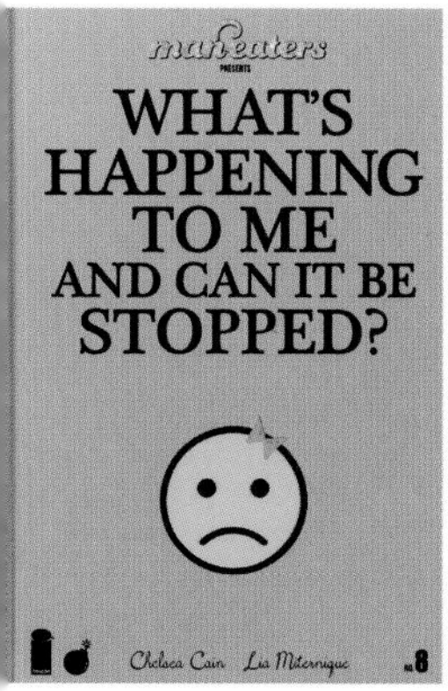
man-eaters
WHAT'S HAPPENING TO ME AND CAN IT BE STOPPED?
Chelsea Cain Lia Miternique
No. 8

B

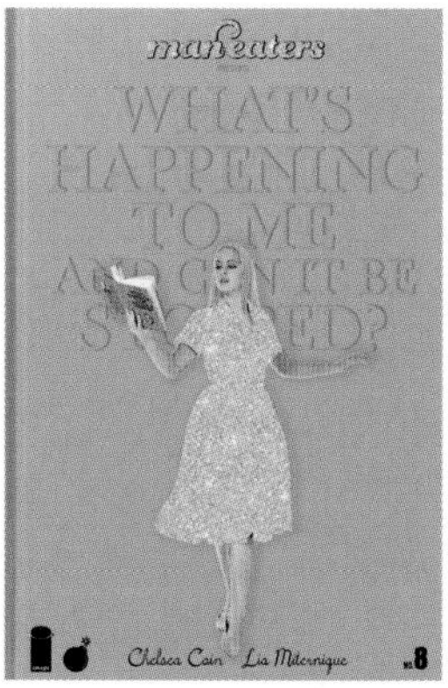
man-eaters
Chelsea Cain Lia Miternique
No. 8

COVER ART DESIGN BY LIA MITERNIQUE, 2018

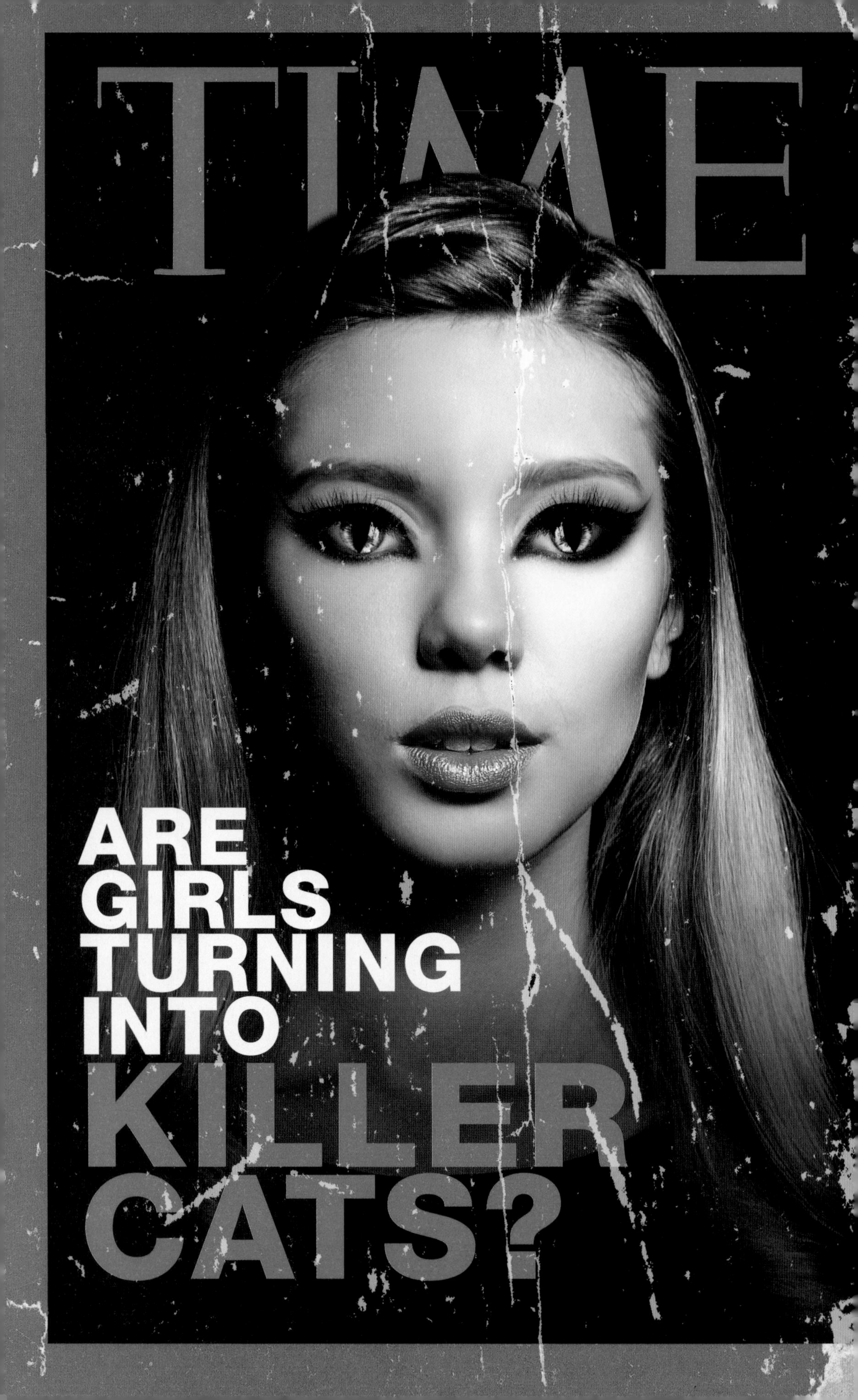
TIME
ARE
GIRLS
TURNING
INTO
KILLER
CATS?